Dead Famous

'One of Ben Elton's many triumphs with *Dead Famous* is
that he is superbly persuasive about the stage of the story: the
characterisation is a joy, the jokes are great, the structuring is very
clever and the thriller parts are ingenious and full of suspense.
And not only that – the satire (of Big Brother, of the television
industry, of the arrogant ignorance and rabid inarticulacy of yoof
culture) is scathing, intelligent and cherishable. As *House Arrest's*
twerpy contestants would put it, wicked. Double wicked. Big up
to Ben Elton and respect, big time. Top, top book'
Mail on Sunday

Inconceivable

'Extremely funny without ever being tasteless or
cruel . . . this is Elton at his best – mature, humane,
and still a laugh a minute. At least'
Daily Telegraph

'A very funny book about a sensitive subject. The characters
are well-developed, the action is page-turning and it's
beginning to seem as if Ben Elton the writer might
be even funnier than Ben Elton the comic'
Daily Mail

Blast from the Past

'Elton at his most outrageously entertaining . . . Elton is a
master of the snappy one-liner, and here the witty
repartee hides a surprisingly romantic core'
Cosmopolitan

'Only Ben Elton could combine uncomfortable questions about
gender politics with a gripping, page-turning narrative
and jokes that make you laugh out loud'
Tony Parsons

Ben Elton's multi-award-winning career as both performer and writer encompasses some of the most memorable and incisive comedy of the past thirty-five years. In addition to his hugely influential work as a stand-up comic, he was co-writer of TV hits *The Young Ones* and *Blackadder* and sole creator of *The Thin Blue Line* and *Upstart Crow*. He has written fifteen major bestsellers, including *Stark, Popcorn, Inconceivable, Dead Famous, High Society, Two Brothers* and *Time and Time Again*, three West End plays and three musicals, including global phenomenon *We Will Rock You*. He has written and directed two feature films, *Maybe Baby* and *Three Summers,* and wrote the screenplay of the film *All Is True,* directed by Kenneth Branagh.

He is married and has three children.

www.penguin.co.uk

Identity Crisis

Ben Elton

BLACK SWAN

TRANSWORLD PUBLISHERS
61–63 Uxbridge Road, London W5 5SA
www.penguin.co.uk

Transworld is part of the Penguin Random House group of companies
whose addresses can be found at global.penguinrandomhouse.com

First published in Great Britain in 2019 by Bantam Press
an imprint of Transworld Publishers
Black Swan edition published 2019

A CIP catalogue record for this book
is available from the British Library.

ISBN
9780552771290
9780552771764

Typeset in 11.16/14.3pt Minion by Jouve (UK), Milton Keynes.
Printed and bound in Great Britain by Clays Ltd, Elcograf S.p.A.

Penguin Random House is committed to a sustainable
future for our business, our readers and our planet. This book
is made from Forest Stewardship Council® certified paper.

1 3 5 7 9 10 8 6 4 2

For my wife Sophie and our children,
Bert, Lottie and Fred

1. #NotHerFault

DETECTIVE CHIEF Inspector Michael Matlock watched himself with the queasy distaste that always overtook him when he was required to review his media appearances. He could never quite get used to how old he looked. That the craggy-faced, fifty-something behind the microphone was actually him.

It wasn't that he hated how he looked. In fact, privately, he thought he wasn't so bad. Still lean, still sharp. Still rock 'n' roll. People said he was a bit like The Edge from U2 but that was probably only because he wore the same type of woolly hat as The Edge did. And you couldn't wear a woolly hat in a police press briefing anyway. Not an indoors briefing.

You just had to admit you were going bald.

'The victim's name was Sammy Hill,' Matlock was saying. 'A young woman, who was assaulted and killed some time shortly after midnight while crossing Conway Park.'

He could hear himself doing a telephone voice for the occasion. Trying to reinstate his *t*s and stop his glottal. As if somehow his natural Kilburn High Road accent lacked sufficient gravitas for the appalling message it was his duty to deliver. How did you give the news nobody wanted to hear? What words or tone could possibly speak to the sadness and the fury that the people watching would be feeling? The utter frustration at the horrible inevitability of it all. How many similar announcements had he made over the years? A lifetime of police work and nothing ever changed.

'This was a brutal murder. A vile and senseless act. And we want to assure the public that we are doing all we can to catch the per-petrator. However, in the meantime there is a killer on the loose, and while we can't rule out the possibility that Sammy knew her attacker, the current indications are that this was a random assault. A case of being in the wrong place at the wrong time.'

The assistant deputy commissioner tapped a key on his laptop. The image froze. Matlock had been in the process of drawing breath but looked as if he was howling. Like the figure in Edvard Munch's *The Scream*. Except he wasn't *that* bald and he didn't have his hands over his ears.

But he was that appalled. And he was that confused.

Funny how the freeze frame seemed to tear away his mask, capturing the fearful anger and agonized impotence previously hidden by his forced tone and official manner. Matlock had felt just like the man in *The Scream* at that press conference. It was how he felt at all of them. He was only human after all.

' "Wrong place at the wrong time"?'

The assistant deputy commissioner spoke slowly. Coldly. Mat-lock sensed he was in trouble, although he couldn't think why.

'Yeah. Very sad, sir,' Matlock said, for want of any other reply.

'What did you mean?'

'What did I mean?'

' "Wrong place wrong time." What did you mean?'

Matlock felt a little surge of anger. He wanted to say, 'Duh!' like his partner Nancy's teenage daughter was always saying to him. He wanted to say that it was bloody obvious what he meant. That this poor woman's space on earth had been the subject of a cataclysmic random intervention. As if a meteor had fallen on her from the sky. That life was appalling and brutal and com-pletely, cosmically unfair. That the grim and terrible truth was it could have happened to any woman. That an innocent life had crossed paths with a wicked and psychotic one.

'I was emphasizing the random nature of the attack, sir,'

Matlock replied quietly. 'I'm pretty certain it's not a domestic. It looks to me like this killer chanced on his victim. Five minutes either way and it would have been another girl. I think it's important the public is aware of that.'

'That's not what I'm asking, Matlock.'

'Then I don't know what you *are* asking, sir.'

'Really?'

'Really.' And he really didn't. Matlock had simply no idea where this was going.

'Conway Park is a public park, isn't it?' the assistant deputy commissioner asked.

'Yes.'

'And as far as I know there's no curfew in this country.'

'Curfew? Not that I'd heard.'

The assistant deputy commissioner's fragile calm exploded. 'Then how the hell do you explain telling the public that this woman was in the wrong place at the wrong time? You massive, *massive* prat!'

Massive prat? Did he really just say that? When had assistant deputy commissioners started talking like school kids? When prime ministers had, Matlock supposed.

'Well,' he began, 'as I say, I wasn't speaking literally. I was trying to indicate the random nature of . . .'

The assistant deputy commissioner tapped his keyboard again and the silently screaming image of anger and confusion on the screen shuddered back into life, resuming once more the mask of a steady, calm, dependable policeman.

'Unfortunately we have to presume that this man may likely strike again. Therefore I appeal to all women in the area to be extra vigilant. Plan your journey home, where possible avoiding under-populated areas. Consider travelling in pairs . . .'

Another hand tapped the keyboard. One with bright-red-polished fingernails. 'Jesus, Mick! It sounds like you're saying it was her fault.'

Oh, fuck. He got it now.

Janine Treadwell was Scotland Yard's senior press and media liaison officer. Mick Matlock was Scotland Yard's senior murder detective. Most of the time they got on with each other pretty well. This was clearly not one of those times.

'Is that really what you think?' she asked him.

'Yes!' the assistant deputy commissioner snapped. 'Is that *who you are?*'

'Look. I just wanted to . . .'

But it had clearly been a rhetorical question.

'Is it, though?' the assistant deputy commissioner went on, revelling in the opportunity to display his enlightened credentials. 'Are you the sort of person who believes that this young woman shouldn't have been in the park at all?'

'No! I just—'

'This woman was not responsible for her own assault, Mick,' Janine said. 'Her attacker was.'

Her kinder tone was, if anything, more painful for Matlock than the assistant deputy commissioner's self-righteous display. She was right. Of course she was. He felt bad for his stupid choice of words and embarrassed that she didn't think he even understood his mistake.

'Yes, Janine, I absolutely do know that, but—'

'And yet!' the assistant deputy commissioner interrupted, almost shouting now, 'you just went on the television and told half the population of this country that if they don't want to get murdered they should steer clear of public parks after dark because otherwise they'll be in the wrong place at the wrong time. What *century* are you living in?'

Matlock didn't try to explain further. He really should have phrased it better. 'Sorry,' he said and, turning to Janine, 'I imagine the press department's going to be dealing with quite a bit of stick over this.'

'I'm afraid we are.'

'It was a stupid thing to say.'

'Little bit,' Janine agreed.

'Horribly, *horribly* tone deaf,' the assistant deputy commissioner added piously.

Matlock stared at his commanding officer. The posturing little shit was revelling in it. He wasn't thinking about Sammy Hill at all. He was thinking about letting everybody know what a thoroughly wonderful person he was.

'Can I get back to my investigation now?' Matlock asked. 'I was on my way to view the body when I got called in.'

'The investigation? God, no,' the assistant deputy commissioner snapped. 'Not until this utter screw-up has completed its spin cycle.'

Matlock turned and left. He'd made a mistake, and he knew it, but he still couldn't be bothered to talk to a senior police officer who used the term 'spin cycle' in any other context than when doing the laundry.

He returned to the Situation Room. Matlock loved his Situation Room. He loved the tension, the buzz. The sense of shared purpose. The flickering screens, the clattering keyboards. Phones ringing. Kettles boiling. Brains whirring. This was where they took care of business. Where they got the job done. Protecting the innocent. Punishing the guilty. Scotland Yard CID, the heart of the city. This was where they were going to catch the psychotic bastard who murdered Sammy Hill.

'You're trending, boss,' Detective Sergeant Barry Taylor said, looking up from his phone. 'You're actually number one! #NotHerFault.'

There was a good-natured round of applause.

Matlock gave a little bow. It never helped to show your crew that you were rattled. But he was rattled. He read the *Guardian*. He knew that language and attitudes were changing. And he absolutely thought that was a good thing. It was just *so* easy to get it wrong.

''Fraid it's all a bit negative,' Taylor went on. 'People can't believe you said that girl shouldn't have been in the park in the first place.'

'I *did not* say—'

'You said she was in the wrong place at the wrong time, boss,' Taylor reminded him, with a broad smile. 'What part of that sentence am I not getting?'

'It's a turn of phrase, Barry. What about context? Doesn't *anybody* do context any more?'

'No, boss,' Detective Constable Sally Clegg chipped in. 'Nobody does context. You need to get used to that.'

Taylor and Clegg were Matlock's closest colleagues. His basic team. They were a good contrast, the two of them. Taylor was brash and confident, a bit of a 'lad' but with sufficient charm and intelligence to get away with it (usually). Clegg was less obviously self-assured but with a strong core – she needed one: she was the youngest and most junior in their team and, of course, female. CID was no longer exclusively a man's world but women remained very much in the minority.

'Wow.' Taylor frowned. 'This is bad.'

'What? What's bad?' Matlock asked.

'The Mayor of London's calling on you to either apologize or resign. The actual *mayor*. He's tagged it #RapeIsAMaleProblem.'

'Rape? Who said anything about rape? We haven't said anything about rape.'

Taylor shrugged. 'Looks like he just assumed.'

Matlock's phone pinged. It was a text from Nancy: *What the fuck have you done? You're on the news.*

Matlock turned on the office TV. BBC News 24. He was all over it. Various representatives of women's groups and crisis centres, plus MPs from both sides of the House were unanimous in their condemnation of his despicably 'tone-deaf victim blaming'.

'The overwhelming majority of rapes and sexual assaults are carried out by men,' the male MP for the constituency in which Conway Park was located stated firmly. 'If we want to protect women then it is *male* attitudes and choices that we need to be questioning.'

Suddenly Matlock was angry. He knew that, in the broader scheme of things, the MP was making a valid point, but it was a socio-political one and this was a murder investigation. Was he seriously suggesting that the safety of his female constituents would be better served if the police appealed to murderers and rapists to consider their choices? 'That is just bloody mad,' he said. 'It's also dangerous.'

'Come on, boss,' Taylor said gleefully. '*Patriarchal entitlement is the root cause of female vulnerability.*'

He was quoting from a recent set of police guidelines and enjoying watching his chief get tied up in knots over what he himself considered to be 'PC madness'.

'Well, it is, Barry,' Clegg said angrily. 'What the fuck else would it be? We don't beat *ourselves* up, you know.'

'Here we go,' Taylor said, with mock weariness.

'You're right, Sally,' Matlock said. 'Patriarchal entitlement absolutely is the root cause of female vulnerability. It has been since the first caveman dragged a woman into his cave by the hair. And wishing that wasn't the case isn't going to make it happen.'

'Please don't say that in your statement, boss,' Clegg replied. She was fond of her boss, and really hoped he wouldn't dig himself in any deeper.

'Say what?'

'That men are cavemen and women need to just get over it.'

'That is *not* what I said . . . Statement? What bloody statement?'

'Well, they're going to have you make a statement obviously. You'll have to go full *mea culpa*.'

'I'm not going to apologize for anything – and I certainly shan't be making any statement. I've got a murder to investigate.'

Clegg and Taylor looked at him with weary pity.

'Of course you'll be making a statement, boss,' Clegg said. 'What *century* are you living in?'

'Since you ask, Sally, I'm thinking of relocating to the twentieth. For a start the music's better.'

2. Number Cruncher

'I WRITE ALGORITHMS.' Malika Rajput was explaining to her mother, Nasreen, for the umpteenth time what she actually *did*.

'I know you've told me before, darling, but what are algorithms again?'

Malika sighed. 'Mathematical equations that take a problem, ask it a series of questions in the most efficient possible manner and produce a solution.'

'A mathematical equation can ask questions?'

Malika's mother would never really get it.

What Nasreen Rajput did get, however, was that her daughter, who had only graduated the previous summer, now had a highly paid job in London. A city that, like the rest of the country, was in deep financial crisis but which was nonetheless too expensive for almost anybody to live in.

'It's wonderful that we can meet for lunch like this, dear, with you back in London. So many of the girls you were at school with have whizzed off all over the country. Abroad too. Looking for "gigs" apparently. I'm still in touch with some of the mothers and they hardly see their girls at all. Just Skype. Like we did when you were hidden away in Oxford. We're so lucky. The only one of your old crowd I've heard about who managed to find work in town is Sally. You remember Sally Clegg?'

'Of course I do, Mum. We were mates. We're still mates. Sort of. You know, on Facebook, that sort of thing.'

'A police detective too. Fancy. Of course you know she's a lesbian?'

'Yes, Mum. I know she's a lesbian. I knew when we were fourteen.'

'I don't see how even she could possibly have known at that age, dear. It's such a big decision, isn't it?'

'I don't think she saw it as a decision, Mum. Just as a thing.'

'Well, I never heard you talking about it.'

'That was because of Bananas.'

'Bananas?'

'It was our code. She didn't want anyone else to know. So we had a code. Whenever she wanted to have a secret talk she'd say, "Bananas", and I'd know.'

'Why Bananas?'

'No idea. Why anything? It just meant secret.'

'Well. Anyway. Good luck to her. *Vive la différence!* And good luck to you with your exciting new life!'

Malika's mother raised her glass of Diet Coke. She really was so proud of her little girl. So poised, so beautiful. When Malika had first begun to demonstrate her extraordinary mathematical powers, Nasreen and her husband had worried it might lead her to turn out dowdy and bookish but she'd grown into a glamorous young woman. Hair and make-up always perfect. Stylish, fashionable clothes. A real heartbreaker. No current boyfriend, admittedly, but actually Nasreen was pleased about that. There had been a couple of pretty wild boys at Oxford of whom she had *not* approved. Plenty of time for romance later. Now it was better for her brilliant daughter to focus on her brilliant career. The only downside Nasreen could think of was that the company Malika worked for had such a ridiculous name.

'I mean really – Communication Sandwich? What on earth does it *mean*?'

Malika's mother could never get past the Sandwich bit. Malika found it confusing too. In fact she thought it was an awful name, even though she cheered it and punched the air whenever the director of policy shouted it at a company motivation session.

'Communication Sandwich! Fuck, yeah! Let's *do* this!'

It was so embarrassing, but a small price to pay for what was definitely a dream job. A job that put mathematics at the heart of commerce and made it a medium for the distribution and manipulation of *ideas*. A job that, more importantly, was extremely well paid. Malika liked being extremely well paid.

'Sandwiches,' she explained, with a weary sigh, 'contain a series of ingredients in a stack. Like today you've ordered cold beef, cheese and pickle.'

'I always do.'

'Shut up, Mum, I'm explaining. And I've ordered Brie, cranberry, watercress, salt and pepper. Different ingredients produce different sandwiches. Following so far?'

'Obviously, dear. I'm not an idiot, whatever your father might tell you.'

'But a sandwich isn't just its internal ingredients, it's also two slices of bread, a top slice and a bottom slice. Call them the problem and the solution.'

'Why?'

'Do *not* ask that, Mum. Every time we go through this I ask you not to ask that. I did not name the company I work for, and the fact that its name is a desperately stretched sandwich metaphor that doesn't work on any level is not my responsibility. Now, are you going to be quiet and listen?'

'All right. All right.'

'OK, you've got your two slices of bread. Your problem and your solution. The problem, the top slice of bread, is selling your product. The solution, the bottom slice of bread, is finding the people who want to buy it. We do that for them, with our layers in between.'

'The beef, cheese and pickle.'

'Exactly. The algorithms, which I, being brilliant, write. For example, a client comes to us saying, "I publish print copies of dictionaries."'

'I don't see what that's got to do with sandwiches.'

'That's because I haven't told you yet.'

'Then I wish you'd get on with it.'

Malika took a deep breath. 'The print-dictionary-using community is a small and specific market. Our client can't afford newspaper ads and, anyway, nobody reads newspapers these days.'

'Dad and I do.'

'Apart from you and Dad. And even if people did, our man's marketing budget would be spent reaching millions of readers, 99.99 per cent of whom will never buy another print dictionary because they look up everything on their phones. An incredibly inefficient method of communication, I think you'll agree.'

'Is this going anywhere, dear?'

'Yes, it's going somewhere! Just shut up and listen!'

'Don't snap at me. I'm still your mother, for all your great big salary.'

Malika took a deep swig of her cappuccino. 'Our client needs to find the small demographic who *do* still use hard-copy reference books, or crucially – because, let's face it, most people who like to use a dictionary have already got one – who might be persuaded to upgrade their existing version, which they had *thought* they were happy with. Communication Sandwich can do that. Our search engines start by endlessly trawling social media, harvesting personal information.'

'You mean spying?'

'Not spying, Mum. It's just the digital equivalent of people-watching.'

'Oh, come on, darling.'

'No, it is. Like when we sit here studying other diners. We're gathering their information and using it to form an opinion about their characters. That's what I do on the net.'

'Except when we look at a couple and say, "Ooh, I bet they're having an affair," or "Look what she's ordered – I could never be a vegetarian," we don't use that information to bombard them with adverts for relationship counselling or vegetarian cookbooks.'

Malika was getting annoyed. Her mum came from a generation when it had been useful for a woman like her to affect a certain lovable dizziness to make their husbands feel clever. But Nasreen Rajput was actually bloody sharp. It was really a bit irritating. And Malika was supposed to be the clever one.

'Do you want me to explain my company name or not?' she asked.

'I'm not sure you can.'

Malika drank the last of her coffee. She'd need another. 'OK. You remember the man who wants to find a customer for his books?'

'His print dictionaries. Yes.'

'Well, to find those customers for him we gather random information and analyse it, comparing and collating billions of posts, likes and searches made online. By asking the right question at the top of the sandwich we can identify members of the print-dictionary-buying community at the bottom. They never actually searched for a new dictionary because they're happy with the one they have, but through other choices they've made, like searching for other retro technologies, such as vinyl records, or *not* searching for word-processing updates, my algorithms can find likely print-dictionary users and my client can bombard those specific people with adverts for a brand new one.'

At that point their food finally arrived.

'Ah,' said Malika's mother. 'Real sandwiches. Lovely.'

'But most of our work is in political sampling,' Malika went on. 'If you're running a political campaign you want to spend your budget getting your message directly to the people who might be most susceptible to it. Not the people who are already going to vote for you and certainly not the people who are never going to vote for you. You're interested in the people who might be *persuaded* to vote for you. So, for instance, immigration seems to be a central issue in every election everywhere, right?'

'I know,' Malika's mum said sadly. 'I remember the days when we thought it would slowly go away.'

'Then you were spectacularly naive, Mum. It's never going to go away. Anyway. It's election time and everybody's focusing on immigration. You've got your multicultural party trying to motivate people to get out and vote for open borders. Who is their target? Probably no point sending an advert to someone who searches for anti-Semitic sites online.'

'You want someone who just searched for holidays in India, right?'

'Well done, Mum! But my algorithms are much subtler than that. Don't forget we're looking for *swing* voters. We don't want to waste our time with people who have made up their minds. For instance, that anti-Semitic-searching guy is almost certain to be anti-immigration – he may even admit to being racist. If I was looking for people who might be *persuaded* to vote anti-immigration I'd ignore him. I'm looking for people who absolutely don't think of themselves as racist but deep down are probably a little bit racist.'

'I think we all are, really.'

'So my algorithm looks for clues. With men, I'd be looking for someone who's a bit nostalgic and retro, loves a curry but also enjoys old-school English food. Maybe has a bit of a war-and-history thing, buys books on Churchill, plays historical battle games online. Nostalgic for the music of his youth, that sort of thing. Not necessarily *remotely* a real racist, just someone who's feeling a bit out of place. Someone who might respond to dog-whistle posts hinting at the disappearance of traditional English culture.'

'And you can do that with mathematics?'

'Yes.'

'And are you currently searching for people who might be per-suaded to be a little bit racist, Malika? And that English culture is disappearing? Or was it just an example, like the print dictionary?'

Malika did not meet her mother's eye. 'I don't choose our cli-ents, Mum.'

3. Professional Confessional

MICK MATLOCK was on a break. Eating a bag of salt and vinegar crisps, listening to a bit of Paul Weller on Spotify and browsing an online historical gaming website.

He was feeling slightly irritated.

Battle Craft Britain Inc., the creators of virtual-reality games based on real British battles, had announced that, beginning with their upcoming Battle of Edington (AD 878, Anglo-Saxons v. Vikings), the armies they created would be more inclusive of female combatants. This hotly contested decision had been based on some much-disputed historical research by a Cambridge postgraduate named Cressida Baynes. She claimed that many more female soldiers (and soldiers of colour) had fought in battles in the British Isles over the centuries than had previously been recognized, and their contribution to history had been wilfully ignored by white male historians. Mindful of the changing nature of the 'national conversation', BCB Inc. had decided to adjust the gender balance in their games accordingly.

Mick Matlock just couldn't help feeling annoyed. He knew he shouldn't be. He considered himself a feminist. He had had a poster of Annie Lennox on his wall at Hendon Police College. He had met Nancy while policing a 'Reclaim the Night' women's march. As far as he was concerned, BCB Inc. could create as many female Saxon and Viking soldiers as they liked. It was probably a good thing. A useful bit of social adjustment. Like not always giving little girls pink toys. What he found hard to handle was the idea that this development represented a historical truth, as opposed to the nakedly revisionist wishful thinking that it so clearly was. Matlock didn't really know why it bothered him. He'd talked about it with Nancy and she couldn't fathom why he gave a single solitary fuck about it – but he did.

Just then Matlock's phone rang and he was forced to unplug Paul Weller from his ears, put the gender balance of the Battle of Edington (AD 878) from his mind and focus on salvaging his career. Janine Treadwell was calling from the press and media office to inform him that the assistant deputy commissioner was insisting that he 'fronted' the media at 2 p.m. A second press conference to sort out the 'clusterfuck' he'd made of the first.

He tried his best to refuse. 'Janine,' he protested, 'all I wanted to do was point out that since we have an unidentified killer on the loose the people most at risk should act in their own interests to minimize the chances of becoming his next victim.'

'Women *know* they're at risk, Mick,' Janine Treadwell replied. 'We walk through life with our car keys in our hands, listening for every footstep behind us. You won't stop male violence by confining women to their homes.'

'I never said—'

'I know you didn't mean it, Mick, but that's how it came across.'

Put that way, it sounded reasonable. He was pretty sure Nancy would agree with her. He was absolutely certain that Nancy's seventeen-year-old daughter Kym would. Although that wouldn't stop Nancy telling Kym never to use the park at night and always to try to travel home with a friend.

Matlock had made the mistake of taking the call on speakerphone and he could see DC Clegg listening in. She gave him a sympathetic shrug. He knew what she was thinking. That he was just another bewildered old dad-man floundering about in the unfamiliar waters of a society he no longer 'got'.

Pretty hurtful for a guy who still considered himself to be

100 per cent rock 'n' roll. Although, of course, he also under-stood that rock 'n' roll was something only dad-men continued to aspire to be.

Matlock gave in. Apart from anything else it was clearly the only way he was going to be allowed back to work. Also, Nancy had called to say that a number of members of her women's book club had tweeted, questioning her silence over her despicably victim-blaming partner with the hashtag #CallOutTheOneYouLove.

Kym had texted him twice with the simple message *Wtf!*

Matlock knew that something had to be done. All of the news websites were carrying the story. Also mainstream telly. On top-rated show *Good Morning Britain* Piers Morgan had told Susanna Reid that Matlock was an embarrassment with no place in a mod-ern police force. Morgan had added that it wasn't often he sided with 'feminazis' but on this occasion 'I got your backs, girls.' The nation never found out exactly what Susanna Reid thought of this offer of solidarity because Morgan just kept on shouting, but her wry glance at the camera gave the audience a pretty good idea.

'Just tell me what the assistant deputy commissioner wants me to say,' Matlock told Janine, and shortly after lunch he found himself appearing before the media for the second time in less than five hours.

This time there were a lot more media to appear before.

Previously Matlock had been offering a situation report on a murder, something pretty routine for London's most senior homicide detective. Now he was at the sharp end of an urgent exercise in damage control.

Matlock was not the first to speak.

To his astonishment, the mayor had found the time to cycle over to New Scotland Yard, followed by his 'team' in a Toyota people-mover, to distance himself, publicly, from Matlock's depressingly patriarchal views.

'London should and must be a safe space for all its citizens,' the mayor intoned solemnly, 'particularly women. Women deserve respect and security in their own city. We will not compromise on that. Ever. Full stop. No argument. End of. Thank you. Chief Inspector Matlock will now address the media.'

Matlock apologized absolutely and unreservedly.

He knew it was his only option. The chorus of condemnation had grown so loud that any effort to apply context and nuance was pointless. He knew he was out of his depth in an age of outrage. Quite an irony, considering that as a proud schoolboy punk rocker he'd *been* the outrage.

In the end he had let Janine prepare a statement on his behalf and read it out.

'I wish to make it clear that any suggestion, which might have been inferred, that I believe men have the right to attack and murder women, if they can find a vulnerable one in a park late at night, was the deeply unfortunate result of a clumsy and unforgivable misspeak. I make no excuses. On the contrary, I own my misspoke. I am all over it. Because that is who I am. I shall be seeking counselling and taking time to reflect and I hope to emerge a better, stronger and more inclusive police chief inspector. I should like to conclude by saying that I hope the public will put this behind them and give me the chance to grow into being the policeman I know I can be. Thank you.'

'Brilliant,' DC Clegg said, handing him a much-needed cup of tea as he got down from the podium. 'That was a proper professional confessional. I almost believed you.'

As Matlock took the mug from her he felt his phone buzz in his pocket. He thought it would be Nancy, calling to comment on his performance. It wasn't: it was an unsolicited post from a source he didn't recognize informing him that Battle Craft Britain Inc. had been forced by feminist academics to declare that King Alfred the Great was probably a woman. Having only that morning read the actual facts, Matlock knew this was a gross exaggeration of the story. A lie, in fact. Amazing how quickly a small irritation had morphed into a completely distorted online outrage.

Where had it come from?

Who had the time for that shit?

4. #ProudMeninist

SITTING IN his little bed-sitting room in Stoke Newington, a room no other person had entered since he had begun renting it, Wotan Orc Slayer was reading the same unsolicited news post as Matlock.

So were ex-US Navy SEAL Cody Strong and Confederate General Stonewall Jackson.

They were all the same person, online gaming avatars used by Oliver Tollett, a supermarket manager and occasional Uber driver from Tunbridge Wells. Unlike Matlock, Wotan, as he liked to be called in day-to-day life, was taking the post at face value and he was furious.

This was it. This was the absolute chuffing limit.

He had been aware that Battle Craft Britain Inc., to which he was a long-time subscriber, had made the decision to embrace the madness that claimed numerous women had been employed as soldiers throughout Britain's history. That much had been banging round the chat rooms for weeks. However, he could now see that this crazed PC madness had bitten much deeper than BCB were admitting. According to the news post, Battle Craft Britain Inc. were secretly planning to fully 'feminize' all their games to address the 'unacceptable' gender imbalance in the armies of previous eras. Furthermore, with reference to new research being presented by respected academic Cressida Baynes, going forward, Alfred the Great would be represented as a female character.

Chillingly, the unsolicited post informed Wotan that none of this information had been included in recent official BCB postings – evidence that a 'deep state' existed within the organization, which was dedicated to covering up its blatant social engineering.

Wotan wanted to cry. He really did.

What was *happening* to the world? When would this end?

He wanted to shout. He wanted to fight. He wanted to smash someone's brains out. Why did these shadowy deep-stated liberal forces *hate men* so much?

Wasn't it enough that the entire resources of the state were being deployed to make the *current* British Army all women? Wotan could not *remember* the last army recruitment advert he'd seen that had any men in it. Maybe in the background. Maybe as blurry out-of-focus goons following in the wake of some clear-eyed and determined-looking lady officer pursuing her army dream. Maybe as a pathetic orderly standing to one side while some feisty, oil-covered cutie mechanic fixed the engine on a three-ton truck.

Why? Why was there this conspiracy to pretend that women were as good at being soldiers as men? Or better. Because obviously the Normandy landings would have been a doddle if half the landing craft had been full of girls. Even his favourite Second World War sniper game had suddenly supplied the Wehrmacht with lady snipers for the Battle of Stalingrad. The Wehrmacht hadn't had any women in combat. IT WAS A FACT! What was going on? Why did every fucking TV drama, every super-hero movie, every rebooted much-loved franchise have to be *all* about kung-fu kickin', no-shit-takin', ball-bustin', bad-assin', fucking wimmin!

And now this! Now the Battle of Edington in 878 was going to be all about women soldiers with a girl King Alfred.

Wotan was just so *angry*.

He tweeted a rape threat to Cressida Baynes and went back to stock-checking the frozen goods. #ProudMeninist.

5. 'Can We Please Not Talk About the Fucking Referendum?'

IT WAS time to view the corpse of Sammy Hill.

Matlock drove, Taylor sat in the front passenger seat and Clegg in the back. She always sat in the back because she had the shortest legs. She'd always accepted the logic of that. Lately, however, she had begun to wonder. After all, if she were to sit in the front passenger seat she could pull it forward to create more room in the back very easily. Why shouldn't Taylor sit in the back sometimes? Clegg had recently come to feel that her presumed position in the car was a really good example of the tiny assumptions that shored up the patriarchy. Boys in the front, girls in the back. That was a really interesting aspect of the whole post-MeToo thing. Actual harassment aside, it was funny how different *everything* looked in the wake of the more general re-examination of gender presumptions that was occurring throughout the world. As a woman she just *noticed* shit more. Or maybe she'd always noticed it but now she was less inclined to put up with it.

On the other hand, could she really be arsed with the whole confrontation of telling Taylor it was his turn to sit in the back?

Not really. Life was too short. Clegg had learned to pick her battles.

*

Taylor was scrolling through what was still called paperwork, even though it was done on an iPad. 'Not much in the initial autopsy, boss,' he said. 'Pathologist says she's got some semen out of the corpse but I reckon it had to have been deposited there consensually because there's no mention of tissue damage around the victim's anus.'

'Anus?'

'Yeah.'

'The semen was in her anus?'

'That's what I'm telling you, boss.'

Matlock sucked a boiled sweet and resisted the powerful urge to crunch it up all at once. He wished it was still OK to smoke in cars. 'Well, that might give us a *possible* lead, I suppose,' he said.

'Boss?'

'You know. A bit wild. Bit kinky and all that.'

'Wild and kinky?'

'Anal sex.'

'Is anal sex wild and kinky?'

There was a moment's uncomfortable silence.

'Well, no. Not really. Isn't it?' Matlock replied. 'I mean in – you know – heterosexual terms. The victim is a woman.'

He crunched his sweet. He was aware, of course, that internet porn had familiarized and anaesthetized an entire generation to sexual practices that his own generation, post-punk or not, had considered at the very least exotic and at most downright pervy. But he still wasn't quite *used* to it. It hadn't been a 'thing' in his day. When he'd been a student he and his girlfriend, whom he'd met at a Simple Minds gig, had felt very grown-up buying a paperback book called *The Joy of Sex*. This was principally a series of drawings depicting various positions for heterosexual coupling. Matlock recalled that the book had mentioned anal sex as an option, but only briefly, at the very end, and only then with some pretty strict advice about hygiene. There certainly hadn't been a drawing. He would have remembered. Nancy felt the same way as he did about it, if anything even more strongly, assuring him that, even should he wish to, he was '*never* going there'.

DC Clegg broke the silence from the back seat. 'Don't ask me, boss. Not really my department, as you know. Barry? Is anal sex a thing among heterosexual couples?' She was gratified to see that the back of Taylor's neck had gone a shade pinker. It wasn't easy to embarrass Barry Taylor on sexual matters so this was a small victory.

'I don't believe it's considered *particularly* unusual, Sally. Don't think you could call it a point of interest in our investigation.'

'Actually, they did a whole episode of *Sex and the City* on it,' said Clegg, 'and that was literally decades ago. Then there was that bit at the start of *Fleabag* where she does a monologue to the camera while being nastied round the back.'

There was another awkward silence, which Taylor filled by putting the radio on. It was tuned to a talk channel.

Fortunately the notoriety of #NotHerFault and Matlock's public shaming had dropped from the news cycle as quickly as it had appeared.

Unfortunately the talk was now once more all about the forth-coming referendum, which was due at the end of September, slightly less than four months away. English independence was proving to be a more popular notion than the prime minister had expected. She had called the referendum in an effort to lance the boil of English nationalism that was growing ever angrier and more pustulent on the right wing of her party. The same trick that David Cameron had once tried to pull over Brexit. And it was beginning to look like an equally massive miscalculation.

'Bunter's right,' a voice was saying, as indeed did most of the voices on talk radio that summer. 'I think it's about time we went it alone. Churchill and 1966 and all that.'

'Bunter's a dickhead,' Matlock muttered.

The 'Bunter' he and the caller were referring to was chief among the three political heavyweights who had lent their support to the England Out campaign. Bunter Jolly, Guppy Toad and Plantagenet Greased-Hogg. 'Big beasts' as the press liked to call them, with 'fine minds' – a term that, on the available evidence, appeared to indicate a passing ability to make weak jokes in worse Latin. Statesmen of proven substance and ability who had resigned cabinet posts to add their 'massive popularity' and 'vast political experience' to the task of reinventing England as an 'optimistic, outward-looking, global trading nation, fit for purpose to meet the challenges of the twenty-first century'.

Any suggestion that the three might have joined England Out because it offered them the only realistic chance of ever reinventing their careers, which were faltering due to their vanity, hubris and utter incompetence, was drowned in the clamour of star-struck approval that their much-remarked-on big-beast status provoked.

Matlock turned off the radio. 'I am so bored with that stupid referendum.'

'You and the rest of the country, boss,' Taylor agreed. 'Still, we can't ignore it. It's happening.'

'Nobody wanted another,' Clegg complained from the back. 'I thought we elected a government to govern, not to be bothering us every five minutes to make decisions for them.'

'Bloody right,' said Matlock.

'I don't know about that,' Taylor said. 'If they really are thinking about breaking up the UK, I reckon it's a bit too important to leave to a bunch of politicians, don't you? Is this what democracy *should* look like? Politicians listening to the people.'

'Jesus!' Matlock exclaimed, shaking his head. 'Are you listening to yourself, Barry? Why elect politicians at all if they're going to pass the buck straight back to the mob?'

'Mob, boss?' Taylor said. 'Bit snobby, don't you think? Not very inclusive. Not very *politically correct*.'

'We know what mobs look like, Barry!' Matlock snapped. 'We've policed enough of them. Do you really want one making snap decisions about the future of the country?'

'Yeah! Why not?'

'Are you actually *serious*?' Matlock demanded. 'If we referred every important and difficult decision to "the people", the first thing they'd do would be to bring back hanging.'

'And that would be a bad thing?' Taylor asked.

'I reckon the chief's totally right,' Clegg put in from the back. 'Who are these "people" anyway? These "people" politicians are supposed to be listening to? I'm a person and I don't agree with any of those idiots who phone in on the radio. And I certainly didn't want a referendum to break up the UK.'

'The Germans ban referendums in their constitution,' Matlock said. 'Do you know why? Because Hitler found them a useful tool.'

Taylor shrugged, clearly bored with the conversation.

Clegg plugged in her earphones.

It was all bollocks anyway and shit would happen whatever you did.

Matlock seethed.

When he was young back in the eighties he'd been pretty politically motivated. Anti-establishment, even. He'd joined the police because he'd thought it would be a good base for having a stab at a career in politics. Even after he'd decided he liked being a copper, he'd still considered himself a bit of a radical. As a young constable, policing the poll-tax riots had been a genuinely conflicting experience for him because basically he agreed with the protesters.

But now. Now! Things had gone so far to the right that the status quo had to be defended! The very things he'd questioned as a student – constitutional government, the mainstream press, judges and the courts – were under threat! This stupid referendum was just the next step in the gradual shattering of any semblance of normal society. Of belief in *anything*. It had opened a floodgate of petty nationalism and covert racism. It was appalling.

And, personally, he blamed the fucking Scots.

They'd started it, trying to break up a perfectly functioning country that had won two world wars, produced the Beatles and invented the steam engine. Why? Hadn't they realized that the inevitable result of Scottish nationalism would be English nationalism? How much nationalism could one small island take? He'd read somewhere that *London* should be going for independence because its economy was so big. What about just Knightsbridge, then? Or the top three levels of the Shard? Matlock reflected that it was actually quite surprising it had taken so long for things to get as nasty as they had. At the time of the first Scottish referendum, in what now felt like a different age and a different country, he had expected a resentful England to immediately follow suit and shout, 'Well, bugger off, then.' But, apart from a bit of banter, England had pretty much ignored it at the time. Now, of course, after the disastrous fudge of Brexit, which had satisfied no one, England was having its moment. There were those stupid St George flags absolutely everywhere. Just like Edinburgh and Glasgow were hung end to end with those stupid bloody Saltires. No one except Buckingham Palace flew the Union flag any more.

How had it all come to this?

Ten years ago the UK had been a relatively successful European nation with a world-beating Olympic team and an enviable reputation for general tolerance. Now a country that had been united since 1707 had absolutely no idea who or what it was.

How had it all gone so wrong so quickly?

Did anybody really *want* this chaos?

It was almost as if somebody was deliberately stirring the pot. But that was just paranoid.

Matlock did not believe in conspiracy theories.

6. #DontBookBedsFromBigots

FREDDIE AND Jacob Whitely-Enfield pressed send. Their holiday had been ruined. They'd been severely inconvenienced and horribly humiliated. Turned away from a legitimate booking at ten o'clock at night and forced to check into a Travelodge in Penrith. It had utterly spoiled their week's hiking in the Lake District.

Jocham and Brenda Macroon, the Christian couple who ran the Wee Nook Guest House, had offered to provide them with separate rooms at the same price but, not surprisingly, Freddie and Jacob, who were on their honeymoon, wanted the double room Freddie had booked.

It had been a stand-off. In a horribly tense, semi-polite, terribly 'English' sort of way. Voices struggling to be calm but shaking with emotion on both sides.

'Excuse me, but it is illegal to discriminate against same-sex couples.'

'We ask you to respect our religious beliefs and either sleep separately or seek accommodation elsewhere.'

'We will not. We've booked this place because we want to climb Great Gable tomorrow.'

'When we accepted the booking we were unaware of its nature.'

'We ask you to respect our sexual orientation.'

'We ask you to respect our faith. We are evangelical Christians and believe homosexuality is a sin.'

'That is a disgusting and offensive thing to say.'

'We will pray for you.'

'We don't want your fucking prayers.'

'Please leave.'

Freddie and Jacob had been forced to return to their car, shaken and distressed, and search for accommodation elsewhere. Getting through to the Travelodge had not been easy because 4G reception was terrible in the hills.

(Jocham and Brenda Macroon had been as good as their word and, having gone online to refund the Whitely-Enfields' deposit, had knelt together in their lounge to pray for two sinners.)

When Freddie and Jacob finally arrived at the Travelodge, it was too late to get even a glass of wine, let alone anything to eat. They were utterly miserable. And while they were naturally people-people and not comfortable picking fights, they really felt that the way they had been treated could not go unchallenged. They thought about reporting it to the police but, frankly, didn't want to further ruin their holiday. So they wrote a scathing review on Trip-Advisor and copied it into a tweet, #DontBookBedsFromBigots.

7. A Smooth Operator

WHEN MALIKA returned from having lunch with her mother she had been quite surprised to see Tommy Spoon and Xavier Arron, the two most vocal backers of the England Out campaign, in the offices of Communication Sandwich. She knew that England Out were their clients – by far their biggest clients, in fact – but the chumminess with which her boss, Julian, was showing them round the office suggested more of a partnership to her.

That was a bit weird.

They weren't an obvious fit, the three of them. Not really mates material. Spoon and Arron were loudly and proudly 'rough diamonds'. Self-made multi-millionaires full of swagger and bling. The opposite of the super-cool Julian Carter, founder and CEO of Communication Sandwich. Malika's private name for Julian was the Smooth Operator because he liked to describe his job as 'just like an old-time telephone operator – pulling out a plug here, rerouting it into a socket there and creating a whole new paradigm of commerce, *millions* of times a second'.

He was soft-spoken, self-effacing and discreetly posh. A bit of a Hugh Grant type, with a dash of Bill Nighy, very attractive in a slightly dishevelled way. His glasses looked like NHS black plastic ones from the sixties but they were, of course, eye-wateringly expensive, super-hip Calvin Kleins. His hair was definitely too long for his age – he was over fifty – but he got away with it because he somehow made it look like he'd just forgotten to have it cut rather than that he thought it looked really cool and sexy (which Malika could see he *so* did). Julian affected a bit of a hapless-posh-boy act but he was obviously extremely sharp. There was a slightly anarchic air about him, like he didn't give a shit. He looked like the sort of bloke who'd been thrown out of a minor public school. In fact, he'd been thrown out of Eton.

Malika liked him. She wouldn't trust him, but she liked him. He was charming, confident and funny. He'd also given her a brilliant job for which he paid her far more than he needed to. Of course, he could afford to be generous – he was clearly very rich. Malika was honest enough with herself to know she found that attractive. She'd grown up quite poor, watching her parents work every waking hour to make a place for themselves in Britain, to build a future for her and her brothers. At Oxford she'd met lots of rich kids, who didn't need to worry about the massive loans that people like Malika were acquiring. Many of her fellow students resented the rich kids. Malika didn't; she envied them.

When she had first joined the firm, Malika had asked Julian why it was called Communication Sandwich. 'Not that it's not a lovely name.'

'That is an unnecessary double negative, Malika,' he had replied, 'because it is *not* a lovely name. It's meaningless post-ironic drivel designed to please a juvenilized society obsessed with pretending everything in life, including long hours of mind-numbingly complex mathematics, is funky and fun. Personally I blame Steve Jobs. He started it all by wearing T-shirts to work and calling a series of technological innovations that would *literally* remake human society in a single decade "just a bunch of cool stuff". I mean, *do* fuck off, Steve. There's humble-bragging and then there's just pure *wank*.'

That was Julian all over. Wry. Apparently fiercely honest. *Probably* a bit of a bastard underneath the chic, crumpled surface but fun to work for. And he always opened lots of champagne on Friday afternoons, which was so important in a boss.

'Malika,' Julian said, as the three of them passed her. 'Let me introduce Tommy and Xavier, or The Zax, as we call him. Great guys. You've probably heard of them.'

Of course she'd heard of them. Everyone had heard of Tommy Spoon and Xavier 'The Zax' Arron in that divided and divisive summer. The loudest English nationalists, they were rarely out of the news.

Tommy owned a much-loved chain of pub-restaurants called Spoons, which served a deliberately retro 1970s English menu consisting of prawn cocktail, steak and chips, and Black Forest gateau. The Zax was a property developer. A 'proud Londoner' who sold London real estate to foreign investors – yacht-dwelling itinerant super-rich in need of apartment blocks to hide their money.

Tommy and The Zax: two straight-talking English patriots, who had had enough of the 'Brussels super-state', to which England was still very much linked even though the UK had sort of half left it. They had also had enough of 'political correctness', which, in their view, was crippling what it even meant to be English.

'Hello, Mr Spoon. Hello, Mr Arron,' Malika said politely.

'Don't be fooled by her youth and beauty,' Julian said, 'which I know I'm not allowed to say but I shall anyway because it's a simple statement of fact. Malika is our Queen of Maths. She is, quite simply, a number-crunching genius. Got a double first from Oxford. I had to poach her from Magdalen College – they were trying to keep her to do a PhD. Well, you would, wouldn't you? Asian *and* a woman *and* state-educated. Talk about ticking all the boxes! In terms of corporate-virtue signalling she's the full triple threat. She's also the reason you pay so much fucking money for my services. Every single England Out vote we bring on board is linked directly to Malika via her extraordinary algorithms. Pretty damned impressive for the daughter of immigrants, don't you think?'

Malika could see Julian was enjoying himself. He loved a bit of mischief and it was certainly mischievous to tell Tommy Spoon and Xavier Arron that they owed their current success in the opinion polls to a brown person. Both men had recently stood in front of a large billboard featuring 'hordes' of brown people 'swarming' to get into England, with the stark headline 'Bursting Point'.

'Julian's exaggerating,' Malika said. 'We're a team here. I'm part of it.'

Spoon grunted a greeting. Arron deigned a nod.

Julian walked them to the lift. 'Brilliant of you guys to drop in,' Malika heard him saying. '*Sooo* good to have your input. Let's do it at beer o'clock next time, eh? Or, better still, a boozy lunch and we'll write the afternoon off, eh? *Eh?*'

She could hear their loud laughter from the lobby – Tommy and The Zax letting everyone know what bloody good blokes they were.

'What a couple of absolute *cunts*,' Julian said when he returned, causing all Malika's busy programmers to grin broadly over their flickering screens.

'You seemed to be getting on with them pretty well,' Malika suggested.

'I can get on with anyone,' Julian replied. 'It's a gift. But really ouchy-wah-wah. I mean seriously. *Such* cunts. Which I *know* is a word I'm not supposed to use but, really, which other word would do? Cunty fucking cunting cunts, the pair of them. Anyway. Fuck 'em. They're cunts. But they pay. A lot. Which is literally all we care about. Anyhoo, Malika, old scout, would you pop through to my office and have a word?'

Julian was the only one who had an office. Everybody else had to hot-desk, constantly migrating amid a vast open-plan sea of computers. Even Malika had to log on at any available screen, which she absolutely hated. At Oxford she'd had her own beautiful oak-lined study.

She followed Julian into his splendid office.

'Well, now, Professor Rajput. How are we getting along with #ProudMeninist and the terrifying threat that men are being written out of history?' he asked.

'Great,' Malika replied. 'It's running like wildfire. So many genuine re-posts we hardly needed to push it with bots at all after the first hour or two. I'll do myself out of a job.'

'Not in the slightest. If it's hit its mark, it's only because of the extreme accuracy of your targeting.'

'Well, my bit's pretty simple, really. If you can do the maths.'

'That being rather the point, my darling. *If* you can do the maths.'

There was a pause. Malika waited. She had guessed that he hadn't brought her to his office just to ask how one of their chosen hashtags was going. He needed only to glance at a screen for that.

'Malika?' he said finally. 'Do you ever wonder where we get our raw data from? You know, the *real* information, which your algorithms then mix and match to find fertile ground for our lovely posts and tweets?'

'It might have crossed my mind, I suppose,' Malika replied warily. 'Should I have done?'

Julian smiled what was clearly intended to be an inscrutable smile. 'All right. Let me put it differently. Supposing I told you that the process wasn't *strictly* above board. What would you say?'

It felt like a test. A test Malika was determined to pass. She was a twenty-two-year-old mathematician earning a six-figure salary at a super-modern, super-hip, cutting-edge company at the heart of the City. Life was an adventure and she wasn't going to screw up the gig of a lifetime on grounds of petty morality. Nobody did morals post-Trump anyway. As long as she kept herself in the clear she was happy not to ask too many questions.

'I'd say *duh*. Obviously it's not above board because we deal in private data. The clue's in the name.'

Julian laughed appreciatively. 'Absolutely! Well *done*, old scout. Good answer.'

'And, for what it's worth, I'm pretty sure I know how you do it too,' she said, pressing her advantage.

'Really? Do tell.'

'I presume it's a version of the trick Cambridge Analytica worked over the first Brexit vote a few years ago. You establish your initial sample in a legitimate way – I'm guessing some sort of pop-up online survey.'

'Correctomundo! Give the girl a coconut. Over a quarter of a million of them, in fact. At an average of between five and ten US dollars each. Not cheap.'

'So you offered a payment. Thought so.'

'Did you now?' Julian ran his fingers through his lovely hair. 'And what made you think that?'

'Because to get that money they have to click your app to receive the payment code. Bingo! You're inside their computer! Suddenly those quarter of a million anonymous questionnaires are linked to actual individuals. You know who they are and where they live.'

Julian didn't reply. He was still smiling, encouraging her to go on.

'*And* you're inside their Facebook profiles,' Malika said.

'Yes.' He nodded.

'Meaning you can match the details on each person's questionnaire with that person's entire online life. Every "like", every post, every search. You're building up incredibly sophisticated profiles of real physical people. People who have no idea that a funny little company with a rather silly name knows literally as much about them as they know themselves.'

'You are a clever girl, aren't you?'

'And better yet,' Malika went on, 'much, *much* better yet. We also have, through that one payment app click, direct access to all their *friends'* Facebooks.'

'We?'

She'd said it deliberately and was pleased he'd picked up on it.

'Yes, us, Julian. We have a quarter of a million unsuspecting people about whom we know everything, plus their hundreds of online friends, about whom we can deduce almost as much, giving us a bank of about twenty-five million people, whose names and addresses we know and whose Facebook pages we can access. That allows us to target any product our clients may wish to sell to the people most likely to be influenced into buying it.' She paused for a moment. 'In this case, English independence.'

Julian smiled a big wicked smile. 'Very good,' he said. 'You worked it all out. I thought you probably had.'

Of course he had. He was testing her. If she'd played the innocent he might have decided he couldn't trust her. Instead, he was binding her to him. Making her complicit. She wasn't a lawyer and didn't know whether this sort of practice was actually criminal, but it was certainly unethical and against every code of practice. From now on, if she was ever minded to blow a whistle on him she'd have to think about whether she needed to strike a plea bargain first.

'Yes,' said Malika. 'I worked out on probably my first day that every search result I produce for you is based directly on stolen data. And, to compound matters further, *expensive* stolen data. An expense that clearly isn't being declared in England Out's accounting for its election spending.'

'And you don't mind?'

'*Possibly* I mind. But I can put up with a lot for what you pay me.'

'Well done. Good answer. Worth a twenty-five per cent rise, I think. Starting now.'

'Thanks, I'll take it. Although you don't have to bribe me, Julian. I like my job. Besides, it isn't *really* a crime, is it? The internet's an absolute sieve. Everybody knows that. And everybody pinches data.'

'Of course they do. And it's not a bribe, Malika,' Julian said. 'It's a reward. You've earned it. And speaking of which, be a good girl and put this through your number-cruncher, will you? Find me a million people to send it to.'

Julian had taken up his beautiful Montblanc fountain pen, an accessory Malika hadn't believed anybody actually owned. She'd only ever seen one in huge displays at Dubai Airport Duty Free, clasped between Johnny Depp's tattooed fingers. Julian paused for a moment, apparently to appreciate the weight and feel of the lovely object, and then, applying its solid gold nib to a sheet of thick creamy paper he wrote, #DontBookBedsFromBigots.

'Sad story,' he went on. 'A very sweet gay couple had their holiday ruined by a couple of religious Nazis. I think their story needs to be heard.'

'Wow,' said Malika. 'Are people still refusing rooms to gay guys? I haven't heard of an incident like that in years.'

'Yes, it's less common, these days, as we all embrace the rainbow. Which is why it's *so* important people hear about this one.'

'It's lucky Muslims don't run many country guest houses. None of the people my parents know would rent a room to a gay couple.'

'Hm. That would be an interesting crisis for the liberal left, wouldn't it? They never mind having a pop at the poor old Christian bigots but I don't think they'd be quite so eager to take on the mullahs, eh? Gay holidaymakers pitted against Muslim hoteliers? What *would* the lovely liberals do? They'd be in *knots*. Sadly, for now we must make do with Christian zealots, whom everybody can agree to shit on. So run along and design me a nice long equation to get that hashtag to the sort of people who will get very, *very* angry about it.'

'Well, that's both sides, isn't it? The gay community and the Christians.'

'Exactly, my darling. Exactly.'

'You want me to send it to both sides?'

'Yes, absolutely. Must be fair.'

'Any particular reason you want me to do this, Julian?'

'I've told you. So they'll all get very, *very* angry about it.'

8. Love, Spelled L-U-V

MATLOCK, CLEGG and Taylor were still making their slow progress through London on their way to the police morgue.

'At this rate,' Matlock observed, 'whoever killed Sammy will have died of old age before we have a chance to catch him.'

Neither Clegg nor Taylor replied. They were both plugged into their phones. The only answer was the tinny tinkling of leaking earbuds.

'Or her,' he added. 'I suppose she *could* have been killed by a woman. We should keep an open mind. Jesus, this traffic is terrible.'

Taylor momentarily unplugged his earphones. 'Stick the blue light on, boss. Give it a bit of siren.'

'Visiting a corpse is not an emergency, Barry. It's already dead.'

He'd thought about using the siren. He'd already had to text Nancy to tell her he was running late *again* and couldn't pick up her daughter from netball. A desertion of a shared responsibility that had *not* gone down well. But Matlock felt rules were important and sirens were for emergencies. Not late school pick-ups.

'Oh, my God!' Taylor exclaimed.

'What?' Matlock demanded. He didn't like sudden noises when he was driving.

'Sorry, boss, but you have *got* to see this. I don't know whether to laugh or cry.' Taylor reached across, holding up his phone.

'I'm driving, Barry.'

'We're at a red light.'

'I'm a policeman. I'm not going to look at a mobile phone while I'm behind the wheel of a car.'

'I thought that was one of the perks. Hey, Sally!' Taylor called, turning and waving his phone at Clegg. 'Check your newsfeed.'

Clegg unplugged her earbuds and looked at her phone. 'Oh, my God, that's *hilarious*.'

'What? What?' Matlock enquired irritably.

'The #LetsStickTogether lot are calling their pro-UK campaign Luv Island,' Taylor said gleefully.

'Luv Island? How try-hard is that?' Clegg joined in. 'L-U-V.'

'To distinguish it from the programme?' Matlock asked.

'Well, obviously.'

Love Island had been *the* reality television event of the previous year and for many years before that too.

'Never watched it,' said Matlock.

'You are joking me!' said Taylor. 'Never watched *Love Island*? It's utterly brilliant.'

'What? A bunch of idiots shagging each other on an island? Jesus, Barry, are you eleven?'

'You are so wrong, chief. It's all about the relationships and human interaction. It's actually really subtle.'

'Is it bollocks.'

'Put the radio back on,' Clegg demanded from behind. 'Maybe they'll bring it up.'

Matlock did as he was bid.

The station they'd been tuned to had briefly moved on from discussing the referendum to venting their fury on a new 'radical gay agenda', which it seemed was based around the hashtag #DontBookBedsFromBigots. This, the apoplectic host claimed, in tones of highest outrage, appeared to be a concerted effort by highly organized homosexual activists to close down all Christian businesses in revenge for two of their number having had to spend the night in a Travelodge.

Matlock tried another channel.

The leader of the opposition was tying himself in knots trying to explain that his party's referendum policy was that England should remain a part of the UK while not being *too* fervent about it. 'Now, let me make this absolutely clear,' the hapless leader burbled. 'We totally believe in the United Kingdom but that does not mean we do not respect absolutely the aspirations of self-determination felt so strongly in all parts of our great nation. This is why we are pledged to ever more comprehensive measures of devolution so that the four great nations of our one great nation may be assured that under our government they'll be as separate and divided as they can possibly be without making it actually official. Basically, really, only the name and the monarch will remain.'

'So much for Luv Island, then?' the host asked testily.

'I'm sorry? Do you mean the TV programme?'

'No. *Luv* Island. L-U-V. Your new slogan.'

There could now be heard the rustling of papers as the leader of the opposition was brought up to speed on the Team UK campaign's latest PR initiative.

Matlock turned off the radio for the second time. 'I can't stand it any more. How about I dial up a bit of Smiths on Spotify?' he said. 'Continue you philistines' education in proper music?'

But neither DS Taylor nor DC Clegg heard him. They were both plugged back in. Clegg was listening to her own music and Taylor was deep in Facebook. He'd just 'liked' a meme that a friend had put up about foreign superstars clogging up the Premier League.

Across town the computers of Communication Sandwich harvested that 'like' and added it to Taylor's profile.

Of course it wasn't racist to laugh about how all the famous English sides were made up almost entirely of players whose names the commentators could not pronounce. But it was certainly within the spectrum of Malika's latest algorithm.

Ping! Taylor got an unsolicited 'news' alert informing him that more immigrants had got jobs last year than the English. The post wasn't backed up by any source but it did contain a link to the England Out webpage.

9. Harnessing the Zeitgeist

DEEP IN an airless bunker in the basement at the Home Office, the campaign to keep England within the United Kingdom (#LetsStickTogether) was holding the latest in a daily series of crisis meetings.

Team UK, as it styled itself, was a cross-party initiative supported by both the government and the opposition. It was led by Jim, the minister for referendums, and Beryl, his opposition shadow – surnames were no longer used in Whitehall to avoid any whiff of posh-snob elitism. Jim and Beryl were two diligent career politicians, two fantastically boring people, who had none of the 'star quality' of England Out's celebrated big beasts.

Conscious that they lacked charisma, Jim and Beryl had engaged the services of an incredibly expensive marketing company, which assured them that, for several million pounds of public money, they could get the Team UK 'brand' 'hard-wired into the zeitgeist'.

The need for this was urgent. Team UK's back was against the wall.

The clock was ticking and England Out were running rings around them.

The reason for this, as Toby, the guy from the incredibly expensive marketing company, explained, was because Team UK's 'brand' was just too negative.

'All you've been doing is telling people that breaking up the

UK would lead to a certain economic meltdown due to a pointless act of wilful self-harm.'

'Because it's true,' Jim protested.

'True? What's true? What does "true" even mean?' Toby asked.

'It means something that is factually correct.'

'Ha!' Toby replied. 'Bunter Jolly says you're just pursuing "Project Gloomy Guts" and failing to recognize the "sunlit uplands" ahead.' He put down the enormous frothy latte he'd been swigging at and tapped a key on his computer.

A YouTube clip appeared of Bunter Jolly standing on a pavement making one of his periodic 'statesmanlike' interventions, which he liked to deliver while out jogging in his enormous St George's flag rugger shorts. 'I may be thicker than a tuckshop lardy cake,' he blithered breathlessly to the devoted press pack, who followed his every move, 'but I know Project Gloomy Guts when I see it. I say to these doom-mongers, just believe in England! There are sunlit uplands ahead.'

Toby tapped the keyboard once more and the image froze. 'We need to be as positive and proactive as they are,' he said. 'And the key to that is connecting with the Millennials and Gen Zedders.'

Jim and Beryl perked up at this. Millennials and Gen Zedders were the demographic who, polling suggested, were most likely to be supportive of keeping England within an outward-looking, Euro-friendly UK.

They also adored the TV show *Love Island*.

The 'connect' was, as Toby explained, a no-brainer. What, he enquired, was not to brain?

'Love Island spelled L-U-V. I love it. What's not to love? It really taps into the zeitgeist.'

'Zeitgeist. I like that,' said Beryl. 'Zeitgeist is good.'

'*Love Island* the TV show is a real unifying force in the nation,' Toby went on, 'and we are going to hitch a ride.'

'Brilliant,' said Beryl happily.

'It does sound promising,' Jim admitted.

'You bet your sweet ass it sounds promising,' Toby pronounced authoritatively. '*Love Island*'s brought back appointment television. For the first time in fifteen years we're all watching and talking about the same TV show.'

'All of us?' asked Jim, who was old enough to remember *Only Fools and Horses* getting twenty million viewers at Christmas.

'Well, three million of us, but they're *all* Millennials and Gen Zedders and, demographic-wise, that's your holy grail right there. Check out the logo, guys. We're *very* pleased.'

Toby punched up a graphic on his PowerPoint. A rainbow-coloured British Isle set within a heart-shaped Union Jack. 'We see the campaign as taking the undeniable geographical fact that England, Scotland and Wales are all part of *one island* and keep doubling down on that. *One* island. Whole and absolute. A unity and a fellowship, contained within a *single* glorious coastline, which has stood the test of centuries. The UK *is* a Luv Island. In the very *realist* sense of the word. England. Scotland. Wales. Three countries. One island. One love. Together and inclusive. This – if you like – *is us*. Fuck, yeah!' Toby punched the air.

Jim and Beryl considered the graphic for a moment. They knew something was missing, of course, but were both wondering whether Toby did.

'This is us . . . plus, of course, Northern Ireland,' Beryl said, almost apologetically.

'Sorry?' Toby asked, returning his fist to his latte.

'What the campaign to keep England in the Union is particularly big on is – well, the Union. Which, as you say, is contained within the whole of *this* island, the one you've coloured with a rainbow, the one with England, Scotland and Wales in it.'

'That's right. The Luv Island.'

'Mm. Plus, the top bit of the island to the left.'

'Sorry?'

'The island of Ireland.'

'The island of island? What does that even mean?'

'Not the island of island. The island of *Ireland*. Which contains one whole nation, the Irish Republic, which is nothing to do with us so we can definitely park that, but also a little bit of *our* nation, which very much *is* to do with us, Northern Ireland.'

'Oh, I see.'

'So actually it's not *quite* as neat as you'd hoped. I mean, still neat. Still brilliant. It's only that we can't say the UK is the Luv Island. We can only say the UK is the Luv Island plus the top bit of the island on the left.'

'Hm. That won't fly. I'm afraid we're going to have to ignore Northern Ireland, if it's all right with you.'

'Well, that is what we did with Brexit,' Jim admitted.

10. The Body in the Drawer

CHIEF INSPECTOR Matlock, DS Taylor and DC Clegg entered the cold room of the police morgue. There they found Dr Katherine Galloway, a bright, enthusiastic young Home Office pathologist, waiting for them.

'Hey, Mike. Or is it Mick?' she said, reaching out a hand. 'I'm Kate.'

Matlock still hadn't got used to people using first names in all circumstances and at all times, no matter how inappropriate it felt. They were in a *morgue*, for Christ's sake. And he was nearly fifty-four. She looked barely old enough even to have graduated. And she wanted to call him Mike, not Chief Inspector Matlock, not even Michael, but Mike – *Mick*, even. She had literally leaped straight to diminutives. He knew he shouldn't be finding this confronting. There was a time when he'd railed against formality, wearing his school tie as loose as he could, going to classes at Hendon Police College in skinny jeans and a Clash T-shirt. But now he really *missed* a few rules of social engagement.

Even an email from his bank began with 'Hi'. *Hi, Michael. About your fixed-term deposit* ... What was the point of this orthodoxy of over-familiarity? Who did it serve? Matlock rather suspected it served people at the top. It was obviously going to be easier to disguise the predatory nature of your politics or your business model if you affected to be on first-name terms with the people you were intent on duping, demeaning and exploiting. Or, in Matlock's case, offering a considerably lower interest rate on an account he'd presumed was locked in at 1.8 per cent.

But try telling that to young people today.

He bit down on another boiled sweet and got on with it, addressing Home Office pathologist Dr Katherine Galloway, whom he'd known for five seconds, like she was a mate.

'Hey, Kate,' he replied. 'This is—'

'Barry. I know, we spoke on the phone. Hey, Barry.'

'Hey, Kate,' said DS Taylor. 'This is Sally.'

'Hey, Sally,' said Kate.

'Hey, Kate,' said DC Clegg.

'So, Kate,' Matlock said, 'Barry tells me you have very little for us.'

'I'm afraid so, Mick. Or if there is anything,' Kate said, 'I can't see it. Sammy suffered only a single clean blow—'

'The victim?'

'Yes, Sammy.' To Kate, first-name terms clearly extended to corpses. 'She was hit hard over the head with what I'm pretty sure was a hammer and that's basically all we know.'

Matlock felt himself shiver a little and it wasn't the cold in the morgue. He'd never really got used to death, which he felt was quite important in a murder detective. He often said that if he ever felt he had become inured to the sight of a corpse he'd apply to be put on Traffic.

'So, if it was a sex attack the perpetrator was satisfied very quickly?' he suggested.

'It would have been a very weird sort of sex attack,' Kate answered. 'Not that they aren't all weird, obviously, but I've never known a sexual assault to be confined to a single blow to a non-intimate part of the body with no other signs of disturbance.'

'DS Taylor tells me that you found semen in the victim's anus?'

'Actually, Mike, gotta say, I don't really use the word "victim",'

Kate said, 'particularly when describing a woman who's suffered an assault. It disempowers her and diminishes her humanity.'

'Oh,' Matlock replied, for want of a better response.

'Victimhood is passive and helpless,' Kate continued. 'It denies the assaulted woman agency over her own self. We prefer "survivor".'

'But this particular woman is dead,' Matlock pointed out.

'Yes.'

'So "survivor" isn't really an appropriate term.'

'I'm aware of that. What we need is a new term for survivors of assault who died.'

'Do you have one?'

'No. But it's an important conversation.'

'Mm,' said Matlock, and he could feel DC Clegg and DS Taylor smirking behind him. 'Maybe one we should have some other time, though. We were discussing the semen.'

'Yes. I have a sample,' Kate said, 'but I don't think it'll be any use to you.'

'No use?'

'It predates the assault by several hours.'

'I see.'

Clegg jotted this information down in her notebook. 'It might be evidence of a prior assault,' she suggested. 'Perhaps our perp had previously assaulted Sammy and subsequently killed her out of guilt or fear of being exposed.'

Kate nodded earnestly. 'Yes, absolutely. Good call, Sal.'

'Thanks, Kate.'

'But your report said there's no physical evidence to suggest that this earlier sexual encounter was a violent one?' Matlock said.

'That's true, but not all rapes involve associated violence.'

'No,' Matlock agreed. 'She might very well have been threatened with further violence or been verbally coerced into consenting to sex.'

'How can sex submitted to under coercion be consensual?' Kate asked, a slight coldness entering her previously breezy tone.

Taylor whistled quietly through his teeth and took a tiny step backwards. Evidently he wanted to make clear that he was taking no part in this conversation. Matlock, too, realized he was on fragile ground. It was just so *tricky*, these days. His press conference debacle was a recent and painful memory.

'I meant coerced into giving *reluctant* consent,' Matlock corrected himself.

'Which is *not* consent, Mick.'

'No.'

'All sex in which the enthusiasm of both partners is not clear and unambiguous is non-consensual.'

'Yes. Of course,' Matlock agreed.

'I.e. rape.'

'Really?'

'Absolutely.'

'Right. Good. OK,' Matlock said. 'So, we can conclude from the presence of semen in the victim's body that she had sex approximately seven hours before she was murdered and that it might have been consensual or she might have been non-violently raped.'

'I think the term "non-violently raped" is weird and a complete contradiction in terms,' Kate replied, 'but OK.'

Matlock decided to get off the subject of rape for a minute. He turned to Taylor. 'And we're absolutely sure there was no robbery?'

'As sure as we can be, boss. Her handbag was still beside her with her money and cards in it. Her watch and earrings were still on her. He didn't even take her phone.'

'So, in terms of motive, we have a possible but entirely hypothetical sex crime and nothing else.' Matlock sighed. 'Let's take a look at her.'

'I hope you can find something. I couldn't,' Kate said, pulling on the handle of one of the cold drawers that were recessed into the wall. 'As I say, I found no features of interest whatsoever.'

Silence fell as the sheet-covered body emerged. All four people present were suddenly conscious that the subject of their abstract discussion was real and present, physically in the room with them. Only recently a living, breathing person like themselves, with hopes and dreams, and love to give. Now cold beneath a sheet in a morgue.

Once the cold drawer was fully extended Kate began to fold back the cover. 'A strong face and prominent jaw set on quite broad shoulders,' she said, as she did so. 'Bodyweight seventy-one kilos. No signs of trauma visible.'

'Shame the cowardly bastard came at her from behind,' Clegg remarked. 'I reckon this girl could have put up a decent fight.'

'Sadly she never got the chance,' Kate went on. 'The fatal wound having been delivered to the back of the head, the front of the corpse is unmarked by violence. Not even a bruise.'

'Even the face is calm,' Matlock observed. 'Almost as if she could open her eyes and climb out of the drawer.'

Kate pulled back the sheet further, revealing quite large but firm-looking breasts. 'Augmented bosom,' she observed. 'Minor associated scarring. At least a year old and unrelated to the assault. Broad torso. Not overweight but with little waist to speak of.'

Another fold of the sheet.

'Prominent penis. Large testicles. Again, no sign of trauma.'

Kate removed the sheet altogether. 'So. Shall we turn her over?'

11. They'll Make Flirting Illegal Next!

FEMINIST HISTORIAN Cressida Baynes took a deep breath and screwed up her courage. It takes a lot of guts to create a public scene and every part of Baynes's character and upbringing screamed against it. She *seriously* did not want to do this but she felt she had no choice. The evening was going to mark a major step up in her self-appointed campaign to redress historic gender imbalance and call out the patriarchy for its past sins. Previously her activism had been largely confined to lobbying on the net and polite Q & As at the occasional literary festival, but now she was determined to take her fight into the physical public arena.

'Ladies and gentlemen!' she said, to the packed theatre foyer. 'The show you have come here to see tonight is nothing more than the celebration of a self-confessed sexual predator! I appeal to you to reconsider your choices and instead join me in protesting it.'

Backstage in his dressing room, the star of the show that Cressida Baynes was protesting had no idea that his life was about to change.

Rodney Watson averted his eyes from the mirror. He must not look. *He must not look.*

They'd get you for that. Oh, they'd get you for that, all right. They'd *hashtag* you in a heartbeat. They'd hash your sodding tag.

How boring. How dull. How *joyless.*

He longed for the days when he could not only stare at his

dresser's breasts as she adjusted his wig, but actually comment on them. 'Bet your boyfriend appreciates those, dear!' Or 'That reminds me, I must buy some melons.'

They'd *enjoyed* it. Girls were tougher in those days. A bit of banter. It was only a laugh.

But now he mustn't even *look*.

He must *not* stare hungrily at the reflection of those T-shirt-clad boobs that brushed against his ear while the hair grips went in or follow the contours of the bra beneath. Search for trace evidence of a nipple. 'I say! Is it cold outside, love? I could hang my hat and coat on those.'

Couldn't do that. Not any more.

You have to stare at the ceiling. It's the only way. Otherwise they'd get you. Those snowflake modern girls with their #MeToo and #TimesUp and #NoShadeOfFuckingGrey. They'd ruin you in a tweet.

A knock at the door interrupted his thoughts.

'Five minutes, please, Mr Watson,' came the stage manager's voice.

'Thank you!' he called back. 'Just getting my face on, darling.'

That was all right. He could still call girls 'darling' because it was the theatre, and theatre people had always called each other darling.

Rodney was giving his *Pepys*. His much celebrated one-man show – sorry! one-*person* show – about the famous seventeenth-century civil servant and diarist. The genius known as the father of the modern navy who had also left first-hand accounts of the Great Fire of London and the Great Plague.

Rodney always gave his *Pepys* between movie and TV engagements. A short regional tour or a season in one of the smaller London playhouses kept him close to a live audience. And it was a *very* nice little earner, thank you very much, *daaaahling*.

Not a bad life either. Give his *Pepys*. Get up late. Spot of lunch somewhere nice. A gallery or the cinema in the afternoon (if there wasn't a matinee), a couple of hours of being adored and applauded, then a lovely little late supper with friends. Of course, it had been more fun when you could try to fuck your dresser in the interval. He used to make sure he got a looker, and it was good sport to have a pop at them even if they wouldn't succumb. The excitement of the chase. Couldn't do *that* any more, of course. How dull. How *joyless*. It had only been a bit of fun. The girls never minded. They could always say no, couldn't they?

What would Pepys have made of Me bloody Too?

Not bloody much.

Pepys had been a proper rogue. A man after Rodney's own heart. Always on the prowl. Because he *loved* women. Rodney loved women too. *Worshipped* them. That was what these Me-bloody-Tooers didn't *get*.

And it was what made playing Pepys so much *fun*, Pepys's love of women. The grand sweep of history was all very well but it was the secret bits of his diary, the ones he'd written in code, that really brought the show to life. The constant grabbing at his serving girls, the forcing of a hand-job in his carriage, the blatant trading of professional favours for sex. The man was incorrigible! Always happy to spring a chap from the navy's press gang if the fellow's wife was pretty enough and willing. Those were the bits the audience loved, the bawdy bits.

Carry on, Pepys! Lock up your daughters!

And, of course, Rodney got a chance to show his *comedy*. People were always surprised by how good at comedy he was. That was because he only ever played villains in movies. Which was the only sort of role the Yanks offered to Brit actors, these days.

Particularly with Harvey gone. God, he missed Harvey. The old shit might have been a bit of a bastard on the sly but he did give Brit actors classy roles. Who in America was going to champion really *classy* Brit films now? Films like *The King's Speech*, *The English Patient*, *Shakespeare in Love*, *My Left Foot*, *The Iron Lady* and *The Queen*? And all the others. Decades of them. Pretty much every Oscar we'd won in thirty years was down to Harvey. Just look at our movie industry without him! Ha! What industry? Non-Yank English-speaking cinema had lost its one champion because the only important American who gave a toss about it had chased a few silly actresses. Jesus! Get some fucking perspective.

It was because of those silly actresses that Rodney was having to give his Pepys at all. By rights he should have had his choice of parts in Hollywood as an Oscar-winning actor. Yes! Oscar-winning, daaahling! Best Supporting Actor.

Because he'd had his chance. His really big break. He'd *got the job.*

A top Brit production house with the typically self-effacingly post-ironic British name of Let's Do Lunch had cast him in *The Royal Closet* and Miramax were going to co-produce and distribute! *Harvey* had been on board! *God*, to quote Meryl Streep, was casting his divine light! The best news *any* little Brit movie could ever get. And this time, he'd be Colin fucking Firth! Just for once somebody apart from Colin fucking Firth was going to get to be Colin fucking Firth. And it was him! Rodney Watson. He had *never* been so excited. His agent had sent him a magnum of Krug.

Then had come that morning, 5 October 2017, and the *New York Times* article detailing the 'decades of harassment'.

Harassment? Pull the other one, love.

Pull the fucking other one, pur-leeeeze.

Those girls knew what they were doing. Had it *really* been so terrible? He would take it up the arse with a broken broomstick for a shot at an Oscar, daaaahling.

Harvey had gone 'toxic' and *The Royal Closet* never got made. Without Harvey's gargantuan clout nobody had been interested in yet another little Brit movie about yet another tortured royal.

So he was back with Pepys. Good old Pepys. His wonderful standby. Self-penned (mainly), self-directed, self-produced. No royalties on the diary quotes because they're four hundred years old. Brilliant.

Lovely little earner and just great bloody fun to do.

He still had Pepys.

The wig was fitted, a cascade of curls around his sagging jowls.

'Shall I put the hat on, Rodney,' his dresser asked, 'or will you?'

'You do it, please, Becky.' He spun his chair round to face her.

Make her put it on from the front. He'd get 'em full in the face. Lovely. He could *smell* her T-shirt.

Be thankful for small pleasures.

Another knock at the door.

'Heard you the first time, darling!' Rodney shouted, with starry irritation.

'Actually, Rodney love, can I come in?' It wasn't the stage manager – pretty little piece but *so* humourless. It was Giles, the theatre manager.

'Bit of a problem, love. Need to have a word.'

Rodney entered and Becky the dresser took the opportunity to leave. 'I'll let you do your own hat, Rodney,' she said, almost running out.

Having been cheated of a close-up of her boobs, Rodney watched her bum as she left. Lovely bum. He still employed lookers whenever he could, even though it was a sort of torture. Small pleasures.

'Problem, love?' he said to Giles, who was hovering at the door.

'Big problem. Can't open the house, love. Foyer's full of protesters.'

'Protesters?'

'Yes, love. Seems it's part of a new hashtag thing started by some feminist historian called Cressida Baynes. #RememberThem.'

'Remember who?'

'Survivors of historical abuse.'

'You mean like Savile's victims? Or Rolf Harris's?'

'No. I mean dead survivors . . . I mean survivors who have since died. Of natural causes. She's calling on all historians and anyone who loves history to make the MeToo movement fully retrospective. #RememberThem. Do you see? She's saying that Pepys was a sexual predator and you're glorifying him. That your show is an apology for a rapist.'

Rodney felt this simply had to be a joke. 'Samuel Pepys is one of the most celebrated figures of the seventeenth century! The Royal Maritime Museum just did a full retrospective on him. I went to the opening. I gave a speech. Couldn't believe it – they served Prosecco instead of proper champ.'

'It seems that's Ms Baynes's point. Not about the Prosecco. The exhibition itself and also your show. The continued lionization of a sex monster. That's what she's protesting about.'

'*Sex monster!* Samuel Pepys?'

'She says his diary is actually a full criminal confession of assaulting his female servants on a daily basis, harassing women in the streets, theatres and churches, and trading professional influence for sex.'

'Well, yes, it is, that's true,' Rodney conceded. 'They are a bit *bawdy*. But people have always thought that side of the diaries was sort of . . . endearing.'

'Endearing? Serial sexual assault?'

'Yes. His candour. He wrote so *wittily* about it. And he's always so *sorry* afterwards. He goes to bed in bits every night, swearing he won't try to touch his servant's cunny ever again. It's sort of sweet.'

'Sweet?'

'Well, that's how it's always been played. In the theatre and films. Steve Coogan did a super one quite recently. *The Private*

Life of Samuel Pepys. Plenty of oom-pah-pah and whoops-a-daisy in that one, let me tell you. It's how I play him too. The brilliant silly old bugger who just can't keep his hands off the girls. And he loves his wife. That's *such* a touching part of the show.'

'Times change, I'm afraid, Rodney.'

'Not for Samuel fucking Pepys, love! Time stopped changing for him in 1703 when he died. He's a national treasure. Now, speaking of times, Giles, we're already five minutes late. How long do you think it will take you to remove them?'

'Remove them?'

'Yes. The protesters. To clear the foyer and get the house in. I've got a table booked at the Ivy for ten fifteen, and if you're late they give it to some recent evictee from *Love Island* having her fifteen minutes.'

'Remove them?' Giles repeated. 'You want me to forcibly evict a legitimate protest in order that a straight white man can portray a serial sex offender as a jovial old cunny-grabbing rogue? Are you crazy? I'm not going to evict them. I'm going to cancel your show and disown you. We've already issued a statement saying that your depiction of Samuel Pepys does not reflect the values of this theatre. It's not who we are.'

Rodney Watson stared at Giles in disbelief. 'You're cancelling my show?'

'Of course we're cancelling it. Pepys was a bloody rapist. Such a shame, but what can I do? Try to see it from my point of view.'

So that was it.

He was being thrown to the wolves on a MeToo-ish whim. Like every management, since Netflix had dumped Kevin Spacey, Giles was looking after number one. Applying the instant and absolute damage control that was now routine in the entertainment industry.

This Baynes woman had done him up like a kipper. Rodney knew he couldn't argue his case. Pepys had been considered a national treasure for three hundred years but, viewed from the perspective of the twenty-first century, he was obviously a disgusting bastard. A seventeenth-century Weinstein, who habitually used his position and power to satisfy his brutish sexual desires. Now that somebody had chosen to point this out, it was clear that the entire Pepys brand – a brand he'd worked so hard to establish and which, in non-movie years, had kept him in champagne and high-end dining – had gone instantly and absolutely toxic.

What could he do?

He couldn't fight it. He couldn't defend a man for crimes that today would land him in prison.

But silence would be just as bad. From this moment every Google search of his name would lead to #RememberThem. Which would, of course, immediately link him to #MeToo, #TimesUp, #NotOK and #CareerFucked.

Guilt by association. His name was about to join the list that routinely followed Weinstein's in the press. It didn't matter what you'd done or were accused of doing: if the bloody media could somehow crowbar you into the list that began with Weinstein they would.

He needed to defend himself. And fast.

Never roll over. Stand up and fight.

'Kindly cancel the performance on *my* insistence, Giles,' Rodney said, 'and invite Ms Baynes backstage. I wish to discuss with her the urgent need to bring a police prosecution against Samuel Pepys.'

12. Never Mind the Bollocks

IF DR Kate Galloway noticed Matlock, Clegg and Taylor's shocked expressions she didn't comment on them. She folded the sheet, put it to one side and asked again if they wanted to turn the body over to inspect the wound.

Matlock found his voice. 'You said in your report that the autopsy had uncovered no obvious new features of interest,' he said.

'Not on the front,' Kate said. 'As I told you, the blow was delivered from behind. You'll need to put on plastic gloves to help me turn her over.'

'Sorry, Kate, but you don't think a dick and two balls are features of interest?'

A beat. A second or two, which seemed much longer.

'No.'

'No?'

The temperature of Kate's attitude was suddenly colder than the cool room itself.

'Why should I find a penis and testicles features of interest? Half the people on the planet have them.'

'But none of the women.'

'None of the *cis* women, Mick.' Kate's expression was now positively frozen. 'But many self-identifying women do.'

Matlock sucked hard at his sweet. Jesus. Why did everything these days have to be so *tricky*? It was a minefield. God, he'd have liked a cigarette. 'And you don't think that in itself is a feature of interest?' he asked.

Kate glared at him. 'Are you suggesting that I should have mentioned it in my first report?'

'Yeah, actually, I am.'

'You don't think that focusing on Sammy's genitals would have been indicative of prejudice?'

'Prejudice?'

'Transphobic prejudice. Which, as you know, is against not only our police code of conduct but, in fact, the law.'

'How the f— How the hell is that transphobic? This is a murder investigation. We're not in a sociology class.'

Kate sighed, clearly making some internal effort to reset her irritation and offence to something approaching tolerance of this sad, ignorant twentieth-century man. 'Sammy was a woman,' she said, with exaggerated patience. 'She identified as a woman and was in the process of transitioning. As you can see, she has acquired breasts and there is evidence of hormone treatment in her system.'

'But in your view that's not relevant to our investigation?'

'The blow was to the back of the head. The body was brought in with the clothing undisturbed. There is absolutely no evidence whatsoever of any interference with Sammy's genitalia. Let me ask *you* a question, Mick. If the victim *had* been a cis woman, as you so predictably presumed she was – surprise surprise – and had she been brought in in *exactly* the same condition and circumstances as Sammy here, would you have expected me to mention in my report that the victim was a woman with a vagina?'

'No, I wouldn't, but—'

'Then why would you require me to mention that Sammy was a woman with a penis?' Kate left this question to hang for a moment, then added coldly, 'You do accept that Sammy *was* a woman, don't you, Mick?'

Matlock knew the answer to that and he replied quickly and firmly. 'Yes, I do, Doctor.'

It was quick and firm enough to save him from professional censure but not quite quick enough to be personally convincing. He had definitely hesitated for the briefest moment before saying it. Kate had spotted this and given him a withering look.

Taylor and Clegg stared at the floor in embarrassment. The investigation was in danger of finding itself on the wrong side of history.

Matlock felt deeply uncomfortable too. He *did* accept that the corpse laid out before him was a woman. He really did. He and Nancy had discussed it endlessly because there seemed to be an article in the *Guardian* on the subject every day. Matlock definitely understood and accepted the difference between sex and gender. It had taken him quite a while to get used to the notion that it was possible to have a penis and be a woman – it was definitely a steep learning curve – but he *did* accept it. He'd read enough and been on enough awareness courses to understand that gender dysphoria was real. That some people felt emotionally and psychologically at odds with their biological sex and that society had chosen to recognize the choices those people made. He understood that and he was happy to applaud it. But he knew, deep down inside, that he didn't *feel* it. He still found it impossibly hard to view a biologically male corpse and feel entirely convinced that the victim was a woman. Politically and publicly he was 100 per cent on it. Privately, it remained a struggle.

'Yes,' he repeated firmly, meeting Kate's eye. 'I absolutely do accept that Sammy was a woman because that was her choice to make.'

'So, therefore, you must also agree that it would have been wrong, intrusive and genitally centric for me to have made her trans status a feature of my report?'

'*Genitally centric?*'

'One of the most offensive things trans people have to put up with is the cis obsession over the status of their genitals.'

'She's *dead*. She's not putting up with anything any more.' Matlock knew he had to stand up for what he perceived to be common sense. He was investigating a murder, not addressing a bloody student union. 'I need to know everything about this case, Kate,' he said. 'I need to know *who Sammy was*.'

'Really?' Kate asked sharply. 'Are you as fascinated with the genital status of all the murder cases you're called upon to investigate? If a male drug addict got knifed while trying to score crystal meth, would you be discussing his cock with the consulting pathologist?'

God, she was relentless. Matlock tried to focus his argument. 'We are looking for a motive for a murder! In most drug- and gang-related killings, the motive is clear. In this case it is not, and I suggest Sammy's transgender status might possibly provide us with one. Sammy could have been the victim of a hate crime.'

He thought it was a winning point. Unanswerable, surely. He was wrong.

'You don't think that cis women can be the victims of hate crimes?' Kate asked.

'Sorry?'

'You're telling me that I was remiss in not mentioning this woman's penis and testicles because they might give you a motive. That her murder could have been a hate crime. Had Sammy been cisgender, would that have ruled out the possibility of her having been the subject of a hate crime for you? Whether they have a vagina or a penis or neither, *all* women are subject to hate crime. Have you heard of the incel movement, Mick? Have you ever been to a women's refuge? Have you? Mick?'

Kate was one of those people who not only liked to use first names but also liked to use them as a combative rhetorical device.

'Yes, Dr Galloway, I have,' Matlock answered, 'and I know very well that there is hate crime against both cis and trans women, but I would suggest that the perpetrators of those crimes fall into different groups. Overlapping, perhaps, but also distinct. And on this occasion it is Sammy's murder that I am investigating.'

'Yes, Mick. And now that you have viewed the corpse you know both this woman's biological sex and her gender identity. Information you have learned in a manner that is respectful to how the deceased self-identified. Do you have a problem, Mick?'

'Let's turn her over and have a look at the wound.'

13. #NotOK

JEMIMA THRING'S finger hovered over the key. Should she press send? She knew it hadn't been in any way a *serious* assault. No violence. No physical coercion. Unless applying a small pressure to her chin to turn her face towards his could be considered physical coercion? She hadn't thought so at the time. But since then she'd wondered.

And even if it wasn't physical, did that make it OK?

Or not OK?

Not quite #MeToo but still #NotOK.

Not rape. Not abuse.

Just #NotOK.

She certainly hadn't wanted that kiss. Not the second one anyway. That was definite. Shouldn't Kurt have realized that? And even if he hadn't, did he have a right to kiss her, knowing that he was lying about wanting them to be a couple? And she had been pretty drunk. He'd certainly known that. He'd brought her the last glass of wine himself.

She *knew* it hadn't been an assault. But she also believed – really, really believed – it was #NotOK.

Jemima pressed send.

14. Storms Gather on Love Island

THE PRODUCERS of *Love Island* were having a difficult morning. The trouble had begun halfway through the daily progress briefing on the upcoming series. The small army of researchers, assistant producers and production assistants had been sharing results and impressions from the audition trawl. Exchanging photos, watching tapes, making small bets on the number of girls who would describe themselves as 'bubbly and outgoing but also strong and fierce', and the number of guys who would claim to be absolutely 'wicked with the ladeez'.

They had been just about to move on to the thorny problem of character identification in the age of ubiquitous cosmetic surgery. Theirs was a show that depended entirely on the audience following the story arcs of each participant, but research indicated that actual facial recognition was becoming problematic, particularly for the female contestants.

'Basically it's getting really hard to tell which blonde, swollen-lipped, side-boob-poppin', eyebrow-bangin' babe is which,' show runner and big boss babe Hayley Bernstein lamented loudly. 'Maybe we could do something with jewellery. A tiara for one? Big earrings for another? Just something to tell them apart.'

There was no chance to debate this issue further, because that was when the news broke that Team UK had co-opted a misspelled version of their programme title for use in their campaign to promote the inclusively joyous nature of the United Kingdom for the purposes of the upcoming English independence referendum.

A nervous junior researcher called Daisy was the first to spot it on her newsfeed. Daisy was only eighteen and the youngest person on the team. In a social-media generational cycle that was measured in months, she was the first to be aware of everything, always linked to the speediest and most relevant apps. She thought Facebook was for grandmas and Instagram for mums. Thus she was best placed to understand the lightning-quick shifts of fashion and focus in internet attitude. On a production like *Love Island*, which existed entirely in the moment, Daisy was the canary in the coal mine, or in net terms the milkshake duck on WhatsApp. Hence it was always Daisy who was first to glance at whatever newsfeed her wafer-thin generational demographic favoured and relay the current nature of the 'national conversation' to the broader team.

'They're calling their Team UK campaign Luv Island,' Daisy read breathlessly from her phone. 'Which is our name. Obviously.'

'Well, they can't,' snapped Hayley. 'We'll sue.'

'They're spelling it differently.'

'Differently?'

'L-U-V.'

'God, that is so sodding *naff*. Anyway, I don't care how they spell it. We were first.'

'The first people to spell "love"?'

'In the context of "Island", which is what they're ripping off. Can we sue, Dave?'

Dave was in compliance, which meant he did law and shit. 'Don't think so,' he said. ' "Love" is kind of in the public domain, however you spell it.'

'Maybe it's a good thing,' Daisy suggested. 'The news is getting a lot of hearts and smiles and party balloons.'

Hayley wasn't convinced. 'It's political. We don't do politics. Except for the thick bird, obviously.'

Everyone nodded wisely. The thick bird was one of the most

popular aspects of the show. The drop-dead gorgeous sex bomb with a vowel-grindingly strong regional accent, who could be relied upon at some point to say something hilariously ill-informed, like 'Is Russia part of New York?'

But the thick bird aside, Hayley was concerned that being associated with one particular camp in a nationally divisive debate might be off message and counter to their brand.

'Every potential England Out voter,' said Hayley, 'is going to hear the phrase Luv Island and instead of thinking sun, sex and sangria they're going to think complacent, snooty, middle-class, city-centric, neo-liberal latte drinkers, who have no idea what's going on in the "real" England.'

'Do you think keeping the UK intact is a "latte" issue, Hayley?' Dave-who-did-law-and-shit asked.

'Of course it's a latte issue!' Hayley barked, sipping her latte. 'The latte-drinking liberal elite and their media mates have absolutely no idea how deeply the "real" people who have to deal with "real" problems resent London, Brussels and the smug bloody Scots! No-offence-Hamish-that-was-just-bantz-you-know-it's-not-who-I-am.'

Hayley spat the last part of her sentence out quickly, having realized halfway through the word 'Scots' (which is a very short word) that she was in serious danger of getting Twittered #every-dayracism and having to be sent on an awareness course. Five years ago if he'd objected she could have sacked the little ginger bastard. But the world had changed.

'No problem, Hayley.' Hamish smiled magnanimously. 'We've been taking shit from the English for a thousand years. We're used to it.' Hamish was very much a 'proud' Scot, meaning he always travelled home from London, where he'd lived and worked since uni, for the regular Scottish independence referendums to vote YES and see his mum.

Another junior member of the team spoke up: Narsti Rimes, a

sullen-looking young man in a black tracksuit with his Nike-clad feet up on the table. 'Yeah. Don't reckon our fans are thinking much about lattes and neo-liberalism shit or whatever, Hayley. It just ain't on the radar.'

Narsti was only twenty and Hayley's PA. He was not really supposed to contradict his boss, but he was the only black person at the table and also, brilliantly and rather scarily, an actual grime artist. He had his own YouTube channel and a track available on iTunes. That sort of life profile carries a lot of cultural capital in a room full of middle-class white people in a permanent state of agony over their privilege. Even Hamish, who was more than happy to play the angry-injured-Scot card when it suited, with all its associated 'rebel' connotations, had to bow to Narsti Rimes's extreme level of street credibility. Except, of course, Narsti would never have called his credibility 'street'. In the language of grime, Narsti was a fully fledged roadman.

'I don't think our base are up for cutting England out of the UK, Hayles. What if the West Country was next? You'd need a passport to play Glastonbury. I reckon we need to *own* this. Put out the word that we're gassed they're ripping our brand for their campaign an' we hope their referendum is half as beautiful as our brilliant show.'

Hayley liked Narsti and thought he was super-cool but she was not happy to be contradicted by her PA in front of the entire staff. She knew she had to stand up for herself.

'I am merely saying,' she replied, 'that above all we are an inclusive show. A national unifier, the brand that's got Britain all round the same TV again. The nation hasn't gossiped so much about the same bunch of harmlessly compelling mediocrities since the last royal wedding. In many ways we *are* Britain. *All* of Britain. Including the half that wants to tear it apart. Dave, issue a statement saying that *Love Island* is above petty politics and shit because we serve a greater ideal. Now, can we *please* get back to trying to find eight hot babes, who look sufficiently different from each other to be distinguishable on telly?'

But it was not to be.

Because at that moment Daisy glanced once more at her phone and gave a little squeak of horror. 'Oh, my God, Hayley,' she gasped. 'Oh, my *God*. Fuck. No, seriously. Fuck!'

Hayley glared furiously at the most junior member of the team. 'What now?'

'Jemima the Whiner's saying that when Kurt kissed her by the firepit it was non-consensual.'

There was a stunned silence.

Little eighteen-year-old Daisy had *never* held the room like this before. Everyone was looking at her. 'Sorry,' she said nervously, ever fearful of the fate of messengers who bring bad news, 'but look.'

She held up her phone, which was so big it was almost a tablet, so that everybody could read the devastating post.

#wtf!!!! Looks like Jemima had something to whine about after all! Hated villa reject goes all #MeToo on Love Island's big tanned ass.

Nobody was in any doubt of the seriousness of such an accusation. They knew what planet they lived on.

'She says when Kurt kissed her she felt uncomfortable,' Daisy went on, in a small apologetic voice, 'and therefore she hadn't sufficiently indicated consent and so . . . it was non-consensual.'

'"Uncomfortable"!' Hayley snarled. 'That bloody word again. When did it become a thing that feeling comfortable was a human right?'

At that moment everybody else's phones caught up with Daisy's and started pinging and buzzing and rattling across the table as their own newsfeeds began humming with the utterly game-changing story.

Narsti's phone trumped all, blasting out the sampled bassline from retro nineties classic 'Gangsta's Paradise'.

A few seconds after that every phone in the room was ringing, with reporters asking for comment.

Then the tsunami of outraged tweeting began to roll over them.

All within a minute of Daisy's first ping.

Hayley and the *Love Island* team knew they had a problem on their hands that would make the English independence referendum look like a mendacious and ill-informed squabble about the internal affairs of an insignificant little country on the edge of Europe.

Love Island was in danger of finding itself on the wrong side of history.

It could actually go toxic. It was that serious.

Shit had got real.

15. A Pronoun By Any Other Name

AFTER HIS delayed visit to the police morgue, and the discovery that he was dealing with the murder of a transgender woman, Matlock went to interview the victim's – or dead survivor's – friend and flatmate, Rob. It was already almost forty-eight hours since the murder and Matlock was extremely anxious to make progress.

Rob's flat was located on a fourth-storey corridor in a low-rise 1970s-built social-housing enclave located in the midst of a rapidly gentrifying area of south London. It was one of the last of the shrinking number of monuments to the post-war social consensus. Matlock was pretty sure that five years hence the people living in the flats would have been forced out beyond the M25 and have to be bussed back in to clean the tube stations. It seemed to him that in the thirty-plus years he'd been with the Met, London had turned into one vast investment portfolio.

He pushed the electric doorbell, still marked 'Sammy and Rob', and reminded himself once again that during the interview he must absolutely refer to Sammy as a female. She was a woman and he was going to respect that 100 per cent. He was nervous, of course, scared that he would make a mistake and say 'him' and 'his', which would be very disrespectful. But the cock and balls that seemed almost to have leaped out at him from the pathologist's slab continued to loom large in his consciousness. He couldn't get them out of his head and had more than once referred to Sammy as a man on the drive back from the morgue. Fortunately DC Clegg had been there to remind him. He would absolutely keep trying, committing himself to an ongoing process of self-correction. He understood that in trans politics, genitals had nothing to do with gender and you weren't supposed to focus on them. Sammy was a 'her' and Matlock was going to get used to that if it killed him.

He was therefore surprised and completely thrown to be politely but firmly informed by Sammy's tearful friend Rob that her chosen pronouns were not 'she', 'her' and 'hers' but 'zie', 'zir' and 'zirs'.

'But I thought she was a woman,' Matlock asked.

'Thought *zie* was a woman,' Rob prompted.

'Thought zie was a woman.'

'Zie was.'

'Then wouldn't she – sorry, zie – want to be referred to as a woman? I thought that was the whole point.'

'Zie identified as a woman but zie rejected a binary view of gender. And zie certainly rejected gender-specific language. Don't you?'

'I never really thought about it. Sorry.'

'Don't say sorry. It's not offensive to be wrong, only to refuse to listen and consider other points of view. But do think about it. That would be good.'

Rob had a kind of calm intensity that was quite intimidating. What people had called passive-aggressive before the term got overused.

'Right. Yeah. I will. No problem.'

'Sugar?' Rob was pouring tea.

Matlock had declined the offer of refreshment but Rob was very upset and clearly happier keeping busy. Without waiting for an answer he put a teaspoonful in each cup.

'Sammy identified as a woman,' Rob went on, stirring slightly manically, as if he'd forgotten to stop, 'like I identify as a man. But gender is a spectrum, obviously, so it's all fluid. Who knows what we were yesterday or might become tomorrow? Don't you think language should reflect that? Wouldn't it be better if it was gender neutral? To have one set of pronouns for both sexes? It would certainly be easier for foreigners to learn English.'

Rob finally stopped his tinkly stirring and brought over the tea.

'But harder for me to unlearn it,' Matlock answered. He'd meant it as a bit of a self-effacing 'dad' joke but Rob didn't take it that way.

'Yes, well,' he said sharply, 'just for once white cisgender men are being asked to make a small effort on behalf of a less-privileged identity group. Would that be so terrible?'

Matlock couldn't quite work out what his colour had to do with anything but he knew Rob was upset so he let it go. 'Right. Yes. Absolutely. Now. Just a few questions. Sammy was a trans woman. Could you tell me what zir sexual orientation was?'

'I don't really like definitions such as gay and straight. Nor did Sammy. As I say, it's all a—'

'Spectrum. Yeah. Got that, but I need to *know* Sammy. I'm investigating her murder.'

'*Zir* murder,' Rob corrected. 'Please respect zir choices.' He was becoming a little tearful.

'Sorry. Zir murder. I need to know everything about zir.'

'All right. If you insist on a label I guess zie was straight.'

Matlock *knew* he should understand what that meant. He knew he should be able to work out what 'straight' meant when referring to a woman who was biologically male. He took a guess.

'So . . . that means zie was attracted to men?'

'Yes. If it's really relevant.'

Matlock was pleased he'd got it right. But he still found it hard to get his head around. He knew that he must simply accept that he now lived in a world where the correct term for one person with a penis being sexually attracted to another person with a penis – if one of those individuals identified as a woman – was 'straight'. He presumed that if two people with penises both of whom identified as women were in a sexual relationship they would be lesbians. But he wasn't sure.

'Sammy had unprotected anal sex with someone about seven hours before zie was killed,' Matlock went on.

'Yes, that was me,' Rob said, tears forming in his eyes. 'We made love before zie got ready to go out.'

'So you were in a relationship?'

'God,' Rob exclaimed, blowing his nose, 'you want everything in a little box, don't you? We were friends. Friends with benefits. Great friends with fantastic benefits. And now zie's dead! Some bastard killed zir. Why don't you just fucking catch him?'

Why indeed? Because there were absolutely no clues.

No trace left at the scene. Nothing on the body. No CCTV footage identifying anything other than hundreds of blurry people in the streets that surrounded the park around the time of the murder. The killer had either been incredibly lucky or very clever and very prepared.

'We're doing everything we can,' Matlock said rather pathetically, sipping his sugary tea.

Just then his phone rang. The screen told him Janine Treadwell was on the line. Matlock apologized to Rob and took the call, expecting further fallout from his victim-blaming scandal.

'When you're back at the Yard can you pop in and see me, Mick?' Janine said. 'I want your views on a cold case we're being asked to look at. Bit of political pressure on this one. They want us to reopen Yewtree.'

'Yewtree? Again?' Matlock was surprised. 'Jesus. Another one?'

He recalled very well the police operation that had been mounted following the Jimmy Savile revelations of 2012, famously pursuing celebrity sex offenders for past crimes. A few

years previously it had seemed to him that scarcely a day had
gone by without some ageing ex-DJ appearing at the gate of his
country cottage to blame the 1970s.

'I thought we'd done with that. Who's the celebrity this time?'

'Samuel Pepys.'

16. Woke-Up Call

RODNEY WATSON, actor, had assumed his 'listening' face. Focused. Engaged. Inclusive. The face he imagined flattered journalists when they interviewed him. Eager to learn. Respectful of the intelligence and merit of whoever it was he was talking to. Sometimes he held that face for as long as forty-five seconds before launching into his next ten-minute monologue.

On this occasion his calm, clear-eyed engagement also masked an inner glee.

He had only gone and turned it fucking round. A career disaster that would have finished off a lesser man had not got the better of Rodney Watson.

Not only was his new Pepys show *Monster! The Trial of Samuel Pepys* already pencilled in for a major regional tour, prior to an expected *significant* London run, but courtesy of his new bestie, historian Cressida Baynes's #RememberThem initiative, he had turned into the poster boy for middle-aged male wokeness. One straight old white guy who actually *got* it.

Already that morning he and Cressida had done Radio 4 and LBC together, and now they were on ITV's *Lorraine*. A plum gig. Lorraine was a mid-morning legend with a huge mum following. Rodney flattered himself he was big with mums. They still remembered his turn as Heathcliff in a sexed-up 1990s Channel 4 *Wuthering Heights*, during which he'd been required to show his bottom on the wild moors. A gig with Lorraine was a classic chance to get some mum trade for his *Monster!* tour. Maybe on their next girls' theatre night out the ladies of the provinces would choose him instead of *Mamma* fucking *Mia!*.

Rodney needed Lorraine to help flog those tickets, but in his view that morning Lorraine needed him more. Because, sadly, his earnest little sidekick Cressida Baynes was *not* a great TV performer. *Lovely* lady. *Such* a sweetie when you got to know her. But too earnest. Lighten the fuck up, girlfriend. She'd already gone completely off message and was banging on about how she had found evidence that there had been many, *many* female combatants at the Battle of Hastings in 1066 (what utter bollocks!) and was in danger of moving off women altogether and on to Britain's historically *enormous* black population.

Rodney could see Lorraine was worried. In the new multi-channel environment you couldn't afford a dull second. There was no programme loyalty any more, even for a popular star like Lorraine. Drop the ball for an instant and they'd be straight over to the Shopping Channel. Time to get involved. Time to save the interview.

'I think what Cressida's trying to say, Lorraine,' Rodney butted in, 'and I am *so* grateful to her for opening this particular straight white man's eyes on the issue, is that just as we have the Alan Turing law, which quite rightly and properly pardons all the homosexuals in history who were convicted of criminal offences, just as we are seeing calls for similar pardons to be issued for our wonderful, heroic, *fierce* suffragettes, it's now time to say, "Yes! OK! Come on now! Pardons are all very well but what about *prosecutions*?" if we are to honour and celebrate those innocents who were once thought criminal. Isn't it time also for the full force of the law to be brought against those *criminals*, who were once thought innocent?'

Rodney presumed that Lorraine would be grateful to him for having successfully rebooted the interview with his sexy charisma. But if she was she didn't show it. In fact she turned straight back to Cressida Baynes. Yet another example of suffocating political correctness: interviewing the woman even when the man was so obviously better.

'So, are you honestly saying, Cressida, that you want the police to bring a prosecution against Samuel Pepys?' Lorraine asked.

'Yes, I am, Lorraine, and they are taking the suggestion very seriously. If we can pardon we can prosecute, and I want that awful man posthumously convicted of crimes against women. If he were alive today he would be in prison and his incriminating diaries would be removed from reading lists.'

'But Pepys's diary is almost the *only* account of everyday life in London in the seventeenth century that we have,' Lorraine pointed out. 'It's an incredibly important historic document.'

'If Jimmy Savile had written a diary detailing London life in the sixties and seventies, Lorraine,' Cressida replied, 'would we think it appropriate to teach it in schools? To celebrate it? I don't think so.'

'We have lots of accounts of modern life, Cressida. Pepys's gives us the *only* first-hand descriptions of the Great Fire, the Great Plague and so much else. Would you seriously ban it?'

'I would certainly teach it in the context that it was written by a brutal and serial sex offender rather than a hero of the navy and a much-loved and -admired national treasure.'

Lorraine was clearly torn. She could see both sides. Cressida's suggestion was pretty problematic but it was also kind of fair: Pepys had been an absolute shit to lots of women.

Rodney was squirming in his seat. He wanted to sell tickets for his show but Lorraine was *perversely* refusing to bring him in.

'You're a historian, Cressida,' Lorraine went on. 'Isn't history going to be a bit difficult to teach if we start to try to remake the past in our own image? Would you prosecute Henry the Eighth, for instance? I mean, men don't cut off their wives' heads any more when they want to divorce them.'

'I'd certainly like to see the Tudor period taught from a more female-centric perspective. But, Lorraine, I'm not seeking the prosecution of King Henry the Eighth. Horrific though they were, the executions of Anne Boleyn and Catherine Howard were the result of due legal process and conducted by order of Parliament. Henry Tudor did not himself swing the axe. My #RememberThem campaign—'

'*Our* #RememberThem campaign, Cressie,' Rodney interrupted.

'—is simply about placing male entitlement and criminality in a historic context. I see it as the retrospective arm of the MeToo movement. Samuel Pepys is recognizable as a modern sex criminal. A domestic and workplace harasser. What is more he left us a full confession. He describes digitally raping his servant girl—'

'Well, he talks of getting his hand up her skirt,' Lorraine said.

'Yes, and I think we can make presumptions about what he was doing with his fingers, Lorraine.'

Lorraine frowned. This was an important topic but it was also mid-morning. She didn't want her viewers making presumptions about what Samuel Pepys did with his fingers while they were up serving girls' skirts.

Rodney frowned also. *Why didn't she bring him in?* She was letting a bloody *historian* do an actor's job.

'I want to convict Samuel Pepys in a court of law,' Cressida said, 'and I want that court to impose an appropriate, if theoretical, prison sentence on him. It is high time we began to view past events from other perspectives than that of powerful white men. I have the full support of Deborah Willet's MP, who has made an official complaint to the police on her behalf.'

'Deborah Willet?'

'Mrs Pepys's lady's companion, whom Pepys routinely molested.'

'Who died over three hundred years ago.'

'Does that make the crimes committed against her any less significant? As Rodney mentioned earlier, Alan Turing was pardoned posthumously. Why cannot Deb Willet get justice posthumously?'

'Absolutely, Cressie!' Rodney butted in, grabbing his chance. 'Pepys was a monster, pure and simple, as I make *very* clear in my new show *Monster*—'

But once again Lorraine refused to shift the interview his way. Bloody women, they stick together. It was like a cult.

'Tell us about your #RememberThem campaign, Cressida,' Lorraine said.

Cressida smiled and drew breath. That was her mistake. It was dog-eat-dog on morning TV. If you stop to breathe, don't be surprised if somebody grabs the air time from between your teeth.

Rodney ignored Lorraine and ploughed right in. 'We're appealing to all history students, teachers, academics, also actors like myself who appear in historical dramas, museum curators, visitors to museums and libraries – in fact anyone who has ever so much as watched an episode of *Poldark* – to wear a #RememberThem badge, honouring the countless victims of past abuse. As a woke white man, Lorraine, I feel *very* strongly about this. It's a wake-up call. A "woke-up" call, if you like. A chance to re-evaluate and reconsider the *millions* of women who, had they had a mobile phone in their crinolines or an iPad hidden under their corset, would have been hashtagging "MeToo" on the likes of Samuel Pepys in a heartbeat. I like to think of it as *Them*Too, Lorraine, I like to think of—'

'Thanks for that, Rodney,' said Lorraine, 'but I'd just like to turn back to—'

No chance, Lozzer, thought Rodney. This is *my* gig now.

'I believe strongly in a woman's right to be heard,' he pressed on. 'Enough with mansplaining! It's time for us men to shut the hell up and listen for once. As men, we need to take stock, reflect, shut our mouths, open our minds and bloody well *listen*. We need to learn the lessons of the past. Which is why I have developed my show *Monster! The Trial of Samuel Pepys*, which is booking now on Ticketec dot com and—'

'I'm afraid that's all we have time for now,' Lorraine announced. 'After the break, how far would *you* go to get that bikini body for the beach? We talk to a doctor and a slimming guru. Thank you, Cressida Baynes, thank you, Rodney Watson. You've certainly given us all something to think about this morning.'

One person watching *Lorraine* that morning had certainly been given something to think about: Ruth Collins, a theatre seamstress and company dresser.

She was still in bed. She worked evenings, so mid-morning *Lorraine* was breakfast TV to her. She was propped up on her pillows, sipping an instant coffee and looking at the badges on the lapel of Rodney Watson's jacket.

The #RememberThem badge. And beneath that the #TimesUp badge. And the #NotOK badge. And one she'd never heard of: #ThisManIsLISTENING.

Maybe if Rodney hadn't worn all those badges Ruth would have kept quiet. Maybe if he hadn't insisted on describing himself as 'woke'. Maybe if he hadn't banged on about women needing to be heard, that historical abuse was still abuse.

Maybe she would have let it lie.

Maybe she wouldn't have found herself revisiting old memories that generally she tried to suppress or ignore. Memories of a job she'd been looking forward to that turned out to be a job from Hell. A job for which she'd begun each day thinking not how to look nice but how to look shapeless. How best to avoid the endless comments, the casual touching. The bullying tone thinly masked as cheerful camaraderie. A job in which she was forced to spend hours alone in a closed room with a bully, who took constant pleasure in embarrassing and demeaning her. For whom there was no other agenda but a sexually predatory one. Whose every look and every comment contained an element of sexual malice. A hint even of physical intimidation. The ever-present possibility that some time, possibly with a drink inside him, he'd pounce.

The funny thing was that she thought Rodney Watson probably regarded himself as just a jolly old bloke. He seemed not to understand that his every casual 'half-accidental' touch, his every creepy comment and disgusting joke made her heart pound and her skin crawl. Or maybe he did. Perhaps that was half the thrill. Watching her go red, look confused, struggle to find a way to counter his pestering without losing her job.

Without losing the job she loved, for which she'd spent three years training. A job she needed. A job for which Rodney Watson clearly had zero respect. A job he scarcely noticed. Because he wasn't capable of seeing past her tits.

On the TV, Rodney had managed somehow to have the last word. Even as the camera cut away from the programme logo prior to the ad break his voice could be heard on his still-live mic saying, 'All I ask is that we remember the victims, Lorraine, that we *remember them.*'

In her bedsit, Ruth Collins was starting to feel that perhaps it was time Rodney Watson remembered the victims of his own past.

17. A Kiss Is Just a Kiss

THE *LOVE Island* production team were preparing to watch 'that' moment from episode thirty-six of the previous series once again. A moment that at the time had been popularly and critically perceived as simply a fantastic bit of telly.

A classic bit of *Love Island* #LoveRatting. A romantic exchange, which appeared to render the girl, Jemima – a.k.a. the Whiner – 'safe' from being 'dumped' at the next 're-coupling'. But which had turned satisfyingly sour when, in a spectacular act of betrayal, Kurt had chosen another girl to save. He had chosen Crystal, one of the mega-fit 'new girls' who had sashayed sassily into the villa earlier that day, their breasts bulging out of their bikini tops and their lips bulging out of their faces.

#TotallyLoveRatted.

Jemima's stunned horror when Kurt had said, 'The girl I want to couple up with is . . .' pause – ad break – more pause '. . . Crystal,' had been one of the defining images of the last series. An absolutely brilliant bit of proper old-school reality TV. The sort of incident for which *Love Island*'s many admirers waited through endless boring bits of filler and stupid games with incomprehensible rules. The absolute reason for the show's success was #LoveRatting. LoveRatting was in *Love Island*'s DNA. Its lifeblood was intrigue and betrayal.

But that had been then.

Now, suddenly and horrifyingly, things were different. What had recently been 'loud and proud' was now 'horribly tone deaf'.

On the wrong side of history.

Or even a little bit rapey.

Suddenly, and in the space of a single morning, everyone was waking up to the post-MeToo implications of a programme format that dealt exclusively with instant hook-ups.

Nervously, Daisy the researcher pressed play.

Episode thirty-six of the previous series leaped once more into life.

Jemima is seen sitting with Kurt at the firepit as she tearfully considers the imminent possibility of being dumped from the island. She and Kurt had been a 'couple' in the house for five days but lately there had been tension. Jemima had been showing interest in Wazzah, a surprise new boy islander who had strutted into the house two days earlier with shoulder muscles so bulging he looked like he was wearing a bronze neck brace. Wazzah totally ticked all of Jemima's boxes and she was caught whispering to the other girls that she wouldn't mind getting to know him.

Kurt had soon been informed by the other boys of Jemima's interest in Wazzah (#brocode) and been properly gutted. However, Kurt had got over his pain quite quickly and begun to chill with some of the other girls, all of whom he now realized ticked all his boxes and whom he would like to get to know.

Meanwhile Wazzah, who had at first appeared to revel in Jemima's attention, had come to feel that in fact she did not tick all his boxes, and had begun to whisper to the other lads that she was totally alienating him with her suffocating neediness.

In the feral hothouse atmosphere of the villa this had, of course, been reported back to Jemima by the other girls (#sistersbeforemisters) and thus Jemima had come to see that her decision to disrespect Kurt had been a mistake. One that left her vulnerable to expulsion in the 'boy-led re-coupling', which had been suddenly announced by the producers. This was the reason she had asked Kurt if she could have a word with him in private by the firepit, and thus had the fateful encounter ensued.

The two of them had been conversing for about a minute. Both had agreed that they really 'got' each other and that, despite recent wobbles, they ticked all of each other's boxes. They had admitted that they both still had 'feelings' for each other and that they would still like to get to know each other.

'So we good, then?' Jemima asks.

'Yeah, course, whatever,' Kurt replies.

Then Kurt hugs Jemima, wrapping his massively muscled arms around her with, a cynic might have thought, an unnecessary flexing of those magnificently contoured, primed, pumped and fully ripped limbs.

Jemima then turns her enormously plump lips, sparkling and shimmering with lip gloss, towards his. And there they quiver. Fat, fleshy, ripe and wet, the lower one hanging a fraction open, revealing a glimpse of perfect teeth.

But it is Kurt who leans in and instigates the kiss. His head moves, not hers.

But then Jemima returns the kiss. There is clear mouth movement.

'Bitch be workin' it,' said a voice from the back of the fully focused production team. A plummy middle-class white girl's voice. 'Bitch be *wahking* it.'

'Sssh!' Hayley snapped. She'd always hated how so many white private-school kids in the media spoke in a sort of grime-influenced Jaffaican but now it was potentially litigious. With Narsti, a real black person, in the room, a white employee trying to sound cool talking black might lay herself open to a charge of cultural appropriation for which the company, the enabler, might be liable.

On screen Jemima turns from Kurt and wipes away a tear.

'If the horny little shit had left it there, we'd be in the clear,' Hayley muttered.

But Kurt doesn't leave it there. He puts his hand on Jemima's chin and turns her mouth back towards his.

'Is he exerting pressure?' Hayley whispered, leaning in.

'She says he did,' said Dave, who did law and shit.

'Gotta believe the victim,' Narsti Rimes said, with a big smile.

'Shut up, Narsti.'

'Just quoting you, Hayley.'

On screen, Kurt leans in and kisses Jemima for a second time.

No matter how hard the *Love Island* team looked it was impossible to tell whether Jemima appreciated having her chin turned or whether she'd returned the second kiss. Her massive hair had fallen in front of her massive mouth, totally obscuring the view.

'She doesn't push him away,' Hayley said hopefully. 'Not for at least five seconds.'

Eventually Jemima disengages, saying, 'I don't know if you should have done that.'

Kurt merely shrugs.

Jemima smiles, takes up her wine glass and walks away.

The kiss was over.

Daisy pressed pause.

'Seriously?' said Hayley. 'I mean seriously. *That*'s put a fifty-million-quid global franchise in crisis? Why didn't she come to us? We'd have paid her off.'

'Maybe this isn't a play for money. Maybe she genuinely feels abused and needs closure,' Daisy suggested.

Hayley gave her a withering look.

The *Love Island* team were not the only people scrutinizing the clip that day. It had been repeated endlessly on both the news and the net all morning. The police were also looking at it in response to a tweeted question from Jemima's local MP who, having noticed the kudos that the MP of Deborah Willet (1650–1678) had been getting online, had tweeted on behalf of Jemima #IStandByAllVictims. The police in turn had tweeted that they were aware of Jemima's allegation and were studying the tape in pursuance of their policy on harassment and abuse, #ZeroTolerance, and their unbreakable commitment to the principle that Britain should and must be a safe space.

In the *Love Island* office Hayley could scarcely believe what was happening to her brilliant, brilliant show.

'It's a kiss!' she exclaimed. 'It's just a fucking kiss.'

But even as she said it Hayley knew that *she could not say that.* Everybody in the room knew that *she could not say that.*

Because once upon a time, and not so very long ago, Hayley had very loudly and very proudly opined that a kiss is *never* just a kiss.

And it had felt so good at the time. Strong. Decisive. *Fierce.*

'Don't you get it?' she'd said back then. 'A kiss is *never* just a kiss. Some are good, some are bad, but *none* are just kisses. They *all* involve the issue of consent.'

For years Hayley had been putting herself on the right side of history and now that same history had caught up with her.

18. #NoShadeOfGrey

AUTUMN 2017. What a time to be alive. Time had been UP, guys. Time had been *UP*!

Hayley had actually been thinking about pitching Netflix to do a massive high-end TV series about it. Well, why not? The world had turned upside down. Who saw *that* coming? Nobody.

Suddenly the men she'd been putting up with all her life had been on the back foot.

Thinking about their behaviour.

Checking their privilege.

Actors, producers, directors, all looking *so nervous*. And it had happened literally overnight. They'd strutted home one evening from their world of power and casual entitlement, their usual cocky selves. Then – boom! – Harvey Weinstein landed, and they'd slunk out the next morning glancing over their shoulders for reporters. Checking the Net to see if they'd been named. Trawling back through old memories, wondering whether some female colleague was going to put a whole new spin on a long-buried and uncomfortable encounter that *could* seem a *bit* dodgy, if looked at in a certain way.

Welcome to the world of feeling vulnerable, guys.

Suddenly women had some power. It had been heady stuff.

And when a group of senior women in film and theatre had rung up and asked Hayley to put her name to a 'statement of intent' on the subject of the British entertainment industry's 'massive' harassment and entitlement problem, which, according to them, 'everybody' had known about *for ever*, she had readily agreed.

A radical set of new guidelines for safe practice in theatre, film and television had been prepared. The stated intention was to make *all* areas of the industry safe-space environments in which brave, fierce and fearless artists could continue to experiment, push the boundaries and tell their radical, empowering stories while remaining absolutely 100 per cent safe, nurtured and comfortable. The guidelines were titled 'No Shade of Grey'.

It was at the media event that had been called to launch this bold new initiative that Hayley had made herself a hostage to fortune. During the panel discussion that followed the photo shoot and was live-streamed on the net, Hayley had stated she believed absolutely that clear, unambiguous consent in *all* circumstances and at *all* times was the number-one issue in the entertainment industry.

'Even if it's just a kiss,' she said, 'it's never just a kiss. There are absolutely no shades of grey.'

She had believed it too. There would be time for nuance later, but this was a revolution, and in revolutions you drew your battle lines. In the heady excitement of those extraordinary days Hayley, like many others, had persuaded herself that it was legitimate to dispense with all sense of proportion and context in pursuit of a national conversation that had to be had. This was a seriously big gear change. It would necessarily be a rough ride.

The high point of that wild year for many had been the British Entertainment Arts Awards. An electrifying evening in which *everyone* had worn black and white as requested, making it very clear in one stunningly glamorous and sophisticated visual metaphor that, as far as British film and TV were concerned, there were no shades of grey.

What a night it had been.

Hayley, who was nominated for Best Reality Production, had

felt a new spirit in the room. The champagne had seemed some-how more sparkly when consumed in the warm glow of collective moral righteousness. The little trays of nibbles, served almost exclusively by gorgeous young out-of-work actresses in tiny black and white dresses, were somehow even yummier for being eaten in the knowledge that, for once, an awards night was doing something really important.

Gone was the usual red-carpet tittle-tattle about designer dresses. Instead there was a series of fierce, strong and fearless pronouncements about being fierce, strong and fearless. The star-spangled presenters, both male and female, eschewed all the usual gushing introductions in favour of making wryly amused comments about the lack of sexual and racial diversity in the nominations. Each one was greeted with warm, knowing applause from a massed industry audience, all wearing their elegant little pins and badges.

#NoShadeOfGrey.

The male winners were all sheepish and self-effacing, talking about how it was the most humbling but also exciting time they had ever known in the industry, while in post-victory interviews avoiding questions about how much they earned compared with their female co-stars.

The female winners in their fabulous frocks, of which, for the younger ones, the top half was often little more than a pair of braces, made forceful statements about the need for less sexual-ization of young women on the screen.

Hayley herself, at the podium, holding her Best Reality Pro-duction gong, was particularly forceful in her call to arms. 'No shade of grey!' she shouted, waving her award. 'No shade of grey!'

To occupy the professional high ground and the moral high ground simultaneously is a rare and heady combination and Hayley had been on top of her world.

But now.

Now it was a few years later.

And in one incendiary post an angry wannabe model and Instagram 'influencer' from Essex had pissed mightily on Hayley's parade.

Because it turned out that on *Love Island*, despite the copper-toned bodies, the golden bikinis, the blue sky, green hills and the bright pink cocktails, it was nothing *but* shades of grey. How could a series based entirely on flirting, gossip, backbiting, infatuation, betrayal, compromise, endless ambiguity and, above all, #LoveRatting possibly be otherwise?

'It was just a fucking kiss,' Hayley said, staring yet again at the frozen image of Kurt and Jemima on the screen, both almost entirely naked, their lips locked together.

'A kiss ain't *never* just a kiss,' Narsti Rimes happily reminded her.

19. Dead Famous

AFTER THE scandal provoked by Matlock's victim-blaming misspeak had died down, there was little further public interest in the Sammy Hill case.

The murder of a woman in a park was not sufficiently unusual or interesting to gain national attention. Particularly in a week in which so many column inches were being given over to the crisis at *Love Island* and the furious debate about whether 'Kocky' Kurt was a sex criminal or Jemima the Whiner an opportunistic little bitch hitching a free ride on the #NotOK movement to settle an old score. The most agonizing divisions of opinion of all were among MeToo activists, some of whom felt that Jemima's claims were spurious and hence highly damaging to an already fragile cause while others felt that all accusations of abusive behaviours were of equal value and importance and that there could be no compromise when it came to supporting the survivor.

Second to #NotOK in trending terms came #RememberThem, the fast-accelerating debate concerning which dead white men should join Samuel Pepys in facing notional prison sentences for historical sex offences. Matlock had been approached to join the police task force on this issue but had declined on the grounds that attempting to prosecute dead people for crimes that had not been crimes when they were committed would place unreasonable demand on police resources.

Trending third on Twitter was #DontBookBedsFromBigots. This had been a bit of a sleeper but had recently started gathering real traction. The horrible experience that Freddie and Jacob had had on their Cumbrian holiday at the hands of Jocham and Brenda Macroon, the evangelical Christian couple who'd refused them a double bed, had suddenly caught the nation's attention and unleashed a Twitter storm of anti-homophobic outrage. An online campaign calling for justice had gained the support of numerous celebrities and MPs, and the police had let it be known that they were considering taking action against the Macroons' business. Freddie and Jacob had then let it be known that they had no wish to see anybody ruined, and they certainly didn't support the numerous threats of death and arson being made against the couple, but they were still hoping for an apology. The Macroons were unable to capitalize on this semi-olive branch: that sodomy was a sin was not their *personal* opinion, they argued, but God's, and thus their hands were tied on the issue.

The fourth biggest-trending topic was #BangUpPepys, a kind of adjunct to #RememberThem, and had been established out of fear that the actual prosecution of Pepys might get sidelined in the general pursuit of other dead criminals. Every history department in the country was throwing up new examples and interpretations of retrospective villainy, and #RememberThem was expanding at an exponential rate – particularly since it had been pointed out that the entire British Empire had been in clear breach of the Race Discrimination Act, thus criminalizing every single civil servant who had ever worked for the Colonial Office. By now Pepys had come to be seen as very much the Harvey Weinstein of the RememberThem movement, the single shocking case that had kicked off the resetting of the nation's view of its own past.

Hashtag-wise, poor dead Sammy didn't even make the top ten.

All that changed, though, with the news that Sammy had not been just any woman killed in a park. She had been a transgender woman killed in a park. A few years before, that would have made no difference to the public interest in the case: trans men and women had suffered and indeed died in anonymity, unmourned by indifferent, even hostile media. But in the long, hot build-up to the English referendum, a period in which the UK had become a melting pot of conflicting identity groups vying for attention, Sammy's death was a touchstone for both outrage and counter-outrage.

Everyone was looking for martyrs.

Everyone was looking for scapegoats.

No one seemed to be in any mood to compromise.

The police had not released the information about Sammy's gender identity. In fact, they had been extremely careful *not* to. Following Home Office guidelines, Janine Treadwell, with her press and media department, had taken the same position as Kate the pathologist. They subscribed absolutely to the principle that, since Sammy Hill had identified as a woman, she *was* a woman, and that was all the public needed to know. Any other position would be tantamount to trolling Sammy's memory by focusing on her prior life as a man and would thus be shamefully transphobic.

The assistant deputy commissioner was particularly sensitive to these charges. He did not want the Metropolitan Police's hard-earned rainbow status to be compromised. He was proud that, after two centuries of institutionalized homophobia, the Met had, in an extraordinarily short space of time, become – at least on the face of it – massively LGBTQ-friendly. No Mardi Gras was complete without joyful photos of burly officers in traditional tit helmets dancing with seven-foot-tall drag queens in G-strings and ostrich feathers, plus some fresh-faced, handsome young constable running into the crowd to propose to his boyfriend.

And now that the boring old G in LGBTQ had been overshadowed by the exotic and challenging T and Q (full definition of Q still under construction), the assistant deputy commissioner was not going to allow the Met's new feel-good profile to be ruined by any suspicion that London's coppers considered Sammy any different from any other female victim.

But, of course, inevitably word had got out. Sammy's friends wanted to celebrate zir life, and the small shrine they established at the place of zir death was festooned with rainbow-themed tributes, which identified Sammy very much as a member of the trans community.

The assistant deputy commissioner was confident that he and the police would attract high praise for their commendable discretion and strictly proper treatment of Sammy's gender status.

He was wrong.

Instead he was horrified to discover that his highly principled stance had backfired entirely. He and his force found themselves being accused of having actively *suppressed* Sammy's gender status.

'Police cover-up!' shouted a thousand tweets, and then the ten thousand retweets that followed.

'Another transphobic hate crime goes unrecorded!'

A posting on the Stonewall site made grim reading for the ADC and Janine from the press and media department.

'Yet again trans individuals who are statistically so likely to be attacked are ignored, marginalized and rendered invisible by the very people their taxes pay to protect them.'

In the increasingly complex landscape of identity politics the Home Office and the Met had made the wrong call. The police were now officially tone deaf and on the wrong side of history.

Matlock, Taylor and Clegg were having lunch at their desks when this particular shit-storm broke.

'Screwed if you do, screwed if you don't,' Taylor said happily, over his all-day-breakfast roll. 'What's the betting if we *had* announced that Sammy the Tranny was a man—'

'Do *not* call her Sammy the Tranny, Barry!' Clegg protested, opening her avocado and alfalfa gluten-free wrap. 'I mean it. Seriously, don't do it. I find it offensive. I really do.'

'All right! All right!' Taylor said. 'Just a bit of bantz. Jesus. You don't mind me calling you a lezzah.'

In fact, Clegg *did* mind him calling her a lezzah but she'd been accepting it for so long now that she couldn't think of a strategy to confront it. She liked Taylor and enjoyed their sparring. She knew he wasn't *trying* to be offensive. And she didn't want to look humourless. But he was definitely wrong.

'I'm just saying,' Taylor continued, 'that if we *had* let on that the sainted Sammy was trans we'd be getting the same level of crap thrown at us as we are cos we didn't.'

'But from different people,' Clegg suggested.

'The *same* people I'd bet,' Taylor replied. 'They're going to get you whatever you say because they *love* being angry.'

'Maybe they just have a lot to be angry about,' Clegg responded.

'We've all got a lot to be angry about, Sally,' Taylor said. His phone pinged. 'Speaking of anger, here you go.' He held up his phone. 'This makes *me* angry. A highly organized, foreign-funded, gay-trans lobby are coordinating an anti-police campaign on Twitter.'

'What bollocks!' Clegg exclaimed. 'Who says?'

'It's a bulletin from the England Out lot.'

'England Out?' Clegg wondered. 'What are they doing tweeting about a trans conspiracy? What's that got to do with the referendum? Shouldn't they be tweeting about jobs and services?'

'Maybe,' Taylor answered, through a mouthful of sausage and bacon. 'Dunno.'

'And also, by the way,' Clegg went on, 'why are you getting England Out posts?'

'Dunno,' Taylor repeated. 'I didn't ask for them. They just seem to have found me. Some are quite interesting, though.'

Now it was Clegg's phone that pinged. Another unbidden

news bulletin. 'Wow,' she said. 'A transgender ballerina's stopped traffic on London Bridge by dancing *Swan Lake* in support of Sammy. Go, girl!'

'That's gonna win 'em a lot of friends, isn't it?' Taylor said. 'Stopping the traffic.'

Clegg turned to Matlock, who was peeling a hard-boiled egg. Matlock was possibly the last person in England who still put one into his lunchbox. Clegg told him that they were back in fashion and you could buy them at Pret, but to Matlock, the idea of *buying* a hard-boiled egg rather than boiling your own was just potty. He boiled his, let it cool and put it in beside his sarnies, with a pinch of salt in a twist of paper. Just as his mum had done before him. He loved old-school stuff. Like a lot of the post-punk generation, he had a weird nostalgia for a post-war, black-and-white 1950s Britain that he'd been born ten years too late to experience.

'I think we're going to find we're working under quite a lot of scrutiny with the Sammy gig, boss,' Clegg remarked.

'I wish you wouldn't call it a "gig", Sally,' Matlock said. 'A gig is something you go to, like the Clash.'

'The *Clash*?'

She and Taylor laughed. Matlock knew he had to update his terms of reference but he never seemed to get round to it. Oasis, maybe? Jesus, even they were nearly thirty years ago. *Thirty years* since *Definitely Maybe*. God, he was getting old. He did quite like the Arctic Monkeys but the truth was they were 'dad' music, too, these days.

'A gig is a concert,' he said, 'not a murder investigation.'

'You are so wrong, boss,' Clegg said, as if she was addressing her father rather than the edgy dude Matlock still wanted to be. 'A gig hasn't been exclusively a performance thing since literally last century. A gig is anything anybody does. Brain surgery is a gig. Washing cars at traffic lights is a gig.'

Matlock knew that, of course. He just didn't like it. He also knew that not liking it put him in exactly the same company as the old farts of his own youth, who had so pathetically objected to the changing meaning of the word 'gay'. It was all so depressing.

'Anyway,' Clegg went on, 'all I'm saying is that we seem to be at the centre of another major outrage frenzy.'

Matlock was aware of the rapidly escalating notoriety that was engulfing his current gig. He'd been reading the BBC News site over lunch. He knew how many columnists, personalities and politicians had begun – in what to him looked like a conspicuous display of opportunistic virtue signalling – to attach themselves to the grief and anger being expressed among trans people over Sammy's murder. It occurred to him that many of these same public-opinion formers had spent the better part of their careers either ignoring or actively obstructing LGBTQ advancement but opinion formers are nothing if not flexible. In an unspoken but universally acknowledged shift in the centre ground of identity politics, it had suddenly been accepted that trans rights were now definitely a very big thing.

Matlock, Taylor and Clegg were all staring at their phones.

'The mayor says the traffic-stopping ballerina is exercising his democratic right to protest,' Taylor said gleefully. 'Well, that's lost him the motorists' vote. He is so screwed at the next election.'

'God, I hate that term, "the motorists' vote",' Clegg said. 'I mean, we're all fucking motorists, aren't we? You don't turn into a small-minded, climate-change-denying wanker just because you have to use a car sometimes. And it's *her* democratic rights, Barry. This ballerina identifies as a woman.'

'Sorry, Sally, but I'll choose my own pronouns while it's still legal to do so, if that's all right with you.'

Taylor wondered how long it would in fact be legal. He had only that morning received a bulletin from England Out, which had informed him that the #LetsStickTogether lot were committed to imposing gender-neutral pronouns in the UK by law as a thank-you for the financial support being given to them by a Europe-wide radical LGBTQ lobbying network, funded by Jewish financier George Soros. In what could only be seen as a major legal contradiction in terms, England Out were also suggesting that #LetsStickTogether were committed to imposing sharia law to assuage the Muslim vote.

'Let's put the television on, see what the news is saying about all this,' Matlock said.

'Wooh. Old-school media,' Clegg said. 'Vintage. Maybe we should listen to it on the "wireless".'

'It's the lunchtime news,' Matlock replied defensively.

'Which literally *nobody* watches any more,' Clegg said, switching on the office TV. 'It's such a weird concept. "Oh, it's lunchtime. I'll have some news." How random is that? Just look at your phone.'

The rapidly spreading outrage over the murder of a trans woman and the subsequent disgustingly transphobic police cover-up was, of course, the lead story. It seemed that the brief halting of traffic on London Bridge was not the only public protest being made over what was now set in the public mind as a transphobic hate crime to which the authorities had proved offensively indifferent. In the space of a single morning, Sammy Hill, a previously entirely private individual mourned only by those who had known and loved zir, had become a martyr to the cause of exposing and confronting trans intolerance. Pop stars and politicians alike were falling over one another to tweet their sorrow, their outrage and possibly, in some cases, to make sure everyone was aware of what wonderful people they were.

#hero #gutted #angel #inspiration and of course #IamSammy.

A sea of flowers and soggy teddy bears had grown vast around the small personal tribute that Sammy's friends had made at the murder spot. Badges were being sold at tube stations, saying, 'I am Sammy'. The mayor commissioned a banner to be hung outside City Hall that said, 'London is Sammy'. And once more Facebook had covered itself with rainbows, hearts and teddy bears.

The orthodox view at lunchtime was definitely that, as a society, we shared the grief and the responsibility for the death of an LGBTQ hero. It seemed the whole country was united in its sadness and shame.

That, of course, was not the case.

Millions of people didn't really give a toss about Sammy and resented being told that they ought to.

And millions more got properly angry about it. Secretly, of course. Because you weren't allowed to *say* anything, were you?

But they were sick of being told all trans people were heroic survivors. That Churchill was actually a horrible racist. That you mustn't make jokes about poofs and the Irish any more. Or feel a bit confronted that the local state primary school spoke forty-seven languages but the local MP who voted for open borders sent his kids private. They were sick of a lot of things.

And the big computer at Communication Sandwich was friends on Facebook with every single one of them.

20. I am Latifa

WINNIE JOSEPH was attending her grief-counselling session. It was part of the police-funded victim-support network. She was entitled to three free sessions and this was her third.

'I am Sammy,' Winnie said. 'What about "I am Latifa"? Where's the hashtag for my Latifa?'

Her counsellor shifted uncomfortably in her seat but said nothing.

'I've got nothing against this Sammy woman or man or whatever she is, but I don't see no badges for my Latifa. I don't see no police press conferences and I don't see no Mayor of London putting up a banner neither.'

Clearly Winnie wasn't going to drop it. Well, it was her session. She only had another twenty minutes. 'I'm sure that Sammy's family are grieving just as you are, Winnie,' the counsellor said gently. 'You have to focus on your own sorrow, not another person's tragedy.'

'Latifa *told* the police our block wasn't safe,' Winnie said, starting to cry now. 'She told them the gangs was running every corridor. But they didn't have the officers, they said. They didn't have enough cops to even *visit* our block, let alone take on them boys what run it. Latifa was getting harassed all the time cos she didn't want to go with them. Didn't want to be one of their girls. One gang-banger roughed her up good when she wouldn't be nice to him.'

'I know, Winnie—'

'You don't know! I'm sorry but you don't. You ain't black and you ain't living in a place where the cops can't be bothered to even police no more. I bet if you was to go to the police all beat-up, a *white* woman from a nice house who got beaten up by a black man, they'd have the officers.'

'Winnie, this is about grief. Anger won't help you.'

'But they got the officers now, haven't they? They was on the telly saying they'd do everything they could to get justice for that Sammy batti-boy.'

'Winnie! I'm afraid you can't say something like that even if you're in pain.'

'I'm sorry,' Winnie said, tears flowing. 'I don't know this Sammy and I don't want to disrespect no one. But my Latifa couldn't even feel safe in her own home or walkin' down her own corridor, and she was right not to cos some gangman wanted sex and to share her with his mates and killed her when she fought back. One more dead woman. One more dead black woman and I don't see nobody starting no hashtag IamLatifa.'

21. The Fishing Fleet

'MALIKA, YOU gorgeous thing, join me in my office, would you? There's a darling.'

She really should have minded him talking to her like that. From most men it would have sounded completely inappropriate and horribly patronizing. Which, of course, it was. But Julian somehow managed to imbue it with a post-ironic spin. As if they were both in on the same joke. Rebelling against the suffocating constraints of the PC fun police. Like those comedians who managed to get away with sexist jokes by adding a touch of irony. Making it into a joke *on* a joke, thus having their cake and eating it. Julian just had such easy, natural confidence. Malika knew that it wasn't *entirely* natural: attending a school where they drip-fed you effortlessly urbane self-assuredness with your morning porridge helped. But she'd met lots of posh boys at Oxford and thought them wankers. Bunter Jolly types, most of them. Julian was in a totally different league. The man had a voice and manner so charmingly posh and self-effacingly entitled that he made Hugh Grant sound like Janet Street-Porter. Malika enjoyed it. He was a lot more fun than most bosses. In good shape too.

'Here's a challenge,' Julian said, when he'd closed the door behind them.

He handed her a page from his notepad on which he'd written #IamLatifa.

'Who's Latifa?' Malika asked.

'You are.'

'I am?'

'Yes, and so am I. We all are. That's the point of the hashtag.'

'Yes, but who actually are we? I mean, who is she?'

'*Exactly*. Smart girl! Who is she? Nobody's heard of her. But she got beaten to death by a random gang-banger in the public stairwell of a grotty council block because she wouldn't suck him off while he recorded it on his phone to share with his mates, and her mother thinks no one cares.'

Malika typed the hashtag into Twitter. 'Her mother's right. Nobody does care. Only twelve retweets.'

'Yes,' Julian replied, almost dreamily. 'Amazing what the Fishing Fleet can drag up. I mean, how the hell did they find that? I just wouldn't have had the patience.'

He was looking at Malika in a rather enigmatic way, as if he was expecting a reaction.

'Fishing Fleet?' she asked.

'Yes. Our Fishing Fleet.'

Again that sideways look. All a bit naughty-boy. Impressive that he could pull it off at over fifty.

'All right,' she said, attempting a joke. 'I'll take the bait. What's our Fishing Fleet?'

'I'll tell you if you'll have dinner with me.'

She hadn't been expecting that. Which was part of his technique, of course. She paused for a moment, considering her reply. 'Isn't that sort of thing a bit harassey, Julian? You being my boss and me being thirty years younger than you. Do we really *do* that any more? I thought time was up.' She'd presumed that might make him think a bit. But he just laughed. 'I certainly do,' he said, 'and if you do, then I suppose we do. Your call, my darling.'

She tried to make him sweat a bit. A man could be *too* confident. 'Sorry, Julian? Did the last ten years not happen? Boss hits on junior chick in closed office? Power imbalance and all that? Not appropriate.'

'Oh, you don't care about all that bollocks, Malika! I know you. You're a Tory bird. Sick of all that political correctness. Whatever happened to good old-fashioned flirting? Didn't you write that somewhere?'

'Have you been looking at my Instagram, Julian?'

'*Duh*. Of course I've been looking at your Instagram. This is Communication Sandwich, for fuck's sake. It's what we do.'

'It's set to private. You would have had to hack it.'

'Uhm, *hello*?'

Malika said nothing. Of course he'd looked: he fancied her so obviously he was going to check her out online. That's what you did when you fancied someone.

'You looked amazing in that polka-dot bikini, by the way,' Julian went on.

'That is definitely inappropriate.'

'I know. I know! Slap wrist! Naughty boy! MeToo-boo-hoo and all that malarkey. But just bantz, old girl.'

She couldn't help smiling. He was just so fucking shameless.

'So,' he went on, 'what about it?'

'What about what?'

'That dinner.'

She decided she'd just go with it. Why not? He was a laugh. And quite attractive. And she'd been working so hard since she'd come to London she hardly had a social life at all. She had met up once with Sally Clegg, her one remaining old school friend still living in town. But Sally had brought her wife with her and Malika never liked being the third wheel on any cart. Besides, it was funny but now Sally was a police officer it just didn't feel the *same*. Hard to say why. But the fact that she was a cop had seemed to loom large over the reunion. They'd once been such bad girls together. Shoplifting make-up. Teasing boys. Now Sally was a married policewoman. Ugh.

And apart from seeing Sally, her social life had been pretty much confined to a few shouty youths who hit on her when she occasionally ventured out to a club with work colleagues.

And what was currently available on Tinder was just, well, yuk.

All in all, party-wise, a night out with Julian would be a massive step up.

'All right. If you want,' she said.

'Good call, that girl! Excellent.'

'If it's somewhere *very* high end.'

'Please, Malika, this is me you're talking to,' he said, affecting mock-offence. 'I do not *do* low-end dining.'

'I mean very high. Eye-watering. Vertigo-inducing. Somewhere I definitely could not afford to go myself even on what you pay me, which, I admit, is extremely not bad at all.'

'All right. How about Le Canard Charmant?'

'I don't know it.'

'It's in Geneva.'

This was definitely a moment. And a very sudden one at that. He was basically asking her to sleep with him straight off the bat. A dirty weekend in Switzerland. That *was* fast. There'd been a bit of flirting, certainly, but then lots of men flirted with her, or tried to, particularly successful middle-aged ones. Probably because they were less challenged by her double first in maths, which she had found put off a lot of younger men. But it was still unexpected. Julian had lots of women – gorgeous posh babes were always drifting through the office. He was a rogue, a player. A serial monogamist, as he put it, but with a *high* turnover.

'Basically I'm faithful on a night-by-night basis.'

Malika decided she needed to do a quick mental calculation. Fortunately she was good at those.

Did she fancy him? Yes. As it happened. He was very good-looking.

Did she enjoy his company? Absolutely. He was smart and

confident. His slightly smug shtick might get dull but it hadn't yet.

Would it make working for him uncomfortable? Maybe – but probably not. He had his own office and, besides, he was such an easy-going guy. If anyone could screw someone and move on without awkwardness, it was him.

And she really did quite like the idea of a mega-posh mini-break with a dashing bad boy.

And, quite frankly, if when the time came she decided not to shag him, she just wouldn't. She was pretty sure Julian would be far too proud to get spiteful over a knockback. All in the game. Gotta be in it to win it. No hard feelings.

'All right,' she said. 'I'll let you take me to dinner in Geneva.'

Julian smiled a big, sweet smile, which looked genuinely warm – as opposed to triumphant.

'Now what's the Fishing Fleet?' she asked.

'Gosh. I'd actually forgotten we were talking about that.'

'I hadn't. It's why I've agreed to dinner.'

'I would have told you anyway.'

'So tell me.'

Julian threw comical glances over his shoulders, as if to check that they weren't being overheard. 'It's another department of the company. They're on the floor above us.'

'You lease the next floor as well as this one?'

'Own, darling, not lease. That would be grubby. I own the whole building.'

'Impressive.' She'd genuinely had no idea he was that rich. 'But, parking that for a moment, what is it?'

'Well, how can I put this?' he said, chewing the cap of his Montblanc pen. 'The Fishing Fleet identifies trends and issues before they've even become trends and issues. It's their job to dig up today what people need to be getting angry about tomorrow. Hot-button topics, which, if properly manipulated, might play into whatever narrative our clients are trying to establish. The Fishing Fleet are *agents provocateurs*. They search out potential controversy for us to massage and develop.'

'So, basically, shit-stirring.'

'Exactly. They find the shit. You stir it.'

'Charming. Doesn't really sound like a job for an adult.'

'Oh, but it *is*. A deadly serious job. For instance, this obscure little hashtag, #IamLatifa. It's the angry cry of a mother who has lost her daughter. A black mother whose daughter died at the hands of an angry and entitled man, with whom she had no connection, apart from him wanting something from her that she didn't wish to give. Latifa's mother has looked at the current national conversation, which is focused on the unfortunate Sammy, and is wondering why the whole nation appears to be wringing its hands over a dead white trans woman while ignoring a dead black cis woman.'

'And why does that interest us?'

'Isn't it obvious? It could be very useful to the England Out campaign.'

'England Out? Don't get it.'

'Tommy and The Zax need black and brown votes. Or at the very least they need black and brown people not to vote pro UK.'

'Well, they might start by not demonizing black and brown people.'

'They can't do that, Malika. A large part of their campaign strategy is based on discreetly fanning racism. That's their base. Racism is their covert tool. The dirty little secret they share with some of their supporters and with which they stealthily manipulate the frustrations of millions more. This, of course, gives them two big problems. First, how to attract, or at least not further alienate, the five million votes belonging to black and brown people and, second, how to stop Team UK grabbing the moral high ground. All of which means they, and by "they" I mean "we", have to start blurring the lines. Confusing the issues. Dividing and ruling. Particularly in London. London's hard for England Out. It's a big #LetsStickTogether city. Very multi-racial. Very cosmopolitan. Well, look at you. You're a Londoner and you're a bleeding ethnic. Indian, isn't it?'

'I'm British, Julian. But if you're talking about my parents, originally Pakistani.'

'And you're pro UK, aren't you? Your parents too.'

'Of course.'

'Well, there you go, then. Most BAME folk in London see no reason to break up the UK. They tend to see themselves as British, not English. We need to rattle their cage. Confuse them. Stir 'em up a bit. The average non-white Londoner is unlikely to be moved by the likes of Tommy Spoon and Xavier Arron. But if it gets pointed out to them that the #LetsStickTogether-supporting latte-drinking London elite care more about a dead white trans woman than a dead black cis woman they might feel more conflicted about giving them their vote.'

'Is the #LetsStickTogether campaign particularly trans-friendly, then?' Malika asked.

'No idea. But there's a *perception* that it is. Pro-UK voters are seen as cosmopolitan and progressive. Little England voters are dismissed as reactionaries. That's the vibe. Whether it's true or not is irrelevant. What we can provoke by fanning the Latifa flame isn't so much a vote *for* English independence – whatever that means in a global economy – but a vote *against* the sort of people who champion it. Against the idea of a PC world where people agonize over trans rights, which emerged five minutes ago, and ignore endemic racism, which has been around since whenever.'

'That's pretty clever,' Malika conceded. 'Wicked and really quite massively shitty but definitely clever.'

'Isn't it? So just you run along and task a friendly bot or two to let the UK's five or six million BAME voters know all about #IamLatifa.'

'I'll see what I can do.'

'Good girl. And remember to bring an overnight bag to work on Friday. We'll need to leave early if we don't want to get stuck in traffic on the way to the airport.'

Oooh. He was fast. Fast and too bloody confident by half.

Did she object to his casual naming of a day for their date without even checking she was free? Did she mind that he was underlining the obvious point that this was an overnight trip? Not really. Actually, she found it quite exciting. She knew it wasn't an attitude that would do her any credit among most of the women she'd known at university, women whose opinions she respected, but sod 'em. She liked decisive men. And she needed an adventure. That happened sometimes if you were a professional mathematician.

'We'd be better off on the Heathrow Express,' she replied.

'Darling, *please*,' Julian admonished her. 'Public fucking transport? But, anyway, we're not going to Heathrow. We're going to Farnborough. Private plane, old scout. Only way to travel.'

22. To Zie or Not to Zie

'Sammy hill was returning home from a night out with friends.' Matlock took a deep breath before continuing. He needed to get this right. He *had* to get this right. Not merely out of respect for the victim but because if he didn't there was every possibility that he'd start getting death threats again via Nancy's book-club Twitter feed.

Who *were* these people, these furious tweeters?

Matlock never ceased to be amazed at the violence of the abuse. He had met a number of transgender individuals in the course of his duties and without exception they had been polite, considerate and seemingly without any unusual degree of malice. Yet somewhere out in the ether there appeared to be a small group of non-binary people who were in a permanent state of blind fury and a hair trigger away from taking massive, absolute and unforgiving offence. And of course it wasn't just transgender people: the same thing seemed to be the case for *all* self-defining groups, which, in the current identity-focused social landscape, appeared to include absolutely everyone. From men to women. From cis to trans. From new-age Travellers to white supremacists. From vegans to pagans. From Celts to carnivores. From anti-vaxxers to enlightened humanists. From the proudly plus-sized to the assertively anorexic. The long, the short and the tall. The good, the bad and the ugly.

The entire population appeared to be *itching* for a fight because everybody else afforded them insufficient respect. At least, they were once they got on the net. That was the strange thing. Everyone seemed perfectly normal when you talked to them personally, in the street or on the bus. No one called him a body fascist or threatened to rape his girlfriend or shouted in his face that he should stay in his lane or check his fucking privilege. But in the virtual social universe of the internet everything had gone completely potty. Matlock knew, of course, that people were always likely to be a little bolder in their nastiness when feeling safely anonymous, but there was nasty and then there was this *new* nasty, which was, in DC Clegg's words, 'proper nasty'.

Why? How? Where was all this fury coming from?

At risk of online outrage, it had to be faced. Matlock could not put off delivering his statement any longer. He focused himself by repeating his opening line.

'Sammy Hill was returning home from a night out with friends.'

The audience shifted uneasily. Hadn't he already said that?

Now the hard part.

'Zie decided to use zir usual route home, which zie often took by zirself. The attacker approached zir from behind and struck a single blow to the back of zir head. Zir clothing was undisturbed and zir wallet was not taken. Sammy was a vibrant young woman with so much to live for and the Metropolitan Police extend their sympathies to zir family and friends and assure them that we are doing everything in our power to bring zir killer to justice.'

Done it! Result. Not a single pronoun wrong.

It hadn't been easy. Overcoming the linguistic habits of more than fifty years was quite a challenge. A fortnight earlier Matlock had had only the vaguest idea that pronouns were even a political issue. Now he was attempting to relearn crucial parts of the English language while conducting a press conference. He was proud of himself: he felt that he had paid a small personal tribute to the memory of Sammy.

Unfortunately, apart from a more correct and appropriate use of language, Matlock had nothing new to offer. The only real way to respect zir was to bring zir killer to justice and Matlock was as far away from that as ever. To date, his investigation had yielded nothing. More than a week had passed without even a hint of a breakthrough. The crime scene had been forensically searched and then re-searched. Every door in the area had been knocked on in an effort to find a witness. Every unsolved murder from the previous ten years had been checked against what little the police knew about Sammy's death. The files of every known sex offender in London had been revisited and their whereabouts established. But there had been nothing. The killer had simply vanished into thin air.

Which was why Matlock was going through the grim process of fronting another press conference, to appeal yet again for witnesses and also to issue a *very* carefully worded warning about personal security.

'There are no suspects as of yet,' he said, 'and very few lines of enquiry. So it's very possible that Sammy was chosen at random and that zir killer will strike again. Therefore I urge risk-appropriate avoidance strategies.'

Having delivered this press-department-approved safety warning, Matlock took another deep breath. The assistant deputy commissioner himself had decided to attend the press conference to ensure that there were no further PR 'clusterfucks', and Matlock could feel the man's eyes drilling into him.

'I would like to conclude,' Matlock said, 'by assuring the public that the Metropolitan Police accept that violence against women is a male problem, the result of sexist inequality and patriarchal entitlement, and that the ultimate solution is the re-education of men and the eradication of gender stereotypes.'

Matlock said this because the ADC had told him he must and had come down to watch him do it. It wasn't that he didn't believe what he'd said. In fact, he saw a lot of sense in it. He just didn't quite understand where it got him specifically as a policeman. He'd been a copper for thirty years and in his experience a small but significant number of men were just violent. The majority of male violence was male on male. In pubs, in clubs and in gangs. And of those men some would always represent a particular danger to women. His job was to catch those men and put them out of harm's way. Let educators and policy-makers consider the causes of male violence. On the front line you had to focus on its consequences.

He'd made the statement because he was nothing if not practical. For him to be in a position to catch Sammy's killer he needed to be in charge of the investigation, and that depended on him toeing the ADC's line, which he strongly suspected had a great deal to do with the ADC's ambitions to drop the A and the D from his title, leaving just the C word. Which in this case was 'commissioner'. Among other things.

Anyway, he'd done what he'd needed to do and it was time to get the rest of the conference over with as quickly as possible.

'I will now answer a very limited number of questions.'

'Inspector!' boomed a loud, confident female voice from the back. 'If the police consider violence against women to be the product of world historical male entitlement then could it not be argued that you yourself have just made a significant contribution to the problem?'

'Sorry? Not following,' Matlock replied. 'Is this a question?'

There was a visible shifting in the crowd. Clearly a lot of people knew who the questioner was. In fact, peering through the television lights, Matlock himself thought he recognized the late-middle-aged woman who had stood up so quickly.

'By continuing to insist that Samuel, a.k.a. Sammy, Hill, a gay man who had swallowed a few hormone pills and was considering having his dick cut off on the National Health is a woman, I suggest you are perpetrating the ultimate male entitlement.'

'I'm sorry? Is this relevant?'

'Historically men have been allowed to do pretty much what they liked to women – own them, steal their property, beat, rape and murder them. However, it's only recently that apparently they are also entitled to *become* them. If male entitlement killed Samuel Hill then, as the ultimate example of male entitlement, in a broad sense, he had only himself to blame.'

This unexpected intervention produced the uproar that, clearly, it was intended to. There were a few cheers and many more howls of protest. Sammy's friend Rob, who had appeared until now to be the gentlest of souls, leaped to his feet and hurled a nearly full cup of Starbucks soy milk chai latte in the general direction of the speaker.

'Don't you dare deadname Sammy, you TERF witch! Sammy was a woman and a hero. Fuck you!'

The room descended into mayhem. Soy or dairy, a nearly full cup of Starbucks is a lot of latte, particularly since Rob had chosen a 'venti' size, which appeared to be Italian for 'bucket'. Almost a litre of creamy froth had arced out over the heads of the assembled journalists and interested parties, and while none had hit its intended target, it certainly hit plenty of other people. Instant uproar ensued. Matlock took the opportunity to suggest that any further questions should be submitted in writing and declared the conference closed.

Later that evening, at home discussing the events of the day with Nancy, Matlock looked up TERF on the net.

'Trans-exclusionary radical feminist,' he said.

'Yeah. Knew that,' Nancy said. 'It's what trans people call feminists like Geraldine Giffard.'

'That was her? I *thought* I recognized her.'

'Didn't you know? It's been on the news and all over the net.'

'I haven't looked. Had a bit of Bruce Springsteen on in the car. Sometimes you have to take a little break from the present.'

'Oh, it was her, all right,' Nancy said. 'I was wondering if she was going to get herself involved with this. Pretty aggressive move to turn up at a police murder briefing and deadname the victim. That was definitely a choice. She wanted to spark outrage.'

Matlock started to type into Google again. Nancy stopped him. 'Deadnaming means using a transitioned person's previous name, Mick,' she explained. 'It's a really shitty thing to do, intentionally de-legitimizing their identity choice. You need to get up to speed on all this, love, or you're going to put your foot in it again.'

Matlock refilled their wine glasses. Nancy was right. He did need to get up to speed on all that stuff. And not just because he didn't want to put his foot in it again: either Sammy's murder had been the random act of an insane psychopath, which, in the absence of further attacks or any connection with previous unsolved murders, Matlock was beginning to doubt, or somebody had wanted Sammy dead. And if that was the case he needed to understand Sammy.

And also the people who hated Sammy.

23. TERF Witch

GERALDINE GIFFARD had been a medium-level celebrity for as long as anybody could remember. A celebrated feminist intellectual whose seminal work *Cockbuster* had been essential reading among female university students in the days when feminists still had hairy armpits and female pop stars had still worn clothes.

Probably the thing most people knew about Geraldine Giffard was that she had once been introduced on some smug artsy panel discussion as being 'a poor man's Germaine Greer'. To which she had famously responded, 'That is a deeply sexist remark. I am a poor *person*'s Germaine Greer.' This sort of ballsy (her term) self-deprecating humour had endeared her to the public and made her a dependable booking for any 'celebrity'-led TV endeavour looking for telegenic eccentrics. Baking cakes, living on an island in a stone-age manner, learning to ballroom dance. And, of course, talking about feminism on *Newsnight* and Radio 4 whenever the subject was in the news.

As a famous second-wave feminist, Geraldine Giffard ought to have been a hero to young modern feminists. But, of course, trans politics had changed the nature of the women's debate in a wholly unexpected and radical way. Quite suddenly feminists under thirty had unilaterally and comprehensively embraced the previously fringe idea that, politically and socially, trans women were no different from cis women (or 'women', as Geraldine Giffard insisted on calling cis women).

'I will not use the term "cis",' she'd told John Humphrys on the *Today* programme. 'I am a *woman*. Full stop. Quite apart from anything else, it's such a horrid little word. Like cissy or cyst! Trans is a *doing* word. It's positive, empowering. Cis, on the other hand, is dismissive and demeaning. A mealy-mouthed word. I think it was deliberate! They couldn't even give us a decent word.'

Giffard's noisy interjection at the Sammy Hill press conference was only the most recent in a series of high-profile interventions on gender issues, which her many youthful feminist critics claimed 'put her on the wrong side of history'.

It had all kicked off for Geraldine Giffard when a man called Bruce Jenner, the famous American reality-television star, macho sports hero and patriarch of the Kardashian Klan had announced quite suddenly that she was a woman called Caitlyn. This expertly organized coming-out, which began with a glamorous shot of Caitlyn on the cover of *Vanity Fair*, was for many people the first they knew of the sea change in social attitudes that was about to sweep the Western world and lead to the 'bathroom wars' becoming a feature of all subsequent American elections. At the time, the general reaction to Jenner's decision from almost all sides of politics and in the media had been hugely supportive. President Obama himself had joined the chorus of praise, hailing Caitlyn for her inspirational courage.

Glamour magazine made her Woman of the Year.

There had been, of course, some carping voices from conservative-minded individuals, but far fewer than might have been expected. In fact, the sudden announcement that a previously world-famous male Olympian and reality-TV star was now a woman, and that there could and should be no argument about it, seemed to cause the most outrage among older left-leaning feminists. Germaine Greer famously commented that just because you cut your cock off it didn't make you a woman and, inevitably, Geraldine Giffard lent her voice to the small but vocal group of objectors to the new transgender orthodoxy.

'This person has never menstruated,' Geraldine proclaimed loudly and angrily of Caitlyn Jenner on *Newsnight*. 'This person has never borne children but has, on the other hand, *fathered* them. This person has never suffered the pain of being barren, has not experienced male sexual violence or any of the casual sexism that women suffer on a daily basis throughout their lives. Indeed, this person has been a willing *collaborator* in that sexism, not just as a hugely famous sportsMAN but also as an integral part of the Kardashian Klan, which exists to perpetrate little else but impossible female body types and impossibly unrealistic social expectations on impressionable young women.'

It was not a popular point of view. In a very real sense she was pissing on the parade.

'But surely you don't deny gender dysphoria?' the *Newsnight* interviewer challenged, making no effort to conceal her disapproval. 'Or the pain and prejudice experienced by people who live with it?'

'Well, I don't believe they're getting beaten up on a daily basis as they always like to claim.'

'Really? *Really*, Professor Giffard?'

'Not like a black man in custody in Alabama or a woman on the streets without a *niqab* in Saudi Arabia. But, no, I don't deny their isolation or their suffering or their right to sympathy and understanding. What I do deny is the idea that biological males can, must and should be defined legally as women simply because that is what they claim they are and that I, as a *biological* woman, have no right to offer a contradictory point of view.'

As a result of this single interview Geraldine Giffard had instantly gone from being a lovable, slightly dotty old darling of the left to a fully fledged Nazi whorebitch. Young radical women, whose mothers and grandmothers had taken *Cockbuster* with them to the Greenham Common Women's Peace Camp, insisted that the book be removed from university reading lists.

Matlock found the whole thing bewildering. The shift in attitudes had happened at such astonishing speed. Even five years earlier no one would have *imagined* that a whole generation of women with vaginas would unite in defence of women with penises to take down a woman with a vagina who had previously been a feminist icon.

But if Geraldine Giffard was hurt by her new pariah status she didn't show it. If anything, the abuse seemed to spur her on. Some people, perhaps unkindly, claimed that Geraldine's most contentious outbursts tended to coincide with her having a new book out. But since she usually had a new book out it was difficult to tell whether this was cynicism or coincidence.

24. Mixed Motives

O<small>N THE</small> morning after the disrupted press conference, Matlock, Taylor and Clegg assembled in the Situation Room for a progress meeting. It was the ninth such meeting since the Sammy Hill murder and it was no more encouraging than the previous eight had been. The word 'progress' was beginning to look somewhat redundant.

'House-to-house interviews?' Matlock asked, although he already knew the answer.

'Nothing, boss,' Taylor replied. 'The team's logged up hundreds and hundreds of hours and not a hint of a lead. A few people have admitted to being in the park around the time of the murder but none seem likely suspects and no one saw anything.'

'CCTV?' Matlock asked wearily.

'Still checking, still nothing,' Clegg replied. 'We've been round every shop, every pub looking for something, anything, a man with a hammer for choice, but so far there's nothing even remotely suspicious. We've moved on from street cameras, and we're checking all the cabs, the buses, shops. Everything.'

'So the killer could still be absolutely anyone.' Matlock sighed. 'And the motive could be absolutely anything.'

'Sex seems most likely to me,' Taylor said. 'A rape gone wrong. The perp struck, found out the victim didn't have what he wanted under his or her skirt so he ran, leaving him or her for dead.'

'Stop saying him or her, Barry,' Clegg said. 'It's *her*, you know that. Or zir, in Sammy's case.'

'Oh, for fuck's sake, Sally. It's all so stupid.'

'It's not stupid. It's about respect!'

'Jesus! Fucking *pronouns*? Seriously? Anyway, all I'm saying is that whatever she or zie had in her or zir knickers, I don't reckon it was what your usual sex attacker assaulting a woman is looking for.'

'And if it *was* an aborted sex attack,' Matlock added, 'it was done by someone new, someone not on our radar, in which case all we can do is wait for him to strike again, which is a pretty depressing prospect.'

'Maybe it was robbery after all. A botched attempt,' Clegg said. 'The killer was after Sammy's purse and jewellery but he got disturbed.'

'Then who disturbed him?' Taylor asked. 'Why haven't they come forward? We've talked to everybody in the entire borough. Personally I think hate crime is still the most likely motive. Sammy was killed because she was trans.'

'Toxic masculinity as a motive?' Clegg asked. 'An angry man? One of those incel weirdos who blame women for not having sex with them?'

'But why would he attack a *trans* woman?' Taylor asked. 'I'm telling you. Trans women are not the sort of women incel men are angry about.'

'You don't know that,' Clegg suggested. 'It's all got so complex. It might not be as simple a thing as straight sexual jealousy. There's a lot of blokes out there just getting really, really angry over the changing sex and gender fault lines, which trans recognition represents.'

'Well, we've got a lot to be angry about, haven't we?' Taylor said. 'Joking! *Joking!* Please don't have me castrated!' He cupped his balls in a mock-defensive gesture.

'Hilarious, Barry,' Clegg commented. 'Relax, your bollocks are safe with me. I'm just saying that you only have to look online to see that, these days, *some* men are terrified and *seething* with anger. They think that what little status they feel they have in society is being undermined. Sammy was a living symbol of the loosening grip that straight men have on power in society. Maybe one of them killed zir because of it.'

'Well, it all sounds pretty stretched to me,' Taylor said, with a shrug.

'Just trying to look at all the angles,' Clegg replied.

'And one of those angles,' Matlock said, 'is that the killer was a woman.' He let the thought land for a moment before continuing. 'A disaffected feminist who objected to Sammy's incursion on her gender territory.'

'I can see where you're going with that, boss,' Clegg said, 'after the coffee shower at the press conference. Geraldine Giffard.'

'Yeah. Geraldine Giffard. I did a lot of reading last night,' Matlock went on, 'googling all sorts of trans stuff and anti-trans stuff, and it seems to me that male anger towards transsexuals is mainly lazy and pretty ill-informed, not much more than mean-spirited prejudice really. *Female* anger towards trans women is more focused, more urgent. There's some women who feel that their very sense of *self* is under siege. From what I could see, browsing a few chat rooms, there's no gender parity in the reactions of cis people to trans. Disaffected cis men tended to hold trans *men* in contempt. Disaffected cis women seem to view trans *women* as a threat. And they can get very angry about it.'

'As we saw at that press conference,' Clegg agreed. 'Anger from both sides.'

'Yes,' Matlock said. 'Sammy and Geraldine Giffard had history.' He tapped his computer and YouTubed up a clip of news footage from the previous day's press conference: the moment when Rob threw his coffee and called Giffard a TERF bitch. 'He knows her and he's furious with her,' he said. 'And clearly it's reciprocated. You can understand why, too. Geraldine Giffard's life has been utterly and unexpectedly hijacked by trans politics.

Her entire radical credentials, the banner she carried for forty years, destroyed *overnight* by trans politics. She was completely blindsided. Sucker-punched. *Nobody* could have seen it coming. After *one* interview on *Newsnight* about Caitlyn Jenner she got no-platformed at universities, banned from literary festivals, and her books were defaced in radical bookshops.'

'Some shops refuse to stock them at all,' Clegg agreed.

'It must feel catastrophic for Giffard,' Matlock mused. 'Just about every girlfriend I've ever had owned a copy of *Cockbuster*, but now young feminists dismiss it as a historical irrelevance written by a sad, mad, out-of-touch old white woman who simply *doesn't get it.*'

'Well, she doesn't get it – sort of,' Clegg said. 'It's actually sad. I mean, I wouldn't chuck coffee over her but I do wish she'd shut up.'

'You see?' Matlock said. 'This completely unforeseen and unexpected issue has destroyed her life's work. Women like you used to be her core constituency. Now at best you want her to shut up. God, that must hurt. What's more, I don't imagine the ultra-sensitive and highly PC BBC are going to let a known transphobe compete in any cooking or travel shows any time soon. That's got to mean a huge drop in personal income. Her opposition to the changing nature of gender hasn't just destroyed her reputation, it's seriously threatened her livelihood. Gotta say, I've known a lot less obvious motives for murder.'

'Wow,' said Clegg. 'Did Geraldine Giffard kill Sammy? Big thought.'

'I reckon she's capable,' Taylor observed. 'I once saw her kill, skin and gut a deer on a TV show called *The Caring Carnivore*. It was impressive.'

'Let's not jump too far with this,' Matlock said. 'We don't have a shred of evidence. All we know is that Sammy's friend Rob hated Geraldine and Sammy almost certainly hated her. The question is, how much did Geraldine hate Sammy?'

25. Kiss Chase

IN THE interview Jemima from *Love Island* gave to *Cherry Sundae*, an online girl-centric 'zine 'for fierce babes who just don't give a fuck', she explained that she now believed Kurt had forced both kisses on her. Whether she drew this conclusion herself or whether it was the result of grooming by the *Cherry Sundae* journalist who interviewed her would be hotly debated in the coming weeks.

In the incendiary interview Jemima admitted that she had responded to the first kiss, during which her mouth could clearly be seen moving, but now explained that she had only done this because she'd found herself confused and disoriented. She felt Kurt should have understood this from her clear, if unspoken, signs. During the second kiss she claimed she had been quite obviously uncomfortable. At the very least there had been no unambiguous consent on her part – the type of consent which, *Cherry Sundae* pointed out, was the bottom-line prerequisite for any entertainment-industry kiss, as outlined in the Industry Code of Practice, *No Shade of Grey*. A code of practice that had been fulsomely endorsed by Hayley Bernstein, #SexTraitor.

Jemima admitted that her reactions had been more confused at the time. Which was why her statement, made in the Confession Room shortly afterwards, that it had been 'nice to have a kiss and make up' no longer reflected her feelings about the incident. Retrospectively Jemima had concluded that Kurt should have understood that any sexual advance would be unwanted.

Clearly she had been in a tearful and vulnerable state. Further-more, Kurt had been in a position of power over her. His decision to remain coupled with her would save her from being dumped, thus greatly enhancing her prospects of becoming an Instagram 'influencer' when she left the island. That Kurt had subsequently selected new girl Crystal proved he had solicited a kiss under false pretences. This, in Jemima and *Cherry Sundae*'s view, con-stituted grooming and abuse of power.

The *Love Island* team studied the online interview with horror.

'So is she saying it was non-consensual at the time?' Hayley asked. 'Or is she saying that it *became* non-consensual after Kurt broke an unspoken contract to keep her on the island? That it was *retrospectively* non-consensual.'

'Both, I think,' said Dave, who did law and shit. 'She didn't want it, but if she *had* wanted it, she certainly wouldn't have wanted it if she'd known he was going to cop off with Crystal at the next coup-ling. Anyway, and either way, the truth is, Hayley, it doesn't matter because it's out there now. The damage is done. Kurt is joining the names that get trotted out in the media whenever Harvey Weinstein is mentioned. And that means us too. We're on the list. The list that starts with Weinstein, Kevin Spacey and Louis CK – whoever he is – and now ends with Kurt and *Love Island*.'

'Oh, shit,' said Hayley. 'We've gone toxic.'

'Yes,' agreed Dave, who did law and shit. 'We've gone toxic.'

Britain's most talked-about and much-loved TV show was now linked irrevocably with the enablement of sexual abuse. Whether people agreed with that view or not was irrelevant. The link was there and would come up in every single mention of the show from then until the end of time.

26. Just Another Battle of Britain

MATLOCK HAD called Sammy's flatmate Rob and arranged to meet him again at his home. He explained that he wanted to talk to him about Geraldine Giffard.

On his way out of the office DC Clegg stopped him. 'Have you heard of Latifa Joseph, boss?' she asked.

'Yeah. Think so. She got murdered, didn't she? Gang-bashing in Hammersmith, wasn't it?'

'The subject's building up quite a head of steam on social media. Just entered the Twitter top five.'

Matlock didn't do Twitter. He thought it was stupid. He used to like saying that people on Twitter were twats until DC Clegg told him that everybody had done that gag about fifteen years ago. 'Why are you telling me this?' he asked.

'We've had a memo from Janine in Press and Media. Apparently the assistant deputy commissioner wants to know if there's anything we can do to show that we're fully focused on the murder?'

'Focused on it? Did they arrest anyone?'

'No chance. Dead girl found in stairwell in a gang-run tower block. Like anybody's going to talk to us. Nobody saw anything. Nobody knows anything. The case is a dead end.'

'So what are we supposed to do about it?'

'More. Apparently.'

'That's bloody stupid. The local plod'll know the local gangs.

If they can't get anywhere I don't see how we can, parachuting in from Scotland Yard.'

'Oh, she doesn't want us to *investigate* it, boss. She just wants us to show that we care.'

'What does she mean, "care"?'

Clegg shrugged. 'Say something, I suppose. Apparently we're not displaying the same empathy to Latifa as we have done to Sammy. That's why the ADC wants you to reach out to the family. You're the police face of Sammy, and it would prove we don't have favourites.'

'Oh, for God's sake!' Matlock snapped.

He was already heading for the door.

'The mayor's already made a statement about it,' Clegg called after him, 'saying London stands with all brave survivors and victims of male violence. He's put a "London is Latifa" banner up next to his "London is Sammy" banner. Janine thinks we need to get in on it. She wants you to—'

'Tell her I'm busy on a murder that we might have some chance of solving,' Matlock called, over his shoulder.

Matlock found Rob in a very fragile state. It was not only those, like Latifa's mother, who felt confronted by the bewildering level of attention suddenly being forced upon Sammy Hill. Zir family, friends and lover were feeling it too.

They knew that Sammy had not been a 'hero' – unless the simple fact of suffering from cruelty and prejudice makes you one. They knew that Sammy had merely been a decent person who had, on occasion, suffered at the hands of a society that now seemed to have collectively appropriated zir name for the purposes of placing themselves in a flatteringly virtuous light. Suddenly it seemed that if you *didn't* feature a rainbow heart with a small tear falling from it on your Facebook profile (the emoji that, by instant osmosis, had come to mean Sammy) you were by default a transphobic shit.

Rob, in particular, found this radical refocusing of Sammy's death almost unbearable, not least because he now found himself very much at the centre of it. He had made the mistake of speaking at a small vigil, which happened to have been held at the exact moment that Sammy's gender status had gone viral. He'd assembled with two dozen or so of Sammy's friends at the place where zie had been murdered and read that poem everybody loves from *Four Weddings and a Funeral* about clocks. After which he'd said he hoped they would all keep their murdered friend for ever in their hearts. 'Always find a moment in your day to think about Sammy,' he'd said, through his tears. 'Lest we forget.'

News of the event had been reported on the Stonewall website. From there it had been picked up by the Communication Sandwich Fishing Fleet, ever diligent in finding ways to shape the English referendum campaign as a battle between latte-drinking snowflakes and common-sense patriots. Sitting on beanbags in his private space, Julian and his team of copy-writers had noted that the phrase 'Lest we forget' had so far been reserved for fallen soldiers. In minutes they had created a viral post accusing 'crazed trans multi-cultural zealots' of claiming that a dead transsexual was as much an English hero as the fighter pilots who had died during the Battle of Britain. Malika's algorithms then swiftly sent the message to the people most likely to be annoyed by it.

DS Barry Taylor had been quite annoyed about it.

Wotan Orc Slayer had been absolutely furious about it. Genuinely, violently furious. He could scarcely control his shaking thumbs as he tweeted that these trannies should try being sent to a Nazi death camp before they went around insulting our fighter pilots who had died so that they could have the freedom to even *be* trannies.

Between Taylor and Wotan's reactions were various degrees of outrage. But everybody who received the post was affected by it, feeling as if the very fabric of what it meant to be English was under attack.

All this, of course, had come as a complete surprise to Rob who, while trying to process the devastating loss of his friend and lover, had found himself suddenly public property. He was regularly hugged and applauded when he did his shopping by people who wanted everybody to know how wonderful they were, and just as regularly spat at by people who were equally anxious for everyone to know how angry they were about every tiny thing. Particularly the idea that trans women were braver than Spitfire pilots. Which, to his astonishment, Rob discovered was what a lot of people thought he'd said at Sammy's vigil.

Thus when Matlock went to interview Rob for a second time he found him extremely shaky indeed.

'Sammy wanted to blend in,' Rob explained, struggling to keep his voice steady. 'Zie just wanted to be accepted. It was a process. A slow process. Zie'd only just told zir parents.'

Matlock was sympathetic but he wanted to talk about the murder. About whether Sammy had had any enemies who might have killed zir in a moment of rage. Whether it was possible that Sammy had led a secret life, one of which perhaps Rob was only vaguely aware. He also wanted to talk about Geraldine Giffard. But he knew he would have to go slowly: Rob was grieving.

'Have you seen this thing about Latifa?' Rob asked. 'The black girl who got killed by thugs in a tower block? What's that got to do with Sammy? One tragedy doesn't cancel out another. And what about the stuff they've been saying on Mumsnet? Why is Sammy *their* problem?'

Rob was referring to yet another group who had taken offence at the 'I am Sammy' movement, questioning, as Latifa's mum had, why the murder of a transgender woman was being seen as a more urgent and significant part of the national conversation than the numerous murders of cis women. After all, women were being beaten and killed every day all over the country and the mayor had not called for any traffic-stopping ballet dancers to rally to their cause. Neither had he hung any banners outside City Hall.

'What about ordinary women?' a nervous but forceful group complained, in a subject thread on the famous mums' site.

Inevitably in the age of outrage this thread became the focus of its own controversy after an online campaign had forced the Mumsnet moderators to ban the phrase 'ordinary woman' as 'hate-speak'. Cis 'mums' were sent a series of memes and posts pointing out that the term 'ordinary' demeaned and diminished biologically female women because 'it suggested that they were somehow boring and not special compared to their biologically male sisters'.

Trans women and their supporters were sent furious posts pointing out that if cis women were 'ordinary' then trans women were by definition 'not' ordinary, which was, of course, a small step from 'abnormal', then only a skip and a jump to 'weird' or 'perverted'.

Matlock was aware of the now multiple strands of outrage that were emanating from the murder of Sammy, and he kept wondering who was getting so angry. Yet again he noted that real people on real streets seemed pretty much the same as ever while online the nation appeared to be degenerating into a viral tribal bloodbath.

Who *were* these people?

Rob had quite a lot of sympathy for the Mumsnet complainers and also for those who were grieving Latifa. 'Sammy would *never* have wanted to be seen as more significant than other women. Zie wanted to be accepted. Zie wanted to be just like any other woman.'

Matlock nodded into the sugared tea that Rob had made for him, although he had, again, declined it. He did not for a moment doubt the truth or sincerity of what Rob said, or feel any personal antipathy to it. If Sammy had wanted to be accepted as just like any other woman that was fine by Matlock. But he knew within himself that he could never personally *understand* such an ambition. He just did not believe that wishful thinking could permanently defy the laws of nature. How could people who were biologically male, many of whom had previously fathered children, ever imagine that they could be regarded as *just like any other woman*? To Matlock it was simply a contradiction in terms.

Rob seemed to read his thoughts. 'I guess it's just a generational thing,' he said.

'What?'

'I know what you're thinking. I saw the same look in my parents' eyes when I introduced them to Sammy,' he said. 'They're good people. They *wanted* to believe. You *want* to believe. You *want* to be supportive, I know that. But you're *never* going to truly *feel* it.'

'I suppose that's true,' Matlock conceded. 'It's probably generational. My partner's daughter talks trans issues at school all the time. She seems to think it's the most natural thing in the world.'

'But you can't. That's OK. It's not your fault,' Rob said. 'It's a process. Sammy never wanted a fight about it. Zie certainly didn't want to fight Geraldine Giffard.'

'And *did* zie fight Geraldine, Rob? I mean, did they clash personally?'

'Of course they did!' Rob replied hotly. 'That TERF bitch tried to stop Sammy swimming in her pond! But Sammy never wanted a fight. Zie just wanted a fucking swim.'

27. Hate Island

As JUNE turned into July, the result of the upcoming English referendum seemed to hang more and more in the balance. The England Out campaign had understood immediately the value of the *Love Island* controversy as a weapon with which to attack the opposition. There were now only three months left till the vote and every opportunity to undermine the credibility of Team UK had to be exploited ruthlessly.

Tommy Spoon and Xavier Arron had rushed around to Communication Sandwich filled with malicious glee.

'This'll fire up our base for fucking sure!' Tommy shouted, as he strode past the hot desk that Malika was occupying on his way to Julian's office. 'Pardon my language, ladies.'

'We'll hammer them hard!' The Zax agreed, in an equally shouty manner. 'It's fucking perfect. Do people really want to live in a country where the number-one reality dating show can be ruined by a bunch of PC snowflakes, who think a bloke kissing a bird is sexual assault? Fucking brilliant. Absolutely proves our point. Stay in the UK, and the latte-drinking middle-class liberal London elite'll put men in prison for wolf-whistling and hand 'em a life sentence for giving a girl a pat on the arse.'

'Yeah!' shouted Tommy. 'We'll spray 'em with memes and tweets. We'll say there are Europe-wide plans to ban men altogether.'

Tommy and The Zax were surprised to discover that Julian only partly agreed with them. 'Of course the *Love Island* #NotOK business is a gift to us, guys,' he said, pouring them bourbon. (Tommy and The Zax drank American whiskey, of course, not Scotch, because, as they liked everybody to know, they thought globally.) 'But you've got the wrong target,' he added.

'Wrong target?' Tommy shouted.

'What do you mean?' The Zax shouted, even louder.

'We don't need to go after our base vote on this,' Julian explained gently. 'They're already furious about political correctness and MeToo. Of course this will make them angrier but they don't need our help for that. We need to go after the other side. The progressives. The liberals. The people who now believe *Love Island* is irredeemably toxic. Don't you see? Because Team UK have deliberately linked their brand to it with their #LuvIsland campaign, they are irredeemably toxic too. The first rule of social media is that, once made, a toxic connection is unbreakable. After the way *Love Island* treated poor traumatized Jemima, a vote for #LuvIsland is a vote for the abuse of an innocent girl or woman and in support of non-consensual kissing.'

'Fuck, that's genius,' said Tommy.

'It's what I do,' Julian replied. 'Malika! Fire up the mainframe.'

Malika duly did so, and an hour later England Out unleashed a barrage of tweets and memes aimed at the sort of people Malika's algorithms had identified as probably being pro UK. They pointed out that Team UK had been revealed as little better than a cheerleader for harassment and sexual abuse. The utter hypocrisy of their shameless association with the sick and abusive date-rape show *Love Island* was surely clear for all to see. The disconnect between the slick, rainbow-hued PR and the seedy reality of their indifference to grooming, harassment and the ongoing trauma of the brave survivor exposed the latte-drinking urban elite for what they were.

UTTERLY SHAMELESS HYPOCRITES.

Or, at least, that was what the headline in the most popular mid-market tabloid called them the following day. It devoted much copy to the fact that, while the leftist London media elite were so anxious to force their PC social engineering on the rest of us, they were happy to sit back while one of their own indulged in Weinstein-level behaviour. It had certainly not gone unnoticed that *Love Island* producer Hayley Bernstein, who had happily lectured the nation about shades of grey and zero tolerance, was now revealed as a despicable enabler of abuse.

#HypocriticalLatteDrinkingBitch.

28. Changing Hashtags in Midstream

TEAM UK were in meltdown.

Toby, the incredibly expensive taxpayer-funded marketing guy, was summoned urgently to another meeting in the basement at the Home Office where he did his best to put a positive spin on developments. 'At least people are talking about us,' he suggested. 'Awareness is gold dust.'

Jim, the minister for referendums, and Beryl, his opposition shadow, were not convinced.

'They may be talking about us,' said Jim, 'but when they do they're calling us elitist latte-drinking hypocrites.'

'What *is* it with the latte thing?' Beryl chipped in. 'Why is drinking lattes so terrible? Don't most people drink lattes? I mean, it's just milky coffee, isn't it?'

'The act and the image,' Toby said. 'Two different things. Like masturbation. Everybody likes to do it but calling someone a wanker still carries deeply negative connotations.'

Beryl would have preferred Toby to choose a different illustration. Particularly while he was holding a creamy latte.

'Anyway,' Toby concluded, with a shrug, 'it's a thing. *Love Island*'s gone toxic. Live with it.'

'Living with it is not an option. I'm afraid you're going to have to shut down the #LuvIsland campaign,' Jim said. 'People don't associate *Love Island* with love and togetherness any more. They associate it with #MeToo and #NotOK. Team UK cannot afford that kind of connection. You need to come up with a new brand

and fast. It's July the fifth and the referendum's at the end of September.'

'I've got it! It's a no-brainer!' said Toby, almost spilling his latte in his eagerness. 'We reboot the "Britain Is Great" campaign.'

Jim frowned. Toby was referring to a much-loathed and entirely desperate David Cameron-led initiative, dating from 2012, launched during the prelude to the first Scottish referendum. This campaign truly *had* been a no-brainer, in the sense that anyone with a brain could see how shit it was, consisting of a series of huge billboards and glossy advertisements featuring the word 'Great' attached to some abstract concept or activity. As in 'Creativity Is Great', 'Engineering Is Great', 'Innovation Is Great' and 'Countryside Is Great'. These ungainly statements were displayed against Union flags and beautifully presented pictures that reflected whatever was great.

Jim's frown deepened. 'I found that campaign a *tiny* bit forced, didn't you?' he said. 'I mean, as phrasing goes it's *quite* clunky and ugly, isn't it? Just sticking "is great" after a lot of random things that every other country does just as well as we do.'

Now it was Toby's turn to frown. It was a slogan. Obviously it wouldn't stand up even to cursory scrutiny. You just had to go with it.

'I mean, engineering?' Jim went on, pressing his point. 'Culture? Countryside? Kind of universal, really, don't you think? Obviously I get the *idea*. We're called Great Britain, so our stuff is great. It's a sort of play on words. But, apart from anything else, most countries don't even call us Great Britain any more. Just the UK. So it didn't really work on any level, did it? And *such* an ugly sentence construction. It's still going, you know. They've got them all over Heathrow at Arrivals. Can you *imagine* the cost? Ye gods.'

Toby did not break his stride. 'OK,' he said, happy in the knowledge that developing an alternative campaign, even if it was only a revamp, meant double-bubble fee-wise. 'Let's take the basic concept and give it a new spin. How about this! #GREATBritainTheCluesInTheName. Fuck, yeah! It's witty, it's punchy, it's not too grand or retro. What do you think?'

Jim and Beryl loved it. Although they'd have loved anything even halfway coherent. They were desperate.

'That is utterly brilliant,' said Beryl.

'What's more,' Jim added, 'I think we've had enough of this lovey-dovey, touchy-feely stuff. Enough with the rainbows and whatnot. We've got to get away from this urban elite latte-drinking image we've been stuck with. We need to talk *real* issues and *real* patriotism. Focus on what truly makes Britain great.'

'Absolutely! Fuck, yeah!' Toby agreed. 'And what exactly is that?'

There was a pause while they all thought about it.

'Well, our shared history, I think,' Beryl suggested. 'We should double down on that.'

'Yes,' Jim agreed. 'It's the anniversary of the end of the Falklands war next June. A glorious victory for Britain. Britain as a *whole*. A plucky little nation sent a task force halfway round the world to protect our common values and won. How about we use the anniversary as a catalyst to launch #GREATBritainThe-CluesInTheName as the voice of British patriotism?'

'Good thought,' Beryl said. '*Great* thought.'

They all laughed, relieved to have taken back control of the agenda.

'And in the meantime you want me to disassociate us from *Love Island*?' Toby asked.

'Oh, yes. That's urgent. A top priority. Make it clear that the campaign to keep England in the United Kingdom stands squarely by all survivors of abuse and as such we disassociate ourselves absolutely from the enablers at *Love Island*, who are tone deaf and on the wrong side of history.'

The news that Team UK were cancelling their #LuvIsland campaign hit the net as Malika and Julian were putting their bags into the limo to head out to Farnborough for their private flight to Geneva.

'It's actually pretty cheap to get your own plane,' Julian explained, as he opened the door for Malika to get in. 'The people who own private planes rarely use them so they're desperate to rent them out. If you ring on the day you can usually take your pick for a few grand. I mean, I could probably afford to own a small one, but why bother with all the hassle when I can rent one for next to nothing?'

Once in the car Julian phoned Tommy Spoon and Xavier Arron. 'Congratulations, gentlemen,' he said, raising a plastic flute of Taittinger to the phone mouthpiece. 'We can now switch targets and go after those England Out supporters you wanted me to shake up. I thought the first Facebook post could be something like *Millennial snowflake UK Remainers buckle to PC madness and reject much-loved people's show* Love Island. *Break the union before they make flirting illegal and arrest you for not fancying trannies.* Bit long, I know, but pretty convincing, don't you think?'

Malika could hear laughing and cheering at the other end.

Julian turned off his phone, clunked his flute against Malika's and sat back in the plush seat. 'You're going to love Le Canard Charmant,' he said. 'The foie gras is like melted butter. You don't mind cruel food, do you? Of course not! Your lot slit sheep's throats in the back garden, don't they? Kidding, obvs. But, really, the foie gras is sensational.'

29. Troll in a Pond

MATLOCK ACCEPTED the mug of tea brought to him by Nancy's daughter, Kym. She was sixteen and the last remaining child in his and Nancy's blended nest.

'What ya lookin' at, Mick?' Kym asked, staring at his computer screen. Kym liked Matlock. They often clashed, of course, as any grown-up and teenager living in the same house will do, but on the whole she approved of him. Not least because, unlike her mum, he made an effort to get on with her real dad.

'The *Highgate Post*,' Matlock answered.

'What's that?'

'Used to be a local newspaper. Now it's a website.'

'Very sad,' Kym said, staring at the screen. 'Taking an old-tech cultural model and just stickin' it on the Net is not going to save them or their jobs.'

'I don't know, Kym. Local papers and their websites are still the only place to go for proper local news. Facebook feeds don't really cover council meetings.'

Kim was reading the headline of an article on the screen. 'What's the Pond War?'

'That's what I'm trying to find out. Had you heard of it?'

'Don't think so. What is it? Americans screwing up the world again?'

Kym and Matlock occasionally talked politics, which Matlock really enjoyed, Kym less so, not least because of Matlock's irritating habit of dragging up what he claimed were much more passionate demos and fights from the ancient past whenever they discussed just about *anything*. Race? The environment? Western militarism? Anti-capitalism? He'd been there and done it all thirty-five years ago and, what was more, *insisted* on YouTubing her the appropriate music. She really did *not* want to watch clips of ancient groups she'd never heard of, with stupid names like Madness and the Blockheads, performing at Rock Against Racism concerts in the early 1980s.

'No. Highgate Ladies' Pond,' Matlock explained. 'It's a women-only swimming pool. They had a protest there last summer over trans access.'

'Bet I know which side you'd be on,' Kym said, leaning in and reading the article.

Kym was big on trans rights and liked to challenge Matlock and her mum on what she saw as their ill-concealed ambivalence on the subject. With all their Greenpeace and anti-racism and gay rights stories from the eighties, it was good to have one cause on which she was properly more radical and liberated than them.

'A women-only public pond?' she said. 'Do they mean an actual *pond*, not a proper swimming pool? Is that even a thing?'

'Absolutely.'

'People swim in a *real* pond? In London?'

'Yep. And only women in this one. Ever heard of Geraldine Giffard?'

'Uh, yeah? She's a TERF bitch.'

'Used to be a feminist icon.'

'So did Florence Nightingale and she was an elitist Tory stooge who took all the credit when a black nurse called Mary Seacole had done all the work.'

'I don't think that's entirely true.'

'Well, actually, it entirely is.'

They let it go.

'So what's up with this pond, then?' Kym asked.

'Back in the eighties,' Matlock replied, 'Geraldine Giffard saved it for women. It had been single sex for ever, but when sex-discrimination legislation started to dismantle the world of all-male clubs and societies, some blokes got arsey about it . . .'

'No shit, Sherlock.'

'. . . and tried to turn the tables.'

Matlock typed in a search: *Geraldine Giffard. Highgate Pond confrontation 80s.*

Instantly a YouTube link came up for an ancient BBC *Panorama* report.

'Incredible,' Matlock murmured. 'You can literally find anything. Truly incredible.'

'And even more truly incredible that you still find it truly incredible that you can literally find anything, and even *more* truly incredible that you *still* say "truly incredible" every single time you do. You have really got to get used to the internet, Mick. It was around years before I was even born.'

Matlock knew she was right. But he knew he would never *quite* get used to the wonder of it. He would never find Skyping people into dinner parties a natural thing to do.

He played the link.

On the little screen a bunch of what, back in the 1980s, would have been called 'Hooray Henrys' were standing around High-gate Pond. A plummy old-fashioned BBC documentary voice explained that they were attempting to occupy the pond on the grounds that an all-women space was reverse sexism. Matlock was surprised at how old-fashioned the *Panorama* man sounded. He'd thought that the 'BBC voice' had gone by the time he was young, but the evidence seemed to be that it hadn't.

On the screen the long-ago Hoorays were looking very pleased with themselves. Having come along in Victorian-style swimsuits, inflatable armbands and comical 'duck' lifebelts round their waists, they had also brought beer.

'What a bunch of wankers,' Kym remarked.

'Wankers indeed,' Matlock agreed.

Now Geraldine Giffard appeared, young and passionate, with massive amounts of long curly hair. She was leading a spirited group of swimsuit-clad female defenders who, having armed themselves with nail scissors and hairpins, were marching about puncturing the protesting men's inflatables.

'The reason *men* gather together is to perpetrate male entitlement!' the young Geraldine shouted, into the boozy, bewildered male faces of those long-gone binary days. 'The reason *women* gather together is a *defence* against male entitlement! You stupid pricks! They're completely different things. This is the one place in London where I can be a fat bird with saggy tits in a bikini and not worry about men making me feel ashamed of my body. Now fuck off.'

The *Panorama* clip had bleeped out the swearing but it was clear what she'd said. Matlock pressed pause. 'I remember all that happening. I think I saw this programme.'

'Fair play,' Kym said. 'She was pretty cool back then.'

'She was considered inspirational by every student fem soc in the country,' Matlock said. 'And not just feminists. She was really popular. Pretty much everybody, barring a few geriatric arseholes, could see that women needed spaces without men more than men needed spaces without women.'

'Obvs,' Kym agreed.

Matlock typed in another search. YouTube produced another instant result. Another news report. 'Truly incredible,' Matlock murmured.

Kym dropped her head in mock-despair.

The news footage was again covering a confrontation at Highgate Pond but this time it was a *Sky News* special from the previous summer. Thirty-five years on, Geraldine Giffard and a small group of like-minded women were once again seen attempting to defend their pond – not against a gang of arrogant, sexist men but against a single trans woman.

Sammy Hill.

'This time,' the Sky reporter explains, 'Geraldine Giffard is on the wrong side of history.' The reporter turns to a local councillor, who states that Sammy's efforts to use the pond were entirely within the rules, the committee who run it having unanimously agreed that self-defining women were women and therefore entitled to swim in it.

'Fucking right too,' Kym said.

Next the reporter interviews some of the protesters, who voice their fears that it might now be possible for a pervert, or worse, to come to the pond simply by claiming to be a woman. They said they felt unsafe.

'As if!' Kym exclaimed. 'Just get the fuck over yourselves.'

A scared but defiant Sammy zirself then tells the reporter zie also felt unsafe, all the time in fact and particularly while swimming, because as a trans woman zie was the subject of constant abuse and some threats. Sammy is seen appealing to the objectors to allow trans women the same sanctuary as cis women are afforded since they were all similarly the targets of male violence.

Zir argument won over many, but not all.

'It just feels that in order to cater to the needs of a very, very tiny group of people,' a nervous-looking young mother states, 'the whole concept of what it is to be a woman is being sacrificed. Womanhood is special. It's precious. What happens next? Trans women competing against cis women in sports? I heard that the NHS has been lobbied to stop using the word "women" in its cervical-cancer ads and say "people with a cervix" instead. Well, I'm sorry but a person with a cervix is a woman and a woman is a person with a cervix.'

The reporter suggests that the story about the NHS is false but the young mum insists that posts on her mums' website say it's true.

Now Geraldine, dressed in a black one-piece bathing suit, pushes her way in front of the camera. 'I defended this pool thirty-five years ago against male entitlement and I am doing so again. I sympathize with those who suffer from gender dysphoria but self-definition without full transition is a step too far. There should be no penises in this pond!'

Geraldine shouts the last point directly into Sammy's anguished, tearful face as zie cowers behind zir towel.

Matlock pressed pause.

'What a nasty, bullying bitch,' was Kym's conclusion.

'Yes,' Matlock said. 'That's what most people said. Geraldine Giffard came out of that conflict looking very bad indeed.'

'And she deserved to.'

Matlock stared at the frozen image of Sammy on the screen. Tears on zir cheeks. 'Geraldine must have hated Sammy for that,' he murmured.

'I imagine she did. She got more than she bargained for. I signed a petition against her online.'

'Yes, she was pretty much vilified. Her own students even stopped attending her lectures.'

'Good for them. She deserved it.'

'She had a number of lucrative speaking engagements cancelled.'

'Why would you care?' said Kym, firmly. 'She's a TERF and I hate her.'

'And she must really have hated Sammy,' Matlock said, almost to himself.

Kym shrugged. Geraldine Giffard's opinions were a matter of supreme indifference to her. She left him staring at the screen.

At Sammy's tearful face. At the tears that had played a part in ending Geraldine's forty-year run as feminist icon and national treasure.

The following morning, while driving back to Scotland Yard, Matlock called Taylor and Clegg. 'We definitely need to talk to Geraldine Giffard.'

'Obviously, boss,' Taylor replied.

Matlock was a bit taken aback. It did seem obvious, now he came to think of it, but there was no need to be rude. 'Don't be a smartarse with me, Barry. I may be a nice bloke but I'm also your boss.'

'Not being a smartarse,' Taylor replied. 'The assistant deputy commissioner's been on about it, and Janine from Press.'

'About interviewing Giffard? Why?'

'Why? It's only the fastest-trending hashtag in UK Twitter history.'

'Hashtag? What hashtag?'

'What hashtag? I thought you said we needed to talk to Geraldine Giffard.'

'Yeah. It seems to me that the person with the biggest grievance against Sammy was Geraldine Giffard. I think she's a genuine suspect.'

'Yeah, boss. You and the entire internet. Just search #GerryKilledSammy. You'll see.'

30. Good Old-fashioned Date

JULIAN HAD been right. Dinner was spectacular. And Malika had the foie gras, even though she knew she shouldn't. It really was pretty awful forcing food down geese's necks like that.

'Any more awful than factory-farming Kentucky Fried Chickens?' Julian had enquired, without looking up from the wine list. 'Really? I don't think so. More awful than destroying rainforests to make pasture to grow hamburger ingredients? More awful than palm oil, which is literally killing orangutans so we can have lipstick and pizza crusts? God, I hate whining liberals and their selective bleeding hearts. The world is cruel and the world is fucked, and unless you're prepared to be a vegan monk, don't tell me you can have your organic artisan Cumbrian sausage delivered to your door by the Real Banger Company, or some other grimly retro-branded hipster start-up, but I can't have my foie gras because the pig only got its brain fried with an electric stun gun while the goose got choked on funnels full of corn.'

'Wow,' Malika had said. 'I feel even better about eating it than I did already.'

'Good girl! And the caramelized pears go so well with it, don't you think? As does this cheeky little dessert wine I ordered so cleverly.'

'Bit decadent, having a dessert wine with a starter.'

'Decadence is a bourgeois concept, darling. Those with class do what the fuck they like without apology. If your starter features caramelized pear, have it with a sweet wine. Obviously.'

Julian was fun.

People who seriously didn't give a toss about anything often were.

On the whole Malika tended to prefer right-wing men to lefties, even at university where Tory boys were treated like pariahs. Having dinner with people who *cared* about stuff was so *tiring*. Everything was terrible. Everything was insoluble. The world's dying and it's all our fault. Dinner with a left-wing bloke was so *draining*. Right-wing guys just wanted to eat and drink and fuck. And, no, they weren't going to check their privilege because somebody was always going to be privileged and, frankly, they'd prefer it was them.

Not that she liked idiots: she'd soon tired of drinking-club rugger buggers. But *clever* right-wing men. Rich, confident, erudite players, who made no apology for being players. That was fun. And older – she quite liked older too.

She'd let him order dinner for them both.

Why not? She also quite liked being seduced – on occasion and always on her terms. She liked being wined and dined and flattered, if it was by an absolute expert like Julian. That was what so many of her women friends at uni hadn't *got*. She *liked* it. She didn't *submit* to it, she welcomed it. And if she got tired of it she'd disengage, politely or otherwise. Sure, she wanted to be paid the same as a man for doing the same job. But did she mind a man paying for her dinner? Like hell.

Besides, she wanted to know more about what Julian did at Communication Sandwich, and she felt he'd be more communicative if he felt flattered.

'So I did a good job getting #IamLatifa out, didn't I?'

'You certainly did, my darling,' Julian agreed. 'A quarter of a million retweets.'

'And how many of those retweets were about a genuine empathy for this murdered woman who lived in an awful council

block? And how many were about antipathy towards the murdered trans woman? About people getting sick of being told they
had to love the whole trans thing, whether they liked it or not?'

'Well, I hope it's very much weighted to the latter, Malika. I'm
not interested in empathy. Empathy is literally the last thing I
want to promote. I'm interested in fury.'

The foie gras was replaced with grilled sole and Dom Pérignon.

'Most people don't serve champagne as a table wine,' Julian
said. 'They give you a poxy glass or two with a canapé and then
it's fucking Chablis or Chardy all night. Personally, I think fizz is
the perfect accompaniment to all food. Including beef. Or even
venison. But particularly fish. Cheers.'

He was showing off appallingly, revelling in the doe-eyed
adoration of a twenty-two-year-old recent graduate who was
born in a council flat. Malika did good doe eyes and she knew it.
Good enough even to keep his attention from flitting down to
check out her elegantly displayed bosom. He was classy like that:
she'd only caught him looking at her tits two or three dozen
times all evening.

'I noticed a lot of my Latifa tweets getting linked up with other
hashtags,' she said, raising her glass to his. 'Have you seen this
whole #VictimSoWhite thing that's happening?'

Malika was referring to a grass-roots initiative that appeared
to have grown spontaneously out of the #IamSammy anger and
which was calling out a white establishment for prioritizing
white over black women who had been assaulted.

'Yes! Absolutely. Awful, isn't it?' Julian agreed. 'The statistics
are *so* depressing. The police and the government obviously care
more about white than they do about black people. No wonder
black people are angry. I mean what did #MeToo do for Latifa?
Why is it #NotOK to kiss a white princess in a bikini on a reality-
TV game show but OK to murder a black girl in a filthy
stairwell?'

'Except nobody ever said that ever,' Malika replied.

'Well, people seem to *think* they did.' Julian smiled.

'Yes. They do, don't they?' Malika said, raising her eyebrows.

'You can't argue with statistics, can you?' Julian returned her look with one of exaggerated innocence.

'Julian, I'm a mathematician. Arguing with statistics is what I do. And Newton's third law of statistics states that for every statistic there is an equal and opposite statistic. And while I don't deny for a second that black people have traditionally had a harder time with the police than white people, is it *really* true that the law systematically ignores black victims as a matter of *policy*?'

'I don't know, Malika. It's out there, isn't it? So perhaps it is true.'

He was smiling at her but it was no longer quite as warm. There was an edge of steel in it. Something of a challenge. His eyebrows were raised very slightly, asking their own question. It seemed to Malika that they were saying, 'Are you with us? Or against us?'

'Those #VictimSoWhite tags all ended up linked to the Sammy ones,' she said, dodging the unspoken question, 'the ones my algorithm marketed directly to BAME Facebook and Twitter accounts. Millions of people are getting told that the current status quo institutionally discriminates against them. The government, the opposition, the *United Kingdom*, in fact, doesn't care about them.'

'Yes. That's right.'

'Julian, did Communication Sandwich create #VictimSoWhite?'

'Do you know, old scout?' he said. 'As a matter of fact I rather think it might have done.'

Even though it was very warm in the restaurant Malika could feel herself shiver a little. The dress she was wearing was somewhat brief and goose bumps were forming on her skin. She had thought she understood her job, understood its essentially cynical nature. Now she realized she'd had no idea. Perhaps she should have guessed long ago that things were as dodgy as they now seemed to be. After all, they'd travelled to dinner in a private jet, booked into the Grand Hôtel Kempinski, which was going to be beyond expensive. Marketing people could be rich but Julian was *criminal* rich.

'So the Fishing Fleet doesn't just spread grievances, or even just embellish them, it actually *creates* them?'

'We *do* give them a nudge, my darling. Just wait till we start #VictimSoBlack and tell all the potential England Out voters that, due to the outrage over #IamLatifa, the police have been told to prioritize black victims and forget white ones.'

'You really think people will believe that?'

'Well, some will. Lots in fact. And for the rest, it's all part of the whole fake-news project, isn't it? Just an ongoing assault on the primacy of evidence. Trump started it years ago. At first he simply denied facts but very quickly he and everybody else realized that it was even easier to make up new ones. For some reason the more confused people get, the more *nervous* and alienated they feel, the more likely they are to vote for reactionary right-wing solutions. Often against their own interests. They circle the wagons, close their borders and close their minds. I don't know why but they do. Jolly good news for us, don't you think? 'Nother bottle?'

Once more Malika felt that Julian was initiating her, bringing her into the fold, just as he had done previously in his office, making her a true creature of Communication Sandwich. She didn't know quite why he was at such pains to show the depths of his cynicism. He hadn't needed to: she was a mathematician; she worked according to a clear brief; she didn't need to know its purpose. Perhaps he thought it would make her more likely to go to bed with him. But why would he feel the need? She'd agreed to the trip. She'd worn a very sexy dress. Why talk shop? That wasn't hot. That wasn't steamy. Except, actually, it was. Because it was so immoral. Semi-criminal at the very least. And he was letting her in on it, which was really very flattering. Testing her mettle against petty morality. That was fun too. He was saying, 'Look at me. I'm a *very* bad boy who makes obscene amounts of *very* dodgy money in pursuit of hedonistic pleasure. Wanna join me?'

And she did. She loved it. It was secret. It was wicked. It was almost industrial espionage. Julian had clearly enjoyed telling her this stuff and she had enjoyed being told. They were a team now, him in his perfect dinner jacket, her in a seriously fabulous dress, dining at a billionaires' restaurant, drinking champagne and drifting towards having sex in a suite that overlooked Lake Geneva. She was a freakin' Bond girl.

And as for that other voice, the one in the very back of her head (which, annoyingly, sounded very like her mother's), saying, 'Malika! Get out! This is ridiculous! It's dangerous. And it's wrong! Get out now, you silly, *silly* girl!', well, that voice could shut the hell up. Mathematicians, even young and attractive ones, didn't get a lot of chances to star in their own private Bond movies. In the real world you only lived *once*.

'Absolutely,' she said, putting her hand on his. 'Another bottle would be lovely.'

He leaned across the table and kissed her. 'This is rather fun,' he said.

'Yes, it is,' Malika agreed. 'Tell me, what have we been dropping on to people's Facebook pages today?'

'We?'

He'd picked up on the very same word he'd picked up on when they'd discussed company business before. She was definitely being tested.

'I'm a part of the team, aren't I?' Malika said. 'It's my numbers that deliver your lies.'

'Oh, don't say lies, darling. That implies there's such a thing as truth, and I think we've all known for at least a decade that that is simply not the case.'

Malika knew very well this was a Faustian moment: she would be making the decision to join the dark side. Her mother certainly wouldn't approve, and was currently making quite a racket about it at the back of her head. But if she'd only ever done things her mother would approve of, she'd have missed out on a lot of fun over the years.

'So? What alternative facts have we dropped today, Julian?' she asked. 'What lies have we turned into truth?'

'Well, interestingly, you'll be happy to hear that the Sammy-the-tranny murder case has been solved.'

She thought he used the derogatory term 'tranny' with a certain glee. Perhaps another challenge, goading her to represent her 'hyper-sensitive generation' and object to abusive language. Hate-speak. Just letting her know that she was joining the proper naughty boys, who hailed from another less pious century and didn't give a fuck about how anybody 'felt'. Malika decided not to call him out on it. Even though she didn't like him calling Sammy Hill a tranny. Any more than she would have liked him calling her a Paki.

'Solved? Really?' she asked.

'No. *Not* really, my sweet,' he said, with a slightly patronizing smirk. 'Not actually solved. But who cares about that? As of this afternoon plenty of people *believe* they know who did it and surely that's what really matters.'

31. The Fallen Women

THE SUDDEN and inexplicable national consensus around #GerryKilledSammy came as a huge relief for Team UK. For a whole morning they had been the number-one trend on Twitter but, as Toby the incredibly expensive marketing bloke was forced to admit, 'not in a good way'.

It turned out that the bold refocusing of their campaign to keep England in the UK rebranded as #GREATBritainTheCluesInTheName had proved more controversial and less popular than Jim and Beryl had hoped.

The plan had been simple enough. Following the announcement of the new hashtag, Team UK were going to ditch the now 'tone deaf' #LuvIsland concept and focus instead on a robust new patriotic appeal that would unify the nation around an idea of an England that everybody could identify with: its shared history with other parts of the United Kingdom.

In vain did junior members of Team UK plead that they should surely be trying to keep the debate around real issues, like jobs, services and the economy. England Out was weak on this issue, they argued. Their model of a low-tax, low-income society was generally viewed as likely to turn an independent England into the sweatshop of the world. England Out's only real argument against this charge was the continued repetition of the phrase 'Project Gloomy Guts', which, despite its success, was wearing a bit thin.

But those voices fell on deaf ears. Toby, the incredibly expensive marketing guy, convinced Jim and Beryl that words like 'jobs', 'services' and 'economy' were 'negative' and their brand needed 'positive' words. And what word could possibly be more positive than GREAT?

'We need to own GREAT,' he stated. 'Double down on GREAT. Let the people know that GREAT is our word by right and that GREAT is who we are.'

Therefore Team UK announced that they would be unapologetically laying full claim to the upcoming anniversary of the Falklands War as a truly GREAT British celebration commemorating a GREAT British achievement in defence of GREAT British citizens in a tiny and vulnerable GREAT British Overseas Territory as the launch pad for their GREAT new campaign #GREATBritainTheCluesInTheName.

After all, who could argue with simple, honest patriotism? What? Toby added, happily trousering another enormous fee, was not to love?

The answer was Cressida Baynes, champion of 'woke' history and founder of the 'game-changing' #RememberThem movement, and her charismatic spokesperson, ex-Heathcliff, and *Heat* magazine 'Bum of the Year 1998', Rodney Watson, who was revelling in his status as the wokest middle-aged white guy since Bono.

Cressida and Rodney had become very famous. Their prosecution of Samuel Pepys was getting closer to becoming a reality each day and was proving to be a popular idea. Even a cursory reading of the juiciest bits from Pepys's diary revealed the man had been, by any modern standards, a sexual predator. The general view was that it was time he faced the judgement of the twenty-first century: #WhyStopAtSavile?

Much progress had been made in Cressida's campaign. A standing committee of the House of Commons was looking into extending the statute of limitations to four hundred years and the police had prepared a full and damning case against the now disgraced diarist. Whether Pepys's long-dead bones would be dug up and reassembled in a court of law was still in question: the legality of prosecuting someone who was dead and thus no longer capable of defending themselves was proving less clear-cut than had at first been imagined. Certainly more complex than simply pardoning dead gay geniuses and fierce, feisty suffragettes.

But, actual prosecution or not, Pepys had been roundly convicted in the court of public opinion, and future historians would see him first and foremost as a sexual predator. The British Library announced that it would put a trigger warning on the cover of its original copy of the diary, and Penguin Books promised to do likewise when they next reprinted, adding that it was unlikely they ever would.

Cressida Baynes and Rodney Watson had become near-permanent fixtures on morning TV, tirelessly pursuing the #RememberThem agenda.

Lobbying for change in schools' history curriculum.

Announcing new research that suggested key members of Scott's doomed Antarctic expedition *may* have been female.

Calling out the massive gender disparity of Britain's statues.

This last issue was a particularly *personal* crusade for Rodney because, as he liked to tell every interviewer, he was a dedicated London walker. 'I walk everywhere in London, Susanna,' he told Susanna Reid on *Good Morning Britain*, 'and do you know? Every time I see a plinth I think, Here we go. Another dead white guy with a pigeon on his head. It's just so *wrong*, Susie, really it is. London is just one big museum to abusive dead white murderers and predators. We need people to "woke" up and smell the historical sexism!'

Rodney just *loved* showing off on morning telly. What was not to love? Free croissant, a lovely latte from a perky little runner, a bit of chat with *gorgeous* Susanna or *heavenly* Lorraine, then lunch.

He knew what his flashing eyes and greying sideburns did to all the watching yummy mummies. These days, as the booze took its toll, he had to put a couple of drops of Optrex in for extra sparkle, but he was still *devilishly* attractive. A famous ex-Heathcliff *and* a famous male feminist, it was a mum-melting package for sure. In fact, it was crossing his mind as he spoke that he might have a crack at pulling Susanna after the broadcast. Wouldn't *they* make a fabulous couple at the next Pride of Britain Awards? And at only twenty years younger than him, she was *so* much more age appropriate than his usual arm candy.

'I am just *so* angry about the statues,' Rodney went on, cutting off Cressida's efforts to get a word in edgeways. 'When we say #RememberThem, let's not just remember the girl *survivors*, let's remember the girl *heroes* too! Where are the statues to the girl artists? Girl scientists? Girl industrialists? The girl soldiers, seafarers, great administrators and law-givers? There aren't any, Sue! And why? Because of a patriarchal conspiracy to write these magnificent girls out of history. That's why I'm calling for statue parity! #CloseTheStatueGap!'

'I'm a bit confused, Rodney,' Susanna said. Piers Morgan was on holiday so she was no longer required to communicate solely through wry glances at the camera. 'You're saying women have been historically brutalized and enslaved but at the same time were also responsible for half the art and science?'

'Absolutely! Yes!' Rodney said, gripping Susanna's knee in a manner that he was confident indicated cross-gender solidarity and definitely *not* that he was a creep and fancied her.

Susanna forcefully removed his hand and turned to Cressida. 'Professor Baynes, tell us a little bit about your response to Team UK's Falklands memorial initiative.'

'Ah, now, I'd actually like to answer that if I may . . .' said Rodney.

'I SAID *Professor Baynes*, tell us a little bit about your response to Team UK's Falklands memorial initiative,' Susanna repeated, with a look that penetrated even Rodney Watson's rhino hide.

Finally given a chance to speak, Cressida Baynes explained the intervention that had done so much to take the shine off Team UK's radical relaunch around the word GREAT.

'In the light of Team UK's decision to use the Cenotaph as a focus for their new campaign, Susanna, how about just this once we take the emphasis off the soldiers who died and remember the women who were murdered and raped? Often, I might add, by those very soldiers.'

'But surely you're not suggesting, Professor, that all soldiers are rapists?' Susanna asked.

'No. But I am saying that rape has been a part of war since war began. As have soldiers. You do the maths.'

Susanna tried coming at the issue from a different direction. 'But is the Falklands War the best example of your point, Professor?' she asked. 'I can see that, historically, women must certainly have suffered in so many wars, perhaps as much as the combatants – the Hundred Years' War, for instance, or the Nazi invasion of the USSR – but the Falklands War wasn't *really* that sort of war, was it? As far as I know, there weren't any rapes during the Falklands campaign at all.'

'And I'm saying that's irrelevant,' Cressida replied. 'My point is that if Team UK want to use the Cenotaph as a symbol of what's great about the UK they might think about focusing on women's suffering in war and not men's for once. By all means honour the fallen soldiers, but also honour the millions of anonymous victims of war for whom there are no memorials and no ceremonies of remembrance.'

Faced with this unexpected intervention, Team UK had acted quickly. They were all too conscious of the success of Cressida Baynes's Pepys campaign and, anxious not to get caught on the wrong side of history again, they decided to broaden the remit of their Cenotaph-based initiative. It was decided to commission a completely new poppy, which would feature multi-coloured petals. A red petal for the soldiers who died, a white one for the women who were murdered and abused, a pink petal for the LGBTQ+ community, who had been forced to hide their true selves while dying for (and being abused by) a nation that denied them legal status, and, finally, a black one for all the African and Asian people who had died as a result of British militarism and colonialism (and also all the African and Asian soldiers who had fought for British militarism and colonialism).

As an effort to unify the nation behind a single idea of Britishness this initiative proved a spectacular failure.

Or as one much re-posted meme put it, 'a GREAT big cock-up'.

The new poppy provoked far more outrage than it did applause and, very quickly, the story took on a life of its own. Millions of smartphones pinged with 'news' that Team UK were planning to prosecute all Britain's war dead for rape and murder. Somehow the belief took hold among large swathes of the population that every name on every war memorial in Britain was to be reported to the police as a war criminal. The mainstream press quickly picked up on the story and pretty soon what had been an effort merely to acknowledge the suffering of one group was perceived as a campaign to denigrate the integrity of another.

A shit-tsunami engulfed Jim and Beryl and everyone at #GREATBritainTheCluesInTheName as front page after front page accused Team UK of using the Cenotaph to disrespect everything it represented. The Glorious Dead had been shamefully slandered.

IS NOTHING SACRED TO LOONY LATTE-DRINKING REMAINERS?

It was for this reason that a shell-shocked Jim and Beryl had been so pleased to discover that #GerryKilledSammy had replaced them as the nation's top Twitter trend.

Well, it was certainly big news that the mad old feminist, who'd been such a reliable female guest host on *Have I Got News For You?*, had turned out to be a murderer.

How weird was that?

32. EARF (Extremely Annoyed Radical Feminist)

'GERALDINE GIFFARD?' My name is Chief Inspector Mick Matlock.'

It had actually taken quite some time to track down a number for her. Not surprisingly, the one she offered on her webpage wasn't responding to calls. She still had a landline but it was ex-directory. Faced with having to wait for a magistrate's warrant to obtain the number from BT, Matlock rang a contact at a popular newspaper.

They had absolutely everybody's number.

'Good. About time,' Geraldine snapped, when he called. 'I was actually going to ring you because this is just getting silly. I'm used to being slagged off by nutters but this is off the scale.'

'You're being abused?'

'Just a bit.'

'Any death threats?'

'A couple of thousand.'

'Thousand?'

'An hour. And rape. Usually both, actually. Rape followed by death. Occasionally the other way round, which is a bit of worry, don't you think? But only tweets. You get used to those. The real problem is I've been getting *so* much shit.'

'Online?'

'Through the letterbox. I've had to nail it up. I want a constable to stand outside my door till these crazies move on to their next target.'

'I'd like to come and talk to you, if I may.'

'Why? I don't want to talk to you. Unless you're going to guard my house personally, Chief Inspector. Just send a sodding bobby.'

'I'd like to come and talk to you, Ms Giffard. Or, if you'd prefer, I could send a car and we can talk here. At Scotland Yard.'

There was a pause. 'You're not suggesting that I'm actually a suspect?'

'As I say, I'd like to have a chat.'

'Oh, my sodding Christ. This isn't even funny. I do not believe this. Is that what you do now with murders? Sit on your arses until the collective lunacy of the internet decides which witch it wants to burn?'

'Ms Giffard—'

'Oh, for Christ's sake.'

'Ms Giffard. You're not a suspect. Just a person of interest. We're looking into all of Sammy's interactions, particularly those involving conflict.'

'So I'm a suspect because I didn't want dicks in my pond?'

'Can I come round and have a chat?'

'Of course you can come round! You're a fucking policeman, and if you haven't worked out yet that that means you can do whatever you want, you must be a pretty shit one.'

'I'll come now, then.'

'Can't wait. I'll put the kettle on.' She hung up.

DC Clegg had been listening to Matlock's half of the conversation. 'She's not too happy, then?'

'No. And nor am I,' Matlock replied. 'Bit depressing to be drawing the same conclusions as the crazier reaches of the internet. How come everybody suddenly decided it was Geraldine Giffard?'

'I don't really know. It just dropped on to a load of people's Facebook newsfeeds and exploded. I suppose you're not the only person who's noticed that she and Sammy had history.'

'Yes, but that doesn't mean she did it.'

'People seem to have decided it does.'

Clegg showed Matlock the Twitter feed. It was pinging away with retweets of the confrontation at Highgate Pond, particularly an ugly photograph of Geraldine shouting into Sammy's face. There were also numerous GIFs of the coffee-throwing moment at the press conference where Rob had confronted Geraldine.

'People seem to have put two and two together,' she said, with a grim smile. 'Geraldine Giffard had a row with Sammy Hill. Sammy Hill got murdered. Thus Geraldine Giffard killed Sammy Hill. Dunno why we even bother *having* detectives now we've got the Net.'

'Look, we mustn't get ahead of ourselves. I know we had our own thoughts on this, but just because you've had a barney with someone doesn't mean you murdered them,' Matlock said.

'Doesn't mean you didn't, though,' Taylor remarked happily from his desk, 'and surely the main point is that taking on Sammy seriously affected Giffard financially and professionally. It cost her plenty. That's your motive right there. Sammy ruined her.'

'Yeah, I know. Still, it'd be a big leap to kill zir for it.'

'She's a nutty feminist. Maybe it was PMT.'

'Barry!' Clegg shouted. 'She's about sixty! I can*not* believe you actually brought periods into it!'

'Just saying.'

'Just being a complete prick.'

'Right,' said Matlock. 'I'm going to go and talk to her then. You can come too, Sally, if you want. Probably be good to have a woman with me.'

'Can I come?' Taylor asked.

None of them had anything better to do, the investigation being as stalled as it had been since the murder. There were only so many times you could ask the same questions of the same indifferent residents and review the same useless CCTV footage. In TV detective series the action cuts from one penny-dropping moment to another. If they showed the bits in between, audiences would be as bored as most detectives are almost all of the time.

'Three of us might look a bit heavy-handed,' Matlock objected.

'Nah. It'll make her feel important. Feminists are always complaining women's voices ain't heard.'

As they got up to leave Clegg glanced at her phone. 'Geraldine's tweeted.'

'You follow her?' Matlock asked.

'Yeah. Have done for years. She can be really funny sometimes and, anyway, she's an important feminist. I don't like what she says about trans issues, but with someone as provocative as her, you're never going to like everything they say, are you? Of course, if it turns out she really did murder Sammy, I'm definitely unfollowing her.'

'What's the tweet?'

Clegg read from her phone. ' "I definitely did not kill Sammy, OK? #LeaveMeAlone!" '

Geraldine Giffard lived in Brixton and the traffic, as ever, was terrible.

'Should have used the tube,' Matlock said. He was always saying that. Why didn't he just do it?

They were crawling along Brixton High Street. Ahead of them a massive billboard had been placed on the railway bridge that crosses the road. The heavy congestion gave them plenty of time to study it as they inched their way forward. It was sponsored by an organization called 'Break the Union'. The group was in no way whatsoever connected to the official England Out campaign, which would have contravened the rules on electoral funding, something Tommy Spoon and Xavier Arron were at constant pains to insist on, despite mounting evidence to the contrary. The poster, which stretched from one side of the street to the other, said, 'Every Scotsman costs an Englishman four hundred pounds a week. Let's spend that money on our own sick kiddies instead.'

'That has to be complete bollocks,' Matlock remarked.

'I reckon it's true,' said Taylor.

'True? *Four hundred quid?* Why would all those English MPs vote to spend that much extra on the Scots? It defies logic.'

'It's a bribe so that the Scots don't vote for independence.'

'But they do that anyway once a year, and they never get quite enough votes to go through with it.'

'Because they're canny Jocks and they know they're on to a bloody good thing, that's why,' Taylor insisted. 'English mugs like you and me pay our taxes so's a bunch of bleeding Bravehearts can get four hundred quid a week in their pocket. *And* the Taffs *and* the Paddies are doing it. We're getting robbed blind.'

'Jock, Taff and Paddy are hate-words, Barry,' said Matlock. 'Don't use them.'

'Why?'

'Because it's against code of practice,' Matlock said.

'And more to the point, Barry,' Clegg added, 'it makes you sound like a stupid ignorant dipshit.'

'Yeah, well, I'll tell you what I hate if we're talking about hate-words. I hate paying so Scotsmen can sit on their arses and impose a PC Euro-style agenda by the back door. That's what I hate.'

Taylor knew that was happening because he'd been receiving detailed news posts from England Out on the subject. They explained that while England Out were in no way associated with Break the Union, its claim that each Scotsman cost an Englishman four hundred pounds a week was fundamentally true – if looked at using specific alternative analysis, based on selected contra-facts working with private think-tank-approved substitute modelling, and information obtained from confidential sources, which the Deep State had attempted to suppress.

Clegg couldn't be bothered to argue. Once more she put in her earphones. Taylor put in his.

Matlock concentrated on the traffic and stared at the ridiculous poster. The campaigning was getting more fevered. The election, which for so long had been a distant prospect, seemed suddenly very close. It was mid-July already. Christ knew what sort of country he'd be living in in just ten weeks' time. Confused. Fractured. Embittered. Divided. Increasingly impoverished with the poor shouldering most of the burden.

So, no change there, then.

What a complete waste of time it all was.

Geraldine Giffard's house was in a pleasant Victorian terrace and she'd lived there for more than thirty years. She was therefore largely insulated from the current plethora of accusations of despicable hipster gentrification, a highly active movement that had already succeeded in achieving the closure of a café called Proper Beans on Toast, which offered nothing except Heinz beans on sliced Wonder White bread and a mug of builders' tea at twenty-five pounds a serve. There were, of course, some radical anti-gentrifiers, who claimed it was bitches like Geraldine who'd started the rot. In a typically robust defence, she had argued, 'If you blame me for gentrifying London you might as well blame the Romans.'

Geraldine's house looked less under attack than Matlock had expected. He had presumed there'd be a regiment of chanting protesters but, apart from some suspicious-looking smears around the nailed-up letterbox and one or two bits of graffiti stating that this was the residence of a TERF WITCH, everything was peaceful. Even the two small trees in moulded lead boxes on either side of the front step were undisturbed. The doorbell worked too: they could hear it ringing inside.

After a couple of minutes Matlock rang it again. 'I think she's in,' he said. 'She knew I was coming straight round. She said she'd put the kettle on.'

'Maybe she's popped out for some biccies,' Taylor suggested. 'Hope so.'

Matlock rang again.

'Try ringing her landline,' Clegg said.

Matlock did. They could hear that ringing too.

Clegg felt her phone go *ping* in her pocket. 'She's tweeting.'

'Read it out.'

'It's a long one . . . It's in two parts . . . "I can't take it any more. I have been hounded and vilified for no greater crime than maintaining that being a woman is the unique preserve and privilege of the female sex. I did not murder Sammy. Nor did I question his/her right to claim that he/she was a woman. I merely maintain my right to maintain that he/she wasn't. Goodbye. #OldAndTired."'

'Goodbye?' Matlock repeated.

'That's what it says.'

A terrible suspicion gripped Matlock. 'We need to break in,' he said.

'We can't do that, boss,' Clegg said. 'We haven't got a warrant.'

'No time.'

Matlock tried the door. 'Too solid. We'd need a battering ram.'

'Maybe there's an open window round the back,' Taylor suggested.

'It's a terraced house, Barry. Round the back is behind the houses of a whole other street. Anyone got a baton?'

No one had. Matlock took off his jacket, wrapped it round his fist and broke a downstairs window.

'You'd better hope she's in, boss, or she can press charges for breaking and entering.'

Geraldine Giffard was in. They found her hanging by the neck in the stairwell.

33. Further Storms on *Love Island*

NOBODY IN the *Love Island* production team could quite believe the speed with which their beautiful show had gone from being much-loved good-hearted TV nonsense to the despised and vilified enabler of abuse.

As they assembled for their morning meeting they were in a state of shock.

'It's like when that American woman got on a plane to Africa,' Narsti Rimes remarked, 'and tweeted she hoped she don't catch no AIDS. Then when she got off the plane she's like the most hated bitch on the planet. That's *us*.'

Narsti was so dripping with credibility that for a moment he managed to make this sound almost like a good thing. Sort of rebel.

'*Love Island* 'gainst the *world*,' he added, and raised his fist to Daisy, offering a bump, which she gleefully accepted. He was just so cool. An actual grime artist with a track on iTunes.

Dave, who did law and shit, suggested they take some small comfort from having been, for the time being, knocked off the number-one hate trend by the general consensus that ex-national treasure Geraldine Giffard had murdered trans woman Sammy Hill. They had experienced further respite from the splenetic outrage which greeted the news that Team UK considered the men who had liberated the Normandy beaches to be war criminals.

But they all knew that *Love Island* would soon be back at the top. *Love Island* was such a well-loved national institution – much more so than Geraldine Giffard or the army – and its dramatic fall from grace would fascinate the nation for a while yet.

And it was getting worse. The focus of their shame was no longer even the now infamous non-consensual kiss. The nation had tasted blood and wanted more, as with any modern-day hate figure. Once villainy had been discovered, further evidence of it must also be found. The news cycle was non-stop and insatiable. The beast needed feeding.

Suddenly tweets and Facebook posts were pointing out how depressingly, predictably, shamefully *tone deaf* the whole tawdry business clearly was. How grimly *twentieth century* its attitudes and prejudices. Boys copping off with girls and girls copping off with boys? What was all that about? How utterly divisively, exclusively and excludingly *binary*.

Where was the rest of the sexual spectrum? Where was the glorious gender jigsaw? Where were the gay kids? The queers? The bis and the tris? Where was the glorious bandwidth of joyful non-conforming, non-specific, non-defining, exuberant sexual *curiosity* that so defined Generation Rainbow in all its myriad multi-coloured hues?

What planet was *Love Island* living on and in what century?

It was as if Madonna had never kissed Britney at the Video Music Awards. Like Kristen Stewart and Cara Delevingne had never strutted the carpet at Cannes with their ever-changing 'gal pals'.

Like Elton and David had never had babies.

It was all so horribly *two-dimensional*.

Nothing but men chasing women and women chasing men.

Men and women? Was that really the best they could do?

What about literally *everybody* else? Or didn't they matter?

Did *Love Island* imagine the whole world was straight? *Nobody* was straight. Was straight even a thing?

The *Love Island* production team were sufficiently tuned into the national conversation to know that, for all the other outrages battling for space on the internet, *Love Island* was the biggest. It was now fully exposed as being on the wrong side of history and thus hurtling down the dumper towards Shows We Used To Love.

The morning's production meeting was crunch time.

Hayley was last to arrive. That was unusual and worrying in itself. Hayley prided herself on her brusque efficiency. She liked to be first, sipping a peppermint tea and strumming her perfectly lacquered nails on the vast shiny table top while her staff bustled in fifteen seconds late, their lattes spilling down their arms due to hurriedly fastened lids at the Costa in the lobby. Today it had taken Hayley two double espressos and a caramel flapjack from Costa before she could face getting into the lift.

She knew she was a part of the problem. A *big* part.

Her perceived hypocrisy over the whole No Shade of Grey business had left her vulnerable. A lesser person might have buckled under the pressure but Hayley Bernstein did not get to head up the most successful reality-TV franchise in the world by being a lesser person. She was a fighter. And with two double espressos and a caramel flapjack inside her she was ready to fight.

'All right,' she said. 'We've got a franchise to save. How are we going to do it? Who's first?'

'Well,' said Dave, who did law and shit, 'I think we have to distance ourselves from Kocky Kurt. Edit him from the Netflix stream of last year's series. Crop him out of all the group photos. Issue a statement making it clear that we have severed all connection with him because he does not reflect us or our values and he is not who we are.'

'Yes. Because that'd work, wouldn't it, Dave?' Hayley snapped. 'Great big multi-million-pound global franchise throws bewildered scapegoat to the wolves in an effort to dodge responsibility for creating the culture of abuse that corrupted him in the first place.'

Dave, who did law and shit, looked crestfallen.

'Any other brilliant suggestions?'

'Well, I was thinking,' said Daisy, momentarily putting down her phone, which was evidence of how serious she recognized the crisis to be, 'supposing we say that we were all bullied at school?'

There was silence.

Daisy took this as encouragement. 'I mean, that's always a good one, isn't it? When a famous person's done something wrong or maybe they're worried people just don't *like* them very much, they say they were bullied at school. Gorgeous actresses always do. Have you noticed? At some point every gorgeous actress will do an interview with the *Guardian* and say she was bullied at school. Maybe we could try that. I know I'd feel sorry for us if I heard we'd been bullied at school.'

Hayley wanted to tell her to fuck off but she knew that would be bullying. 'Thank you, Daisy,' she said icily. 'I'll bear the idea in mind.'

Daisy didn't hear as she was already back to staring at her phone.

'Or we could play the bipolar card?' Dave, who did law and shit, suggested. 'It worked for Mel Gibson, and his arse was *toast* over the Jew thing.'

'Don't use "toast" in that context, Dave,' Hayley said. 'Nobody's done that since the noughties.'

'Besides, Dave,' Daisy said, without looking up from her phone, 'I think *everybody*'s a bit bipolar, aren't they?'

'Shut up, Dave. Shut up, Daisy,' Hayley said.

She turned to Narsti Rimes. Well, she turned her body but her eyes remained firmly staring at the ceiling. That was because on the previous evening she and Narsti Rimes had drunkenly had it off on her living-room floor. Therefore, on top of all her other problems, Hayley now had to deal with the inevitable resetting of the office dynamic that shagging a colleague entails.

All those questions.

Had it been a mistake?

Was it going to happen again?

Were they some sort of *thing* now?

And, most important of all, was he going to denounce her to HR for sexual misconduct?

She was his boss, after all, in a clear position of power and authority. She was forty-five and he only twenty. Hayley knew she was definitely vulnerable. The press absolutely loved it when they could expose a woman for sexual misconduct amid the constant denunciations of appalling men. It just made everyone feel so much *better* about MeToo if we were all in it together.

Narsti Rimes knew what she was thinking because usually it was him who was thinking it. He thought it whenever a night out clubbing ended in a casual hook-up. Booze, drugs, sex. Then afterwards the unspoken fear of discovering that she took a different view of the evening from his. Sometimes girls were really sweet and actually brought it up: 'Don't worry, Narsti. I ain't going to tweet that I was too drunk to say yes.'

It was nice when they did that. Just a quick answer to the unspoken question.

'Safe, girl. That's really sweet.'

Should he say that to Hayley? Tell her it's all fine?

Maybe later, but probably not in a meeting.

'I s'pose we've got to do what everybody else does, Hayles,' he said, focusing on the job. 'We grovel. We say sorry. Like the police keep doing. We say, "Hey. We're listening. We're learning. This is not who we are." We say that we're working through our issues and focusing on being a better version of ourselves an' shit.'

Daisy emerged from her phone as she usually did when Narsti Rimes was speaking. 'I think that's brilliant!' she said. 'Perhaps we should all spend a week at the Priory before we announce! You know, make our personal reinvention look properly real.'

Dave, who did law and shit, wasn't having it. 'I just don't think simply saying sorry is going to be enough,' he said. 'I think to be forgiven there has to be some *semblance* of change. Even Mel Gibson stopped drinking. We're taking heat for enabling toxic masculinity and being too binary in our programme model. We're *Love Island*. How can we change that?'

Hayley swallowed hard. Quite suddenly her blood was racing and her eyes were flashing. It wasn't the espressos. It was an idea. A brilliant idea. She'd seen a way out. 'Oh, my God,' she said. 'I know what we have to do.'

'What have we got to do, Hayles?' Narsti asked.

'We embrace the rainbow! We don't just apologize for our tone-deafness. We *own* it. We eat it and we let it *nourish* us! We make it the engine for real social change. We make the next series one big, glorious celebration of Generation Curious. A technicolour exploration of the full and fabulous nature of the sex and gender spectrum.'

The room burst into spontaneous applause. Everyone could see that it was a stunning reinvention that would put their franchise slap back at the heart of the national conversation and on the right side of history.

Hayley allowed herself a brief moment to bask in the clapping, cheering and air-punching. Then she got down to business. 'Right, everybody,' she said. 'Clear the audition schedule, chuck out all the generic, formulaic geezers and slappers, they are just *so* last year. We are now searching for contestants across the whole rainbow and we have less than a week to find them before our season launch.'

'Wait a minute, Hayles,' Narsti said. 'Shouldn't we keep two of the heteros? One geezer and one slapper? I mean, they're in the rainbow too, right?'

Hayley paused for a moment. Then, once more, her pulse raced and her eyes flashed. 'You're right, Narsti,' she said, and this time she looked him happily in the eye. 'We do need one of each of the old model. So we'll keep a geezer from the last trawl.'

'And a slapper?' Narsti asked. 'We need one of each?'

'Exactly!' said Hayley triumphantly. 'And we already have one because here's the kicker, team! We'll invite Jemima back! Talk about owning your misstep. This is off the scale!'

This time the room fell silent for a moment of awe. No clapping or air-punching. The idea was just too stunning for anything but respectful silence. This, they knew, was why Hayley was the boss.

'*Love Island* is dead!' Hayley shouted. 'Long live *Rainbow Island*!'

Now the room burst into cheering.

In a moment of pure joy Hayley offered Narsti a high five. Even the fact that he continued with a series of slaps, strokes, fists and thumb hooks, all of which she failed to match, could not diminish her joy.

34. Dead Popular

THE THREE big beasts of the England Out campaign sat deep in the leather-bound comfort of the Glutton Club. Bunter Jolly sipped his vintage brandy, Plantagenet Greased-Hogg his glass of finest claret, Guppy Toad his kale, celery and asparagus smoothie. Three 'fine minds' discussing weighty matters of state just as generation after generation of those born to rule had done before them in those same deep armchairs.

'Fucking Bank of England,' Jolly boomed furiously, resting the huge bubble glass on his bulging stomach.

Greased-Hogg wished Jolly wouldn't boom so much. He also wished Jolly wouldn't lounge back like that in his chair. Quite apart from anything else it made his trousers ride up, revealing the St George's Cross socks and enormous white calves, a sartorial disaster that Greased-Hogg, in perfect patrician pinstripe with a faultless English rose in his buttonhole, found jarring. 'Yes. They aren't really playing the game, are they, Bunter?' he replied, in his softest, most donnish tones.

The Bank of England certainly wasn't playing the game. That very morning it had published a report on the extreme likelihood that total economic meltdown would follow the break-up of the United Kingdom. The collective opinion of the most senior financial experts in the country was that the implosion of a sovereign state with all the infrastructure paralysis that would follow could result only in absolute financial disaster. Capital would haemorrhage from the nations' arteries as foreign investors and credit agencies contemplated the prospect of four nations that had previously been one, struggling to make practical sense of the Balkanization of their tiny little island (plus a bit of the one next door).

Jolly, Toad and Greased-Hogg could feel the chances of one of them becoming the next prime minister slipping away.

It was that serious.

'We must brace ourselves for difficult days ahead,' Guppy Toad opined sombrely, perching on the edge of his armchair like a particularly pompous garden gnome. He was sipping his smoothie, his pouting little lips sucking gently at the straw, his big fish eyes staring over the rim of his glass.

Toad, in common with Greased-Hogg, half believed in the England Out dream, seeing it as a chance to return to proper English values. They genuinely longed for a day when employment protection, workers' rights, the welfare state and all the odious apparatus of state socialism could be consigned to history. Then England would be returned to its natural, early-nineteenth-century state when the members of the Glutton Club owned absolutely everything and the impoverished peasantry and industrial slave labourers were very grateful to them for shouldering that burden and loved them for it. Toad and Greased-Hogg were both enormous fans of *Downton Abbey*, seeing it not so much as drama but as a political blueprint. Bunter Jolly had quite enjoyed *Downton*, but deep down he was really only an enormous fan of Bunter Jolly.

'I issued a statement during my jog,' he boomed.

'Yes. I saw,' Greased-Hogg murmured, with the hint of a sneer. He did hate the way Jolly monopolized the cameras. It was so un-English.

'I bloody told them,' Jolly went on. 'I told them it's all very well those muggly mugwump brainy boffins at the bank presenting their irrefutable evidence that the self-destruction of a highly successful and stable democracy will trigger a flight of capital from the City – but as far as I'm concerned it's just more of Project Gloomy Guts and they should all just bog off back to the tuck shop.'

'I made a statement too,' Toad chipped in, so eagerly that he almost fell off his perch and spilled his smoothie. 'I said the people have had enough of clever dicks who bloody well think they know everything.'

'Yes, Guppy, we know. *Again*,' Greased-Hogg replied, with weary contempt, 'and the collective response was that in fact the people have actually had enough of you saying they've had enough of clever dicks who bloody well think they know everything.'

Toad looked like he might cry. The line had been his one really effective contribution to the debate so far. For a while its simple brilliance and honest common sense had even caused the press to begin to refer to him as future prime-ministerial material. Bunter Jolly, for whom Toad had fagged at Eton, had been apoplectic with rage.

The line had been the result of a desperate improvisation. After Toad had declared himself for England Out he had found himself doorstepped by a positive phalanx of experts confronting him with irrefutable evidence that the predicted sunlit uplands did not exist. Not having the balls to go for the straight Trumpian attack of calling them all lying low-lifes in the pay of the opposition, Toad had produced a weary patrician sneer and said, 'I think we've all had enough of clever dicks who bloody well think they know everything. I prefer to trust the people. They generally get it right, you know.'

To everyone's surprise, this blatant abdication of intellectual responsibility and grimly patronizing effort to curry favour with voters by making their ignorance a virtue had proved an effective tactic. For some time afterwards, whenever Guppy Toad was faced with evidence or informed analysis that contradicted the theory of the sunlit uplands, he had put on an ever-smugger and sneerier face and trotted out the same mantra.

Unfortunately for Toad, one day an enterprising journalist had had a rather good idea. They had decided to track Toad's movements over a single morning and discovered that Toad had *not* had enough of clever dicks who bloody well think they know everything. Toad was recorded as having visited his heart specialist, his chiropodist, his vintner, his investment banker, his tax accountant and his 'wellness' guru, all between the hours of 8 a.m. and noon. The journalist published this busy itinerary and asked why, if Toad had had enough of clever dicks, he had visited six of them before lunch. Surely when seeking advice on his heart, his verrucas, his fine wines, his hedge funds, his offshore tax havens and the balance between his yin and his yang he would be better off simply putting his trust in 'the people'. Why didn't he just go to Clapham, hail an omnibus and ask the man on it?

'I'm afraid,' Greased-Hogg said, staring at his own speckled reflection in the deep shine of his faultless Lobb brogues, 'the public may perhaps be tiring of our talk of sunlit uplands, and Project Gloomy Guts. It seems likely that this time they will listen to the experts. I have instructed my private secretary to inform the BBC that I will shortly be available to them to present a documentary about English castles. I suggest that you also begin considering your post-referendum media options.'

Jolly drained his cognac and ordered another. He'd already been in touch with the producers of satirical political panel shows and informed them that he might soon be free to host.

Guppy Toad blinked back the tears. He knew that, of the three of them, he'd be the first to have to resort to dancing on *Strictly*.

As it turned out, none of those options would prove necessary because, despite the Bank of England report and Greased-Hogg's fears, England Out were not required to engage in any serious economic debate that morning. Yet again the nation's attention was focused elsewhere.

Even as Jolly, Toad and Greased-Hogg sipped their drinks in gloomy silence, Geraldine Giffard's suicide was electrifying the Twittersphere, the Facebook bubble and the Insta echo chamber. This, of course, meant that shortly afterwards it electrified what remained of the mainstream media, which now did the majority of its investigative journalism by looking at Twitter, Facebook and Instagram. By lunchtime on the day after Geraldine had been discovered hanging in her stairwell – the day of the Bank of England's economic report – it seemed that the whole country was talking about nothing but her death.

The whole country wasn't, but that was how it seemed.

And in death Geraldine's popularity ratings had skyrocketed. The previously despised transphobic troll had been instantly transformed into an icon of free speech, a martyr to plurality of opinion. If 'likes' and heart emojis could raise the dead, Geraldine would have been flying high over London. Yesterday's mad murdering femmo was today's hounded victim – hounded by trans zealots and a politically correct establishment for no greater crime than having an opinion that ran contrary to the views of the latte-drinking neo-liberal elite.

The news that the police had *not* been about to charge her with Sammy's murder added fuel to the flames of outrage. It seemed that, despite the best efforts of #GerryKilledSammy to claim otherwise, there was not a single shred of actual evidence connecting Geraldine Giffard to Sammy's murder, beyond the fact that she had clashed with zir at Highgate Pond.

A highly respected feminist and popular runner-up on *Strictly* had been bullied into taking her own life.

There could be no greater indication of the way the public mood had changed than the mayor's decision to add a banner stating 'We Are All Geraldine' alongside the other banners already decorating City Hall.

Geraldine's suicide had stunned everybody.

Or not quite everybody.

Matlock was not stunned by Geraldine's suicide because he did not believe that Geraldine Giffard had killed herself. He did not believe that she was the sort of person to allow herself to be bullied by anyone. What was more, when he had spoken to her an hour or so before her death she had absolutely not sounded like a woman in danger of hanging herself in despair. What she had wanted was a bobby to stand outside her door and stop people putting shit through her letterbox.

She had promised to put the kettle on.

She had not sounded old and tired.

And, to Matlock's ear at least, her last tweet appeared to have been written by a completely different person from the one they all knew.

But if she *hadn't* killed herself he now had two murders to solve.

And the only person he could currently think of who connected the two was Sammy's flatmate Rob.

35. Not a CHUT

MATLOCK AND Clegg did not interview Rob at his home, the upside of which being that Matlock was not required to drink a large mug of unwanted sugary tea.

They saw him instead at Scotland Yard, where the coffee was excellent: since its privatization, the reception area now featured three separate coffee franchises.

'Yes, I hated Geraldine Giffard,' Rob said, in answer to Matlock's question. 'I hated her because she was a cruel and heartless TERF bitch. But I hope you don't think I'm responsible for her death, because I'm not.'

'Take it easy, Rob,' Matlock said. 'Of course we're not saying you murdered her.'

Rob glared at Matlock. 'What does that mean? That you think I'm in some other way responsible?'

Matlock said nothing, letting it sit for a moment.

'Well, you wouldn't be alone,' Rob went on. 'It's what lots of people are saying on the net.'

'People say all sorts of stupid things on the net.'

Rob glanced at him angrily. 'Do you mean me?'

'Not specifically. Although you have tweeted some pretty angry stuff.' DC Clegg pushed a transcript across the table.

' "Sammy deserved to live. Geraldine Giffard deserves to die," ' she quoted.

Rob looked genuinely mortified. 'It was late. I was drunk. I shouldn't have said that. But it was just a tweet.'

He was fidgety and strung out, more so even than usual. Clegg wanted to put her hand on his to stop it shaking, but you couldn't do that sort of thing any more. Couldn't pat a suspect. It was inappropriate, like hugging other people's children.

'And I'm certainly paying for it now,' Rob went on. 'The trolls are horrible. Horrible. They're saying I thought Sammy was a war hero, braver than a Spitfire pilot, which I *never* said. And that zie was a better woman than a cis woman, when I only ever said zie was *as good as* one. And that I'm a crazy murdering queer because I hounded Geraldine Giffard and despised her for her vagina, which I didn't because I respect all women, including those with vaginas. I am not a CHUT!'

'Cis-Hating Ultra Trans,' Clegg murmured for Matlock's benefit.

'I don't hate cis people and I'm not trans,' Rob almost wailed. 'I'm BMGFGP.'

'Biologically Male Gender Fluid Gay Person,' Clegg whispered.

'And I respect everybody,' Rob concluded bitterly.

Matlock couldn't help wondering whether BMGFGP was really a thing. He felt it would need a vowel somewhere if it was going to catch on properly.

'They say I killed her. *I'm a vegan!*' Rob howled. 'I don't kill anything!'

'You shouldn't read all that stuff on the net, Rob,' Clegg said.

'I can't help it! It's all so ridiculous.'

'Yes. It is.'

'Although I am glad the bitch is dead.'

'Don't tweet that,' Clegg advised.

'Because I still believe she murdered Sammy.'

'Maybe don't tweet that either.'

'Maybe don't tweet anything,' Matlock suggested.

Conversation lagged. Matlock pushed his bag of assorted fruit drops across the table. To his surprise, Rob took one. Nobody *ever* accepted his offer of a boiled sweet. Boiled sweets were the runt of the confectionery litter. Boring to suck, tooth-gluing to bite and simply not as nice as literally *any* other treat you could buy in the half of each supermarket that was now given over to sweets, crisps and chocolate. Matlock only ate them because he wasn't allowed to smoke but, despite this, Rob took one and, to Matlock's annoyance, fossicked about for a red one.

'There's no evidence to suggest Geraldine killed Sammy, Rob,' Matlock said gently. 'In fact, there's no evidence to suggest any culprit at all.'

'So why are you talking to me about it? Shouldn't you be out there looking?'

'I'm not talking to you about Sammy's death. I'm talking to you about Geraldine's.'

'She killed herself, good riddance. What's it got to do with me?'

'Because there is always the possibility that she didn't kill herself.'

It took a moment for this to sink in. 'You mean,' and Rob could scarcely bring himself to say it, 'you think somebody *killed* her?'

'I don't think anything. I have an open mind.'

'Well, I didn't kill her! I did not kill her! Jesus! Are you fucking brain dead?'

This was a new Rob. Angry. Suddenly very angry. Furious, even. And Matlock couldn't help wondering if he was also scared. 'I'm not saying you did. Just that it seems very possible to me that at some level Sammy's and Geraldine's deaths are connected. I believe that Sammy died because zie was a trans woman and I think that Geraldine died because she was an outspoken old-school feminist critic of trans women. I'm looking for someone who is linked to both of them. You fit that bill, Rob, but no doubt there are many others. I need your help to find them.'

'How? I can't help you. I don't know anything.'

'You know a lot of people in the trans community, and I'm sure you're aware of a lot of feminists who are critics of trans women.'

'Ha!' He almost laughed. 'You don't need to be some ancient old feminist to hate trans women. In fact, you can hate trans women *and* feminists equally and loads of nasty people do. There's one particular nutter who trolls *every* type of woman for, as far as I can see, the simple reason that he can't get a single one to have sex with him.'

'Incel,' said Clegg.

'Yeah. It never seems to *occur* to Wotan Orc Slayer that he is in fact *not* involuntarily celibate, he's *voluntarily* celibate. No woman will fuck him because he's such a complete and utter cunt.'

Clegg winced slightly. She found it slightly depressing that, for all their concentration on finding new non-offensive terms for every aspect of the sex and gender spectrum, the rainbow generation still used female genitalia as the ultimate term of abuse. So depressing that 'cunt' remained the go-to hate-word across all genders and sexualities. She let it go. Life was just too short.

Besides, this was a police interview.

'In the meantime,' Clegg said, 'we need you to give us a detailed account of your movements this morning. If possible with corroborating witnesses.'

'All right.'

'And we'll need the same for the evening of the second of June.'

'Second of June?' Rob looked startled. 'But that's . . .'

'Yes, Rob,' said Clegg. 'That's the evening Sammy was killed. Just procedure.'

36. Soppy Bastard

MALIKA WAS beginning to suspect that Julian might be falling in love with her.

It was quite a surprise for her even to be entertaining the thought. He was so hugely arrogant, so confident, such a consummate controller that it would be most out of character for him to cede power in any relationship, let alone one with a twenty-two-year-old employee, whom he'd been using for sex. And there could be no doubt that allowing yourself to fall in love deprived you of a whole lot of leverage.

Malika certainly wasn't in love with Julian. She fancied him, although curiously slightly less now that she suspected him of developing feelings for her. She knew enough about herself to understand that strong, powerful, decisive (and, yes, rich) men turned her on, and she was honest enough to acknowledge that weakness, even romantic weakness, didn't. At least, not in guys more than twice her age with whom she was only having a stupid naughty fling. It wasn't that she wanted to be dominated or pushed around, but she had never felt that strength in one partner required compliance in the other. Quite the opposite. She liked sparks. She liked edge. She liked a bit of a jousting match over dinner and in bed. She was a Shakespeare lover, and in Shakespearian terms, she wanted a Benedick not a Romeo. A Petruchio to her Katherine. Or when she was messing around with a supremely ambitious amoral cynic, like Julian, a Macbeth to her Lady Macbeth.

And Julian had really been that guy.

So exciting.

Arrogant, dismissive, selfish. A proper smooth criminal. Not good husband material, obviously, either in terms of age or character, but *very* jolly for a wild, impetuous fling. That was how it had felt when he demanded she be ready to leave according to his timetable and under his terms for their glorious trip to Geneva. And how it had felt when he took her in his arms on the balcony of their suite overlooking the lake. Also when he had led her straight back inside to bed, not even asking but taking her laughter and the fact that she had gathered up the champagne bottle on the way as consent.

And it was how it had felt in the various frenzied shags and the second fabulous fling they'd had subsequently.

A wild, heady few weeks. Wonderful dinners at exclusive members' clubs. Another luxury weekend.

'Bring nothing but a bikini. We're going to Necker Island to spend the weekend with Richard. Kate Moss will be there and she's a *dream*.'

Wow. That had been *fun*. She didn't really know much about Kate Moss but Kate Moss had brought Cara Delevingne, whom Malika loved, and there were a couple of the old *Twilight* cast there, too. Not K-Stew and R-Patz but only one tier down. That had been just brilliant. Malika was definitely Generation *Twilight*: she'd watched it secretly in her room when she was eight. And now a childhood dream had come true. She'd been skinny-dipping with a real vampire.

Yes. There could be no doubt that hanging out in Julian's life was fun.

But just as swiftly as it had begun it had changed. The silly fool's tone had started to soften. Damn it.

He was no longer so brusque or so commanding. The gentle sneer that had previously been ever present, playing on his lips and *lazing* in his glance, had been replaced by long stares, which were almost . . . if not actually puppyish, definitely a long way from wolfish. And wolfish was what she preferred. If a seriously inappropriate man was going to gaze at her over a glass of £500-a-bottle champagne she wanted him to do it lustfully, not longingly.

Malika had quite a thing for retro kitsch and Sean Connery was her favourite Bond. She had no desire for a 'woke' 007.

Julian was even talking about taking a cottage for their next weekend away. A *cottage*! And cooking for themselves! From a man who only a fortnight previously had booked Necker Island without telling her and arranged for caviar, lobster and Dom P to be served on the private plane that flew them there.

It wasn't that Malika didn't want devotion in a man. Or that she wouldn't enjoy cosy, fireside weekends cooking simple meals *à deux*.

Just not with Julian.

If and when she allowed herself to fall in love, it would be with someone sweet, considerate and kind. And of a similar age.

Not a wicked old swine like Julian.

What she wanted from Julian was wild times, rich pickings and dirty sex in exotic locations.

Malika was thinking about ending the affair. And, of course, wondering how best to do it without jeopardizing her job. Her previous confidence that breaking up with him would not affect their office relationship had been based on *him* tiring of *her*. Not the other way round. Julian was a very proud man: he would not take kindly to being made to feel foolish by someone he'd opened up to. But she knew she needed to get on with it. Things would only get more difficult the longer she left it. If he fell in love with her properly – as opposed to what she now considered to be just a soppy Instacrush based mainly on her youth – breaking up with him and remaining in her job would be near impossible.

So, she had decided to cool things down. Take a step back.

Gently let him know that she was not interested in an exclusive relationship.

She decided to begin the process on the next Champagne Friday when, after the usual end-of-week drinks at work, Julian would no doubt be expecting to take her for an early dinner at Soho House.

He was in a good mood. He'd seemed particularly pleased with everyone as he went from hot desk to hot desk, pouring the fizz, and as they took their seats in the restaurant, Malika asked him why he was so perky.

It seemed that the success of what he called the 'Sammy and Gerry Circus' had exceeded even his rosy expectations. 'It's really kicking off,' he said, glancing at the wine list with his usual studiedly cursory glance of bored semi-interest. 'So many fault lines opening up. And all of them on the left! Isn't it wonderful watching the righteous little fuckers squirm? A dead tranny and a dead feminazi. Something to conflict everyone! Did the femmo kill the tranny, and did the tranny's crazed tribe hound the femmo to death? Talk about divide and rule. I love it. It's looking like total cultural war out there.'

'Only *looking* like,' Malika reminded him. 'Eighty per cent of that outrage is generated by us.'

'Doesn't matter once the mainstream media have reported it, which, of course, they always fucking do, like the pathetic sheep they are. Then it'll be totally out there. Which is very good news for us. The more confused and conflicted UK voters are the better, eh? Bring me a bottle of the Château Lafite Rothschild Pauillac.'

The waiter had appeared, and Malika knew from Julian's casual and dismissive tone that he was ordering something that would cost many hundreds of pounds.

'Something decent to toast your magnificent algorithms,' he

said, 'and if you want to take that as a euphemism you're very welcome because, Ms Rajput, your tits are also smoking!'

He was a bit drunk, very frisky and *sooo* pleased with himself, which, frankly, Malika no longer found quite as attractive as she had just a few weeks earlier. In fact, he was turning into a bit of a twat. She decided that now was as good a time as any to broach the subject of establishing a little distance between them. She drew breath, her opening line (something along the lines of being young and confused and in need of a bit of space) was already on her lips. Just one more sip of fizzy water and she'd tell him.

And then Julian mentioned Russia.

Perhaps he'd sensed her cooling ardour and wanted to regain some of his bad-boy swagger. Maybe he, too, was missing the magic of that first dinner they'd shared when he'd held her in thrall with languid hints at the secret, lawless side of his business. As he spoke she could feel his hand on her leg under the table.

'Now look here, old scout,' he said, still drinking in her cleavage, 'disappointing news, I'm afraid. Going to have put our cottage-weekend idea on hold. Need to make a business trip to Moscow.'

'Moscow? Sounds fun.'

'It is. Muskovi, my darling, home of all things *very* naughty! Tomorrow morning, in fact. A car's picking me up at my apartment at seven a.m., but don't worry, we can grab some clothes for you at the airport.' He let it land for a moment, transferring his glance from her boobs to her eyes. 'I hate flying commercial, but at least they have some decent shops at Heathrow.'

He'd clearly meant it to have an effect and it did. Although perhaps not in quite the way he'd hoped. It was certainly more like the old Julian, Malika thought. Commanding and imperious. Arrogant, in fact. The absolute presumption that not only would she be coming with him but that she'd be leaving early from his flat with nothing more than the heels and the LBD she was currently wearing. For the time being he seemed to have got his mojo back, and that was an improvement certainly. But Malika found that her old gleefully superficial attraction to him didn't just snap back on demand. She'd had a glimpse of the end-game and that's not something you can ignore. Soufflés don't rise twice. She was still clear in her mind that she'd have to dump him *quite* soon. But maybe not tonight. He was still a very amusing man. And still quite attractive. And still very rich.

And she'd never been to Russia.

'I'm game,' she said.

'Good girl!'

'Any particular reason to go to Moscow?'

'I thought you might like to meet my boss. And, of course, yours.'

37. Latifa's Mum

WINNIE JOSEPH lived in a flat in one of the numerous social-housing tower blocks that clustered round the Westway just past Hammersmith en route to Heathrow Airport. Sad grey sentinels, standing silent witness to everybody else in England buggering off to somewhere else. Depressed, crumbling, danger-ous, bleak. The residents caught in decades of limbo, for ever in danger of being herded out of London altogether if the property-developing dreams of a post-Brexit 'bounce' ever came to pass. But also for ever hanging on the hope of the radical improve-ment promised by left-wing councils waiting for sufficient signs of life in the UK economy to make borrowing something other than a fantasy.

Meanwhile the only thriving industry and local employer remained drugs and its associated trades of sex and violence. Gang rule brought equal misery to members and non-members alike.

Not many police officers ever ventured beyond the front entrance of Barbara Castle Tower, but DC Sally Clegg didn't look much like a police officer. As she ascended the stairs to the eighth floor – the lift worked, but she didn't fancy getting trapped in a confined space – she wondered whether she'd feel more or less safe if she was wearing a uniform.

Clegg was deputizing for Matlock. He had absolutely refused to take time off from investigating an unsolved murder to 'reach out', as Janine from Press had put it, to the mother of the victim of a completely different one. But #VictimSoWhite was refusing to go away and Janine had been insistent that somebody officially linked to the Sammy investigation should visit the principal surviving victim of the Latifa investigation. The idea, as ever, was to reassure her that the Metropolitan Police considered the murder of a black cis woman as seriously as they took that of a white trans woman.

Clegg found Winnie among her photographs and memories. It was a cosy flat. There was a constant throb of contrasting drums and basses, hips and hops emanating from surrounding flats, but Winnie's was a place of calm. She had the TV on but with the sound down. 'It keeps me company,' she explained. 'My husband's gone and my two sons only come around every now and then. Latifa used to visit each day. She was living with me at the end, which was why she got killed. A nice good-looking girl like her was always going to be a target. We asked you for more policemen to come around. We asked you to stop the gang-bangers hangin' about and scarin' us all. But you never did a thing. Then one day one of them killed my girl.'

Clegg could only stare into the peppermint tea she'd been offered and mumble something about stretched resources.

'Not so stretched you ain't got time for a chief inspector to get on the TV every five minutes sayin' some white woman was a hero because she used to be a man, apparently.'

There wasn't much Clegg could say, except reassure Winnie that the police really did think black deaths were as important as white ones. She could see that Winnie didn't really believe her. In deep conscience she wondered if she even believed it herself.

But they talked for forty minutes or more. Winnie was obviously very, very lonely and glad of Clegg's company, even though she resented the reason she'd come to visit. Clegg was happy to give the time. As a member of the force that had failed to find justice for Winnie's daughter, Clegg certainly owed her that.

They talked about Latifa and the possible future of the Barbara Castle Tower. And whether life might be better or worse if England left the UK. Winnie said she didn't feel things could be any worse but they probably wouldn't get any better either.

'I'd been going to vote Remain,' she said. 'Just because the UK is the country I came to as a baby and the only one I've ever known. But now I'll vote Out.'

'Why did you change your mind?' Clegg asked. She was only making conversation but she was actually quite interested.

'Cos they cared about my Latifa,' Winnie answered. 'They stuck her name all over their Facebook ads and asked why nobody thought she mattered. They did that hashtag, IamLatifa. And lots of people started talking about it and it made me feel better that someone remembered.'

'Wow,' Clegg said. 'I just presumed you started that hashtag.'

'Yeah. Everybody did but I don't know nothing about hashtags. Latifa used to say a smartphone was wasted on me because I only talked on it. But after they did that hashtag I learned all about Twitter and there was so much love for my girl.'

38. Phoenix Rising

HAYLEY AND Narsti Rimes were having a well-earned break-fast in bed. The first episode of the hastily reconfigured *Rainbow Island* had been broadcast on the previous evening to what appeared to have been universal acclaim. The concept of rejecting the 'binary obsession' that had held back dating shows for years was seen as a major, long-overdue cultural break-through, and consequently Hayley's star was rising again.

Here was a woman who had 'owned her misstep' on the issue of consent last season, taken time to 'listen and to learn' and returned in a blaze of virtue-trumpeting glory with a wake-up call for the nation. It had been a massive and unprecedented effort, researching and recasting the entire island cohort in less than a week, but it had certainly been worth it.

'Best season launch in years,' Hayley said, snuggling up to Narsti under the sheets and nuzzling his arm.

Goodness, a twenty-year-old body felt good. She decided not to dwell on what he might be thinking about forty-five-year-old bodies. He certainly seemed happy enough when shagging one.

'Safe,' Narsti agreed, sipping coffee and thumbing through his phone.

Hayley tried not to mind that. She knew that she hailed from a prehistoric generation that did not reach instantly for their phones after having sex. In her day it had still been the tail end of reaching for a ciggy and actually talking to each other. She accepted, however, that times had changed, and that if she was going to have a lover half her age, he would spend a lot of time looking at his phone.

'Of course, we're going to have to sort of work out where we take the show from here,' Hayley said.

'Wazzat?'

Narsti had actually started playing a game now, which was *slightly* irritating.

'Could you put your phone away for a minute, please, Narsti?'

'Yeah. Safe,' he murmured.

'No. I meant now.'

With a slight sigh, Narsti turned it off. 'Yeah? What?'

'I was just talking about our show. What do we do with it now? I mean format-wise.'

'Not getting it, girl. It is what it is and it does what it does, don' it?'

'Mm. Well, yes. But it *is* a dating show, of course. The whole point is who hooks up with whom and who dumps whom.'

'Yeah?'

'Which, with exclusively binary heterosexual islanders, left a lot of room for manoeuvre.'

'Yeah?'

'I'm just wondering, now we've embraced a rainbow of different gender identities and sexualities, how things are going to play out if nobody actually fancies each other?'

But Narsti wasn't listening. He was back on his phone, along with the rest of humanity.

39. Out of the Closet

WITH LESS than two months to go until the referendum vote, the announcement by prominent Team UK supporters Tom and Bill of Let's Do Lunch Films that they were reviving stalled-movie project *The Royal Closet* was a welcome bit of good news for Team UK and their faltering #GREATBritainTheCluesInTheName campaign.

By rights they should have been, as Toby the marketing guy said, 'owning the giddy fuck out of England Out's arse'. Every possible economic indicator was flashing red for danger as polls showed that the nation had begun to flirt seriously with self-destruction. Following the Bank of England's lead, financial experts were unanimous in their prediction that chaos and confusion, which dismantling the shared infrastructure and institutions of a four-hundred-year-old union must entail, would cripple the economy for years to come. And that was without factoring in the inevitable punitive measures that Europe and the rest of the world, including Scotland, Wales and Northern Ireland, would take against the zero tax, zero tariff, sweatshop economy that England Out's organizers claimed would enable 'Project England' to undercut global trade.

Nonetheless, despite these apocalyptic predictions, the England Out 'base', as it had come to be called, remained stubbornly solid.

Of course, everybody knew that the reason England Out's vote was not collapsing had nothing to do with the actual campaign.

And certainly not the chinless witterings of England Out heavy-weights Bunter Jolly, Guppy Toad and Plantagenet Greased-Hogg. England was sleepwalking towards secession because nobody gave a toss about the referendum any more. The years of ever more surreal instability that had begun with the first Scottish referendum had simply exhausted everybody. Most people just didn't want to talk about England, Scotland, the Irish border or fucking Europe ever again. (Nobody had talked about Wales anyway, except of course the Welsh.)

Besides, there was just *so much else* to talk about. With the identity wars being fanned by an ever more splenetic social media, the nation seemed already to be as fragmented as it could possibly get – so who really cared if it physically broke up as well?

The nation wasn't a nation. Just a collection of tribes.

During the evacuation of Dunkirk, Britain had acted as one. When the great big enormous movie of *Dunkirk* was released, Britain had debated the absence of black characters on the beaches.

Team UK's efforts to bring the country together as a single identity group around the upcoming Falklands War anniversary had imploded spectacularly. They were losing the history war on all fronts and were in desperate need of a new symbol of national focus.

Thus the announcement that Let's Do Lunch Films were to produce yet another unashamedly patriotic, romantic and just really bloody *classy* fictional history of real events that didn't actually happen about the British royal family – the sort of movie we do *so well* – was welcome news. As was Tom and Bill of Let's Do Lunch's offer to hold the premiere in support of #GREAT-BritainTheCluesInTheName, and in the firm expectation of knighthoods after the referendum had been won.

The revival of the long-stalled project was also great news for actor Rodney Watson, who had become, against some stiff competition, the wokest actor in the country. In fact, it was Rodney's status as celebrity ambassador of the #RememberThem movement that had reignited *The Royal Closet* in the first place.

Let's Do Lunch had been looking for some easy virtue-signalling. The famous production company had been as shaken by the various waves of socio-political change sweeping the entertainment industry as any other company. 'More diversity!' was the constant deafening cry, leaving movie and TV bosses in despair. Every effort was deemed too-little-too-late, and no amount of tough lady cops, sweary sitcoms centred around kooky women saying 'vagina', or black actors playing lawyers and judges seemed to satisfy calls for real and significant diversity.

Tom and Bill at Let's Do Lunch were particularly vulnerable to criticism, making, as they did, movies set in an almost exclusively white upper-middle-class Never-Never Land of quaintly nostalgic Englishness. Only recently these movies had been considered '*so* classy' and 'what we do best', but now they were considered 'tone deaf', bereft of even a single tough female cop, a black judge or a kooky woman making lots of comic references to her vagina.

Therefore reviving *The Royal Closet* seemed to offer an opportunity to Tom and Bill to make the sort of movie they were *so good at* and also to be seen as favouring diversity. The story featured a gender-curious King George VI, a tortured gay character in his valet, three fabulous female leads in his queen and the two princesses, and since the movie was set two years after the arrival of the *Windrush*, the chance to make all the servants at Buckingham Palace black.

Add to that the immense moral authority that Rodney Watson, creator of *Monster! The Trial of Samuel Pepys* and famed spokesperson for #RememberThem brought to the project, and switching the green light back on for *The Royal Closet* was a serious no-brainer.

40. A Girl's Got to Do

Rodney Watson had not been the only actor who had lost out on a role when its Miramax/Weinstein association had caused *The Royal Closet* to go toxic. Far away in a tiny apartment in Los Angeles, which she shared with five other struggling Brits, Cassie Trinder, a twenty-five-year-old actress, had heard about the revival of the project and was wondering.

Every day now the news seemed to be full of payback. Skeletons rattled. Old wrongs righted. Careers ruined overnight. Just as hers had been.

But was what had gone around finally about to come around?

Could it be that her time was no longer up?

Was it possible that there was a way out of her current hell?

Because that was what she was in. Hell.

That special hell of being a broke, out-of-work actress stranded in LA, who was already lying about her age.

And only a few years earlier it had all been so exciting.

She had just scored a UK TV hit playing a teenage drug addict in a Channel 4 Gen Z comedy drama called *Pants*, and off the back of it she had been cast as the young female lead in a major US-backed movie.

Well, off the back of *Pants* and something else.

Something else. Something undertaken with the deepest and most painful reluctance. A horrible, horrible memory that still caught her unawares and made her sick to her stomach. That she pushed hurriedly from her mind whenever it came to her un-bidden in the night.

A hateful experience. But she didn't hate herself for doing it.

What she *hated* was being cheated out of the reward. She hated that deeply. It gnawed at her soul. *Doing* it had made her feel hor-ribly used. But being cheated afterwards made her feel *ab*used. Its deep injustice was slowly eating her up inside. Therapy hadn't helped and she couldn't afford it any more anyway.

The movie had been *The Royal Closet*, a highly anticipated collaboration between the mighty US production company Miramax and top UK independent Let's Do Lunch.

And the announcement of her involvement had been made in Cannes!

In *Cannes*, for fuck's sake.

In another life *she had been in Cannes*. Partying with the A list! Leonardo had *absolutely* put the hard word on her. Just walked up to her in the hotel lobby and asked her to a party on his yacht.

And she'd knocked him back. Thanks, Leo, but no thanks. She was having dinner that night with an even bigger fish. Bigger in every way. Richer and more powerful. Also fatter, hairier and with a bit of a wonky eye. *That* fish.

She could still feel the breath on her ear as the minion from Miramax had leaned in to whisper Harvey's message. A *female* minion. There's solidarity for you. If there really is a special place in Hell for women who don't help other women, Cassie reckoned it must be quite a crowded place.

'Mr Weinstein would like to talk through the part with you one more time before he signs off on your casting at the press conference tomorrow.'

They were all having dinner on La Croisette. Miramax and Let's Do Lunch were co-hosting the table. It was to celebrate their joint venture and its upcoming announcement, which was scheduled for the following morning.

Harvey was sitting at the very top end of the table, of course, with Tom and Bill. Rodney Watson, the actor, was next to them (he'd had a pop at her too, dirty old bastard – as *if*) and assorted American 'executive producers'. Whatever *they* did.

Cassie was further down among the line producers and press people.

Harvey wasn't even looking at her.

'Oh,' Cassie replied to the Miramax minion, struggling to disguise her sudden sense of alarm. 'I thought it was all signed off.'

'It is. *It is*,' the minion assured her. 'Harvey just needs to hear you read one more time. This is a *very big deal* for you, remember. Harvey is about to change your life.'

Cassie relaxed a little. A final read. OK, she could do that. Stay focused. Dig deep. Fortunately she'd stuck to water all night.

'So. Are we good?' the minion half whispered. 'After dinner. In his suite?'

Cassie swallowed hard. 'In his *suite*?'

'You can be more private there. Comfortable. It's a nice suite.'

Maybe she'd been naive, but she really hadn't seen it coming. The brutal power play had come so late. She'd already been promised the job. It was being announced in the morning.

Cassie had heard all the rumours, of course. That Harvey was a player, dangerous even. He'd almost said so himself when they'd met in London months before. 'I make girls' dreams come true,' he'd said. 'But it's a two-way street. No free lunches in La La Land.'

Maybe that should have told her all she needed to know. But she'd thought he was just fishing. A flirty suggestion. Testing the water. She'd just laughed it off at the time. She could now see that it had been the proper hard word.

'It's just a final read,' the Miramax minion cooed. 'Harvey

takes casting *sooooo* seriously. One last look at the role. More of a chat, really. Just to sign off before tomorrow.'

Now Harvey himself turned, raised his glass to her and offered a wry smile. He was sort of a genius, after all.

What could she do? Say no?

To Harvey fucking Weinstein?

On what grounds? He was only asking for a final read.

She was about to be cast in the role of a lifetime.

Christ, if the most powerful independent producer in Hollywood wanted a final audition, who the hell was she to say no?

Even if he did want to hold it in his bedroom.

'Sure,' she said, trying to sound as breezily professional as was possible with the woman's lips almost touching her ear. 'I'll be there. Have Harvey text me when he wants me. I'll get my script and come up. I should probably change first, right?'

Cassie was wearing an evening gown that rendered her virtually topless.

'Oh, no need to bother,' the minion replied appreciatively, making no secret of drinking in the considerable expanse of the all-natural bosom quivering near her chin as she leaned in at Cassie's shoulder. 'You look just fine.'

'Will anyone else be present?'

'Sure. Of course. I'll be coming up with you.'

And so, an hour later, Cassie joined the list of nervous young women who'd padded down a thick-carpeted hotel corridor towards Harvey Weinstein's suite in anticipation of a 'meeting'.

Standing at the door in her stunning evening gown, Cassie tried to focus.

It was late at night.

This was a *bedroom* door.

And she was alone. The Miramax minion, who had escorted her up in the lift full of happy chatter, had suddenly had to take a call.

'Sorry! Gotta get this,' she'd said, as she backed away. 'You carry on.'

And she was gone.

Now Cassie knew something wasn't right. She knew she should retreat. Send an apology in the morning: 'Sorry. Just so tired. Don't know what came over me.'

But wait one minute. This was her boss. This was *the* boss. The man with the Midas touch who made and broke careers with a single call on his cell phone. The man who, in the morning, was going to give her the *lead* female role in an Oscar-tipped production.

And all he wanted was a final read.

Or he wanted something. A drink? She could do that.

Or more than a drink? Could she do that too?

Or should she turn and run?

But what if she did? Where would she be in the morning? Still in the movie? Still part of the big announcement? Or heading for the airport?

Would Harvey drop her?

It would sound perfectly reasonable if he did.

'So what if it was late? What's late? I was on New York time. I asked for a final read and she was too *tired* to do that one thing for me. Too tired? This is not a nine-to-five industry, and Cassie Trinder is *not* an actress I want to work with.'

Cassie wanted that job. More than anything in her whole life she wanted that job.

She knocked.

The world now knows what Cassie encountered when Harvey Weinstein opened the door of his suite, but at the time Cassie was totally taken aback. She certainly hadn't been expecting the bathrobe.

'Come in,' he said. 'You look great, by the way.'

She did as she was told. You didn't say no to Harvey.

Cassie wasn't proud of what happened next, but actually she

wasn't ashamed either. She didn't make the rules in Hollywood. Louis B. Mayer used to grab Judy Garland's teenage tits in his office. That was how it went for girls. One revolting hour in exchange for a life transformed.

The next morning he'd stood there beaming at the podium. And when Cassie was introduced as the sensational new discovery he smiled at her and gave her a thumbs-up.

Cassie kept the press release which was handed out that morning. She still had it, although she never read it. It was too painful.

> *Let's Do Lunch and Miramax Pictures are proud to announce that with the engagement of celebrated British actor Rodney Watson and newcomer and fellow Brit Cassie Trinder, casting on the upcoming historical romance* The Royal Closet *is complete. A semi-imagined bio-fantasy developed from potentially but not actually true events that might have but did not occur. This is the beautiful and deeply timely story of a royal valet struggling to conceal his homosexuality while forming a deep and passionate bond with King George VI (who dreams of becoming Queen Georgina) in the shadow of the Cold War.*

Cassie was going to play Princess Elizabeth.

The prim and proper teenage virgin who was forced to grow up quickly after finding her father in the closet with his servant.

They'd even done her costumes. The 1950s underwear was *sooo* sexy.

And then, one month before principal photography was scheduled to start, came that morning: 5 October 2017.

Harvey Weinstein was destroyed in a single day. Julius Caesar scarcely went down any faster. And by the end of the week everybody with the slightest connection to him had run for the hills, claiming they scarcely knew the monstrous old bastard.

Including Tom and Bill.

The Royal Closet was pronounced irredeemably toxic by association and cancelled immediately. The cast and crew of that and numerous other projects were just collateral damage.

And now, a few years later, Cassie, who had so nearly been granted a golden Hollywood ticket, was just one of the thousands, *tens* of thousands, of British actors hanging around in LA waiting for pilot season. They were absolutely everywhere, those British actors. There was even one in her bed: Clarice, a photofit of Cassie, very pretty, quite classy, broke and desperate but, crucially, still only nineteen so in with an actual shot. Cassie and Clarice shared a bed out of pure financial expediency and went together to the same auditions along with hundreds of other British girls, whom Cassie was starting to recognize.

And the Aussies.

And the Kiwis.

And the Canadians.

The gorgeous Euros with better English than Cassie's.

And, of course, the Americans. The internet had been supposed to liberate cultures worldwide, enabling people to share in each other's films and television. In reality it had created an entertainment industry even more US-centric than it had been in Hollywood's golden era. Then only movies had been almost exclusively American. At least smaller countries had their own TV industries. But that had been in another century. BN. Before Netflix. Apart from the occasional *noir* thriller from Norway and costume drama from Britain, every major television event was US-funded and made, even if all the actors were British, like in *Game of Thrones*. If you were an actor and you wanted a career in TV, you *had* to go to LA. There wasn't a single out-of-work actor under forty in London during US pilot season. They were all sharing beds and couches in Los Angeles.

You went, you took your classes. You waited your tables and

you joined the ten-mile queue of every half-talented pretty kid on the planet for the next audition.

Cassie had already done *so many years* of it, and she knew in her heart that she was never going to make it now. She'd just carry on living off cereal and occasionally going on dates just to get a nice dinner, despite the grim horror of having to extricate herself at the end of the evening, until finally she gave up and retrained as a wellness therapist.

She was a broke actress who wasn't even an actress any more because she hadn't had a job in two years and she was twenty-fucking-five years old.

And what was worse, much worse, was that she'd had to sit unemployed in LA through the whole #MeToo era. Had her movie been made she would have accepted that she and the patriarchy were square.

But the movie wasn't made.

Because time had been up.

Oh, time had been up, all right. Time had been up on Cassie's entire career.

Because the appalling gut-wrenching irony was that her life had been utterly *ruined* by #TimesUp.

Couldn't they have waited just another couple of months?

Just till she'd got her movie made? Why did *she* have to be last? The whole of Tinseltown had worshipped at the shrine of Harvey for twenty-five years. Now, suddenly, it was all so shocking! 'Oh, no. He abused his power!' For God's sake! What did anybody *ever* do with power except abuse it?

It was all so incredibly *unfair.*

She'd been screwed by the patriarchy and then she'd been screwed by the sisterhood. How was that for a double whammy?

And now they were going to make *The Royal Closet* after all.

And sleazy, creepy old Rodney Watson was to be retained in the role he had been slated to play the first time around. But *her* role, Princess Elizabeth, that was going to some fresh-faced eighteen-year-old ingénue called Parsley Mulligatawny, who'd recently got her boobs out as an all-conquering magical warrior princess who ruled a vast kingdom but owned very few clothes in a *Game of Thrones*-style rip-off.

But Princess Elizabeth was Cassie's role. And now, sitting in her grotty, scummy digs in LA, she was thinking about that. Thinking hard.

The movie had been a Let's Do Lunch project when it had been announced the first time around and it was *still* a Let's Do Lunch project. Harvey was gone but Tom and Bill were still in charge. Tom and Bill, who could regularly be seen wearing their #NotOK badges at industry events.

She'd show them what was not OK.

It was not OK to cheat Cassie Trinder.

Time was definitely up.

41. Remember Her?

THE MURDER of Cressida Baynes came as a great surprise to everyone. Even more so than the suicide of Geraldine Giffard a fortnight earlier.

It also shifted the balance of the national conversation about the responsibility of dead soldiers for the brutalized women of previous centuries back in #RememberThem's favour. The general consensus on the morning the news broke was that the murder was a perfect example of what the whole movement was about. The brutal killing of a woman for the crime of speaking out on behalf of other brutalized women seemed to go to the very heart of what was wrong with the gender balance in society.

The murder had occurred in a park. Cressida had been hit over the head from behind – in just the same way that Sammy had died. Except that, unlike in the case of Sammy, the killer had left a clue. A very, very big clue. He had dropped his wallet, in which were found his driving licence and his supermarket manager ID. These documents revealed that his name was Oliver Tollett and he was twenty-nine years old. Another document found in the wallet was Tollett's membership card for a fantasy battle re-enactment society, which revealed that his aliases were ex-US Navy SEAL Cody Strong, Confederate General Stonewall Jackson and Wotan Orc Slayer.

Detective Chief Inspector Matlock had already taken an interest in the case because of its similar methodology to the Sammy Hill murder. When he recognized the name Wotan Orc Slayer as the one Rob had mentioned as a particularly virulent example of anti-women trolling, be they cis or trans, Matlock insisted on taking over the case personally.

Clegg and Taylor went to collect Tollett and he was brought into Scotland Yard to be interviewed under caution.

During his interview Tollett claimed that he had been at home playing internet games at the time that the murder had taken place. He did not know how his wallet had found its way to the park.

'Can anyone corroborate that you were at home?' Matlock asked him.

Tollett replied that he lived alone. It was possible that the person who lived below might have heard him moving about but that was unlikely because he didn't move about a lot. 'I sit at my computer. I have a very full life online.'

'Then I'm presuming if we check with your server we'll find that you were online when you say you were?'

'No. You won't, I'm afraid.'

'Why is that, Oliver?'

'Wotan.'

'You want me to call you Wotan?'

'It's my name. My identity.'

Perhaps Wotan caught DS Taylor smirking at this because he became suddenly very angry. 'What? Can't a straight white man have an identity? Oh, I *see*. Talk about double standards. If some gay bloke tells you his name's Susan then big respect to that because it's his or *her* identity. But when I say my name's Wotan and that I identify as a Norse god that's a joke, is it?'

Matlock threw a glance of warning at Taylor. 'No, Wotan,' he said, 'it's not a joke. If your name is Wotan that's fine by me. Now, why do you think your server will not have recorded your activity?'

'Because I log on in a rather convoluted manner, which is not immediately visible to conventional servers.'

'Really? And why would that be?'

'It's not kiddie porn, if that's what you're thinking!' Wotan snapped angrily. 'I'd castrate the lot of them. The paedos, I mean, not the kiddies.'

'I wasn't thinking anything. You tell me.'

'Because of the Deep State. Obviously I'd prefer it if government spooks weren't monitoring my activities. I'm a private individual.'

'Not so private when it comes to making threats online, Wotan. You've been banned three times from Twitter, haven't you? You threatened to kill Cressida Baynes, didn't you?'

'I threaten to kill lots of people. But it doesn't actually mean that in a tweet.'

'Mean what?'

'Mean that you actually want to kill them. It's more like "Oh, I disagree with you. Maybe you should think things through more", that sort of thing.'

'Wotan,' Matlock said, 'your wallet was found at the scene, you have no alibi and you've made numerous death threats against the victim. Can you think of any reason why I shouldn't arrest you for the murder of Professor Cressida Baynes?'

'Only that I didn't do it.'

Clegg opened a sheaf of files and pushed it across the table for Wotan to look at. 'You were a member of the incel movement, weren't you, Wotan?' she said. 'You actively promoted the idea of violence against women as revenge for your lack of a sex life.'

'Sort of,' Wotan admitted, 'although I never would have done anything.'

'You were also a massive critic of #RememberThem and the whole "feminization" of history thing that Cressida Baynes stood for, weren't you?'

'Yes, I bloody well was. That stupid, stupid woman said heroes were traitors and traitors were heroes, and she said Alfred the Great was a woman.'

'Actually, she didn't,' Matlock said. 'I'm a member of Battle Craft too and that was fake news.'

'Ha! That's what they want you to believe.'

Matlock arrested Wotan Orc Slayer, the circumstantial evidence being all but conclusive.

When the news became public it was greatly applauded. There was no doubt in anybody's mind that Matlock had got his man.

Except for the doubts Matlock harboured himself.

He was going to need more than a dropped wallet and a few angry tweets to believe that this strange inadequate little man was any kind of murderer. Let alone a murderer capable of killing with a single blow and leaving no trace, apart from a conveniently placed wallet.

42. Remember Her Too

TOM AND Bill had agreed to see Cassie Trinder out of courtesy. And also some genuine sympathy – as much as could be risked in the diamond-hard world of British movie-making where everybody had to pretend to be as tough as the Americans were. It had been a real shame the way poor Cassie's big break had been ruined like that. They'd felt awful about it at the time. Such a difficult phone call to make. On the other hand, that was showbiz.

Neither of them had set eyes on her for almost five years and, frankly, she'd changed. It wasn't that twenty-five was exactly *old* for an actress, but it wasn't twenty and it certainly wasn't eighteen. Particularly if you're not famous. If a girl's already famous, then, Christ, twenty-five isn't old *at all*. She'll still be good for a romantic lead at thirty, thirty-five, even. But you have to be famous already if you want to be twenty-five and female in the movie business, and Cassie Trinder had missed her chance of being famous years ago. Nothing personal. It was just a fact.

Also she'd acquired that awful LA look. The *amorphous* quality they all assumed after a year or two in La La Hell. Same ubiquitous blonde hair, same copper-toned face from which sus- piciously over-blue eyes shone like sapphires. You didn't need to have any work done to acquire the LA casting-call look (apart from the teeth: everyone had to do the teeth) – it just sort of *seeped* into you. You ended up with that face after auditioning a hundred times for the same part (cute blonde girl). The face that meant your absolute best shot was for a daytime soap, for which you would kill your own mother, incidentally.

Such a shame. And she'd been a real contender at eighteen. Original, sweet. Teeth cute but not perfect. Fresh, witty. *Quirky.* The sort of Brit the Americans loved. The sort of look that had recently got eighteen-year-old Parsley Mulligatawny her role in the *Game of Thrones* rip-off and which had now secured her Princess Elizabeth in *The Royal Closet.*

They were sitting together in the vast boardroom at Let's Do Lunch. On every wall hung framed posters of previous triumphs. A gallery dedicated to Colin Firth plus Gary Oldman for a bit of edge. The table was a great big shiny oval one. Tom and Bill sat at the top and Cassie at the other end, with, between them, Olivia Givenchy, Let's Do Lunch's top female producer. These days, there had to be a woman present in all meetings with totty talent. That was firm company policy. Tom and Bill weren't getting caught out *that* way, thank you very much.

'It's terrific to see you, Cassie,' Tom said. 'You look so great. How's LA? Good? Great. Do you know Olivia? Yeah? She wasn't with us when you . . . when . . . Anyway. She's great, so great. Anyway, very, *very* good to see you. How *are* you?'

'Yeah, how *are* you?' Bill added. 'You look great. LA suits you.'

'I've come for my part,' said Cassie.

They'd *sort* of been expecting it.

The announcement that *The Royal Closet* was being rebooted had been in all the trades and, of course, Cassie's name had featured in many of the articles. Parsley Mulligatawny's casting as Princess Elizabeth had also been announced, but Cassie's name was still coming up first on Google because of the huge press that had surrounded the Cannes launch of the previous Weinstein-connected version. Thus Tom and Bill had guessed that the association of her name once more with Let's Do Lunch had led her back to their door in the hope of work. But they hadn't really believed that she could be so delusional as to try to lobby for her old role. She was *twenty-five*. And *not* famous.

'Your part, Cassie?' Olivia Givenchy asked, before Tom or Bill could respond. Clearly she felt it would be a lot easier if she fronted this tough conversation. The boys were so *nice*.

'Princess Elizabeth in *The Royal Closet*,' Cassie replied calmly. 'It's my part. It was announced at Cannes. Tom and Bill were there.'

Tom and Bill were looking anywhere but at Cassie. Suddenly the ceiling panels appeared to be *fascinating*.

Olivia, on the other hand, was looking straight at her. 'That part has gone to Parsley Mulligatawny,' she said, 'as I'm sure you're aware.'

'Well, I want it back,' Cassie replied. 'I have a contract.'

'No, you don't.' This was Tom speaking. He was hating this conversation a lot and wanted it to be over. 'You *had* a contract, Cassie, but it was with a production that was cancelled. I'm sorry, I really am, but that's how it is. You're welcome to talk to a lawyer, but I can assure you the cancellation rendered all obligations on the part of Let's Do Lunch null and void.'

'Perhaps one of the chambermaids?' Bill said desperately. 'Can't we find Cassie a few lines?'

Olivia shut him down at once. Maybe they could give the girl something later. She wasn't heartless, but this was not the time to show weakness. 'Bit parts are an issue to be discussed with the assistant casting director, Bill,' she said quickly. 'If Ms Trinder wishes to write to our casting people—'

'I was summoned to Harvey Weinstein's hotel bedroom when he was your partner on *The Royal Closet*,' Cassie said very loudly. 'He promised me the role of Princess Elizabeth if I did what he wanted me to do, and I did it. That was a contract, a verbal contract and, legally, a verbal contract is binding, so if you don't give me the role I'm going to sue you.'

Tom and Bill were too surprised and frankly mortified to answer. The poor girl was delusional.

'Cassie,' Olivia said, 'were you threatened?'

'No.'

'Abused in any way either physically or verbally?'

'If you mean did he shout at me or push me around – no.'

'So whatever happened in that room was consensual?'

Cassie shrugged. 'You tell me.'

'Cassie, I'm sorry,' Olivia said. 'I'm really, really sorry. And I know I speak for Tom and Bill also when I say that we feel for you. We feel for you deeply.'

'And we're here for you,' Bill interjected. 'We've got your back.'

'Then give me my part.'

Tom, Bill and Olivia exchanged anguished glances.

'Cassie,' Olivia said gently. 'You don't need an acting job, really you don't, you need therapy. You need to work on you. What you absolutely do not need to do is ruin your career and your reputation by making a public issue out of your willing compliance in a casting-couch assignation. Surely you must see how that would look.'

Cassie smiled. Then, without another word, she got up and left.

Olivia Givenchy had forgotten what century she was living in.

Ten years earlier, seven even, any actress who made a public statement that she had been intimate with a fat, ugly old man solely in order to land an important role in a movie would have been slut-shamed into career oblivion. Such tawdry transactions were a sniggering, dirty little secret between predator and *ingénue* never to be referred to again. All the power lay with the man, all the shame with the women. That was how it had always been and, as far as anybody could see, how it always *would* be.

Except, of course, it wasn't. Rules of gender engagement that had stood solidly since the dawn of time were suddenly challenged.

Women began to tell their stories.

But even then, no one told a story like Cassie's. Making her complaint *not* just against a corrupt system, which left young women with only hard choices, but against the fact that having *made* that hard choice she had not been fucking paid.

As Cassie told the world, *that* was seriously #NotOK.

It was a game-changing step up in the whole #MeToo saga, and Cassie Trinder's timing was perfect.

She couldn't have known that she would be making her case at the very moment the latte-drinking social-justice warriors of Team UK had lashed their latest desperate branding initiative to the mast of the Let's Do Lunch ship. It ensured that, when Cassie spoke out against her tawdry treatment at the hands of Let's Do Lunch, her words would be gleefully leaped upon by England Out and what remained of the mainstream media as further evidence of the infuriating hypocrisy of the holier-than-thou Team UK neo-liberal elite.

Cassie's argument was just *such* a compelling one. And she had such a *great* story to tell. It had everything: sex, power, money and, at its heart, a fierce, feisty, can-do lady, who just wasn't going to take it any more.

When Cassie's publicist announced that another Weinstein survivor was ready to talk, the media, of course, had gone crazy for it: that particular well had dried up years ago and the emergence of a new victim of the legendary Ground Zero monster of the #MeToo era was news gold.

'Except I'm not coming to you as a victim,' Cassie told the panel on *Loose Women*. 'And the only thing I'm a survivor of is getting ripped off.'

'You was proper mugged, girlfriend,' said Janet Street-Porter. 'Let's Do Lunch pimped you aht, then done you over.'

'Too bloody right,' Coleen Nolan agreed. 'Men! Am I right, ladies?'

The audience applauded and Cassie pressed her point. 'These days, we all say "everybody knew". These days, we all say Harvey and people like him were an open secret. Well, if everybody knew, Tom and Bill from Let's Do Lunch knew. They knew all about Harvey Weinstein. It isn't me who should feel ashamed! It's them! I did what I felt I had to do to survive in a brutal patriarchal world of male entitlement and I want my contract honoured! A verbal contract was made. An *oral* contract was made. Miramax is gone but Let's Do Lunch is still around, making *my* movie without me and it is *not* OK. Janet? Coleen? Am I right?'

'Damn right.'

'You go, girl!'

It was the first standing ovation in the history of *Loose Women*. Cassie's use of 'oral contract' when she meant 'verbal contract' might have been a mistake or it might have been deliberate. Either way it cemented her reputation as the toughest, fiercest, feistiest sex survivor in the whole depressing history of the showbiz patriarchy. She didn't have a legal contract but suddenly, and in contravention of all previous standards, she occupied the moral high ground. This was an invigorating new side to the Hollywood sex saga.

Let's Do Lunch found themselves absolutely the villains. Enablers. Renegers. Abusers. Cheats. And, worse, for a company whose house style was charming Englishness, people were accusing them of not being *gentlemen*.

Colin Firth announced that Let's Do Lunch must now join Woody Allen on the list of filmmakers with whom he would not work again.

Tom and Bill were in agony. They had a massive movie about to begin principal photography and an enraged internet demanding that they sack Parsley Mulligatawny and cast a *twenty-five-year-old* self-confessed slut, who looked like a barmaid in *The Young and the Restless*, as the virginal Princess Elizabeth.

Parsley Mulligatawny was in absolute bits, issuing statement after statement that she stood with all survivors of absolutely everything. Telling anyone who would listen that Cassie Trinder was her hero and that, out of respect for both Cassie and herself as strong, fierce, feisty women, she would still be taking the role in *The Royal Closet* but she would be dedicating her performance to #NotOK and donating part of her fee to a women's refuge in Mumbai. Probably.

And, of course, Team UK were absolutely buggered.

Yet again a PR initiative designed to bring people together was proving hopelessly divisive. Yet again they had found themselves tone deaf to the national conversation and on the wrong side of history. An absolute avalanche of memes, tweets and news posts was sowing further division in an already hopelessly fractured situation. One thing was for sure, as Jim from Team UK (speaking with the full authority of the prime minister) made clear: if Tom and Bill wanted even a sniff of those knighthoods they'd better sort out the mess and pronto.

Tom and Bill sorted out the mess.

Parsley kept her part in *The Royal Closet* but Cassie was given the lead in *Black Cobra*, a new series for Netflix, playing the fiercely incorruptible speaker of the House of Commons, who begins a lesbian affair with the married Muslim head of the SAS anti-terrorist squad, Cobra Force Black. At twenty-five, Netflix had thought Cassie perhaps a tad too old to play the speaker of the House of Commons but, as proud feminist men, Tom and Bill had stuck to their principles and Cassie's long hell was over.

43. Without a Clue

MATLOCK, CLEGG and Taylor were back at the morgue, the same place they'd been almost seven weeks earlier with the corpse of Sammy Hill. And two weeks ago with that of Geraldine Giffard. The summer was long and hot, but the trail of whoever and whatever they were looking for was as cold as ever.

'Any DNA, Kate?' Matlock asked.

'If you mean from Wotan Orc Slayer, Mick,' Home Office pathologist Dr Katherine 'Kate' Galloway replied, 'no.'

If Matlock had found addressing Dr Galloway, a professional associate whom he didn't know and who was less than half his age, as 'Kate' a bit uncomfortable, he *really* hated having to refer to Oliver Tollett as Wotan Orc Slayer. But police guidelines on self-identification were very clear and people had the right to be addressed in the identity they chose even when, in his opinion, they were just taking the piss. Matlock knew for a fact that Oliver Tollett had never slain an orc. Although he would no doubt argue that he felt like he had.

'Cressida Baynes was killed in much the same manner as Sammy Hill, right?' he asked.

'Yes, Mick, very similar. Both suffered a single fatal blow to the back of the head with a hammer-like instrument.'

'The same hammer?'

'It's possible, I suppose. You think it might be the same killer?'

'Well, they're very similar killings.'

'Lots of women get knocked over the head,' Kate replied. 'I

can't see any reason to presume Sammy and Cressida were killed by the same man.'

'I'm not presuming anything, but one clean blow, no other violence or interference whatsoever and absolutely no trace of a single clue, that's pretty rare even once, let alone twice.'

'There was Wotan's wallet,' Taylor suggested.

'Yes. There was his wallet. Quite strange to manage to leave absolutely no trace of your presence whatsoever with the exception of your ID. Personally I'd be very surprised if Wotan Orc Slayer was capable of slaying anything, but all I'm saying is that if he did kill Cressida, then, based on the similarities, I think it's reasonable to ask ourselves whether he also killed Sammy.'

'His profile certainly sets him up for both as hate crimes,' Clegg said. 'He sure hates women.'

'From what I can see,' Matlock observed, 'Wotan seems to hate pretty much everything.'

'Yeah, but women most of all.'

'Sammy was a trans woman,' Taylor insisted. 'I keep saying. Incel blokes kill women because they think women have a duty to have sex with them, which they have not delivered on. Incel blokes don't want to have sex with trans women.'

Kate stiffened, ever alert for offence and speech crime, in this case the binary presumption of the nature of a person's sexuality. 'That's a very questionable observation, Barry,' she said. 'There's no reason why a straight cis man wouldn't be attracted to a trans woman.'

'No reason in *principle*,' Taylor replied. 'But, in my admittedly limited experience, my guess is they wouldn't be.'

'That may be a factor of social conditioning,' Kate observed tartly.

'Or it may be a factor of not fancying chicks with dicks,' Taylor snapped back, 'or chicks who previously had dicks.'

'I don't like that language at all, Barry,' Kate said. ' "Chicks with dicks" is hate-speak and I'm asking you not to repeat it. Have you ever considered the possibility that a cis man might be attracted to a trans woman but fears social ridicule if he admits to it?'

'Oh, for Christ's sake!'

'I believe it all comes down to blue toys and pink toys establishing rigid gender identification in pre-schoolers.'

'Yeah. Right. Whatever.' Taylor sighed.

'We're getting off the point!' Matlock said, more loudly than he had expected to, but he was trying to stop his head spinning. 'Wotan Orc Slayer. Now we know he hates women. And he also hates the left in general. He hates all forms of feminism and, to use his own term, he hates all types of "queer". I think it's pretty clear that he didn't have to resent trans women denying him sex to hate them too. So he does have a hate motive for both of these identical murders, and his wallet ties him to one of them.'

But Matlock was just going through the motions of establishing a case. Inside he was certain it wasn't Wotan. The man was clearly filled with spite, malice and ignorant delusion on a near-cosmic scale, but Matlock didn't think he was capable of *any* murder, let alone the kind of cool precision and ruthless resolve that murders like those of Sammy Hill and Cressida Baynes would have required, *twice*. He would have screwed it up at his first attempt and got nicked at the scene.

'OK,' Matlock went on. 'Let's park Wotan for a minute. I'd like to take another look at Geraldine Giffard.'

Even though it had now been some weeks since Giffard's death, Matlock had applied for her body to remain in the morgue. She had no close family anxious to bury her and, as far as Matlock was concerned, the cause of death was a long way from being established, whatever appearances might suggest.

Kate pulled out a corpse drawer to reveal Geraldine looking much more peaceful than she had ever done in life. Hard to believe that the still, lifeless form lying chilled before them had once been the terror of talk shows, shouty, sweary and slightly terrifying. A woman who had at various times in her life successfully danced, baked and gardened her way into the nation's hearts, let alone stalked, killed and butchered wild game. And who, of course, had also been fundamental in setting the feminist agenda of the 1980s.

'Funny,' Matlock said, staring at the nasty rope bruising at her neck, 'how the noose didn't work.'

'What do you mean?' Kate asked.

'Yeah, boss,' Taylor put in. 'She's dead, isn't she?'

'Yeah, but hanging's supposed to break the neck, isn't it? That's the purpose of a noose, a quick painless snap. It's what you'd want if you were killing yourself. A painless snap, not a slow choke.'

'Well, this one didn't work properly, that's all,' Kate replied. 'Amateur nooses often don't. The poor woman died of suffocation. Horrible.'

'Yeah, I know. I can see that just by looking at how deep the bruising is. That noose tightened and she struggled. Very nasty.'

Matlock leaned in and inspected the two rows of tiny little quarter-moon-shaped wounds visible on Geraldine's neck.

'Those fingernail marks,' he said. 'You're sure it's only *her* skin under the nail?'

'Yes. Only Geraldine's. Not that of an assailant, if that's what you're suggesting,' Kate replied. 'It's all in my report. There's skin and blood under all her nails and it's all hers. Clearly she hanged herself, then changed her mind as she struggled at the noose. Not the first time I've seen that.'

'From what I know of Geraldine Giffard,' Matlock said, 'if she changed her mind it would have been the first time she ever did.'

44. Remembering Her.
And Her. And Her and Her.

INEVITABLY RODNEY Watson was centre stage at Cressida Baynes's funeral. The only man invited to speak.

'She was a warrior,' he intoned, relishing the deep cadences of his fabulously mellow voice, 'and a fierce, *fierce* advocate of retrospective justice for women. She was my inspiration. My teacher. And my friend. Her brave crusade was, put simply, to "woke" up the past. She did not simply wish to consign sexism to history. She wanted to remove sexism *from* history. Yes! That was her *fierce*, brave crusade. A crusade on which I was privileged to join her and to which I here and now dedicate my current touring production of *Monster! The Trial of Samuel Pepys*. A show Cressida inspired and which I will continue to develop, franchising productions globally until justice is finally done by the deceased survivors of that appalling man. And to Cressida herself I dedicate my upcoming movie, *The Royal Closet*, which I know she was *so* excited about. Cressida was my guiding light and I know that I was hers. She said, "Remember them." I say, "Remember her!" Yes! Remember her! Remember her! Remember her!'

He'd rather expected a round of applause and was disappointed not to get one. On the other hand it was a funeral, and Heaven knew it wasn't all about *him*. People were simply being respectful, and quite right too.

Rodney was a bit pissed by the time he got back to his flat. The

Baynes family had put on quite a decent wake, and since he had a firm rule that he *never* walked away from free champagne, it was late afternoon before he got home.

He'd nodded off in his big leather chair and was only awoken when his phone rang. Good thing it did because God knew how long he'd have slept and he had a lovely dinner planned with friends at the Wolseley.

The call was from his agent.

'Daphne!' Rodney said sleepily. 'Good of you to call. Has there been anything in the *Standard* yet? About my funeral speech? I know they were there because I spotted that absolute tart from the diary column who said I was pissed at the opening night of Andrew's new *Superstar*.'

'Rodders darling,' Daphne replied, ignoring his question, 'who's Ruth Collins?'

Rodney thought for a moment. His head was not at its clearest. 'Ruth Collins?' he replied blearily. 'Name vaguely rings a bell.'

In fact it wasn't ringing a bell at all. It was tolling one. 'Did she give her Beatrice to my Benedick at Chichester back in the eighties?' Rodney asked, trying to think back.

'She's not an actress. She's a dresser. Apparently she worked for you on *Run For Your Wife* in Tunbridge Wells and one tour of *Pepys*.'

'God, yes, *of course*,' Rodney replied, now feeling the tiniest hint of unease. 'Yes, that would be her. *Sweet* girl. How *is* she?'

'She's just tweeted that you used to masturbate in front of her while she did your wig.'

'Ah.' Long, deep breath. 'Has she?'

'She's hashtagged it #IRememberHim.'

Rodney got up out of his big leather chair and poured himself an eighteen-year-old single malt from the exquisite decanter (a gift from the Theatre Royal Haymarket) that stood on the embossed leather coaster (from a fan, so silly, must have cost a fortune) on the lovely little walnut-inlaid side table (bargain, antique market on the King's Road, only went in to browse but could *not* resist).

He had such a lovely, lovely life. Surely it couldn't all get fucked up. Could it?

'Rodney?' Daphne said. 'Are you there?'

'Yes. I'm here.'

'*Did* you masturbate in front of Ruth Collins while she did your wig during the Tunbridge run of *Run For Your Wife*, darling? It's important I know.'

He'd *sort* of been expecting it.

Ever since #MeToo had begun he'd wondered. Of course he had. What red-blooded good old bloke hadn't? Occasionally, late at night, he'd suffered twinges of fear at the memory of some of his more *banterish* behaviour. Behaviour that had been perfectly acceptable *then*.

Yes. He'd *sort* of been expecting it. Even Rodney, with his monumental self-righteous self-assurance, had *wondered*.

But she'd waited so long. He'd begun to imagine he was in the clear.

Of course he'd known it was a risk becoming the public face of #RememberThem. He'd thought it might rattle a few skeletons in long-buried closets. But he'd had no choice: closing his *Pepys* show would have ruined him. And, besides, he'd never actually touched her. Well, not much. He'd never touched any of them. Well, not much. Just his own cock. And he'd really only been *washing* it. A vigorous wash was a very different thing from masturbation. People had such dirty minds.

'Oh, for Heaven's sake, Daphne!' Rodney replied, draining half a tumbler of Glenmorangie. 'Of course I didn't.'

'Are you quite sure about that, Rodney?'

Rodney poured himself another Scotch. His hand was shaking. He spilled some of the spirit on the inlaid table.

'Rodney?'

'Look! I'd sometimes have a quick whore's bath between shows. Just *washing* the bloody thing, that's all. Christ, you get bloody sweaty under the lights. And *Run For Your Wife* is an absolute marathon. I was in my *dressing* room. A man can wash his cock in his dressing room, can't he? If she was bloody looking that's her business.'

'She claims you regularly asked her if she fancied washing it between her lovely big melons.'

Rodney took another swig. He *had* probably said that. But as a joke. Banter. Nothing more. But you weren't allowed to have a fucking joke now. Oh dear no. Banter was fucking *harassment* these days, darling.

'The girl's lying. As if I would *ever*. God, she must have been young enough to be my granddaughter.'

'Hm. I think that's possibly not a good thing to remind people, Rodders. Kind of part of the problem, really. Looking at our past diaries, you'd have been fifty-three and she was eighteen.'

'Ah.'

'Hm. Do you want me to issue a statement of denial, darling?'

'Can't we just ignore it and hope it goes away?'

'I don't think things do go away these days. Certainly not this sort of thing. And certainly not for the woke bloke face of #RememberThem.'

'Then yes. Fucking yes! Issue a vigorous and absolute denial.'

'Hang on a second, Rodders.'

There was a pause. Rodney wondered if he could hear a faint series of buzzes coming from the other end of the connection.

As if Daphne's phone was receiving messages.

'Not good, darling,' Daphne said finally. 'I've got you on news alert. Four other girls have tweeted that you wanked in front of them too.'

'Washed! Washed, not wanked.'

Another faint buzz.

'Five now, love.'

45. Too Many Victims, Not Enough Suspects

MATLOCK WROTE out three names.

Sammy Hill.

Geraldine Giffard.

Cressida Baynes.

Were the deaths connected? And, if so, how?

He wrote down two more names.

Rob.

Wotan.

Beside Rob's name he wrote: 'Loved Sammy. Hated Geraldine. No obvious connection to Cressida.'

Beside Wotan's name he wrote: 'Hated trans women (Sammy). Hated feminists (Geraldine and Cressida). Threatened Cressida with death.'

It was something to tell the boss but nothing more. And, after nearly seven weeks, precious little at that. And, even more depressing, it wasn't actually anything at all because, as far as Matlock was concerned, neither Rob nor Wotan had killed anyone.

He didn't believe for a moment that either the sensitive Rob or the idiotic and inadequate Wotan was capable of murder. Let alone such efficient murders as Sammy's and Cressida's, both of which had been carried out with remarkable speed and efficiency, leaving no forensic evidence whatsoever. Matlock could believe that one frenzied hate attack could *conceivably* result in such a frustratingly barren crime scene. But two? That suggested a pretty efficient killer to say the least.

And Geraldine? At one point she had been suspected of involvement in Sammy's death. Was that still a possibility? Had Gerry killed Sammy, then killed herself out of remorse? Had she bollocks.

Geraldine was a strong, proud woman. It was *just* possible that she was capable of murdering the trans woman responsible for her public shaming and career collapse, but every single thing Matlock knew about her suggested that if she had committed such a crime the last thing she would do about it was kill herself afterwards out of remorse. And as for that ridiculous final tweet, saying she was killing herself because she was being hounded, that was even more absurd. Geraldine Giffard did not surrender a principle. She'd never done it before in her whole life. Why start on her last day?

In which case someone else had sent the text using her phone.

Only Geraldine's prints were found on it. Had that somebody *forced* her to send it? Or even written it using her dead hand?

If any of that was true, Geraldine's death had been an even more impressive killing than Sammy's and Cressida's. For, once again, no incriminating trace of anyone but the deceased had been found at the scene.

Matlock crossed out the names of Rob and Wotan.

Leaving him with no suspects.

And three victims.

Of whom? Of what?

46. Fallen Hero

RODNEY WATSON'S fall from grace was, of course, massive news. There was just *so* much to enjoy about it. Far more so than the usual bog-standard sense of *Schadenfreude* that grips the nation when a rich and famous person screws up mightily. This, after all, was Rodney Watson: pompous, smug, virtue-trumpeting windbag of #RememberThem. The man who spoke on behalf of all mistreated women had turned out to be a proper Harvey. Could it even *get* any juicier?

Ruth Collins had now been joined by eight other theatre dressers, who had come forward with sincere and angry complaints of wandering hands, creepy over-long hugs, sexually charged inappropriate language and, of course, a lot of 'washing' of the genitals.

Rodney's excuse was a gift to the tabloid headline writers.

'What a WASHER.'

'Rodney COMES Clean!'

'Working Up a Lather.'

But a cornered actor is a dangerous animal and, despite the ridicule, the disgraced spokesman of #RememberThem was putting up a fight.

'I am beyond saddened and deeply appalled,' read the statement made by Rodney Watson to the press, 'that what was an entirely innocent dressing-room hygiene routine should have been interpreted in this manner. As an actor, I sweat profusely in pursuit of my deeply challenging and exhausting art, particularly when playing historic costume roles as I am so often required to do. I live in fear of falling prey to that ancient curse of the cod-piece, which every actor knows as Stinky Dick, and I sponge and flannel both at the interval and straight after final curtain. The fact that my dressers found this entirely innocent practice sug-gestive and inappropriate is a complete surprise to me and a matter of deep distress and regret. However, my conscience is clear.'

It was a bold effort but the fact that numerous young women were able to testify separately that a distinct and common element of Rodney's 'innocent hygiene routine' involved loud shouts of 'Say hello to Captain Bigfellow' and 'How's this for a standing ova-tion, love?', somewhat undermining the famous actor's defence.

But Rodney continued to protest his innocence.

'Don't give an inch, darling,' he said, to his shaving mirror. 'Deny, deny, deny.'

When the ex-dressers claimed he reached around and patted their bottoms as they adjusted his period collars, he said that he was merely practising his theatrical gestures and unfortunately their bottoms had got in the way. Any other suggestion was out-rageous and simply not who he was.

When five separate women mentioned his habit of blowing down their cleavages when they leaned in to pin his wig, he claimed that he was a lifelong semi-borderline-mild-possible asthmatic who was prone to panting.

His absolute and unequivocal denial of any wrongdoing what-soever in the face of consistent and credible near-identical accu-sations from multiple witnesses began to sow doubt in people's minds.

Voices joined in his defence.

Had #NotOK gone too far?

When would the witch-hunt end?

But then young actresses began to come forward to add their

stories to those of Rodney's dressers. In an ironic case of art repeating history, literally, the women who had previously played the serving maid Deborah Willet to Rodney's Pepys emerged with harassment stories of their own. Early productions had featured a proper cast – before budget restrictions had forced Rodney to make it a one-man show – and it now seemed that Rodney had treated the actresses playing Deb Willet in much the same way that Pepys had treated the original Deb Willet. They all told the same story of being summoned to Rodney's dressing room for 'notes', only to discover him 'washing' Captain Bigfellow while he lectured them about stagecraft. Another commonly repeated accusation was that during the part of the show where Rodney, as Pepys, put his hand up Willet's dress, Rodney attempted to take the same advantage that Pepys had written about.

But still Rodney would not give in. He continued to assert (and, it seemed, to believe) that he was innocent of any real wrongdoing and, in fact, was the victim. The victim of a humourless, politically correct world, which couldn't take a bit of bantz.

'Christ al-fucking-mighty,' he said, having phoned his agent in frustration, 'it's not as if I've raped anyone.'

'Please don't use that defence publicly, Rodney.'

'Obviously not. I'm not an idiot, darling.'

Then, after a beat, his agent asked, '*Have* you raped anybody, Rodders?'

'No!'

'Got close?'

'No!'

Although as Rodney said it, for the first time since Ruth Collins had made her initial accusation, he half wondered. Things had changed *so much*. The rules were just so different. God, what they called sexual assault these days could be *anything*. He'd certainly cornered a few squirming poppets in theatres over the years, babbling sweet nothings and blocking their way as they tried to escape. Perhaps *possibly* even holding their wrists a bit. Using his weight to keep them pinned. Had he ever placed a hand over any of their mouths? He didn't *think* he had.

'No!' he said again. 'I have never bloody raped anyone. Now look, the point is, what do I do now? What's our plan?'

'Sorry, Rodders? *Our* plan?'

'Yes. What are we going to do? I suppose I shall have to issue one of those fucking awful statements about taking time out to consider who I am and to reflect on what I've learned and all that bollocks. I think that sort of thing should probably come from you.'

'Rodney. Didn't you read *my* statement? I tweeted it.'

'I'm not looking at Twitter right now for obvious reasons.'

'Oh. Then I should tell you, darling, that I've dropped you. Your actions don't reflect the values of this agency. They are not who we are. Sorry, love, but you've gone toxic, and once you go toxic you're on your own.'

'You utter, utter cunt!' Rodney almost screamed.

'Try to see it from my point of view. Toxic is totally catching.'

'Right! Fine, you cunt. I'll go with Bunty and Pru who are always trying to poach me anyway. And don't expect to take a percentage from my *Royal Closet* fee because I'm not paying it.'

'Oh, Rodders, darling,' his former agent said, and her voice was properly sad, 'you really *don't* get it, do you?'

47. Innocent Troll

MATLOCK HAD been going to release Wotan Orc Slayer anyway. In all conscience he just didn't feel he could hold him any longer, convinced as he was that Wotan hadn't killed anybody. True, the would-be slayer of orcs was tied to the murder of Cressida Baynes by his infamously violent tweets and, of course, his dropped wallet, the single piece of evidence Matlock held, but Matlock just couldn't believe he'd dropped it there himself.

In the end it turned out that Wotan had an alibi anyway. Several alibis, in fact. Thank the Good, Wolfsbane and Sir Lancing Proudblade of Rivermore to name only the first three in a list of many hundreds who had been logged on to the same game that Wotan had been playing at the moment that Cressida Baynes was murdered.

DC Clegg brought Matlock the news.

'Wotan was on the net when he said he was, using his home computer. So, unless he lugged a twenty-four-inch Dell desktop to the park that Cressida Baynes was walking through, found a way to luck into some local unsecured Wi-Fi and then managed to play Dungeon Darkness online while whacking her over the head with a hammer, he's off the hook.'

'How do you know?' Matlock enquired. 'I thought he'd hidden his log-in activities on some phantom Dark Net server.'

'So did he, but most people who think they're invisible online aren't at all. At least, not when a proper expert looks. You need to be a lot cleverer than Wotan Orc Slayer to be capable of covering your cyber tracks. Hope he wasn't looking at anything he shouldn't because Computer Forensics have his entire search history.'

'Jesus, that'll be a depressing read, I imagine,' Matlock said. 'Anyway, we'd better let him go, hadn't we?'

'Seems so,' Clegg agreed. 'And now we literally don't have any suspects for anything, not even the ones that we never believed did it. Not just back to square one, but back to somewhere before square one was even a thing. I'll make some tea.'

'My turn, surely?' Matlock said.

'Boss. You *always* say that.'

'I make it, don't I? Sometimes,' he protested.

'Oh, absolutely. *Some*times.'

'Quite often, I thought.'

'Well,' Clegg conceded, 'more than Barry, certainly. Maybe I'll pop down to the front and get you a coffee from Costa. I've got a feeling you're going to need one.'

Sure enough, half an hour later Matlock was summoned to the assistant deputy commissioner's office. Janine Treadwell from Press and Media was also present. Once again the ADC was not happy.

'What the hell did you let him go for?'

'Because he didn't do it,' Matlock replied.

'His wallet was found at the scene.'

'His internet use puts him at home in front of his computer at the time of the crime.'

'I still think he did it!' the ADC protested.

'Yes, and I'm afraid most of the internet agrees with you,' Janine chipped in.

'Only because we announced his arrest, Janine. Despite me really, *really* asking you not to,' Matlock reminded her.

'I asked her to,' the ADC said defensively. 'The public needed to be reassured that we'd caught this monster.'

'But we hadn't because he didn't do it.'

The ADC clearly wanted to give Matlock a huge bollocking but couldn't quite work out on what grounds. 'This investigation has been getting absolutely nowhere, Chief Inspector, and now you release an incel fanatic! The bastard's very nearly a terrorist!'

'He's clicked on a couple of their sites, but that's all.'

'Very nasty sites, Mick,' Janine pointed out. 'Sites where men talk about wanting to punish women for their own sexual inadequacy.'

'Exactly!' the ADC snapped. 'What more do you want?'

'Some evidence that he did it, sir. Which I won't get because he didn't.'

'Perhaps you're just not looking hard enough!' the ADC said, going red in the face now. 'This man sent the victim death threats online!'

'Oh, come on, sir!' Matlock snapped. Temperatures were now rising on both sides. 'Death threats are the new mild rebuke. People fire them off for a late pizza delivery.'

'Mick's right about that,' Janine admitted. 'One of the *Bake Off* judges has just tweeted she needs police protection because she marked down a popular hazelnut meringue roulade.'

Clearly the assistant deputy commissioner did not want to talk about hazelnut meringue roulades. He was furious. But what could he do? He couldn't *make* Matlock re-arrest Wotan Orc Slayer if the man had an alibi. 'We must get a result,' he growled impotently. 'The public are up in arms.'

'What public?' Matlock demanded. 'The actual public? As in the on-the-street-demonstrating public? Or the online public, as in the nothing-better-to-do-on-a-bus-or-the-loo-than-tweet-angry-shit public?'

'The net is the new streets, Chief Inspector!' the ADC barked. 'We are failing to protect women, and when we *finally* arrest someone, a man who basically self-identifies as a deeply sexist, aggressive, misogynistic, nasty troll shit, we immediately let him go! It's a very, very unfortunate situation.'

'Well, if it's any consolation,' Matlock said, 'he's just phoned to complain that he's now getting numerous death threats. Lots of them. He wants police protection.'

'Don't give it to him! That would look bloody terrible.'

'Of course I'm not going to give it to him. I've told you – online death threats are as unconnected with actual reality as everything else on the bleeding internet.'

48. Great Britain Rebranded (Again)

TOM AND Bill of Let's Do Lunch announced that Rodney Watson had been dropped from his leading role in *The Royal Closet* because his actions did not reflect the values of the company and were not who they were. With Colin Firth having already ruled himself out, they offered the role to Hugh Bonneville. After he said no, they asked Olivia Colman and finally James Corden, but they also turned it down. It was clear that, for the second time in its troubled history, *The Royal Closet* had gone irrevocably toxic.

And since toxic is nothing if not contagious, so also was the movie's association with #GREATBritainTheCluesInTheName.

Yet again Team UK had hitched itself to an image of national unity only to find itself mired in controversy. First *Love Island*, then the Falklands memorial celebrations and now *The Royal Closet* had all proved touchstones for the ongoing re-evaluation of the treatment of women in society. And each time the campaign to keep England in the UK had come out of it looking divisive, hypocritical and out of touch.

Toby, the incredibly expensive marketing guy, had been summoned once more to the joyless basement at the Home Office for yet another crisis meeting with Jim and Beryl, the minister for referendums and his opposition shadow.

'Yes, it's a bit of a clusterfuck,' Toby admitted, 'but, hey, what doesn't kill me makes me stronger. I say we start looking for celebrity endorsements. I'm talking to Take That at the moment.

Can't get a much prouder symbol of national unity than Take That.'

'I think linking with them would be *wonderful* for the UK brand,' said Beryl, who was a huge fan.

'It's complicated, though. I'm pretty sure Gary would do it for a knighthood but then the other two would want knighthoods as well. And I'm really not sure we could get away with knighting *them*. Besides, I wouldn't be surprised if Gary made it a condition that *only* he got a knighthood because, let's face it, it's his band and I think he likes to make that pretty clear.'

'Ooh, that's harsh,' said Beryl.

'But kind of fair,' Toby replied.

'Other two?' said Jim. 'I thought there were five of them.'

Toby and Beryl exchanged pitying glances. Toby was actually quite angry. How was he supposed to plot a course towards national unity if one of its principal spokespeople couldn't even keep up with how many guys were still flanking Gary Barlow in Take That?

Jim was angry too. 'Look!' he said, coming close to raising his voice. 'Is this really the time to be talking about celebrity endorsements?'

'Excuse me?' Toby replied, actually shocked. 'Is it ever *not* a time to be talking about celebrity endorsements?'

'Yes! And this is it. It's time to talk about issues,' Jim insisted. 'It's September already, and at the end of September England is in danger of crashing out of the UK without any kind of plan. Our duty is to put that stark fact before the public. We need to turn the national conversation back to a proper grown-up, joined-up discussion of the actual issues – the catastrophic economic consequences if the UK were to cease to exist as a legal entity. Every single trade deal, every treaty, every international law and association would have to be renegotiated from the UN, the WTO and the IMF down. Literally nothing would be legal any more.

Scotland, Wales and Northern Ireland would retain the lawful status of the UK and England would have to begin from scratch while also having somehow to untangle itself from its internal infrastructure. And for what? Some "sunlit uplands" that exist only in the crazed imagination of the moronic Bunter Jolly, the lost-empire fantasies of Guppy Toad and the imbecilic fogeyism of Greased-Hogg. *That* is what we need to be talking about. And when England Outers shout back, "Project Gloomy Guts!", we must *engage them*. Expose the paucity of their infantile slogan-eering. *Force* them to have an adult conversation on the actual issues. That is what our campaign surely should be doing.'

There was silence.

Toby was rendered momentarily speechless. Was the minister out of his mind? Was this man seriously suggesting that political debate should return to the days of actual discussion of the issues? Was he *literally* raving tonto? Once a government started working on the assumption that content and substance were more important than image and branding, who would be next? The BBC? The NHS? Would all those strange multinationals with names no one had ever heard of stop making incomprehensibly enigmatic corporate adverts to play before the movie started on aeroplanes? This gibbering lunatic had to be stopped. Not just for the sake of Toby's own immensely lucrative contract but for the sake of the millions of contracts like it. Toby was looking into the face of nothing less than an existential threat to the entire marketing industry. Tens of thousands of jobs would be lost and *nobody would even notice*. Except, of course, in the hospitality sphere because lunch in London would simply grind to a halt.

The danger was real and present. Toby had to take down this appalling notion and take it down fast.

Just then his phone buzzed. It was the previous day's TV viewing figures. He had them on email – they were one of the essential tools of his trade. And, on this occasion, a lifeline.

'*Rainbow Island* is number one across all age categories,' he said. 'So, you see, we were right all along.'

'How?' Jim asked. 'How were we right?'

'How? *How?*' Toby asked.

'Yes. How?'

'I agree with Jim,' said Beryl. 'How?'

'Because they're nailing the zeitgeist, that's what! They are taking that zeitgeist and they are *making it their bitch*.'

'Oh. Right,' said Jim.

'The nation has spoken and it is all over the show's glorious rainbow mix of brilliant, mad, sexy, up-for-it party people, who are all shades of gender neutral, gender curious, gay, bi, tri, straight, bent, kink and all things in between. We've been a part of this from the start and now it's paying back big-time.'

'Part of what?' Beryl asked.

'*Love Island*, obviously, or *Rainbow Island*, as in its game-changingly zeitgeisty reinvention. Our whole Luv Island initiative was *exactly* what all this was about. Don't you see? We led *them*!'

'Did we?' Jim asked.

'Absolutely. In a very real sense, their current success was our idea.'

'Was it?' Beryl asked.

'Fuck, yeah! And now we get back on board and share in the spoils.'

'But we cancelled our Luv Island campaign when Jemima made her claims of non-consensual kisses. We disassociated ourselves from it completely.'

'But don't you see? That's what's so perfect. Jemima's back and so are we. We are rebranding. We are #RainbowBritain. Fuck, yeah!'

'But we only recently rebranded as #GREATBritainTheClues-InTheName,' Beryl protested.

'Forget that. We've moved on.'

'You mean moved back.'

'On. Back. Who cares? Surely it all depends on where you're standing anyway.'

'People will say we're flip-flopping and rudderless.'

'And we'll say we've listened and we've learned.'

'People will say we don't know our arse from our elbows.'

'And we'll say we absolutely do know our arse from our elbows and release several detailed studies to prove it. Don't you understand? We're fighting an election here and the first rule is you can say anything you like, then deny you said it, then say it again. There are no rules, only winners and losers, so let's get out there and show the guys at England Out that this referendum is our bitch.'

49. Trollskis

MALIKA LIKED some bits of her Russian trip and hated a lot of others.

She liked the sightseeing. Julian's business had taken them to St Petersburg instead of Moscow, and while Malika was sorry not to see the Kremlin, the Winter Palace certainly made up for it. She was a very romantic person, also a Conservative and a monarchist, so she found the imperial residence achingly evocative and sad. All she could think of when she and Julian visited were those poor imperial princesses. The last of the Romanov line. Doomed daughters of a doomed tsar. So pretty, so innocent, so naive. So vulnerable. They'd run about in those very courtyards where she was standing now, drinking it in, trying not to let Julian's constant staring and tapping at his phone spoil the moment. The princesses had tumbled along those same corridors, skipping and laughing in their matching white dresses. They'd played with their sick, haemophilic brother under those same magnificent ceilings, four devoted sisters ever on guard for anything that might bruise the precious tsarevich.

'Oh, those beautiful princesses,' Malika said, feeling almost teary.

'Actually, they weren't known as princesses,' Julian pointed out, in his easy drawl, which Malika had once found so effortlessly authoritative but now thought sounded patronizing and glib. 'Their actual rank and title was grand duchess.'

'Yeah. Knew that,' Malika replied.

Of course she knew it. She'd read whole books on the awful story. But they *were* princesses. They were the daughters of an emperor and great-granddaughters of Queen Victoria. Calling them grand duchesses made them sound like dowager old maids instead of four fairytale virgins trapped in their royal prison. The story broke Malika's heart. All their gilded privilege couldn't save them from being gunned down by dirty thugs in a filthy cellar just as they were blossoming into beautiful, elegant young ladies.

Malika loved her visit to the Winter Palace.

Particularly once she'd made the decision to leave Julian to his phone and explore it on her own.

The other side of her visit, however – the dining and socializing with his business associates – made her skin crawl.

Malika freely admitted that she had never liked Russians much anyway. Or not the ones she had met. Which were the rich ones. Arrogant, bullying and drunken was how she described them (secure in the knowledge that being a woman of Pakistani descent made her pretty bulletproof when it came to being censured for everyday racism). She was sure that the vast majority of Russians were not like that at all but that was how she'd found the ones she'd encountered and she wasn't going to lie about it. They had been like that in the streets of Zermatt when she'd experienced them during her gap-year season as a chalet girl. And it was how she found the two that she was forced to dine with on both nights of her visit to St Petersburg. They were gangsters in her view, pure and simple, and she found them utterly gross. They could scarcely order from the menu without letting you know they could afford to buy the restaurant if they chose. Also that they could have the waiter killed if he mixed up the plates, and the local police chief if he tried to arrest them for it.

And as for their women – it was just incredible. At least in the ice bars of Zermatt they'd been clothed from head to toe in endangered animals but the two who accompanied what looked like their owners to dinner with her and Julian were almost naked. Malika could hardly believe any woman would leave the house like that or any man would want her to. They looked simply ridiculous, like pet pole dancers. Like they'd bought their entire wardrobe from Ann Summers and Victoria's Secret. They had basically come out for dinner in their underwear and heels. Six-inch heels. Neither spoke a word all evening and neither ate more than a mouthful of each course. Malika hardly spoke because Julian and his loud, brutish, middle-aged companions made no effort at all to engage her. She did, however, eat lots. Malika loved caviar and had it plain with onion, cream and blinis to start, then in a sauce with her fish, and she would have had it for pudding if it had been on the menu. The meal was superb, the men disgusting and the women, in Malika's view, deeply sad.

The conversation made her uneasy. Not that she could understand most of it because it was conducted in Russian (which, rather impressively, Julian spoke) but he and the Russians used enough English words and names for her to gain a pretty good impression of what they were discussing. Tommy Spoon and Xavier Arron were mentioned quite a lot and the sneering, amused contempt, which was both Russians' default attitude, seemed to redouble when they were. The term 'English referendum' came up often, along with various politicians' names, particularly those of Bunter Jolly, Guppy Toad and Plantagenet Greased-Hogg. Also the international word 'hashtag', and from the way in which Julian gestured towards her when it came up, Malika presumed he was explaining the role her algorithms were playing in the business they were discussing.

All in all, by the time the dessert arrived – it appeared to be made entirely of cream flavoured with various types of alcohol – Malika was feeling quite alarmed. Of course, she'd pretty much guessed already what sort of business Julian must have in Russia, but to have it so brutally confirmed and by such brutal people was a bit scary to say the least. It was clear to her that these Russians were discussing the English referendum with a view to influencing the result and that Julian was working with them. Of course, Russia's covert interference in Western democracy was nothing new: it had been a feature of every election since it was first noticed with Trump and Brexit in 2016 and had, no doubt, begun well before that. However, Putin had always vigorously denied it, and the process of suspicion and counter-suspicion had grown so familiar that the seriousness of the threat had largely slipped from the public consciousness.

Now Malika had witnessed it.

Of course she'd known almost from the beginning of her time at Communication Sandwich that Julian ran a dodgy business. The disinformation her algorithms spewed out was obviously morally corrupt and, she imagined, could probably be challenged legally. The England Out campaign was subject to British electoral law and clearly the methods Julian employed as a paid operative must be in contravention of all of it. Then there was the secondary campaign 'Break the Union', which was self-evidently a mere cipher for a more brazenly nasty wing of England Out and thus also an illegal extension of their funding. Malika hadn't really minded any of this. Politics was a rough business, and if you didn't play hardball, you deserved to get what you got.

But this was different. A foreign power gleefully and shamelessly influencing the very internet marketing company employed by one side in an English election was go-to-prison stuff. Julian's two friends were laughing and slapping him on the back in what could only be described as a proprietorial manner, which implied they weren't so much influencing the England Out cyber campaign as controlling it.

Julian had said that if Malika came to Russia with him she would 'meet her bosses', and it was obvious that now she had or, at least, her bosses' representatives. Because influencing foreign elections wasn't about business, it was politics, serious politics. It occurred to Malika as she moved whipped cream around her cut-crystal bowl that indirectly she was working for Putin.

She didn't like it.

Nor did she like the way the conversation seemed finally to have moved on from UK politics to her and the two other women sitting at the table. A conversation that appeared to consist of leering sexual banter in which Julian was clearly joining. All three men were drunk, vodka had replaced champagne and the traditional rounds of toasts and shots were under way. The two girlfriends were matching the men, shot for shot, which Malika could scarcely credit since they were both tiny (apart from their boobs) and had eaten hardly anything. Malika was being encouraged to drink vodka but was refusing to do so, which seemed to annoy Julian's associates. One of them waved the bottle at her angrily – it was golden, with what appeared to be a ring of tiny diamonds round its stopper.

'He says that is a ten-thousand-dollar bottle of vodka,' Julian said.

'Tell him I'm sure that it is but I've had enough to drink.'

'He says just a shot or two.'

'And I say no.'

'Good girl! Rule Britannia.'

Julian was pretending to support her, but when he turned once more to the man with the bottle, Malika strongly suspected that he said something derogatory and sexual about her: both men laughed dirty laughs and raised their glasses to her in an unpleasantly covetous manner.

Bro-skis before ho-skis, she thought. *Not* very classy.

When they got back to their suite, Malika was glad that Julian was too drunk to do anything but collapse unconscious on the bed.

She had a lot to think about.

50. Christian Martyrs

IT OCCURRED to Matlock that, if anyone had been searching for an event that might swing the pendulum of popular opinion back from the feel-good inclusiveness that marked the first weeks of *Rainbow Island* to something much darker, the suicides of Jocham and Brenda Macroon might have been how they chose to do it.

In the days preceding the distressing discovery, it really had seemed that the utterly fractured national mood had finally lightened a little. A consensus appeared to be gathering that the glorious 'otherness' of so many sexual choices and gender identities, lolling about together in their bathing costumes and chatting about life over pink and green cocktails, was rather a good thing.

And a very *British* thing.

Surely this was what we did best, revelling in our glorious eccentricities. Perhaps it wasn't quite the full-blown normalization of the spectrum that some LGBTQ+ activists might have hoped for, but it was friendly and it was accepting, which was a big step in the right direction. As a spokesperson for Stonewall was happy to say, 'We'll take as many likes, hearts and kisses as people want to give us.'

There hadn't been an orgy of life-threatening bile on the net for almost a whole week.

Even Team UK was feeling a boost. Their decision to link the fortunes of the official effort to retain the sovereign integrity of the United Kingdom to a reality-TV show seemed to be paying dividends. In another distant age, say ten years before, the complete reversal of their previous position might have undermined the credibility of Team UK's current association. But that had been then. In the modern era, for a politician to show an absolute lack of consistency on any and all positions was not merely expected but, if properly spun, was seen as evidence of admirable 'flexibility' and an ability to 'listen' and to 'learn' from 'the people'.

In fact it no longer mattered what any politician said because not only did people not believe a word of it but they could also be pretty confident that the politician would say the exact opposite the following day. It only mattered how people *felt* and, for the time being, there was evidence that people were feeling better disposed towards #RainbowBritain.

The prime minister herself had tweeted, 'Welcome, *Rainbow Island*! Welcome, #RainbowUK.' She went on to make the point that, what with the awful divisiveness and identity factionalization caused by the murders of Sammy Hill, Latifa Joseph and Cressida Baynes, and the suicide of Geraldine Giffard, *Rainbow Island* was just the tonic the nation needed to bring everybody together and 'just have a bit of blooming fun'.

However, whatever feel-good factor the initial success of *Rainbow Island* might have engendered, the nation's mood darkened again when the bodies of the Macroons were discovered in the living room of their small Cumbrian guest house (known as 'Wee Nook'). The briefly notorious hoteliers were hanging from a rafter. Beneath their suspended feet were hundreds of letters and printouts of tweets and TripAdvisor reviews, all apparently sent by outraged activists bent on persecuting the elderly Christian couple for refusing married homosexuals a room with a double bed. There was also a neatly written note Blu-Tacked to the TV screen from the dead couple explaining that they simply couldn't take it any more and were going to God.

The Macroon case had been no longer at the forefront of the

national conversation but it seemed that there had been growing frustration in what the media termed the 'gay community' that the Macroons had not been prosecuted although they had broken the law. This had not emanated from Freddie and Jacob, the offended gay couple – they had *declined* to press charges and had appealed to people to be tolerant of the Macroons – but their wishes had either been forgotten or ignored by those who had continued to bombard the couple with threats and abuse.

Inevitably the revelation of this ongoing persecution, as evidenced by the notes that surrounded the dead pair, produced a strong reaction in the media and online.

GAY HATE CRIME was the headline in Britain's biggest tabloid and GAY FUNDAMENTALISTS DRIVE COUPLE TO SUICIDE FOR BEING CHRISTIANS was the lead story in Britain's only remaining broadsheet.

There was an immediate and inevitable, if still shocking, outbreak of anti-gay bile from those who were already prejudiced against homosexuals, and what seemed to be a change in attitude within a broader demographic. It wasn't that most people believed that all gay people could be blamed for the venomous actions of a minority of dedicated trolls but there was a great deal of discussion across all media about just how far the age of identity entitlement had gone.

WHAT IS GOING ON? asked one newspaper.

JUST HOW MUCH DO THESE PEOPLE WANT? asked another.

According to them, the list of socially game-changing demands was endless.

Trans women forcing their penises into women's ponds.

Trans men claiming urinals were transphobic because they couldn't use them.

Gay lovers high-handedly requiring Christian couples to offer them double beds in their own private businesses.

Was it not the case, some commentators suggested, that the ever-expanding demands for access and equality by anyone and everyone had led some minorities to feel that their occupancy of the moral high ground entitled them to hound anybody who disagreed with them to their graves?

Politicians on the right suddenly felt emboldened to speak out against equality legislation, which had only recently been fully accepted and bedded into the national psyche.

'It seems reasonable to me,' Bunter Jolly opined, in an op-ed in the nation's last remaining broadsheet, 'that if I own a double bed I am entitled to deny people the freedom to bugger each other in it.'

Guppy Toad and Plantagenet Greased-Hogg agreed.

Suddenly Team UK's massive new promotion of #Rainbow-Britain was touted as at best appallingly 'tone deaf' to the suffering of Christians and at worst caving in to left-wing gaysexual bully-boys.

The guilt of association soon gave rise to accusations gaining traction online that Team UK had been *part* of the persecution of the Macroons. When it was revealed that many of the notes the Macroons had received had warned 'straight white bigots' of the coming of 'Gaytopia', widespread public unease went up another notch. Was this chilling evidence of a new phase in the remaking of Britain?

What was Gaytopia? Was it the poofter version of Islamic State?

Were they planning a QUEER CALIPHATE?

The England Out campaign was, of course, right at the heart of the outrage, issuing a never-ending stream of memes and posts, which made it absolutely clear that such a thing would never happen in an independent England. The St George's flag was adorning more and more Facebook posts, and England Out revealed its counter to the Team UK #RainbowBritain slogan, which was #EnglandRedWhiteAndProud's great play of the fact that they were 'reclaiming' the words 'proud' and, hence, 'pride' from their association with gay men walking down the high street once a year in nothing but high heels and a G-string.

Working late in the Situation Room at Scotland Yard, Matlock was feeling a growing sense of unease over these latest developments. 'This Macroon thing's a bit weird,' he said, opening beers for Clegg and Taylor, 'and, frankly, a bit bloody sinister.'

'I'll say it's bloody sinister,' Clegg replied. 'I mean, obviously the idiots who were trolling the Macroons should be ashamed of themselves. But the way people are talking as if intolerance is a *gay* problem is a bit ironic to say the least. Suddenly *we're* the bigots because of a few fringe lunatics. It's the same way people generalize about Muslims. Sometimes I just give up. I'm gay and I know loads of gay people and we all thought those Macroons were sad old fossils, but I don't know a single person who actually trolled them.'

'Well, some of your lot did,' Taylor said. 'Sorry, but it's true.'

'I agree with Sally,' Matlock said. 'I never met anybody who writes the sort of hate that's all over the net. On *any* subject. I suppose somebody does but I never met them. I used to think it was just a few nutters like Wotan Orc Slayer, and the problem was that the press were always quoting them and making the world seem more fucked up even than it is. But it really does seem like there actually are a million little trolls lurking behind a million innocent front doors wishing death on everyone else.'

'Yep. Sadly,' Clegg said, chugging deeply at her beer.

'Although in fact,' Matlock went on, 'I wasn't talking about the anti-gay backlash stuff when I said it was all getting a bit sinister.'

'Well, what were you talking about?'

'The Macroons were Christians. That was what got them into trouble, wasn't it? Proper Christians. Not like when people *say* they're Christians because they want to get into a C of E school or because it's nice at Christmas or for something to put on the census form. But committed Christians. People who believed in the Bible. People so committed they were prepared to ruin their tiny little holiday business because they thought homosexuality is a sin.'

'Yeah. Right. So what?'

'Well, *suicide*'s a sin, isn't it? What fully committed Christian ever commits suicide?'

'Maybe they were looking for martyrdom.'

'Maybe.' Then, after a moment's thought, 'Fancy a trip to Cumbria?'

51. Not a Very Colourful Rainbow

THE MACROON tragedy and the outrage that followed became a huge problem for Team UK and its #RainbowBritain campaign. But not for *Rainbow Island*. The effect on the programme of the sudden surge of anti-gay rhetoric on social media and (in a slightly more muted form) in the mainstream press was mostly positive. *Love Island* had been no stranger to controversy. It had always polarized people, copping as much disdain as adoration. So when *Rainbow Island* came in for abuse from those who felt its new spectrum-based approach was either too PC or because they were prejudiced against the various contestants, Hayley embraced it, revelling in the show's status as standard-bearer for the new inclusiveness. The terrible case of the Macroons and the subsequent anti-gay backlash made *Rainbow Island* seem even more zeitgeisty and culturally important than ever. People had to be encouraged to embrace the rainbow. The show was *significant* as well as fun. The problem for Hayley was that, as the days went by, the new-style programme was in danger of being more of the former than the latter.

Because while the sun, hot bodies and booze were all present and correct, as ever, the sexual intrigue was not. The endless coupling and re-coupling of previous seasons, the ongoing desire of most of the islanders, particularly the male ones, to 'get to know' as many members of the opposite sex as possible, had gone. The jealousies, the betrayals, the romantic dramas, the rejections and the conquests were no longer a feature.

The reason was obvious and, of course, it had been on Hayley's mind throughout the whole frenzied process of assembling a non-binary cast for the show. There were simply too few dating options for the islanders to choose from.

The opening cohort consisted of:

One straight cis woman. Jemima.

One straight cis man. Jonathon.

One gay cis woman. Maria.

One gay cis man. Frank.

One lesbian trans woman (likes girls). Storm.

One gay trans man (likes boys). Sebastian.

One straight trans woman (likes boys). Veronique.

One straight trans man (likes girls). Rock.

One biological male non-binary genderqueer (sexual interest in all genders and none). Summer.

One biological female non-binary genderqueer (sexual interest in all genders and none). Kaan.

One intersex person identifying as male (sexual interest in all genders and none). Rupert.

One intersex person identifying as female (sexual interest in all genders and none). Flora.

One biological male asexual aromantic (without sexual feelings or associations and with no interest in romance). Winston.

One biological female asexual aromantic (without sexual feelings or associations and with no interest in romance). Dakota.

This was clearly a revealing and intriguing group of identities, most of which had never before been properly represented in mainstream culture. It made for a genuinely compelling social mix, and the conversation over the first few days had been fascinating. Socially and culturally, the show was lauded as a triumph and there could be no doubt that the vast majority of its audience learned more about the breadth and diversity of the human rainbow in the first hour than in their entire previous lives.

As did Jemima and Jonathon, the cis heterosexual pair. Not surprisingly, they were by far the least well versed in the various complexities and sensibilities of the acronym they were surprised to learn had been extended to LGBTQIAPK+. Although, of course, there was no absolute consensus even on this across all the islanders, and in a fun game round the firepit only three could reel off the meanings of all the letters without pausing for thought. Most stumbled on the last four (intersexual, asexual [and aromantic], pansexual and kink).

To be fair, everybody was pretty pissed.

Another advantage of the new-style *Rainbow Island* was that the old *Love Island* problem of trying to tell a gang of near identikit Barbies and Kens apart was no longer an issue because while all the new islanders were attractive in their own way they did not all fit the conventional *Love Island* norms. A trans woman in a bikini can look very different from a cis woman in a bikini. Also, the presence of bodily and even facial hair on some of the female-identifying islanders was an absolute first. Previously there had not been a *single* female hairy armpit in the entire history of the island. In fact, not one single solitary hair had *ever* appeared on any part of *any* female ever on the show, apart from their ruthlessly plucked and painted eyebrows and their endless flowing locks.

But being able to tell someone apart from an amorphous Barbie-fied and Ken-tastic gaggle of Stepford Islanders doesn't necessarily mean you fancy them, and on the new *Rainbow Island* the opportunities for coupling were soon revealed to be much reduced. Previously, on *Love Island* the equation had been simple. Each boy fancied pretty much all of the girls and each girl fancied at least some of the boys.

On *Rainbow Island* a lot fewer boxes were ticked.

After the first three broadcasts Hayley drew up a little coupling chart and it made pretty grim reading.

Jemima: did not fancy Jonathon. Or anyone else. No options.
Jonathon: did fancy Jemima. Also Maria. No options.
Maria: quite fancied Jemima and Dakota. No options.
Frank: had never seen such a motley bunch in his whole life. No options.
Storm: quite fancied Maria and Kaan. One option.
Sebastian: fancied Frank and Rupert. One option.
Veronique: fancied Kaan, Flora and Dakota. Two options.
Rock: fancied Jemima, Maria and Flora. One option.
Summer: up for anything. One option.
Kaan: up for anything. Three options.
Rupert: fancied Kaan and Sebastian. Two options.
Flora: fancied Kaan and Veronique. Two options.
Winston: no options.
Dakota: no options.

At the first 'coupling' only two actual vague matches were established. All other choices were based on friendship and expedience. *Rainbow Island* was much lauded as a cultural exercise but it was quickly turning out to be a *terrible* dating show. Also, after the initial friendly and inquisitive interactions, a worrying schism was developing in the group.

Jemima and Jonathon were becoming isolated.

Perhaps Hayley had done it deliberately, perhaps it was a coincidence, perhaps it was a function of the culture, but the two cisgender heterosexuals in the villa were soon revealed as by far the most conservatively minded of the group. They simply weren't as liberated in their thinking, politically or sexually, as everyone else. They were constantly putting their foot in it with their lack of linguistic sensibility and inability to respect pronouns. Jonathon in particular *kept* asking the trans islanders about their genitals, which all the other islanders recognized as unacceptable and very rude.

But what to the islanders, who had to live with him 24/7, seemed insensitive, and reactionary to many viewers at home, to others seemed genuine questions from a boy whose only crime was being a confused straight white male in a world that had changed utterly without anybody keeping him up to speed.

Voices on the net began to claim that Jemima and particularly Jonathon were being bullied. Contra voices pointed out that the isolation that 'Jay-Jay', as Jemima and Jonathon had become known collectively, were feeling among a huge majority of LGBTQIAPK+ people was only what LGBTQIAPK+ people felt all the time in the real world. But there was a faintly triumphalist *Schadenfreude* tone to the contra comments, which lent fuel to the bullying lobby's objections. In the absence of sex and flirting the islanders had lots of opportunities for conversation, and while the LGBTQIAPK+ islanders were by no means a politically cohesive unit, they shared a basically liberal world view. Day after day Jay-Jay found themselves on the losing side of every argument, looking marginalized, small-minded and, frankly, a bit stupid.

Pretty much nothing could have played better into the England Out paranoid vision of a UK in which 'normal' people would be social and cultural pariahs. Suddenly the internet was swamped with memes and newsfeeds telling people that if they wanted to know what the United Kingdom would look like tomorrow they need only watch *Rainbow Island* today.

This suggestion seemed to be proved true by the islanders: it emerged during a heated late-night firepit chat that the only people in the villa who were considering voting for English independence were Jay-Jay. Jonathon definitely was and Jemima 'might'. Every other islander was pro UK.

Tommy Spoon and Xavier Arron could scarcely contain their glee as they pushed their #EnglandRedWhiteAndProud agenda.

And Team UK were in despair. In making an effort to give voice to small marginalized groups within society, *Rainbow Island* had succeeded in compounding the myth that those groups were favoured disproportionately and were, in fact, in control.

52. In Russia Without Love

WHEN JULIAN woke up on the morning after their second night in Russia he was in a spiteful mood, although he tried not to show it. Even when heavily hungover and obviously conflicted about the previous evening, as he was now, he always attempted to affect an amused, semi-detached indifference, as if he simply did not give a flying fuck.

'You could have waited, darling,' he said, once his bleary eyes had focused and he'd taken in the scene.

Malika had been awake for some time and had already ordered breakfast. She was sitting in an impossibly thick and fluffy white dressing-gown, picking at the crumbs of a croissant and sipping sparkling water. 'There's still plenty of pastries. They sent enough for ten,' she said. 'But I'm afraid what's left of the coffee will be cold. And I haven't touched either of the raspberry vodka shots so you can have those, if you want.'

'Order some more coffee, will you?' he demanded grumpily. Then, perhaps realizing that wasn't the tone of amused, semi-detached indifference he favoured, he added, 'I mean, do be an angel.' He got out of bed and headed for the bathroom, scooping up one of the vodka shots as he went.

'Ouchy-wah-wah! That's good. Much better than a Bloody Mary.'

He was naked. Men did that, Malika thought. Not that she'd been to bed with a huge number but she had noticed that they always seemed prepared to wander round the bedroom with it all swinging about. Something she would not do herself and she wondered if many women would. Too used to being judged.

He wasn't in bad shape, though, just a very slight paunch, and she'd have been worried if there hadn't been at least a bit of a tum. Any bloke who has a six-pack at over fifty is either a movie star or a complete wanker with too much time on their hands. He could, of course, be both.

She could hear him peeing. That was another thing she'd noticed. Men didn't close the door. Sometimes *even* when taking a dump, which was an absolute red line as far as she was concerned. She wondered if perhaps it was something to do with marking their territory. Like dripping on the floor.

When Julian returned he'd wrapped a towel round his waist rather than use one of the dressing-gowns. She was glad of that. He looked pretty good in his towel and the dressing-gowns were sort of feminine, definitely a better look on women than men. If she had to let him screw her, as she rather suspected she might, she'd have her best shot at looking like she wanted to.

The thing was, Malika knew that the two of them had crossed a Rubicon on the previous evening. Julian knew it too. She could tell by the way he was looking at her now. A hint of suspicion. A hint of malice. Possibly a hint of vulnerability, although only *possibly*. He tended not to do vulnerability.

'Order it?' he asked suddenly.

'Sorry?'

'The coffee? Did you order it? I need coffee. Drank with the Russians last night. If you don't remember.'

'Yes. I remember.'

He'd come to the crux of things quickly. They'd been drinking with Russians last night, and he and his companions, his 'bosses', as he'd put it, had said a very great deal.

'I remember very well,' Malika went on, and then very deliberately, 'because I was sober.'

She ordered the coffee. Julian drained the other vodka shot. She wished she'd done it herself, not because she wanted it but to stop him having it. She didn't want him drunk for this conversation.

'So now you know, then,' he said.

She didn't need to ask what he meant by that. 'Yes. Now I know.'

Much of it had been clear to her anyway. If you're working in internet communications and your boss takes you to Russia to meet his boss, you know you're not in an ordinary marketing company. The dinner on the previous evening had turned uneasy suspicions into the starkest reality. This was no campaign of subtle influence: the Russians were actually running the show.

'Communication Sandwich is an instrument of Russian espionage and covert propaganda,' Malika said, 'and you are basically a Russian operative.'

Julian sat down opposite her at the little breakfast table. He broke off a piece of apricot Danish and ate it. Then he licked the end of his finger and used it to pick up the crumbs and flakes from the crisp linen tablecloth. With the last little flake he leaned across and held his finger to Malika's lips, the greasy piece of pastry hanging on the glistening tip. It was an aggressive gesture, one of ownership and power. The demand that she accept his finger, with its spit-stuck crumb, in her mouth.

She complied, while matching his cold stare with her own. He put his finger into her mouth and she sucked it, succeeding in not communicating any of the nauseous distaste she was feeling.

'And so are you, my darling. So are you,' he said finally, withdrawing his finger, now wet with Malika's saliva, which he then put into his own mouth before adding, 'You are a Russian operative too.'

Malika hoped that her steady, cool stare was holding, but she knew that if it was, it would be a minor miracle because she was sort of crapping herself.

This was heavy stuff.

She'd let her sense of intrigue and adventure lure her into it, thinking she could apply the brakes and get out if it got scary. But last night he'd deliberately forced the pace. He'd made her complicit. Fully. The stark truth was that if she did not take this to the authorities she was indeed a Russian operative. And, from that point onwards, as guilty as he was.

Why had she done it? Damn stupid bravado, that was why. Why hadn't she just taken a year backpacking in South America like all the other girls?

More to the point, why had *he* done it? He was taking a massive risk. Telling a junior employee his darkest secrets, even if he was having a fling with her. Deliberately bringing her into the heart of his web of intrigue, cavorting with criminals and spies in front of her. It was horribly reckless. Crazy. Why?

It seemed to her that there could be only one answer. He wanted to bind her to him. Malika had her fair share of personal vanity. And she knew how silly men could get when they imagined themselves in love. Perhaps Julian had become aware of her growing doubts about their relationship. Had he sensed that she'd already fallen out of fascination with him? He had feelings for her, she believed that, or, at least, that he had developed a selfish and possessive crush on her, which she guessed was the only romantic feeling he was capable of. He wanted to keep her. And what better way of making it impossible for her to leave than to compromise her? To lock her up with a secret so serious that every second she kept it bound her closer to him still.

And it had worked.

She was stuck. Absolutely stuck. This was Russia, fucking Russia, and she was deep in the worst aspect of it. The corrupt, immoral, heartless, criminal bit. And as Julian stared at her across the pastry basket, she knew that if she gave so much as a hint of anything other than excited compliance, if he didn't trust her totally, she was pretty sure she'd never be leaving.

'Terrible tragedy, Mrs Rajput. I blame myself. Malika insisted on going sightseeing alone. I warned her. A beautiful young girl like her. I should have insisted. She was taken. God knows by whom. I can only pray it wasn't sex traffickers. We are doing everything we can . . .'

There'd be a brief flurry of activity, the embassy, the press. A couple of British policemen would fly to Russia to help with the inquiry. Then, slowly, she'd be forgotten, until only her parents and friends remembered, holding annual vigils, wearing 'Find Malika' T-shirts, insisting that they would never give up hope.

Julian would do that. She believed it. He was a man who liked to be in control, particularly over women he was attracted to and wanted to own. The best control was to bed them whenever you wanted and have them decorate the evening at your command. But, failing that, watching them taken in terror from your hotel suite by Russian gangsters might be a pretty good morning's sport.

She knew she must be clever. Really clever. Because he *knew* she was clever. Clever enough to understand that simply sitting in his bedroom made her, at the very least, an accessory to an incredibly serious crime. And that not reporting him would double it. And that continuing to work for him in the full knowledge of the nature of his work would make her a full-blown criminal too.

She couldn't reject him – she honestly believed that would be fatal. But neither should she embrace him too eagerly. He'd never believe it. She had to show some fear, some doubt, alongside growing eagerness and excitement. And she needed to be impressed. Amazed. *Turned on* by it all. Turned on by *him*. That would be her best protection.

There was a knock at the door. She jumped. What the fuck? Christ! How long had she been hesitating? Had they come for her already?

Julian smiled. He clearly enjoyed seeing a woman shaken. Scared. 'The coffee,' he said, with a smug, languid grin. 'Life-saver.'

They let the staff do their thing, wheeling out the breakfast table. Julian wasn't a breakfast guy. 'Just leave the coffee.'

When they'd gone he poured himself a cup. Just himself. Not her. No more Mr Nice Guy until she'd passed her test. And if she didn't pass, no more Mr Nice Guy, period.

'Well?' he said. 'What are you thinking?'

The question gave Malika her strategy. This was all about sex and power. Here was her chance to hand him both and, with it, the best and most convincing indication of her compliance.

And it would give her a bit more time to consider her options.

'Isn't that what boys ask girls *after* they've screwed them?'

She let her dressing-gown fall open.

Even the sex had changed since the last time. He was a little rougher, a tad mean. Not a hate-fuck by any means but certainly a power-fuck. It had an edge. Of course, he did have a massive hangover.

When it was over he went and poured more coffee. This time he brought her a cup. 'So?' he said.

'So what?' she replied, affecting a joyfully sensuous post-coital stretch. 'Apart from "That was amazing."'

What was one more lie?

She could see he was pleased. Turned out men really couldn't tell if a girl was faking it. At least, this one couldn't.

'So. What are you thinking?'

She was ready now. She'd been working on her answer while he was grinding away on top of her.

'I was trying to decide how many laws we're breaking. You know, making a list – it's my ordered mathematical mind. Starting with the littler ones. Is wilfully spreading mendacious misinformation a crime? Or is it just a thing somebody ends up reporting to the Advertising Standards Authority?'

'Hm. Not sure,' he said, sitting on the edge of the bed and putting a proprietorial hand under the duvet and on to her thigh. 'Probably a crime if you do it on behalf of the official campaign in a referendum. But they'd have to prove it. I mean, what is misinformation, after all?'

'Lies?' Malika suggested. 'We send deliberate lies to people's Facebooks and we spread them on Twitter.'

'Oh, don't say lies, old scout,' Julian replied, with mock sadness. 'Such an ugly word and *so* misleading. What exactly *are* lies, after all? If you have lies, you must have truth, and we all know that truth is a myth. An entirely subjective notion, an abstract ideal.'

'All right. We'll call that one a misdemeanour,' Malika said, with a smile. 'Ooh, look, they brought another couple of raspberry vodkas with the coffee and I want mine this time!'

She gave him a playful punch and he got the shots from the coffee tray.

'But election fraud is definitely a crime,' she went on. 'Break the Union is basically a subsidiary of England Out, isn't it?'

'Oh, absolutely. We founded it. We run it.'

'You mean the Stalin brothers run it.'

'Yes, through me. But it masquerades as an independent. A think-tank, God help us.'

'So that's fraud,' Malika said, downing her vodka shot. 'Because it puts Tommy and The Zax way, way over the spending limit.'

'All right. That's a crime. So that's one. What else?'

'Well, let's cut the bullshit and go straight for the biggie, eh?' Malika replied. 'Assisting a foreign power to interfere in a British election. A *hostile* sovereign power.'

Julian smiled his naughty-boy smile. He was getting back to his old smug, happy self. 'Oh, we don't help them *interfere,* old scout. We help them *control.*'

'Which I think you'll find is treason.'

'Treason? Is that really still a thing?' he asked. 'I mean, you know, in a globalized neo-liberal world?'

'Yes. I think it is still a thing. And it's also still a crime.'

'How wicked of us.'

'Christ, I think it might even be a *capital* crime.'

'Ouchy-double-wah-wah.'

Malika took her phone from the bedside table and tapped a question. 'No. We're all right there. They stopped hanging people for treason in 1998. But you can still get life in prison.'

'We'd hate that.'

Julian grinned and nuzzled his face against her shoulder. Malika felt he was starting to believe she was his creature, and she needed him to believe it. It was a matter of life and death. At the very least until they got back to Britain.

She decided to deliver her *coup de grâce*. 'So if I'm in,' she asked, 'what's my cut?'

Julian was delighted. 'Well done, that girl! Good show! Brilliant. I knew you'd be with me. Which was why I've already opened a Swiss bank account in your name.'

'No!'

'Yes!'

'Wow, Julian. You are *bad*!'

She didn't even have to pretend to sound a bit thrilled at that, because actually, despite her changing attitude towards him, she sort of was. He was an extremely dangerous man and she was beginning to find him increasingly unpleasant company, but he undoubtedly had a sort of style. She'd wanted an adventure, and sitting in St Petersburg being told by a smooth criminal that she now had her own Swiss bank account felt pretty adventurous. Her mother would absolutely hate it.

'Very bad, my darling. And so are you. There's a quarter of a million Swiss francs in it. Your quarterly bonus.'

He went to his briefcase. Still naked, she noted. Big man with his dick out. Definitely a power thing. He returned with an old-fashioned bank book. 'They do it old-school in Switzerland, you know. Proper little book,' he said, handing it over, 'with your name on it. Isn't that sweet?'

Malika opened it. The money was there, all right. An incredible amount. But what surprised her more was the date of the deposit. And the town it had been made in.

Not Zürich as she'd expected, but Geneva.

'Julian? You opened this account a month ago. On . . .'

'Yes. That's right. I opened it on the weekend of our first date.'

It was a pretty stunning revelation. Such arrogance. Such confidence.

She knew what reaction was required so she threw her arms around his neck and kissed him hard. 'Thank you. Thank you. Thank you,' she said, directly against his mouth. 'Oh, my God, you did this in Geneva! You knew we'd be together in this. A million a year bonus! Thank you! Thank you! And you *knew all along*!'

'Oh, I knew, all right, old scout. I know you so well.'

No, you fucking don't, she thought.

53. Oppressive Relationship

Hayley now knew for a stone-cold fact that her plan to reinvent her hugely successful gender-binary, heterosexual dating show as a full-spectrum, multiple-sexualities exercise in corporate-virtue signalling had been a massive failure.

Well, she asked herself, as the truth sank in, what was not to fail?

The almost complete absence of sexual intrigue had doomed it. She'd kind of always guessed it would, but in crisis management you deal with one problem at a time.

There were just *so* many different boxes that the chances of two people ticking all of each other's were horribly remote. And if the islanders didn't tick all of each other's boxes there was little chance of them really wanting to get to know each other.

So there were no hook-ups and no dumpings. No backbiting, no whispered trysts, no confidences betrayed and no kisses stolen. No strutting, entitled peacocks declaring their intention to play the field. No tearfully needy identi-babes 'feeling used' while still claiming to be fierce and strong. Instead there was lots of sunbathing and lots of friendly chatter. There was also quite a bit of social and political debate, which was *quite* interesting but no replacement for snogging and counter-snogging.

The show had *sort of* worked for the first week or two while the TV audience familiarized themselves with the 'exotic' areas of the spectrum of which they'd previously been only vaguely aware. But when the penny dropped that people who did not fit the traditional gender/sexual norm were actually completely ordinary in every other way it started to get boring. Lots of the female-identifying islanders had very brightly coloured hair, which made a nice change from the previously ubiquitous blonde with a few brunettes. And there were more piercings and even more ink than usual, particularly on the female-identifying islanders. But beneath the tattooed skin it soon turned out that the *Rainbow Island*ers were pretty much as boring as the *Love Island*ers had been. Without the romantic tension that had been the only reason for the show ever existing, the whole thing was a bust.

There had been a couple of tentative *possible* romances. Storm and Kaan had started to flirt quite a bit while Sebastian and Rupert announced that they *could* be a 'thing' but wanted to take it slow and see what happened. Unfortunately even these tender shoots failed to engage the public's interest because there were no rival suitors for either potential couple. *Love Island* had lived or died by the quality of its #LoveRatting, the passion of its jealousies and betrayals. Fancying someone was not enough: they also had to cheat on them. But no other islanders were jealous of either Storm and Kaan's tentative flirting or Sebastian and Rupert's long-term possibilities so there were no contenders for betrayal. Everybody wished them well and thought it would be 'really sweet' if they hooked up, but that was the extent of the interest. In fact, the general mood among the islanders was that everyone should calm down about it and give them some space to be themselves.

That did *not* make for good reality TV and ratings went through the floor.

Hayley really needed to think. She *had* to find a way out of this mess and make her show interesting again.

But she couldn't concentrate.

Because Narsti was starting to get seriously on her nerves.

Super-cool, laid-back, don't-give-a-fuck Narsti with his Nikes on *her* kitchen table, eating her food, drinking her wine and leaving wee on her toilet floor. *And* the seat up.

Hadn't he ever *seen* a female comedian?

She was angry with her twenty-year-old lover and she was also bored with him. Even if he was a sodding grime artist. She wanted him out of her bed and out of her flat. Apart from anything else, he literally *laughed* at her choice of music in the car to work. What the hell was *wrong* with Tay Tay? She was a lot more cheerful and relaxing than Stormzy, that was for sure.

Hayley decided she needed to end the relationship. She needed a clear head and an uncluttered life. She had a TV show to save.

But it was complicated. What if his feelings were hurt?

What if he decided to boil her bunny?

She'd been screwing him. She still *was* screwing him, for want of an exit strategy, and she was only now learning just how much power she had ceded because of a silly little crush.

It wasn't that Narsti had *said* anything but she knew what he was thinking. She knew from the way he didn't really bother to be very nice any more. Or very charming. From the way he let her know he was bored with the sex and also with her forty-five-year-old body. It was very clear to her that Narsti felt in control.

He'd got a hashtag on her and they both knew it.

Of course she knew that Narsti did not personally give much of a shizzle about #MeToo or #NotOK or, indeed, any other hashtag. He was young and he was cool and he just wanted to party. In fact, the truth was that, beyond the obligatory 'Yo, bruvs! We've got to give big respect to the ladeeez,' Hayley was pretty clear that Narsti *resented* the current focus on female oppression. Why wouldn't he? He was a young, council-estate black man: he knew all about the power of the patriarchy because when it came for him it was usually wearing a police uniform. She knew he'd been stopped and searched a billion times, and roughed up on at least a couple of them. Hayley had been out with him and knew the suspicion and fear that Narsti often encountered simply for being young, male and black. Most of his mates were out of work. They were *still* getting turned away from clubs by bouncers who pretended it was nothing to do with race. And when they got angry about it they were arrested, and when they were arrested they were infinitely more likely to get sent to prison. And sent by a judge who, unlike all the judges on TV, was always white. Yet suddenly victimhood was all about middle-class white women, mostly actresses apparently, wearing ten-grand dresses on red carpets to shout about how unfair their lives were. And, not only that, but suddenly *he* was one of the oppressors! Because he was a bloke! She knew how Narsti felt about all this because he sometimes let his frustration show.

'Yeah, rape's the worst, ain't no argument. I'd castrate every one of them and I wouldn't even care. But if me an' my brothers were to start wearing badges for every time we got beaten up, or didn't get no job, or wasn't paid as much or didn't get a seat on the fucking company board cos of who we were, blud! You wouldn't even *see* us for fuckin' badges!'

And, what was more, it had all happened just as he'd started to get a little cool. To get a little traction. But instead of being able to make the most of it and fuck himself stupid, as should have been the birthright of any hip guy with a track available on iTunes, Narsti was having to watch his back so's not to get MeFuckingToo'd and made instantly toxic. It wasn't fair. Hayley knew that, as far as Narsti was concerned, there weren't no victim like a young working-class black man and there weren't no fiercer survivor than Narsti Rimes.

And surviving was what he was doing now.

Hayley was pretty sure of that. Pretty sure she'd been played.

She came to this conclusion when she'd scrolled through a few of his emails during one of his disgustingly long shits (during which he smoked weed, played on his phone and *always* forgot to put the fan on). He'd left his laptop open and she'd had a cheeky peek. So what? It was a company email account. She had a *right* to look. Thus, having discovered that he didn't even bother to hide his porn history, she also learned that, from his first day on *Love Island*, Narsti had been using his position to try to advance his music and presenting career. Trying to work the vast network of media contacts that his job as her PA afforded him to get a gig in front of camera presenting music videos or making 'road-level' gangsta docos about 'keeping it real' in the 'endz'. Clearly Narsti Rimes had seen being Hayley's assistant as nothing more than a brief stepping stone to better things.

But he hadn't got any other offers. Lots of interest but no offers. Every reply was a rejection. They were looking for black people certainly. Every media company *needed* black people and urgently, not so much to positively discriminate but more as a reversal of the *reverse* discrimination that had previously made things #MediaSoWhite. The problem for Narsti was that they were all looking for black *women*. It was obvious, really. Two boxes ticked. It was simple arithmetics.

So, clearly, Narsti had worked out that, for the time being at least, he needed to look after the job he had in an industry that was hiring fewer people and paying them less every day. Jesus, at twenty he was lucky to be paid at all. Most companies called any-one under twenty-five an intern and made them work for free. Narsti had decided he needed some insurance.

And that would be her. *Stupid* woman.

Stupid, stupid, middle-aged Hayley, developing a crush on a twenty-year-old and letting him know. Giving him the eye. The smile. Letting a hand linger on a shoulder. Leaning in close to check an email.

And now he had her. She knew that. She was already seriously politically tainted over Jemima and the whole #NoShadeOfGrey business. She couldn't afford to get caught up in an inappropriate and power-imbalanced sexual stand-off with a junior employee less than half her age. Narsti would be deciding when to end this relationship, not her.

And the horrible irony was that she was particularly vulnerable to being shamed as a sex predator because she was a *woman*! She knew how the game went: it was just *so* much juicier to expose a power-abusing female sex pest than yet another boring male one. After all, there were so *many* men. Another was just dull and depressing. When would it end? Aren't we done yet? Can't we just move on from this?

But an abusive *bitch*? Now, that's more like it. That was news. *Good* news.

#NotJustMen.

Plus, what was more, a handsome, charming, *young* male victim. A *black* male victim. It was perfect. The press just *loved* a male victim. Whenever the instances of office harassment were mulled over by earnest leader writers, they always wrote that many women *and men* had been abused. What a lot of shit! Oh, no doubt there'd been a *few*, but probably most of those had been gay stuff, still male entitlement. What was the split on men harassing women as opposed to women harassing men? She bet it would be about a thousand to one.

Which was why if she tried to sack Narsti, and he took her to Human Resources for constructive dismissal, the press would run dirty headlines on her for a week.

NO SHADE OF GREY BUT SHE LIKES A BIT OF BLACK! Wey-hey! Woo-hoo! Hypocrite Hayley the sex monster.

The female spider is just so much more *fun* to squash.

Which was why the truth was she'd just have to put up with him till he decided he'd had enough of her. It probably wouldn't be too long now. In fact she'd already noticed he'd started paying a lot of attention to pretty young Daisy in the office who was clearly a puddle of liquid goo at his feet.

Anyway. Never mind Narsti: he was an irritation but not a disaster. The disaster was *Rainbow Island*.

But Hayley had a plan.

54. Waiting on a Train

'HOPE WE get back in time to vote in the referendum. It's only six weeks from now and I'm beginning to think we might not make it.'

Clegg and Matlock were standing on the platform at Penrith station, and the train had already been delayed by four hours. It was a fitting end to a very frustrating trip in which Matlock's growing suspicions, while having not been allayed, had not been confirmed. Not least because he still had no real idea of who or what he was suspicious of.

'It *could* have been suicide,' Clegg said, for the umpteenth time. 'It certainly looked like suicide. The mutual pact. The co-signed letter. All the nasty troll stuff lying around on the floor. Perfect scenario for martyrdom, and Christians may disapprove of suicide but they tend to love a martyr. After all, if they'd wanted to draw attention to their cause and turn the anger back on their persecutors they couldn't have picked a better method.'

'Hm. Or someone else did.'

'But the note. It was definitely in their handwriting. Both of them.'

'They could have been forced,' Matlock answered grimly.

'Wow. Pretty Gothic, boss. Somebody forcing them to sign their own suicide note, then hanging them.'

Matlock shrugged. Put like that, it didn't sound particularly likely.

'And then,' Clegg went on, 'the killers would have had to

extricate themselves without leaving a single trace. That cottage was deep in the country and the weather's been wet but you had Forensics fine-tooth comb it and there wasn't a single trace of a footprint, not a speck of dirt. No recent fingerprints, except the Macroons' own on the doorways. No trace whatsoever of the intimidation and brutal murder of two people and the staging of a suicide.'

'On the other hand,' Matlock pointed out, 'if it was killers, they'd certainly have had time and leisure to do it and clean up properly. Wee Nook was as isolated as the North Pole.'

'True. But it would still be an impressive achievement. What sort of person could pull that off?'

'Somebody bloody good at their job.'

The crowded platform began to stir. The train was finally due. A sign announced it would arrive in three minutes.

'They died in the same way Geraldine Giffard did. Hanged.'

'So?'

'Nothing.' Then, after a beat, 'Their necks were the same. The pathologist's report said there were fingernail punctures above the rope marks.'

'Yeah. I saw the photos. I guess they struggled a bit.'

'So yet again the noose didn't work for either of them. They died of strangulation.'

'Well, who knows how to make a noose?'

'You might look it up and make sure you did it right if you wanted to hang yourself. Besides, if they wanted to die, why were they struggling?'

'Because choking turned out to be nastier than they'd expected, boss. You have literally not one single shred of evidence to suggest these two were murdered. Or that Geraldine Giffard was.'

'Yeah. I know. We don't have one single shred of evidence for anything. Don't you think that's strange?'

55. Crisis Management

HAYLEY WAS waiting for the *Rainbow Island* production team when they arrived. The old Hayley, the first-in-her-seat-jiggling-her-peppermint-teabag-and-looking-at-her-watch Hayley. It was time to get to work.

'Everyone here?' she asked, as the team bustled in, gripping their spilling Costas.

'Not Narsti,' said Daisy, helpfully.

Of course Hayley knew that. She'd left him in her bed an hour before when she'd left for work. She hadn't even bothered to try to wake him.

'I'm sure he'll be here soon,' Daisy added, 'and there's bound to be a good reason.'

'Shut up, Daisy,' Hayley said. She wasn't allowed to say that any more but she really didn't care. 'Right!' she commanded. 'Listen up. We're changing course. Taking a new tack.'

'New tack, Hayley?' said Dave, who did law and shit. 'Sounds exciting.'

'We don't do exciting right now, Dave,' Hayley replied. 'We do desperate. Our show has always worked on sexual tension but, thanks to Jemima the Whiner putting us on the wrong side of history, we chucked that out and cast a group of islanders with conflicting sexuality. My suggestion is that we stop trying to wring one tiny sad bit of gossip out of a gay man vaguely fancying a genderqueer one, for want of anything better, and find something else to interest our audience. I think we should stop looking for *sexual* tension, start bigging up *social* tension.'

'Social tension?' Dave said. 'Sounds brilliant. Fantastic. Although actually I don't get it. What do you mean?'

'Right now we've got a bunch of happy-clappy rainbow campers all congratulating themselves on being queer-this and gender-that and on being so fucking tolerant that they respect every letter of the fucking alphabet equally.'

'Which I think is really, really nice,' Daisy interjected.

'Shut up, Daisy.'

Now Daisy's eyes were beginning to fill.

Hayley didn't care. 'Nice is not what we want, Daisy, my naive young Generation Twatter,' Hayley said impatiently. '*Nice* makes shit telly. *Big Brother* and *I'm a Celebrity* did not get to be world-conquering franchises by doing nice. They did it by being bitchy. By accentuating the irritations. Making people look selfish and self-obsessed. That's what we have to do. If we can't get this bunch to start snogging each other, we'll edit towards them hating each other. We'll make them play games that pit one bloody identity against another. We'll call it Alphabet War! And we'll starve them so they resent each other for eating. We'll get them pissed so that they're maudlin and angry late at night. We'll split them up, mix them up, turn them up and *fuck them up*. That's what we'll do.'

Hayley was in her element.

Pitching.

Spit-balling.

That was why she was a colossus in the industry with a Silver Fellowship from BAFTA in her loo.

'If there's one thing we know about the age of identity it's that everybody's parading their tolerance. Everybody's dancing about in glittery bikinis and hugging each other in the streets because they're so fucking *tolerant*. Everybody's putting hearts and "likes" and rainbows all over their Facebook pages and making smiley faces in their fucking latte froth to make it absolutely clear that they love everything and everybody and, above all, that they're really, really *tolerant*. Well, let's prove they aren't, eh? Let's prove that humanity is basically made up of nasty, spiteful, self-interested, mean-spirited CUNTS. Whatever their gender *or* their precious fucking sexuality, they're all cunts. *We're* all cunts. Let's get out there and shatter the fucking rainbow!'

56. The Dots and How to Join Them

THE TRAIN arrived six hours late. Clegg and Matlock boarded and found their pre-booked seats, which miraculously hadn't been taken by someone else. First class too. Bloody right. Let the press complain if they wanted. They were working. The promised trolley service was running, too, which was a massive bonus.

'Beer and sausage rolls,' Clegg said. 'Food of the gods. Cheers.'

They drank and munched in silence for a while, each immersed in their own thoughts. There was internet on the train and Clegg thought about picking up her phone, then made the tough but rewarding decision to look out of the window instead. The Cumbrian countryside was magical. She glanced around to see if anybody else was enjoying it. No one. Why did people look at their phones *all the time*? Why did she? Was she going to look back on her life and realize she'd actually missed it because she'd been staring at her phone? Clegg had a sudden urge to say something, to stand up, call out the entire carriage and challenge them to give the view five minutes and see if they didn't feel better. She didn't, of course.

Then Matlock's voice intruded on her thoughts: 'So, how did it go with Latifa's mum, then?'

'What?' For a moment Clegg couldn't work out what he was referring to.

'You know. The mother of the murdered black woman. You went and passed on our condolences.'

'Oh, that. Yeah. Very sad.'

'I'll bet.'

'And such a scary building. No wonder she felt resentful towards the police. You could tell they just never go there.'

'I suppose not. I wouldn't want to if I was a young copper. Gangs rule those blocks. Anyway, thanks for doing it.'

The conversation lapsed. Clegg watched some cows. Lots of cows. How often did you see cows? Never, even in the country, if you only ever looked at your phone. Then she remembered something quite interesting.

'One thing,' she said. 'You know the big hoo-hah? The #IamLatifa thing that Janine from Press and Media was so worried about? The actual reason we had to go and express our sympathy?'

'Yeah. That was pretty huge, wasn't it? For its designated fifteen minutes.'

'Well, she never started it.'

'Who?'

'Latifa's mum.'

'Really? I just presumed she did.'

'Yeah. Everybody did. But she didn't. Quite interesting, I thought. I mean, her grief was personal and private. The way grief used to be. The public grief really was an internet phenomenon. Right from its inception that grief came from a virtual not an actual place. Somebody else generated it.'

'Yeah,' Matlock mused. 'And the subsequent fury.'

It *was* interesting. And somehow, to Matlock, it seemed quite significant. He wondered why.

'The funny thing was,' Clegg went on, 'she thought that the England Out campaign started it.'

'Jesus. Really? That's a bit weird, isn't it? Spoon and Arron? Not the most obvious bleeding hearts. Can't see them caring much about other people's sorrows.'

'No,' Clegg agreed. 'Empathy's not really their thing.'

'So why did their referendum campaign care about Latifa or her mum?'

'Dunno. Maybe she just got it wrong. It doesn't make sense.'

'Why did she think they were involved? Did she say?'

'She said she first saw the hashtag on some England Out posts that popped up on her Facebook.'

'Unsolicited? She wasn't a supporter?'

'I didn't ask, but I'm guessing not. She said that till then she'd been pro UK. Then she got this post covered with heart emojis and flowers and all, and a big push on #IamLatifa from the Out lot. She says it was the first she heard of it.'

'Barry Taylor gets England Out postings too,' Matlock said.

'I know. I think it's seriously crap.'

'He's shown me a few. I never saw any hearts for any dead black women on them. And certainly no #IamLatifa.'

'Wow,' Clegg said. 'So it was a targeted campaign.'

'I guess it must have been.'

'That's bloody clever, actually. I'd never have given those two loud-mouthed England Out pricks credit for that. Or Bunter Jolly and his bunch of chinless twats. Targeting black grievance at one part of the country, while sending dog-whistle racism to another. That's fiendish. Actually, that's scary.'

Matlock shrugged. 'Everything's scary these days.' Then, after a moment, a thought occurred to him, a surprising, unlikely and deeply sinister thought. He got out his phone. 'Taylor?' he said. 'You still in the office? Good. I want you to pull the reports on that Latifa killing. You remember? The black woman the net got all fired up about? I think the surname was Joseph . . . Yeah, yeah. The one people said we didn't care about cos she was black . . .' Matlock turned to Clegg. 'Where was it again?'

'Hammersmith. A tower block called Barbara Castle. Whoever she was.'

Matlock couldn't suppress a look of exasperation. Who was

Barbara Castle? Pioneering female cabinet minister and Labour heroine? It never ceased to amaze him the shit that young people didn't know. He turned back to his phone. 'Call Hammersmith CID and ask for a detailed description of the killing. Get back to me ASAP and if you can't get through keep trying. I'm on a train.'

Ten minutes later Taylor called back. 'Not much to tell, boss,' he said. 'Latifa Joseph was—'

The train went into a tunnel. When it emerged Matlock called Taylor.

'Bugger it. He's engaged.'

'Of course he is. You broke the rule,' Clegg said.

'Rule?'

'When someone calls you and you get cut off, you let them call you back. Else you'll clash.'

'Oh, bollocks,' Matlock said, dialling again. 'Aargh! Engaged.'

'Told you. He'll have rung again as well. Don't you get it? He's ringing you.'

'All right. All right! I'll leave it.'

'Yeah, but now he'll be leaving it, too, cos he'll have worked out you're breaking the rule. You should ring him again.'

'You want me to ring? Isn't that against the rule?'

'Not now you've broken it. But hurry up cos in about half a minute he'll have decided you've worked out that you broke the rule and have now stopped breaking it. So he'll try you and you'll clash again. Ring now.'

Matlock did and he got through. 'Yeah, yeah,' he said testily. 'I know, I broke the rule. Clegg's just given me chapter and verse. What about Latifa Joseph's murder? You said there wasn't much to tell. So tell me.'

Matlock listened for a moment, then clicked the button to end the call. He actually looked shocked.

'Boss?'

'Latifa Joseph was killed by a single blow to the back of the head. Absolutely no trace of the killer was found.'

57. Oppressed CGHs (Cisgender Heterosexuals)

Hayley's plan hadn't worked. At least, not in the manner she'd intended. She had totally misunderstood Generation Rainbow. Her idea to manipulate the islanders into revealing that, for all their pretensions of tolerance and inclusiveness they were just as big a bunch of nasty mean-spirited cunts as everybody else, did not play out as she had planned.

It wasn't necessarily that they were any more tolerant than everybody else. In fact, in some ways they were less so, but for them speech had been criminalized and you could be condemned simply for what you *said*.

Which was why they *never* said the wrong thing.

That was Hayley's problem.

Linguistic inclusiveness was hard-wired into their systems. At least in terms of sex and gender issues. The new puritan orthodoxy of 'acceptable' words and phraseology, which older people found a baffling minefield, was second nature to them.

They never made the classic 'dad' mistake of having to backtrack on some banterish bit of prejudice by saying, 'Oops, I'm probably not allowed to say that any more.' Because they never made any mistakes.

Whatever they might have felt inside, the occupants of #RainbowIsland had the approved all-inclusive language of twenty-first-century identity politics locked down harder than

Newspeak had been for the citizens of Airstrip One in George Orwell's *1984*.

There were *tiny* glints of hope for Hayley's plan.

Frank, the gay man, could be a *bit* impatient with *some* trans orthodoxy. Waspish, even. He occasionally revealed small cracks in his default tolerance. He clearly secretly thought that the 'op' *was* important in terms of transitioning, which, of course, was trans heresy. The first rule of trans is that you *never* ask anyone, 'Are you pre- or post-op?' because it implies that if the answer is 'pre' the person's gender identity is invalidated. But evidently Frank didn't quite sympathize. He couldn't *quite* conceal his view that since Sebastian was (by his own admission) still inhabiting a biologically female body he had no right to employ the constant verbal tic 'speaking as a gay man'. But Frank never *verbally* objected. He had no intention of being labelled a transphobe on national TV. He only raised the occasional quizzical eyebrow. Hayley's cameras caught a couple, and subtle viewers suspected what he was thinking but he was far too well versed in the etiquette of universal acceptance to *say* anything.

Likewise the others.

A number of trans islanders clearly had a bit of a problem with Winston and Dakota who, as asexual aromantics, refused to acknowledge that gender was even a 'thing'. If you've spent a lifetime struggling with depression and prejudice because of your conviction about your gender, it was *slightly* confronting to be lumped together in the LGBTQIAPK+ alphabet soup with people who denied gender existed at all. Storm, Sebastian, Veronique and Rock had one or two whispered conversations about Winston and Dakota's airy dismissal of gender being, in their view, a 'bandwagon' fashion affectation. The relatively recent idea that 'gender is over' undermined their own painful gender journeys.

There was one proper row because Flora was a terrible farter. Maria ventured a suggestion that perhaps it was due to some possible mix-up in the downstairs plumbing as a result of gender-corrective surgery. Flora considered this offensive and it kicked off big-time for a few minutes. But just as soon it ended in a group hug.

Then there were the pronouns, of course. Pronouns were always causing a bit of tension, there being so many of them.

But, all in all, it was slim pickings.

The conflict Hayley was searching for simply was not materializing.

With one huge and very juicy exception.

Jay-Jay.

All the LGBTQIAPK+ islanders were starting to hate Jemima and Jonathon.

And when Hayley realized this she knew she'd hit pay-dirt.

It had all started quite subtly. At first the problem had really only been that Jay-Jay were just so *straight*. All the other islanders had much more interesting stories to tell. Stories of heartbreak and isolation. Of despair and triumph. Of confusion and revelation. Of prejudice and redemption.

Some had suffered violence from bigots and bullies. Most had felt isolated and marginalized at various points in their lives.

All had struggled with the moment of coming out. With family. With friends. With colleagues.

Jemima and Jonathon had nothing like that to offer, and Hayley thanked her lucky stars for the choices she'd made. She could easily have found two cisgender heteros with abusive stories to tell. Plenty of straight cisgender people suffered violence and violation. But Hayley hadn't sought that out. She'd wanted her straight couple to be exactly as the *Love Island* boys and girls had always been, which was very, *very* straight and uncomplicated. Jemima, of course, had *been* on *Love Island* and Jonathon had been cast to type: tall, handsome, rippling muscles, firm-jawed, perfectly groomed and manicured and deeply copper-tanned. In fact, as Frank had pointed out on the first day, twenty years ago he could only have been a gay man, but ever since David Beckham had worn a sarong and ushered in the age of the metrosexual, all straight men had looked gay.

'Such is our triumph,' Frank had murmured.

Jonathon was also not the sharpest knife in the drawer. Nice bloke. Decent geezer. Do anything for you. Bit thick.

Right from the very beginning Jay-Jay had been on the outside. They were simply not as sophisticated, not as worldly, not as experienced. Even Jemima's famous brush with harassment and non-consensual kissing paled somewhat in comparison to the stories that other islanders had to tell.

At first it had seemed almost sweet, Jay-Jay breathlessly asking their questions, the others patiently answering them.

But then things began to get sour.

Jonathon simply *could not* get over the genital thing. He understood post-operative (just). If you've had your dick and balls cut off and a sort of hole put in to replace them, then maybe, OK, you can call yourself a woman. Sort of. But he really could not get his head round the concept that you could be a different gender from what was in your trousers.

And he kept *on* about it.

He *kept* coming back to it. Unlike Frank, who secretly shared his opinion, he did not disguise his views. And all the trans islanders got more and more upset about it. And Hayley could see that this was very good telly.

Because in the outside world people like Jonathon were in the majority and the LGBTQIAPK+ were the ones with all the explaining to do, but on *Rainbow Island* it was the exact opposite.

'The perfect flip!' Hayley crowed with glee.

And she worked it with all her might.

First, she 'exposed' Jay-Jay's inherent prejudice by 'challenging' them to go on 'dates' with islanders whose gender identity and sexuality could at least on paper be compatible with theirs. Hayley arranged candle-lit dinners *à deux* (such a feature of the *Love Island* coupling process) for Jemima, with all the straight-male-identifying islanders, and she did the same for Jonathon with all the similar women.

Jemima 'dated' Rock, Summer and Rupert.

Jonathon 'dated' Veronique, Kaan and Flora.

These dates were not a success. Jemima fared better, not well, but better. Two out of three of her dates thought she was attractive, and while Jemima made it clear she did not reciprocate, she didn't give any obvious indication of distaste.

Jonathon wasn't so polite. He wasn't *deliberately* rude. He just completely and massively continued not to 'get' it. He even looked a bit disgusted. 'I mean, come on,' he said to Veronique, 'I mean, fair play to you and all that, and I don't care what you say you are, I think it's brilliant. Be whatever you want. If you're a bird you're a bird. Whatever. I'm not bothered. But you're a bloke. I mean, you *were* a bloke. I mean, you *are* a bloke. Where it counts. Like. And I don't go on dates with blokes.'

All three of Jonathon's dates returned to the villa angry and hurt. Jonathon returned completely bewildered. 'What did I *say*?'

Hayley made it her daily mission to force Jay-Jay to expose their outmoded attitudes. She introduced truth and dare games. Forfeit games with kisses for prizes. The same stuff that had caused crackling sexual tension on *Love Island* but which created only embarrassment and upset on the *Rainbow* version.

One of Hayley's wickedest tricks was to introduce a polygraph game, forcing Jay-Jay into confessions of unreconstructed prejudice and exposing their lies when Jemima, at least, tried to disguise it.

By the end of the game the horrible truth was laid bare for all the islanders to live with. Both Jemima and Jonathon were transphobes. They believed that sex equalled gender. They believed that there were only two genders. And they believed that you were born with either one or the other.

Perhaps most damningly of all, Jay-Jay both said that they thought believing yourself to be another sex from the sex of the body you were born with was a 'mental illness'. Jemima cried buckets when this came out. She knew what she was *supposed* to say and she tried to lie but over and over again the machine caught her out.

Jonathon had no such qualms about his views. 'Well, it's flipping mad, isn't it? Wanting to cut your dick off and have a twat put in instead? What's all that about?'

Of course, Hayley did her best to cover her tracks.

She knew that she was playing with fire and she subjected all the other islanders to similar tough treatment. She even managed to expose the occasional moment of prejudice in others. Under the polygraph test Frank could no longer disguise his frustrations with trans men behind archly raised eyebrows. He had to admit that he personally could never have a sexual interest in a trans man. He disguised the confession with bravado: 'This queer needs boy dick, not trick dick made from clit.' But when the results were read out, it still caused pain and offence. Pretty much everyone was exposed in some minor deviation from their stated principles. But only minor ones. The general and genuine tolerance and acceptance of Maria, Frank, Storm, Sebastian, Veronique, Rock, Summer, Kaan, Rupert, Flora, Winston and Dakota were in stark and confronting contrast to the utterly unreconstructed binary views of Jemima and Jonathon.

Hayley's brutal mischief worked. The show began to climb once more in the ratings. No longer an innocent game of hetero kiss-chase but instead a painful experiment in reverse marginalization. The couple who on paper should have had all the power were now the outcasts, the pariahs. And, to Hayley's delight, the mutual isolation had led them to recognize how many of each other's boxes they ticked (well, two, basically:

cisgender and heterosexual), and they had begun the traditional *Love Island* process of 'getting to know each other'.

For a few days the general view among the viewing public was very much on the side of the rainbow coalition. The obvious, very real hurt and upset that Jay-Jay had caused, with their stubborn inability to embrace other people's gender identities, was seen as insensitive and depressing. Jonathon was obviously a bit of a yob but Jemima really disappointed people. She had, after all, been something of a hero of #NotOK, a brave survivor of a non-consensual kiss and a victim of abuse. Now she was revealed as having learned nothing from her previous ordeal. No empathy and no understanding.

In the third week the pendulum seemed to swing again. Jay-Jay's social isolation started to look a little bit sad. They were alone in a crowded villa. There were whispers as they walked past tight-knit little groups. Merry conversations died when they entered rooms. They started to feel the pressure and clung to each other the more, which was rather touching. In the outside world some commentators began to note that, weirdly, Jay-Jay were now being treated by LGBTQIAPK+ people in the same manner that LGBTQIAPK+ people complained they themselves had been treated for so long. Some columnists took vicious pleasure in what they suggested was clear hypocrisy: 'Where is the tolerance now?' they crowed. 'Where is the sacred spectrum in which there is room for all? Clearly there is no room in the rainbow for this confused and marginalized heterosexual couple, whose only crime is that they adhere to the values with which they were brought up.'

Other commentators took the other side, pointing out that, although they were sorry for Jay-Jay, for viewers it was perhaps the best way to demonstrate the prejudice that LGBTQIAPK+ people suffered. 'Perhaps cisgender heterosexuals need to see it happening to two of their own before they can truly get it.'

One thing was certain. Whoever's side you were on, the show was climbing its way back to the top. And more than that, while before it had been seen as flimsy escapism, its new incarnation was clearly a fascinating social experiment boldly exploring the fault lines of the Rainbow Generation.

Hayley was lauded as a game-changing television genius, brilliantly rebuilding *Love Island* from its #NotOK nadir to this new and revelatory incarnation.

Hayley was incredibly happy. The awards season beckoned.

She decided it was time to seal the deal by shifting things up another gear. To give Jay-Jay a night in the Love Nest.

The Love Nest had always played a huge part in *Love Island*. It contained one double bed and allowed potentially loved-up couples a chance to spend a night alone together instead of in the communal dormitory.

Not surprisingly, there hadn't been a lot of call for it on *Rainbow Island*: this would be the first time it was used. Of course, Hayley was hoping for some sexual fireworks, she never said no to that, but also she'd decided Jay-Jay needed a break from the other islanders and vice versa. Things were beginning to turn a little nasty. The continued hostility that the others were showing to Jay-Jay had produced a bit of a siege mentality in the oppressed 'cis hetties' and Jay-Jay had begun to circle the wagons. Jemima, who had tried for some time to say the right thing, was fed up with being called transphobic and homophobic and interphobic and every kind of phobic so she decided to take a leaf out of Jonathon's book and own it.

No polygraph was needed now: there was open hostility between Jay-Jay and the other islanders. And, on Jonathon's part at least, the beginnings of a physical threat. He was over being sneered at and looked down on and, quite frankly, it was doing his head in. There'd already been a bit of pushing between him and Winston, the only islander who could match Jonathon for weight and strength, and both he and Jemima had been involved in shouting matches with pretty much everybody at some point.

Battle lines were being drawn and Hayley decided everybody needed a period of cooling off. She didn't want her once-more-successful show to be pulled because fights were breaking out. And if Jay-Jay decided on a comfort shag that would be a brilliant bonus.

And so, at the appointed hour, Jay-Jay gathered up their wash-bags and toothbrushes and made their way down the length of the dormitory and out past the bar towards the so-far-redundant Love Nest. In past seasons these progresses had always been accompanied with good-natured encouragement, whoops and whistles as the slightly red-faced couple paraded past their mates.

But there was no such love on *Rainbow Island*.

Jay-Jay walked in silence past sullen, resentful faces, past people who felt deeply that Jay-Jay represented an existential challenge to their very place in society. As far as they were concerned, Jay-Jay were mean, spiteful, hurtful and plain wicked. Jay-Jay denied their legitimacy as human beings.

They hated Jay-Jay. And the entire watching public could see it.

And Jay-Jay hated them, these people who had forced their agenda on them, who sneered at and condemned them for not getting it, for not embracing it, for being confronted by it.

But tonight everybody would get a break.

Jay-Jay entered the Love Nest.

And they loved it.

It was so lovely.

What was not to love?

A crisp white duvet with petals on it. A bottle of fizzy wine in a bucket. And, above all, they were *alone*. Back in the *majority* at last. And so they kissed and kissed. Such warm, passionate kisses as might melt the coldest heart.

And then they went to bed, and although Jemima let Jonathon

understand that she wasn't going to do anything her dad wouldn't approve of, 'cos he'd do his nut', she did have feelings for him and she did want to get to know him because he did tick all of her boxes.

Jonathon replied that he would never want to disrespect her or cause her dad to do his nut but that he felt the same way. *She* ticked *his* boxes. He certainly had feelings for her and he certainly wanted to get to know her.

'So just cuddles, then?' said Jay-Jay.

'Yeah. Just cuddles, promise,' Jay-Jay replied.

'Promise?' said Jay-Jay, with a sweet smile.

'Promise,' said Jay-Jay, with noble sincerity.

And so they cuddled and kissed and eventually they went to sleep.

And then, about two hours later, when all was still in the villa, there was a power cut and all the lights went out. Including the infra-red one through which the cameras had been watching Jay-Jay sleep.

For a few minutes, while the production team struggled to find an electrician, there was complete darkness on *Rainbow Island*.

58. Joined-up Dots

THAT SAME evening Matlock, Clegg and Taylor had been reviewing their meagre progress.

'We now have three identical murders,' Matlock said, writing the names up on a whiteboard with a marker pen. When it came to a situation conference he did things the old-fashioned way. It helped focus his thinking. He couldn't read novels on an iPad. On the other hand, having resisted Spotify for *years* he had to admit it was insanely brilliant. You could find ska and 2 Tone tracks that even the people who'd recorded them had forgotten ever existed.

'Latifa. Sammy. Cressida.' He spoke slowly, like a school teacher, as he wrote. 'Now, apart from a startling similarity of method, these incidents *appear* to be pretty unconnected.'

'Could be a reason for that, boss,' Taylor said sarkily.

Matlock ignored him. 'And as for suspects, we have very little. Nothing at all for Latifa. We *had* Wotan for Cressida, but he now has an alibi. Which leaves us Sammy and her angry association with Geraldine, who is also now dead, *apparently* by suicide. Sammy and Geraldine knew each other and had actually had a proper confrontation. Which, it could be argued, was a factor in ruining Geraldine's career.'

'Yeah, but really only a factor, boss,' Clegg said. 'I mean, Geraldine's clash with trans politics and fourth-wave feminism was much bigger and broader than one shouting match with Sammy over access to a pond.'

'You've lost me already,' Taylor said. 'Fourth-wave feminism? How many waves of it do they want? I thought one was enough.'

'Shut up, Barry,' said Clegg.

'Yeah. Shut up, Barry,' said Matlock.

'You wouldn't say that to me if I was a woman. Double standards, if you ask me.'

'If you were a woman we wouldn't have to say it to you because you wouldn't be such an ignorant dick,' Clegg replied.

'And moving swiftly on,' Matlock said, 'you're right, Sally, the pond confrontation really doesn't give Geraldine sufficient reason to murder Sammy in cold blood so, regrettably, we must scratch it as a motive. Which means we have absolutely nothing. No obvious connection between the three murders at all. No motives, no physical evidence and no suspects.'

'So why're we connecting them?' Taylor asked. 'I mean, just asking.'

'Modus operandi, Barry. On all three occasions a violent attacker administered a single fatal blow to the back of the head and was then able to leave without trace. Now, that means either three separate amateurs, who got very lucky, or *one* expert hitman. I was prepared to accept the very long shot of *two* lucky amateurs when we were only dealing with the deaths of Sammy and Cressida, but when we found out that Latifa had died *in exactly the same way and her killer had left no trace*, my credulity was stretched too far. Common sense leads me to conclude that Sammy, Cressida and Latifa were killed by the same person.'

Clegg and Taylor had both known the way Matlock's mind had been going but it was still quite a shock to hear it pronounced so boldly.

'Why would any one person want to kill those three?' Taylor asked. 'Do you think it's some sort of psycho serial killer?'

'Maybe. Possibly,' Matlock answered. 'But, you see, I think we need to be looking at *six* killings, not three. We need to consider the three suicides. Geraldine Giffard, and Jocham and Brenda Macroon.'

'Since when does Homicide deal with suicide?' Taylor enquired.

'When maybe they're not suicides.'

'Excuse me, boss,' Taylor said. 'You're trying to connect the suicides of a famous loud-mouth femmo in Brixton with two evangelical Christians in Cumbria *and* call 'em murders? Have you been on the wacky baccy?'

'Those suicides were *also* conducted in an identical manner to each other,' Matlock insisted. 'All three victims chose to hang themselves and all three victims appear to have regretted their decision and struggled to stop the rope suffocating them. That is quite a big coincidence.'

'Not particularly,' Taylor observed.

'Well, a coincidence, if not a big one. So, let's presume for a moment that Geraldine did *not* kill herself and that neither did the Macroons.'

'But *why* are we assuming that, boss?' Taylor asked. 'Wishful thinking, if you ask me.'

'No, Barry. I'm a detective. I don't do wishful thinking.'

'Oh, come on! You reckon it's significant that they all hanged themselves? Not that much of a coincidence. There ain't *that* many ways you can kill yourself, are there? And don't forget one of them was a double suicide, so really that's just *two* similar suicides, innit? Cos a loving couple going for a double suicide are hardly going to choose different methods, are they? "You hang yourself if you like, love, but I'm going to slash my wrists"?'

'That's right, Barry. This is good,' Matlock replied, trying to hold on to his authority. 'You're challenging me. I like that. Nothing worse than a detective who can only convince himself.'

He caught Clegg smiling. 'Come on, boss,' she said, trying to sound encouraging but actually coming across as a little patronizing. 'Keep going. Never mind, Barry. I'm following, sort of.'

Now both Clegg and Taylor were smiling.

'Look!' Matlock said. 'The method of suicide isn't the only troubling feature. In my view neither Geraldine nor the Macroons *should* have committed suicide. Geraldine was the toughest old girl that ever went on *Strictly*, and the Macroons were committed Christians. What was more, *they'd* proved themselves pretty tough too. They'd got through the worst of the abuse. They'd faced it down. Weathered the storm. Even the business was back on its feet, because it turns out there are plenty of evangelical born-again hill walkers happy to support a homophobic guest house. Why suddenly top themselves now?'

'Keep going, boss. I'll make some tea,' Clegg said. 'This is better than the Famous Five.' She went to put the kettle on and get the biscuits.

'All right. So we're supposing that the suicides were murders.'

'You are,' Taylor said. 'I'm not.'

'For the purposes of argument, Barry, we all are. And I'm also supposing that the identical nature of their modus operandi ties Geraldine and the Macroons together. Then I'm supposing that the connection between Geraldine and Sammy ties the three suicide/murders to our three other murders. Which means we have Latifa, Sammy, Cressida, Geraldine and the Macroons all killed by the same person or persons.'

Taylor couldn't take it any more.

'Oh, come on, boss!' he almost shouted. '*Why?* For fuck's sake! I know you're a brilliant cop and I love you, boss, I really do, but this is just desperate. I suppose I can *just* follow your logic but the only reason you're saying any of it is because we've got nothing else. We *need* a break because Christ knows we ain't had one yet so you're seeing one where it ain't. I mean, really. What's the common motive? What could any single killer have against this totally mixed-up bunch of weirdos?'

Clegg handed out the tea.

Matlock dunked his biscuit. He stared at the names and the arrows he'd written on his whiteboard. He was thinking. Thinking hard. He was *certain* he was on to something but for the life of him he couldn't begin to work out what.

'I *may* have got an answer for you, Barry,' he said.

'An answer to what?' Taylor replied with a shrug. 'I don't even know what the question is.'

'Why anybody might link these six,' Matlock answered.

'Any custard creams, Sally?' Taylor said.

'No, just digestives,' Clegg replied, with exaggerated patience. 'You could always bring some in, you know.'

'I bring biscuits!' Taylor protested.

'Once, Barry, once! About three years ago and you've been referring to that one packet of chocolate Hobnobs ever since.'

'You two are messing with my train of thought!' Matlock said angrily. 'Just shut up about biscuits and listen.'

Clegg and Taylor sipped their tea and tried not to laugh.

'To answer your question, Barry, I don't think our hypothetical killer had anything *personal* against any of the victims. I think it's possible they died because of what they represented.'

'Represented?'

'Their *identities*. Or their connection to the identity of others.'

'Not following,' Taylor said.

'Me slightly,' said Clegg, 'but only slightly.'

'Sammy was a trans woman, which provokes very, very strong opinions in almost everybody. Some are supportive, some are abusive.'

'Well, we've certainly found that out,' Clegg agreed.

'Latifa was a black woman, an identity that almost always tops the list of least-advantaged groups, which means that recently they've suddenly been imbued with perhaps the most credibility in the identity wars.'

'Identity wars, boss?'

'This whole business of people defining themselves by race, gender and sexuality. Nobody talks about class any more, or even nationality, do they? They talk about who *they* are specifically. It's the age of the individual.'

'Boss? Is this actually going anywhere?' Taylor asked. 'Because I am completely and utterly lost.'

Clegg's silence suggested that she felt the same.

Matlock knew he was floundering. He tried to focus his thoughts. 'My point is that Latifa, like Sammy, was a representative of a very strong *identity*. Now, Geraldine not quite so much. White, wealthy cis woman. Not a lot of points in being that. But by setting herself up in *opposition* to trans she suddenly acquired a life-changing identity.'

'TERF bitch,' said Clegg.

'Exactly. After forty years as a radical feminist overnight she became a TERF bitch, which made her central to the whole world of identity outrage. Her opposition to the new self-defining trans politics absolutely defined *her*. Eclipsed all her other achievements. It was *who she was.*'

'Boss,' objected Taylor, 'are we coppers or fucking sociologists? I reckon you've been reading the *Guardian* for too long.'

'Just let me get through this, Barry. Let's look at Cressida Baynes. Like Geraldine, she wasn't *personally* remarkable in identity terms, just another middle-class white cis woman—'

'Jesus wept!' Taylor moaned. 'What are we *talking* about?'

Matlock pressed on: 'But she was the public face of a movement that was refocusing our entire history with a feminist perspective. She defined herself by her opposition to the patriarchy. She publicly demonized straight white men, living and dead.'

'For Christ's sake, boss!' Taylor exclaimed again. 'No disrespect but are you *listening* to yourself? You think the same bloke killed Sammy Hill and Cressida Baynes because they were both talking about all the modern shit that *everybody* seems to be talking about *all the time*? And which, I might add, as far as I know, nobody but a bunch of crazy wankers on Twitter actually gives a toss about.'

'Yes,' Matlock said. 'That's exactly what I'm suggesting. Let's look at the Macroons. They came to symbolize a classic cultural identity divide. Old-fashioned conservative moral values versus the new acceptance of gays. They were born into a world where white Christian couples were at the absolute all-powerful top of the tree and homosexuality was still illegal, and they died in a world in which they were social pariahs, pretty much universally condemned for being a white Christian couple who objected to homosexuality!'

'So *what*, boss?' Taylor persisted. 'What's that got to do with anything? Particularly our investigation. What are you suggesting this hypothetical single killer is trying to do? If he's trying to stop everybody talking about identity shit – who they are and what they are and why they're a special case and a survivor and a fucking hero – he'll have to kill just about everybody in the country because that's all *anybody* ever talks about. Why would he choose this random bunch? Why would he choose anybody? What is the point?'

Matlock didn't have an answer. He'd said all he had to say and he couldn't get his argument any further. Because Taylor was right. There was no actual connection at all. All he had was a feeling, God help him, a *feeling*. The thing he hated most was when people tried to counter evidence with their *feelings*. Like Nancy's friend who refused to vaccinate her kids because she *felt* it was wrong. And now he was doing the same thing.

He slumped down in his chair with an exasperated shrug.

'With respect, chief,' Taylor said, and it sounded like he was almost sorry for Matlock, 'I think you've done that thing you always tell us *not* to do. You've come up with some out-of-the-box theory and you're trying to fit everything into it. You've been talking about six connected deaths but the truth is only two of those deaths have anything to do with us. Latifa belongs to Hammersmith CID and nobody's suggested passing it on to us. Geraldine killed herself and so did the Macroons. The only murders that we're currently tasked with looking into are Sammy Hill's and Cressida Baynes's, and I reckon we should forget everything else and focus on them. As *separate* murders. Totally unconnected. Maybe if we do that we might come up with something.'

Again Matlock didn't answer because again he couldn't. Now that he'd put his vague suspicions into words it all sounded so weak, so ridiculous. He didn't have a suspect and he didn't have a motive, yet here he was, trying to string together six deaths, three of which weren't even considered murders. Probably Taylor was right. He should get back to the first cases. Look only at Sammy and Cressida. Separately. And start all over again.

Clegg had switched off a bit. After all, she had been aware of Matlock's connection theory, such as it was, since their train journey back from Penrith. In the absence of anything useful to contribute, she'd allowed her eyes to steal to her phone and had begun browsing her newsfeed.

The referendum was just a month away now, and it was truly beginning to look as if England might vote to break up the United Kingdom. Clegg was quite scared about it. The debate had polarized the whole country and appeared to have come down to this: do you believe in a forward-looking, progressive United Kingdom or do you want a more conservative 'traditional-values' England? An England in which the tide of social reform would be rolled back by the likes of Bunter Jolly to the satisfaction of the likes of Tommy Spoon and Xavier Arron. As a married lesbian Clegg knew which country she was voting for, but she wasn't very confident she was going to get it.

Then an item dropped into her newsfeed that drove all thoughts of national referendums from her mind.

Now this *was* news.

This was proper serious.

'Oh, my God! No way! No way! No way!' she exclaimed.

'What?' Matlock asked.

'Jay-Jay just got murdered on *Rainbow Island*.'

59. Guilty As Charged

RODNEY WATSON was a fighter. He never gave up. Not when something was *really* important.

When it was a point of principle.

Then you would find him on the barricades.

He thought it was important that people should know that about him.

And so he told them.

Often.

He also told Cher Basset, fearless hypocrisy exposer, on her satellite news evening show *Full Disclosure YO!*. 'I'm guilty,' he told Cher, in an interview that could best be described as the battle of the 'serious faces'. 'I'm guilty, Cher, guilty of *being a man*, Cher, which apparently is fast becoming a criminal offence in this strange shadow of a country we once felt we knew. And, yes, crime of crimes, a *white* man. White? Is it relevant? Not to me. I'm colour blind, Cher. I do not *see* colour. Who are these racists obsessing on colour? I see only humanity. And humanity, Cher, as we both know, is *not* skin deep.'

'Then why did you use a racial description now?' Cher asked, nodding in agreement with herself as she answered the question for him. 'Because it's become a slur? An abusive epithet? Because you've been condemned for the crime of being white?'

'Yes, Cher, yes! The crime of being a straight white *man*, Cher. That is what they say when they hurl yet another disgusting, abhorrent lie in my direction. They say, "Yet another *straight white man* who abuses women!" Me. Cher, I have never abused a woman in my entire life. Never. I *adore* women, Cher . . .'

'I believe that's actually a matter of record,' Cher agreed, giving some very serious nods.

'Yes! Yes, it is, Cher. It is a matter of public record that I adore women. And yet I am guilty. Guilty as charged. Of being white, male and, God in his Heaven forbid, heterosexual, *robustly* heterosexual.'

'Public enemy number one.'

'Public. Dot. Enemy. Dot. *Numero uno*, Cher. Have we all gone mad?'

'I think we have, Rodney. I think the loopy left latte conspiracy is a *kind* of madness.'

'I *flirt*, Cher. I'm a *guy*. Acting is a *brutally* demanding calling, and when I've put myself through an emotional *mangle*, Cher, so that seven hundred people can have a spiritually uplifting night out, I like to *unwind* when I get back to my dressing room.'

'So you flirt a little.'

'I flirt a little, Cher.'

'Banter.'

'Bantz, Cher. Flirty bantz. So sue me. Kill me. Destroy me. I deserve it all for I am guilty, Cher. Guilty of being white, male and heterosexual. I like a *laugh*, Cher. I like to pull off my cossie, pour myself a cheeky little Chardonnay, rub myself down with a cold flannel and *have a bit of bantz*.'

'And for that you've been destroyed.'

'Destroyed, Cher. My *Pepys* tour has been cancelled. I've been sacked from *The Royal Closet*, which I was perfect for – and it's not me saying that. I've been told so many times.'

'It's a matter of record.'

'I actually think it is, Cher.'

Rodney and Cher's expressions were now so serious that if the Four Horsemen of the Apocalypse had arrived announcing the end of days the two of them would have found it difficult to register any greater degree of anguished self-importance.

'But it's not that I've been ruined *professionally*, Cher, and of course *financially*,' Rodney went on, 'that doesn't matter a fig. I'm a trouper, a poor player. I shall earn a crust somehow. Actors are used to hunger. But it's my *personal* reputation that these women have robbed me of. These women have stolen my good name. And I'm BLOODY ANGRY, Cher. I'm mad as hell. Because I have done *nothing* wrong. This is a witch-hunt of a *good man*, Cher. No complaints were made at the time. Not one of these girls thought to object. Oh, they can say *now* that they were traumatized. That they've buried these memories. But it's a lie, Cher! The reason they didn't report me for washing my penis *in my own dressing room*, Cher, is because at the time they weren't in the least bit offended. I'm a *good guy*. Ask anyone. I'm a *nice person*. I have letters. These girls say they were fearful for their jobs, that I was more important to any theatre than a casual contract dresser on Equity minimum. What nonsense! This is a witch-hunt. Pure and simple. I have been put through hell, Cher. *Hell*. And I'm not going to take it any more.'

It was a spirited effort. Nobody had expected Rodney to issue such a blank denial after a plethora of entirely separate accounts of identical harassment. But in the gladiatorial days of 'like' or 'hate', the rules of engagement for a man in his position were clear. Deny, deny and then deny again. And, of course, as he was so famous, there was no shortage of platforms on which Rodney could issue his robust defence and his accompanying argument that *he* was the victim. Lorraine and *Good Morning Britain* would no longer touch him, choosing to believe his accusers, but plenty of other interviewers did. Suddenly, what had seemed like a rare open-and-shut harassment case was no longer any such thing *simply* because of Rodney's continued and absolute refusal to admit wrongdoing. Through sheer repetition his denials gained a sort of legitimacy. Rodney even announced that he intended to follow Cassie Trinder's example and sue Let's Do Lunch for breach of contract.

'Cassie was unfairly dumped from the first *Royal Closet* due to a sexual predator, and I have been dumped from the second for exactly the same reason.'

The fact that in his case he was the sexual predator was sometimes lost in the righteous anger of his objections, particularly when he was interviewed by Cher Basset on *Full Disclosure YO!* on the satellite evening shift.

Even in the mainstream media some voices were raised in his defence. Rodney's argument that men were being criminalized for being men found fertile ground. Some commentators even went so far as to question the motives of the victims. A bit of research revealed they'd all had multiple sexual partners in their lives and that two had worked as dressers in erotic clubs. Which almost made them ex-sex-workers. Were they as squeaky innocent as they claimed?

On the net, of course, the argument was taken much further. News posts and tweets warning of a 'war on men' grew louder. Grandmothers, it seemed, were terrified for the future of their grandsons. Mothers warned their boys never even to *talk* to girls for fear of being sent to prison.

All in all, while there could be no doubt that Rodney would never be offered a BBC costume drama again and he had certainly blown the 'woke' man reputation he had enjoyed during his time as Cressida Baynes's partner in #RememberThem, parts of the national conversation seemed to be turning back in his favour. He'd even begun to talk about a new one-man show, which he would call *Is This A Man?*, in which he promised to tell *his* side of the story.

It therefore came as a great shock to the nation when Rodney Watson killed himself. He was found hanging in the communal garden of the lovely apartment building where he lived in St John's Wood. Clasped in his hand was a note once more proclaiming his innocence of sexual harassment and his forgiveness of the women who had accused him of it.

'Ladies,' he wrote. 'I forgive you. For you are also victims. Not of me. But of a loony leftist latte-drinking feminazi orthodoxy, which may yet destroy us all.'

60. In Bed With the Devil

IF IT was possible for algorithms, Malika's were throbbing, shaking and causing vibrations that could have been recorded on the Richter scale.

If it was possible for an internet-based spreader of dark propaganda and fake news to have a spring in its step, Communication Sandwich was positively leaping tall buildings.

They were *caning* it. They were *owning* it.

The extraordinary double whammy of the *Rainbow Island* murders and the suicide of 'hounded' national treasure and iconic Heathcliff Rodney Watson had presented hitherto undreamed-of opportunities for mischief.

It was September, and although the English referendum was only three weeks away, it had all but disappeared from the national conversation as these astonishing deaths, the Rodney Watson suicide and particularly the sensational double murder of Jay-Jay dominated new and old media alike.

'Funny, isn't it?' Julian remarked to Malika.

They were sitting together in his great big free-standing enamelled roll-topped bath, which stood on the polished oak floor in the centre of his vast bedroom, which took up an entire floor of the converted riverside warehouse in Wapping that he called home.

'Funny?' asked Malika, wishing he'd get his foot from between her legs. Did he really think she found it sensual having some old man's foot kneading away at her labia?

'Well, all the high-brow commentators and those Team UK arseholes are moaning away that nobody's talking about the referendum because of Jay-Jay and that shitty old ham Rodney Watson. They say that democracy is dead because, instead of discussing the most pressing issue to face Britain since 1707, we're all talking about a couple of dead reality stars and some mincing luvvie who topped himself, when the truth is that actually, subliminally, in *real* terms, the referendum is *all* people are talking about.'

'Not following,' Malika said, through gritted teeth. He was wiggling his toes now. He actually thought he was *stroking* her. Yeah. Right. Because any girl who wanted her twat randomly stroked would choose horny, rough-skinned, thick-nailed, *middle-aged-bloke toes* to do it.

'Every time anyone reads one of our posts,' Julian went on, 'one of our brilliant newsfeeds about plans to make men illegal or force heterosexuals to have a quota of sex with trans people, or the "fact" that calling a member of the Airfix-model-aircraft-building community a nerd was going to be classed as a hate crime – and then says to their friends, "The country's gone mad," is *actually* talking about the referendum.'

He had grasped Malika's feet now and begun to use them to masturbate himself. This process put more pressure on her crotch, which his wiggly-toed foot was still jammed up against. What had previously been merely horribly unerotic was now downright uncomfortable. Astonishingly, he clearly still believed he was doing them both a favour.

'Mm,' he growled, laying his head back on the rolled lip of the bath, which was equipped with a plastic cushion. 'Feel good?' As if the whole grim business was some kind of mutually fulfilling fantasy play.

'Actually, babes,' she replied, 'maybe not so much. You can either have my feet on your cock or your foot in my crotch but I don't think both. Your legs are longer than mine so your foot is actually jammed up against it really hard.'

'Where's your sense of *adventure*?' he said, with mocking reproval, while moving neither her feet from his cock nor his foot from her crotch.

'Julian,' Malika said, trying to sound both jolly and firm, 'move your foot out of my pussy, please.'

'You *love* it,' he said, head still reclined, addressing the ceiling. Working her feet. Working his foot.

Malika had to make a choice about how to react.

She'd been making a lot of choices since they'd got back from Russia.

She knew that she had to get away from Julian and from Communication Sandwich. She was involved with a serious, serious crime. She was knowingly working for a foreign power to influence a British election, which could result in a lot of years in prison. But how to do it? She was herself a conspirator. Julian had made sure of that, first by sharing the fact that Tommy and Xavier were in serious breach of the electoral-funding rules, and then with the infinitely more serious revelation of the Russian connection. And *paying her*. She hadn't touched the enormous sum he'd banked in her name. But it was there and it was hers. She currently owned it so it was seriously incriminating evidence against her.

Which was the point. He wanted her incriminated.

Malika believed that initially Julian had shown his hand out of vanity and a certain erotic excitement. It was fun and powerful to let a beautiful wide-eyed girl know what a bad boy her super-rich lover was. He'd read her correctly in presuming that it would excite her and it had. But by the time he'd taken her to Russia she believed his motives had changed. He had become kind of infatuated with her and he wanted to keep her. That was why he had made them partners in a *serious* crime.

So. What to do now?

She had to get out but she would prefer to do it at the least personal risk. Nobody wanted Vladimir Putin for an enemy.

Everything depended on how she handled Julian, whom she now despised. He was watching her, she knew that. Ever alert for signs that her loyalty might not be absolute. She caught him looking at her sometimes and saw both jealousy and fear in his eyes. He wanted to own her body *and* soul. In a twisted way, he loved her. But he also feared her because she had the power to send him to prison.

And so, until she was ready to make her move (which meant first deciding on what move to make), she must make him believe that she was still his besotted creature. The girl he had utterly corrupted with his sexily sophisticated wickedness. A cute, fuckable little Faustus to his all-conquering, all-macho Mephistopheles.

He had to *believe* in her.

So. How to deal with the fact that he had continued to keep his foot wedged in her crotch while wanking himself off using the soles of her feet?

Put up with it? Let him have his way? Collude in his fantasy that she, too, was enjoying being manipulated in such an uncomfortable and undignified manner, the water sloshing out of the bath, her arse being pulled about on the enamel, making noises that were somewhere between a fart and a foghorn?

No. Not that. Then he'd suspect her. He knew she was tough. He knew she was proud. He knew she would never be either a submissive little ingénue or a pragmatic whore. She'd said it was uncomfortable. If she pretended to enjoy it now he'd know she was lying and probably harbouring secret, resentful thoughts. Thoughts that could make her a threat.

So. Let him continue? Let him manipulate her body? Do with it as he pleased but let him know that it was all about him? That she wasn't enjoying it one little bit but if that was what her big, powerful man wanted that was what he would get? He'd certainly like that. She knew enough about him in bed to have grasped that sex for Julian was, like everything else, about power and domination. In fact she strongly suspected that an unwilling lover might even be more exciting to him than a willing one. Not actual rape, perhaps, but certainly a bit *rapey*. Yes, he would enjoy that but he *still* wouldn't believe her because, for all his vanity, he was a shrewd judge of character and he knew she would *never fucking put up with it*. That was, she believed, why he was attracted to her. Because she was a challenge.

So she pulled her feet from his hands, leaned forward and slapped his face as hard as she could. 'I *said* get your foot out of my cunt!'

Then she got out of the bath, grabbed a towel and started getting dressed.

It was a calculated risk. Julian was proud and vain, and people like that can be fragile too. They can lash out when their egos are threatened. But Malika knew it was the best option. Weakness never works with bullies. Appeasement just stores up trouble for later. She believed that, worst-case scenario, he would be angry and offended, but it wouldn't make him doubt her loyalty to him and to Communication Sandwich.

In fact, he was turned on. She'd thought he might be. Julian was a sophisticated enough bully to want something to kick against. He didn't do milksops. By playing the furious, flashing-eyed, proud temptress she flattered him. She was a conquest worth the effort.

Of course she'd have to fuck him now, which she didn't want to do but it was what the woman she wanted him to believe she was would do. And she *had* to make him trust her until she could find a safe way out. That meant keeping his interest engaged with a dangerous game of carrot and stick. She'd given him the stick so now she'd have to put up with his carrot.

Afterwards, as she lay in his arms, she asked him questions. She believed that the more she knew, the more deeply Julian would feel she was compromised. That shared knowledge was shared guilt. *She* believed that the more she knew, the more collateral she'd have if it came to a plea bargain.

'So do Tommy and The Zax know they're tools of Putin?' she asked. 'Or is it our secret? Please say they don't. They're two of the biggest arseholes in the world and I really, really would prefer them not to be my partners in crime.'

He looked at her for a moment. With suspicion? Had she asked too much? No. She'd pitched it just right. Proud, robust, cynical. Naughty.

He kissed her nose. 'Oh, my dusky temptress.'

Did he actually just *say* that? *Dusky temptress?* OMG. She wanted to punch him. Instead she giggled. 'Mata Hari. That's me. Exotic lady spy. Full of eastern promise.'

'Like Turkish Delight.'

'Very. Very sweet.'

'And milk-chocolate-coloured.'

Did he really just say that? *Chocolate-coloured?*

'To answer your question, no,' Julian told her. 'The two complete pricks you mention do *not* know the extent to which they are pawns of the Russian Ministry of Dirty Tricks. I serve two masters and am *paid* by two masters. If my lesser masters knew about my real master, they might be a tad scared. Or, worse, want some of my roubles for themselves. After all, it's their campaign the Russians are manipulating. But I can assure you that is *not* going to happen.'

'But surely they'd object on principle, wouldn't they? I mean, patriotism is their thing, isn't it?'

'Which is why they're trying to break up the United Kingdom? Hello?'

'Well, I mean *English* patriotism. Red, white and proud, and all that.'

'Goodness, old scout. For such a clever and sophisticated girl you can be awfully thick, can't you? Of course they don't care about England. They think they do but they don't. They care about a low-tax, low-wage, national sweatshop, in which trade unions are banned and workplace safety legislation consists of a packet of Elastoplast in the boss's desk. They care about money and money alone. How to get it and how to keep it. It's the only thing any true Conservative cares about. I've told you before, they'll ditch any other principle. They'll welcome the queers, undermine marriage, sell out the nation state, betray the Church and give up fox-hunting just as long as they can hang on to the money. It's what makes the right wing so trustworthy. They'll always act in their own financial self-interest. It's people who agonize about everybody else you've got to be wary of. You never know what bollocks they'll come up with.'

'So it's really just you and me?' Malika asked. 'We're really the only ones who know?'

Now she sensed a tiny moment of doubt passing across Julian's thoughts. 'Lot of questions, darling. Don't you think it's better *not* to know some things?'

'Maybe you should have thought about that before you told me shit that could land me in prison. Did you ever think about that? Hm? Maybe it would have been better if I'd got myself a boyfriend who didn't seduce me into committing treason.'

The stick. Stand up for yourself. Confront his doubts. Don't dodge them.

'But, of course, that wouldn't have been *quite* so sexy, would it?' she added.

Then she reached down and took hold of him. The carrot again. She could tell at once it was working.

'You knew very well what accepting a trip to Russia might

mean.' He smiled. 'You walked into this with your eyes open, you little Indian minx.'

Malika knew that was partly true. She also knew she needed to walk out again. And soon. 'Pakistani minx,' she said.

'Whatever,' he replied. 'Same difference.'

She really needed to find a way out of this mess and away from this arsehole.

61. The List Gets Longer

MATLOCK HAD insisted on going to Spain himself as head of the British police assisting the local force in investigating the *Rainbow Island* double murder. And all he'd come back with was a bottle of duty-free Scotch.

'Both killed by a single blow with a hammer-like instrument to the back of the head,' he said, opening the bottle and pouring three glasses.

'Jesus,' said Taylor, 'that is so crazy.'

'Poor Jay-Jay,' said Clegg. 'Just when they were falling in love too.'

'Spanish police are holding all the other islanders at the moment but, as far as they can tell, it could have been any and all of them or none. They found absolutely no forensic clues at the murder scene whatsoever. Cheers.'

They sipped their drinks.

It was evening. Matlock had made the trip to Spain and back in a day. There hadn't been any point in hanging around.

'So now we've got nine,' Matlock said, after a moment.

'Nine what, boss?' Taylor asked.

'Nine bodies.'

Matlock went to his whiteboard. The names he had written on it a few days before had not been rubbed off. There were two columns. The first was headed 'Murders'. Under it was written:

> *Latifa Joseph*
> *Sammy Hill*
> *Cressida Baynes*

Underneath, Matlock added *Jemima Thring* and *Jonathon Radcliffe*.

The other column was headed 'Suicides', under which was written:

> *Geraldine Giffard*
> *Jocham and Brenda Macroon*

Beneath this column Matlock wrote:

> *Rodney Watson*

'Sticking with your theory, then, boss?' Taylor asked.

'It's not a theory, Barry. If only it was a theory. I'd kill for a theory. It's just an observation. The two young people who were appearing on *Rainbow Island* died in the same way as Latifa, Sammy and Cressida. Bosh. Back of the head, job done. Clean, quick and no traces. Come *on*, Barry! What are the chances of five different murders happening like that?'

'Better, I reckon, than one bloke doing all five,' Taylor said. 'I mean, these last two were on *Love Island*! For fuck's sake, boss! What's that got to do with Cressida Baynes or Latifa Joseph? There is just no connection. On the other hand, you've got about fifteen very angry people who were living with them and hated their guts. For once we ain't short of suspects.'

Matlock didn't reply to Taylor's point. As with the last time he had tried to make sense of this situation, the best he could do was to talk through his thoughts.

'Then there's the "suicides". Rodney Watson. Why did he suddenly kill himself? He's been all over the news for weeks telling his story and suddenly he hangs himself. And again it seems, according to Kate at the lab, his neck didn't break. He suffocated while trying to loosen the noose. So now we've got four identical suicides. And we've got another link between them and the murders. Before we only had Geraldine Giffard linked to Sammy Hill. But now we've got Rodney Watson linked to Cressida Baynes. They were partners in the RememberThem movement. Rodney spoke at her funeral. So come on. That's pretty weird, isn't it? Last time we went through this I tried to link the suicides to the murders and neither of you were having a bit of it. Now we've had another identical suicide that links to one of our murders.'

'And two more murders that don't link to fucking anything!' Taylor said.

'And one more that does,' Clegg said.

She was staring at her phone, genuinely shocked. 'Wotan Orc Slayer's been murdered.'

62. Bunter's Sunlit Uplands

THE PRIME minister spoke first. It was a big-beast intervention.

Until this point she had largely kept out of the referendum
fray. She was, after all, the prime minister and her job, as she had
made very clear, was to get on with the business of running the
country. 'That,' she liked to point out, 'was what people elected
me to do and I intend to deliver on that promise.'

That she had taken the disastrous decision to call the referendum in the first place and that the job of 'running the country'
wasn't normally thought to include enabling its dismantlement
was something she tried to ignore. If pressed, she claimed, as she
had claimed at the time, that the referendum had been called in
response to the 'will of the people' and their desire to 'settle the
question of English independence for a generation'. Of course,
literally every single person in the UK (the 'people') was aware
that she had *actually* called it in an effort to stop Bunter Jolly
rallying the lunatic wing of her party around the impossible but
seductive fantasy of 'taking control' of a small country in a globalized neo-liberal world. Neither Bunter Jolly nor the PM had
believed for a moment that the referendum would ever deliver a
yes vote. It was merely a question of who could best harness the
festering resentments of a confused and angry party base to pursue their own personal ambitions.

And the funny thing was, as the PM and Bunter Jolly faced
each other from behind their separate lecterns for the first and

final televised debate of the referendum campaign, they were both looking for exactly the same result.

They were *both* hoping for, and confidently anticipating, a narrow victory for Team UK.

For the PM this represented a considerable narrowing in the scope of her personal ambition. When she'd called for the referendum she had been expecting a resounding vote of confidence in the ancient Union, there being *no* serious economic or social arguments to support the Balkanization of the British Isles with all the fractured, mean-spirited, petty nationalism that would inevitably follow. The PM had been hoping that this strong result would finally lance the boil of Bunter Jolly and his 'smart' decision to gamble the country in the hope of winning a better job for himself or, at the very least, a higher fee for his newspaper columns and more regular slots on satirical news programmes. The PM now understood that the result would be much closer than she'd expected. Team UK's inability to get its 'brand' 'out there' had been *very* frustrating. As had England Out's 'doubling down' on the vision of 'sunlit uplands' and its cynical but effective strategy of characterizing all facts and logical argument as Project Gloomy Guts.

But she still thought she'd win. She knew she'd win.

Everybody did.

Including Bunter Jolly. He was counting on it. Whatever the moronic nineteenth-century fantasies of inbred idiots like Guppy Toad and Plantagenet Greased-Hogg might be, the last thing Bunter wanted was to win and to get the blame for the destruction of one of the world's most successful nations. He had never *wanted* to win, just to show off. All he *ever* wanted to do was show off. And an unexpectedly tight poll, which still delivered victory to Team UK, would be his personal dream result. It would 'heal' nothing, 'decide' nothing and yet deeply wound the PM, thus bringing him much closer to seizing the party leadership and becoming the next prime minister of what would still be quite a decent-sized little nation. Result, *my son*!

And so they faced each other, in *literally* the most important televised political debate since the last one.

The PM spoke first, sticking with her tried and tested career-long strategy of using the words 'resolve', 'stability' and 'strength' quite a lot.

Then, just when everybody thought it was finally over, she said them all again.

And again.

Only then did she sit down.

Then Bunter Jolly rose to speak, confident that this was his moment, his best and final chance to ensure a credible England Out result. One last push to hopelessly confuse and divide the nation. It wasn't a 'slam dunk'. He knew that. The polls were still predicting a decent margin for Team UK, not huge but still convincing. This was his last chance to narrow that lead.

Had he been making this speech at the beginning of the campaign, he would have kept it 'on message'. He would have dismissed the PM's speech as being 'the same old Project Gloomy Guts' before laying out his vision for uplands that he was proudly confident would be sunlit.

But it wasn't the beginning of the campaign. The ground beneath the nation's feet had been shifting. Somehow or other, and Bunter did not care how, the fault lines of the national conversation had begun to ricochet in a manner that was passionately divisive even in the post-truth age of outrage. Bunter Jolly, in his cunning weasel brain, had seen an opportunity in the daily headlines. He had decided it was time to make a proper speech.

'This referendum,' he began, 'is about identity. We hear a lot about identity these days, don't we? The prime minister and her bedfellows on the opposition benches talk about it endlessly, lecturing us about the rights of this group or that. But I should like to stand up today for one identity that seems to have been rather ignored in their master plan. Their *Rainbow Britain*, as they call it. And that is the *English* identity. Does the prime minister even believe that such a thing exists? Is Englishness a "thing" at all? Important *of itself*? I believe it is. That England is a proud nation. The proudest, I suggest, on earth. Does the prime minister believe that? Or does she think that England is merely a collectively administered tax and currency zone in which any number of *different* identities look after their own? Identities based not on common nationality, but on sex, gender, race, religion and anything else anybody wants to tell you that they're "proud" of being, but in which *nobody* is proud to be English! Well, I am proud to be English. Yes! How about that, eh? What I *am* is white, straight and a bloke, but what I'm *proud* to be is English! And if I were not a white, straight bloke, if I'd been born gay or black or in the body of a man but with the soul of a woman, or even more plus-sized than I currently am, or vegan or all of those things together, then that is *who* I would be and I would be happy to be it. But what I would be *proud* to be is English. An identity I can share not only with people who look like me, or have sex like me, or purchase the same cruelty-free products as me, or wear the same-sized clothes as me, but with everybody! With *all* the different "identities" of this great and sceptred Albion, which is our collective home! The prime minister and her Team UK love to pit one identity against another, making laws about who you must rent a double bed to, or who you must share your toilet with. And what jokes you can and *can't* tell for fear of being arrested for hate-speak. And that you must give up your job and your culture to anybody who happens to turn up and want it, and if you object you're a racist. England Out recognizes none of these identities as special cases. England Out says we are all the *same* identity and we are all English.'

There was applause. It was warm. It was genuine. The cameras cut away to the prime minister. Her face still bore the look of sceptical respect on which she had fixed at the beginning of Bunter's speech, but now behind her eyes there was fear. For the first time in his tawdry, opportunistic, principle-free career, Bunter Jolly was making a half-decent speech. It was waffle, of course. Beneath the surface it was meaningless guff. But who looked beneath the surface these days? *On* the surface it sounded sort of reasonable. Actually it sounded bloody reasonable. Bunter Jolly was channelling his inner fucking statesman.

He was harnessing the zeitgeist.

He was making the zeitgeist his bitch.

Bunter basked in the applause. But astonishingly he managed to restrain his natural instincts and he didn't blow it. He didn't preen, he didn't crow, and he didn't quote any Latin. Somewhere in his nasty, selfish, bloated, boozy soul he knew that he had a shot at looking a tiny bit Churchillian and he must not screw it up.

'Another word we hear rather a lot these days,' he went on, 'is "community". There are, it seems, any number of communities. Every "identity" has a community. There is this community and that community. There's a community for every type and every taste. And all must be respected! But what actually is a community in our country today? What will a community be in whatever our country is tomorrow? Is it a thing based on shared geography? A street, a village or a town? A thing bound together by common institutions and needs? Services, jobs, the local football team, the pub, the school, the lollipop lady? That's what I think it is. That's what the campaign for English independence thinks a community is.'

The PM wanted to leap from her seat. She wanted to grab the microphone back and shout, YOU FAT FUCKING LIAR! 'It's a lie!' she wanted to shout. 'You don't believe that at all. You think a community is a source of cheap, unprotected, non-unionized labour to attract foreign investment.'

But she couldn't say it. She'd had her chance and all she'd said was 'resolve', 'stability' and 'strength' over and over again.

Bunter had the floor. And astonishingly, incredibly, he *still* wasn't making a mess of it.

'But what does Team UK think a community is?' he asked. 'They think a community doesn't have anything to do with geography. They think a community is something based on body type, on self-image, on gender identity, on race or simply on shared prejudice and ignorance.'

'No!' the PM wanted to shout. 'That's YOU. You're the ones who want to build a consensus based on prejudice and ignorance! That's YOU.'

But she couldn't say it. She'd used up all her time saying the words 'resolve', 'stability' and 'strength'.

'Team UK,' Bunter thundered, 'do not believe that a "community" is a thing of bricks and mortar at all! The terraced houses, the town hall, the library and the school. No! They think of those things as merely a *physical space* in which exist people who belong to hundreds of *different* communities. Not local but *global*. Communities based on anything and everything from vaginas to vegetables. Communities of people whose neighbours are not next door or in the supermarket, in the chip shop or at the school gate, but online and in another town or country. Communities of people who avoid their *actual* neighbours at all costs, rubbing wary and suspicious shoulders with them only when absolutely necessary. Is that the community people wish to live in? A United Kingdom in which the only thing that unites us is our infinitely nuanced differences? Or in an England where every English person of whatever race, creed, gender, sexuality, religion or dress size can march together towards the sunlit uplands that await the bold! The fearless! THE ENGLISH!'

63. Groundhog Corpse

WOTAN ORC Slayer's body had been found slumped over his computer screen, a single fatal blow having been delivered to the back of his head. Technically it was actually General Stonewall Jackson of the Army of the Confederacy who died because that had been the identity in which Wotan was playing his online war games when the killer or killers had struck.

The murderer had then opened a Word document on Wotan's screen and typed, 'This is for the murdered women, you incel piece of shit, #AllMenAreMurderersAllMenAreRapists.'

Orc Slayer's death was an absolute gift for the England Out campaign, occurring as it did on the very night that Bunter Jolly delivered his rousing condemnation of Britain's new tribalism. The killing played perfectly into his thesis that the UK was a hopelessly broken community. That politically correct latte-drinking liberal elitists in their north London ivory towers had created a nation in which tiny special-interest groups such as radical men-hating feminazis considered themselves above the law. Jolly was riding a wave of popular opinion that it had all gone too far and something drastic had to be done.

'I can't believe people are arguing that this idiot getting killed is a reason to break up the UK,' Clegg said, as Matlock drove her and Taylor once more to the police morgue. 'Bunter Jolly and Plantagenet Greased-Hogg must be kissing each other with Guppy Toad in the middle of the arsehole sandwich. Jesus. It couldn't have worked out any better if they'd actually planned it.'

'Yeah. Funny that,' Matlock said thoughtfully.

This was followed by a long silence, which eventually Taylor broke. 'All right, boss,' he said reluctantly. 'I admit it. It *is* a bit weird.'

'You think?' said Matlock.

'Sort of. Yeah.'

'So you've finally spotted the link, have you?' Matlock sighed. 'You and every bleeding journalist in the country.'

'Well. Maybe. I suppose,' said Taylor. 'All this stupid identity stuff does seem to be winding people up. I mean, you could almost say it was *causing* these murders. People get so angry and then finally some nutter snaps.'

'Piers Morgan was on *Good Morning Britain* saying it was a symptom of a cancerous social malaise,' Clegg said, from the back. 'He thinks the nation's gone bonkers and we need a complete reset.'

'Well, ain't that convenient,' Matlock observed, 'seeing as we're all going to get the chance to give it one next week?'

'Susanna Reid asked if he was saying feminism and LGBT rights were a reason to break up the UK, and he said it pained him to say so but somebody had to have the guts to admit it.'

They arrived at the morgue.

'Groundhog Day,' said Taylor, as Matlock parked the car.

'Groundhog Corpse,' Matlock suggested.

Kate Galloway was waiting for them in the cold room. 'Hey, Mick,' she said. 'Hey, Sally. Hey, Barry.'

'Hey, Kate.'

'Hey, Kate.'

'Hey, Kate.'

Wotan was lying in his drawer. Face up he looked completely at peace. Untouched. Like the others.

'General Jackson received a single blow from a hammer-like object to the back of the head,' said Kate.

All three officers were taken aback. They had not expected the pathologist to take her commitment to Home Office rules on respecting identity choices quite this far. Matlock and Taylor let it go but Clegg just had to say something.

'Don't you think maybe referring to him as a nineteenth-century Confederate general might sort of play into the hands of people who say all that stuff is PC gone mad?'

'I don't consider those people or curate my behaviour on their behalf,' Kate replied tartly. 'I respect all identity choices. Full stop.'

'But by doing that you've *got* to be undermining the trans position, surely. The whole respecting-identity thing is about respecting serious choices. Transgender decisions are heartfelt, life-changing acts of the deepest self-awareness, and you're applying the same rules of recognition to a collection of gaming avatars?'

'Many people make multiple identity choices,' Kate replied, eyes blazing with the light of battle. 'It's not for me to judge between them.'

'Well, I think that's fucking stupid,' Clegg said, with a surprising burst of anger, 'and it's sort of why the country's about to be destroyed.'

'You need to manage your anger and consider your verbal choices, Sally, because I'm finding them confronting.'

Matlock broke it up. 'We're here to discuss the death blow, not the referendum. You call him Wotan, Sally, Kate can call him General Jackson and actually, since we're choosing, I'm going to go back to calling him Oliver Tollett. And all three of them are dead. So let's get on with it, shall we? You said he got whacked on the back of the head, right? The same as all the others?'

'Yes,' Kate replied. 'Same as all the others.'

'Quite a coincidence.'

'Mm. Or copycats, I suppose,' Kate added. 'Could be copycats.'

Now Matlock was feeling angry. With himself. He'd had

enough of this. He knew he had to up his game. He felt like he was on a hamster's wheel, treading the same path over and over again and getting nowhere. He was Scotland Yard's senior murder detective. He had to break the cycle. He had to break the wheel. Find some fucking evidence, for God's sake.

'Dr Galloway?' Matlock said.

'Kate,' she corrected.

'No. I've decided I'd prefer Dr Galloway, if it's all right by you. And I'm Chief Inspector Matlock, which I will be until we stop meeting over corpses with the back of their heads stoved in. Then we can do first names if you want. Now, what I require from you, Doctor, is a *detailed* study of the head wounds delivered to Latifa Joseph, Sammy Hill, Cressida Baynes and Oliver Tollett. Also of Jemima Thring and Jonathon Radcliffe, collectively known as Jay-Jay. Please send a team to Spain and—'

'I've told you, they're all—'

'Identical. Yes, I know. We've agreed that many times. *Superficially* identical. But I said I want a detailed study. And I want it seriously detailed. I want the bone and tissue equivalent of a fingerprint.'

'I have given you a detailed study, *Chief Inspector*,' Kate said angrily. 'Are you questioning my work?'

'No. I'm just asking you to give me a *more* detailed study,' Matlock snapped back, 'but much more importantly, I want *comparable* detail. I want you to assemble the six backs of heads and put them side by side and *compare them*. I want every wound analysed in three-dimensional studies. I want computer simulations made of the exact angle of entry for each assault, depth of wound and power of each blow. And then I want the results set against each other. I am looking for a *signature*. OK? *Specific* similarities. Not just that they were all a neat whack on the back of the head. Look at the depth of the wounds and the thickness of the skulls and take a view from that of the strength of the arm that delivered each blow. Was it the *same* arm? Consider the trauma to the bone on each occasion and stop telling me it was a "hammer-like weapon" and tell me if it was a fucking *hammer*. And if not, what? And if it *was* a fucking hammer, was it the *same* fucking hammer each time? Because I think it was. And, whatever that twat Bunter Jolly and the internet might think, these murders were *not* the result of crazed and random bursts of entitlement or copycat killings. They are the work of a single brilliant killer who, for some reason known only to himself, appears to hate all aspects of what is known as "identity culture". A killer who is currently running rings round us.'

64. Mixed Emojis

SALLY CLEGG hadn't particularly wanted to meet Malika again. Just because you go to school with a girl doesn't mean you're obliged to be friends later when you happen to find yourselves back living in the same town. They'd both changed. Moved on. School was school. And they'd already had one obligatory reunion night, which had been a total frost.

Maybe Clegg shouldn't have brought her wife along. But then again, she'd sort of had to. Her life wouldn't have been worth living otherwise. Danielle was the jealous type, and when Clegg had arranged to meet her old school friend Malika, Danielle had insisted on going along.

'I'd just like to *meet* her,' Danielle had insisted.

Yeah. Right.

Of course, when Danielle discovered that Malika just happened to be gorgeous her worst suspicions were confirmed. Obviously Danielle had absolutely no reason to *be* jealous but, as Clegg had discovered long ago, when it came to jealousy, reason had nothing to do with it. Likewise, the fact that Malika was straight appeared to be irrelevant. In Danielle's view this just made Clegg's planned conquest of her even more enticing.

'You want to turn your little school friend. You know you do.'

And, anyway, in Danielle's view no woman was entirely straight.

And now suddenly, having previously said she was done with Malika, Clegg had announced that she wanted to see her again. And the fact that Malika was clearly angling to meet Clegg alone didn't help. Danielle knew this because she and Clegg had each other's Facebook and email passwords, an arrangement that Clegg had long since started to regret. A girl was entitled to *some* private space, surely. Even in a loving and monogamous marriage.

Anyway, Danielle had read Malika's note.

'So great to meet Danielle (heart emoji),' Malika had written, 'but I really think we bored her talking about school (frowny face emoji). I'd so love to see you again but please don't let Danielle feel obliged to come. It was so sweet of her the last time (angel emoji) and I *loved* meeting her (another heart emoji) but I just want to talk about the old days (schoolgirl emoji) and I'd hate to put her through that again (face blowing kisses emoji). I've got some amazing photos to show you, Sally, of you and all the gang. We look *so* eight years ago! Well, duh! There's lots of stuff that I never put on Facebook. You'll love it. So let's do this! (Cocktails emoji. Party hats emoji.) Let's meet up again, you and me (three heart emojis in a row).'

'Ugh, it's so fucking cutesy,' was Danielle's verdict. 'Could she use any *more* emojis?'

Danielle was right, Clegg thought. It *was* a bit cutesy. Weirdly so. Not like the Malika she used to know.

'It's obvious she wants to get with you,' Danielle pronounced.

'She does *not* want to get with me.'

'And the fact you're denying the obvious tells me you want to get with her.'

'I do *not* want to get with her.'

'You kissed her once.'

'Once! And we were fourteen. It was because of Katy Perry.'

'She wants more.'

'She does not want more.'

'Then why's she trying to meet up? Why's she sending hearts and kissy faces?'

'Half of those were for you!'

'Oh, fuck off.'

Danielle had a point, Clegg thought. Why *was* she sending kissy faces? Why was she trying to meet up again when once had so definitely felt like enough? They'd been good friends back in the day but even at school they'd drifted apart before the sixth form. Malika was a Tory girl – it had been her rebel pose. She'd once organized for Plantagenet Greased-Hogg to come and speak to the Debating Soc. Even back in the day Clegg had considered that a red line. What at fourteen had seemed like devilish, in-your-face, go-girl, anti-virtue cynicism – 'Screw being poor, I want to get rich' – at seventeen had looked like selfishness.

And why had Malika suddenly adopted this gushing girly tone? She hadn't been all hearts and kissy faces when they'd had their reunion evening. In fact she'd *never* been a hearts-and-kisses type of communicator.

Now, suddenly, Malika had sent her three emails in three days. All covered in emojis. The first two Clegg had ignored.

But the most recent one had ended with 'Bananas'.

Love you loads
Malika Xoxoxox
PS Bananas! (Scaredy-face emoji.)

Their old code word from when they were fourteen. 'Bananas' had meant a secret. Mainly the secret that Clegg was into girls. But that wasn't a secret any more and hadn't been for a very long time. Last time they'd met she'd brought the wife, for God's sake. Bananas couldn't be referring to her sexuality.

So why had Malika written 'bananas' now?

What was her new secret?

And why the scaredy-face emoji?

65. Expanding the Team

Now that Matlock felt vindicated in his suspicions about the identity-based connectivity between the names on his whiteboard, he felt emboldened to commit every possible resource he could to finding an actual physical connection between them. A connection between ten deaths that were still listed administratively as entirely separate, four of which were not even classed as murders.

But he *knew* they were all part of the same pattern. Politicians and the media were connecting them too, although only as evidence of sickness in society. Matlock, however, was convinced it wasn't about the sickness of society but about the sickness of one (or possibly more) individual. The sickness of a serial killer. However, he needed to prove it. He needed to find *some* physical evidence of a link between them all. That was clearly the only way he could ever hope to arrive at an actual human suspect. A suspect driven by what was probably the weirdest, vaguest and most random 'motive' that he'd ever attached to a crime.

Matlock had no idea why one killer should be behind all these crimes but he knew in his gut that the same person or persons *must* have been present at all six murders *and* all four suicides. The modus operandi was simply *too* similar, the ruthless efficiency too perfect, for it to be the work of anything other than a single killing entity. Even without the results of Kate Galloway's promised closer comparison between the six death blows, he was absolutely sure that the same killer had dealt them all.

So he blew his departmental budget. The team, which had so far been basically just him, Clegg and Taylor, was now a hundred strong and equipped with as many computers. And their first task was to watch and watch again every single moment of CCTV that had been recorded within a thousand metres of all ten deaths during the evenings on which they'd occurred and to describe physically every single person who appeared.

Matlock's idea was that the descriptions were to be noted down using a set of 250 core phrases. *Only* his designated language was to be used.

Over five feet. Over five foot five. Over six feet.

Twenty to twenty-five. Twenty-five to thirty. Thirty to thirty-five. Etc., etc.

Roundish glasses.

Squared-off glasses.

Sunglasses.

Smoking. Chewing.

Clean-shaven. Designer stubble. Short beard. Full hipster beard.

Long hair. Short hair. Dyed hair. Ponytail. Bald.

Nike baseball cap. Adidas baseball cap. Kangol beanie.

T-shirt. Sweatshirt. Hoodie. Scarf. Plain scarf. Patterned scarf.

Bow-legged. Pigeon-toed. Swaggering gait.

Brand of shopping bag. Brand of jeans.

Shoes. Boots. Docs. Crocs.

Every single one of the thousands of individuals had to be described using only phrases from the approved lexicon and with time codes and locations noted. Then it would be a simple computer task to discover matches. There would, of course, be thousands of matches of a single similar element and slightly fewer matches of *two* elements, etc. Two people in a Nike cap did not mean it was the same person. But two people in a Nike cap with a ponytail poking out of the back, of similar age, wearing similar glasses, with bow legs, Dr Marten boots and carrying a Sports Direct carrier bag *might* be the same person.

Because time was of the essence, Matlock had taken a big decision at the beginning of the search and restricted it to men.

Clegg had questioned this, pointing out that it was possible for women to be killers too.

'Yeah,' said Matlock, 'of course they can, and I wouldn't for a moment wish to appear sexist by suggesting that women can't be as mean and nasty as men. But *statistically* the vast, and I mean the *vast*, majority of violent crime is committed by men. It is in fact a male problem, as you will recall my having to spend an entire press conference making clear. And since these killings are occurring at about one a week, I'd suggest we have no time to lose and that's why I have made the purely *pragmatic* decision to presume for the time being that we're looking for a man and hence halve our search remit in a single stroke.'

'Blimey, chief,' said Taylor, gleefully. 'You'll be profiling people at airports next. Then you'll get dismissed from the force for not searching as many little old white grannies for bombs as you do brown blokes with rucksacks.'

'Shut up, Barry,' said Clegg. 'Try being a Muslim in Britain. You wouldn't like it if you were profiled all the time.'

'I am profiled all the time. I'm a straight white bloke. Haven't you heard? Everything's our fault.'

'That's because everything is your fault.'

'In that case can we have back all the good stuff we did too? All the culture, art, science, medicine and central heating?'

'No. Because women and other ethnicities would have

discovered all that stuff themselves if you lot hadn't been in the way. In fact, we probably did and you just took the credit.'

'Shut up, both of you,' said Matlock. 'This is a murder investigation, not—'

'A student debating society,' Clegg and Taylor chorused.

'And don't either of you forget it.'

Alongside the CCTV search, Matlock had also got a court order to pull phone data from the various telecom companies and started his team looking at the tens of thousands of calls that had been made in the vicinities of the killings, trying to find a number match between locations.

Then he served the banks with an order for records of all ATM withdrawals and cashless payments in the area.

Matlock knew it was unlikely that any killer clever and efficient enough to manage to commit numerous murders and stage several suicides without leaving a single trace of themselves would be unlikely to be so stupid as to use their phone or buy a pack of fags near the scene – but there was a chance. And if they had done, he was going to find it.

He needed only one match, photographic or digital, to find a suspect.

After the first day the CCTV was proving the most promising avenue of research. Not surprisingly, football shirts featured heavily in the matches so far produced and numerous men were seen wearing them at multiple murder locations. Away strips were less common, of course, and second away strips even rarer.

Matlock pored over the search results with the intensity of a deer stalker, noting with a small thrill that a man wearing glasses, a woollen hat and the alternative-alternative Tottenham strip had been logged at three of the locations. Of course, it could easily have been three *different* Spurs fans, and the footage was too blurry to produce any certainty, but it was a possible connection.

One of numerous others to be sent along to Digital Forensics to attempt a closer look.

He was pondering those sightings and racking his brains to try to come up with some other line of enquiry when Clegg appeared. She was wearing make-up and a smarter-than-usual coat.

'You look nice,' Matlock observed.

'I'm going out,' she replied.

'Out?' Matlock asked.

'Yeah. For the evening.'

'But we're rebooting the gig,' Matlock protested. 'Refocusing our investigation with renewed vigour.'

'I know, boss. I was here when you gave your pep talk to all the new people. But I'm still going out. You've got a hundred officers staring at CCTV and checking printouts. One more or less isn't going to make any difference. I'm taking the evening off.'

'Well, I just hope you've got a good reason. And it had better not be earache from the wife. My Nancy hasn't seen me in a week but you don't see me taking the evening off.'

'No. I see you pointlessly sitting around fretting while the team does its stuff. And, as it happens, my wife would rather I *was* at work because she's irrationally jealous of who I'm meeting.'

'*Women*, eh?'

'Exactly, but I have to go because I think something's wrong.'

'Does it have anything to do with our investigation?'

'I'd say that was about a billion to one shot.'

'Then who cares? Stay here.'

'See you, boss.'

And Clegg went out.

66. Reaching Out to an Old Friend

MALIKA GUESSED Julian was reading her emails. That was why she'd put in all the heart emojis and kissy faces. And why she'd told him that her old school friend was now a police officer.

He would have found out anyway. That was the net for you. If he was spying on her emails, of course he was going to click on the profile of the cute girl she was going out to meet. And then the first thing he sees is that she's a cop. Best to get the story in first.

'None of us could believe it when we found out.'

Malika was putting on her make-up. She was still in her underwear. She didn't normally do her make-up in her underwear, more practical to do it after you've got your dress over your head, but keeping Julian sweet was now a part of her every move. He'd bought her the matching set himself so seeing her wandering around in it would give him a double dose of ownership. His totty. His bra and pants. They were from Agent Provocateur – yuk. Malika reckoned men buying girls sexy but entirely impractical underwear was seriously naff. A sexy dress certainly, maybe even a cute little nightie, but a girl liked to choose her undies herself. She had honestly thought he had more class.

'I mean a policewoman!' she went on. 'How grim is that? *And* she's a dyke. Talk about a cliché. It's like some horribly PC character in a BBC crime drama. "Carey Mulligan plays a feisty lesbian cop in a *major* new crime series." Jesus, are there are any crime dramas, these days, which *don't* feature feisty gay lady cops?'

Julian laughed, but she could see he was a little uneasy. He'd been getting more and more possessive ever since Russia. It was partly his growing infatuation, she was sure of that – he was sort of in love with her and love for him meant ownership – but there was also an edge of fear in his attitude. She doubted he'd ever been as indiscreet with anyone in his life as he'd been with her. Weird what a middle-age crush can do to a man. He'd been so *desperate* to impress her that he hadn't been able to help himself. Now, however, he had to live with the fact that his twenty-two-year-old squeeze knew stuff about him that could put him away for a long time. Maybe even get him killed if his Russian mates decided he'd become a love-struck liability.

And he knew she hadn't touched the money he'd given her. Of course he did. There was nothing about her online he didn't know. He was her stalker as well as her lover.

Besides, he'd challenged her on it. 'You haven't touched your money.'

'Why would I when I can spend yours?'

'You could buy me something.'

'Fuck that. I'm the girl. We're old-school. You buy me stuff. End of.'

She knew he liked that. Old-school turned him on. Of course Baby didn't buy pressies for Daddy. She *was* the pressie.

Once, when truly drunk, he'd said something particularly horrible. 'You know I *could* fuck a feminist,' he'd slurred into her earhole. 'Of *course* I could. But it could only ever be a hate-fuck.'

He'd thought she'd laugh. And she *did* laugh, of course, but inside she was disgusted. And also surprised at what a poor judge of character he'd turned out to be. Just because she was a money-focused Tory girl didn't mean she wasn't a feminist in her way. Just not a left-wing feminist.

'So when will you be home?' he asked.

'I don't *know*,' she said, trying to sound teasing. 'Jesus, Julian, I haven't been out on my own in a month.'

'Don't you like spending time with me, baby girl?'

It was beginning to get like that. Proprietorial comments dressed up as cutesy little-boy sulks. It wouldn't be long before he was expecting her to be sitting around in a négligée with a cocktail ready for when he came home. Like something out of *Mad Men*.

Then one day, not long after that, he'd bring home another gorgeous twenty-two-year-old and suggest a threesome, which she'd have to agree to or endure a furious drunken scene.

And in the end he'd get sick of her and chuck her out.

Except, with what she knew, he couldn't do that.

So he'd probably kill her and chuck her in the Thames. Shit. Would he? Really? It seemed incredible. A few months ago he'd been her charming, roguish, posh-boy boss. But then she'd met his gangster friends.

She needed to get out now.

'Of *course* I like spending time with you, gorgeous boy,' she said, 'and I wish I didn't have to go. But she is an old friend and, actually, I think she kind of needs a bit of support right now.'

A flicker of doubt on his face.

Fuck! Fuck, fuck, *fuck*.

He was reading her emails: she *had* to presume that. Emails in which *she* had definitely been the one suggesting the meeting. Positively begging for a meeting. Three emails in three days. With heart emojis.

'Your friend's depressed?' he asked, all smooth concern. The lying bastard. 'Didn't know that.'

'Well, she'd never *say*,' Malika replied, casually finishing her make-up, 'but that's why I want to see her. Her mum rang me to say that Sally's avoiding everybody and she's worried she's having one of her dark ones again. She used to get them at school and did a bit of minor arm scratching.'

'God, how grim. Get *over* yourself. I can't *stand* people who bang *on and on* about *fucking* mental health. Imagine if they'd tried that at Dunkirk.'

'Exactly. And she absolutely refuses to take any pills. Why? Just take the pills, girl. Anything to feel good, if you ask me.'

'Hear hear. *Love* a happy pill.'

'But I am fond of her so I've been reaching out, trying to get her to meet up. It took me three emails and about a million heart emojis to get a response.'

He smiled. Result. She could see that she'd got away with it. And not a bad improvisation, though she thought so herself.

'You really are a sweet kid,' Julian said, coming over and squeezing her bottom.

Did he really think she liked being called a kid? Particularly while he slipped his fingers under the edge of her knickers. She wriggled free. 'Ah-ah. None of that! Later.'

With any luck he'd be asleep.

'Your policewoman mate doesn't deserve you. I don't deserve you. Have a good time and don't be out late.'

'I might have to be. She's awful when she's in her moods. I shall probably have to get pissed to get through it.'

'Well, don't forget she's a policewoman. No idle gossip, baby. Probably best to steer clear of Russian trips altogether.'

'I'm going to pretend I didn't hear that because if I *did* hear it you'd be getting another slap. I am *not* a fucking idiot.'

Except, she thought, she was an idiot to have let herself be drawn into this in the first place.

67. Girls' Night Out

MALIKA MET Clegg at Soho House. Julian had wangled her to the top of the applications list and bought her membership as a two-month anniversary present. Pretty good present, she had to admit, a lot better than silk G-strings. She absolutely loved belonging to such an amazingly smart place and intended to find a way to stay a member after she'd done what she needed to do.

Malika also reckoned it was the sort of place where one could have a discreet conversation and be ignored – there were so many glamorous and famous people about that nobody would ever think to look at them. Besides which, everyone was having their *own* discreet conversations. Mainly about proposed co-productions with Netflix, no doubt. Perhaps one or two might even feature plot pitches for drama thrillers about covert Russian cyber-attacks on Western democracy. Wouldn't that be ironic? she thought, as she waited for her guest to arrive.

Clegg had been slightly thrilled when Malika had suggested meeting at Soho House and she wasn't disappointed. She'd never been to anywhere so cool and hip in her life (except once as a young constable and only then as part of a drug raid, which hardly counted). She had already definitely spotted Kate Moss and *possibly* Brooklyn Beckham.

*

Malika gave her old friend about a minute to enjoy ordering an extremely expensive cocktail and some insanely tempting nibbles before getting down to what was on her mind.

'Sally,' she said. 'You noticed I said "PS Bananas" in my last message?'

'Yes.'

'It was to make you see me.'

'I guessed that. I was definitely going to reply to your other emails, by the way.'

'Don't lie. We both know the last time we met up was boring for all of us. Your wife was obviously suspicious of me, which was *so* weird. I mean, *as if*. Neither of us had any intention of ever seeing each other again but I need your help. Hence PS Bananas.'

'You always were a charmer, Mal. I'm presuming bananas doesn't mean we need to be discreet about my sexuality.'

'No. I think Soho House is probably the last place in London anyone needs to be discreet about their sexuality.'

'So what are we being discreet about, then?'

The drinks arrived, giving Malika a moment to collect her thoughts. How on earth to begin? She leaned in a little closer. The music was quite loud, which was good for privacy but meant she had to speak quite loudly and clearly. It felt strange saying things in such bold tones that she'd imagined she'd be delivering in discreet half-whispered allusions.

'I work for a communications company through which the Russian government is trying to pervert the course of the English independence referendum.'

There. She'd said it. She'd crossed the Rubicon. There was no turning back. She'd told a British police officer that she was effectively a Russian *agent provocateur*. It felt very strange. She'd been thinking about nothing else for weeks and now, in a single sentence, it was done. Her life would never be the same again. The secret was out.

'What?' said Clegg, leaning forward, a strained look on her face. 'I didn't hear a word of that.'

Bollocks. She'd have to say it again. She wasn't sure if she had the resolve. Maybe she should take this as a sign. Not blow the whistle. Go back to Julian's flat instead, fuck more money out of him, then run away to South America.

Except no. There was one thing Malika wanted more than to be fabulously rich and that was not to go to prison or be a wanted criminal for the rest of her life. Quite apart from anything else, what would her mum say?

She leaned in once more and spoke into Clegg's ear.

'Now, listen to me, Sally. Can you hear me now? Am I being clear? Because this is very, very fucking important.'

Clegg nodded.

'I am in big trouble. Implicated in serious crimes with very dangerous people. I want to get out. I want to do the right thing. But if they suspect I'm turning on them it's *possible* that they might take quite drastic action. I mean . . . I think I might actually be in proper danger.'

Malika could feel Clegg's tension. Well, at least she'd heard her this time.

'I've come to you because when I make my move I need to get it absolutely right. I'll have one shot to report them and get away. Once I've blown my cover I won't get another chance. So I need advice on who to go to, who to tell. Is it the police? Is it the *Guardian*, God help me? Is it MI-fucking-5?'

Malika realized she was shaking. She was not a girl who scared easily but you didn't need to scare easily to be scared at the shit she'd got herself into. MI5? Just *saying* it sounded truly ridiculous.

'Malika,' Clegg said. 'What is it? You haven't told me what you've done.'

Fuck. Having said it once but not been heard she'd forgotten to say it again. Now she'd have to. This was so hard. She looked around, almost expecting to see Julian behind her, flanked by a couple of goons with bulges under their coats below their armpits.

'I run computer programs for the England Out campaign,' she said. 'They're double-dipping on electoral funding because the fringe organization, known as Break the Union, is not fringe at all but a coordinated part of their work, which makes it electoral fraud.'

'Wow,' Clegg observed. 'That's pretty serious. You're a proper whistle-blower, Malika.'

'Don't say "wow" yet, Sally. That's not the "wow" bit. That's the "I'd be fine reporting this on my own" bit. The "I'd just write to the *Guardian*" bit. *This* is the proper "wow" bit.'

Once more she leaned in as close as she could and for the second time said the proper "wow" bit. 'The company I work for is funded and controlled by the Russian government. It is tasked with sowing dismay and confusion in the UK with the ultimate goal of pushing England towards breaking away from the UK.'

Clegg's eyes widened in a gratifyingly astonished manner. 'OK,' she said. 'That is pretty wow.'

'Isn't it?

'And you're sure of this?'

'Sally, I've been to Russia. I've met my boss's bosses. They are not nice people.'

'And you want to expose them?'

Just then Malika noticed a waitress pointing in her direction. The woman was talking to a smartly dressed man in a suit and tie. Malika froze. The man was staring at her. He started walking towards her, and as he did so, he put his hand inside his jacket. Suddenly Malika was utterly terrified. She wanted to run but she couldn't. She wanted to scream.

'Malika, what's wrong?' Clegg asked.

Before Malika could find her voice the man was standing over her, his hand emerging from his jacket. 'Russell,' he said, offering her a little business card. 'I'm with Soho House. You're Malika?

Super. Julian just wanted me to say hi and check you and your guest are having the *best* fun. Also . . .'

Malika now saw that a waiter had been following with a bucket on a tray.

'Krug, 2011,' Russell went on. 'With our compliments.'

Malika pulled herself together and thanked him as he opened the champagne and poured.

'Our pleasure. Julian's such a mate. Enjoy.'

And Russell was gone.

'Shit, Mal,' Clegg said. 'What it is to have connections. This is amazing.'

'He was checking up on me.'

'What?'

'Never mind. It doesn't matter.' Malika swallowed hard and tried to control her heartbeat. It had been nothing. Well, not nothing. Julian was letting her know how short her leash was. But at least it wasn't worse.

'I was telling you about these fucking Russians I work for indirectly and, no, I don't want to expose "them". I don't know if you really *can* expose them because, well, they're Russians, aren't they? They just do whatever they want, don't they, and then just deny it? They even deny invading countries. From the top man down they seriously do not give a fuck. But I want to expose my boss because if I don't then when he does finally get exposed, as I've got to presume in the end he will – if for no other reason than that he's too arrogant to keep his secrets – I'll be in as much trouble as him. That's right, isn't it?'

'Well, yeah. I guess. An accessory at least. If you've been doing this stuff knowing it's illegal, for sure. And speaking of which, what is it you actually do? Is this about media and advertising standards? Is it actual subversion? Is it cyber-terrorism?'

'I don't know. It's sort of all that, really. Just a massively nasty effort to mess with everybody's heads.'

'How do you do that?'

Once more Malika glanced around the room. She felt vulnerable just saying it.

'We take stuff that's already contentious and divisive and we double down on it. Then we double down again. We exaggerate, we spread lies, we generate tension and mistrust, and then we hang that mistrust on Team UK.'

'Christ, that's you, Mal? My colleague has got some of your posts.'

'Everybody gets our posts. They're not all obvious. You've probably got them yourself. Sometimes we double, triple bluff. For instance, you remember that trans woman who got killed, Sammy Hill? I'm sure you do – it was huge at the time, everyone hurling abuse at each other online. Well, ninety per cent of that abuse was posted by us. We took both sides. We pretended to be outraged feminists and we pretended to be terrified trannies.'

(Even in the middle of this extraordinary conversation Clegg wanted to say, 'Please don't say trannies,' but she didn't. She just nodded.)

'And then you remember the whole thing got linked to that silly old show-off feminist?' Malika went on. 'The one who killed herself because everyone was calling her a murderer? Geraldine Giffard? That was us. We started #GerryKilledSammy. We took all that and we *worked* it.'

'No!'

'Yes. I'm afraid we made it sound like it was trans against the world. And then fems against trans. And, of course, old fems against new—'

'But that's a real thing,' Clegg interrupted. 'You didn't invent that.'

'Of course it's a real thing, Sally. All good disinformation is based on at least half a truth. We just add most of the bile and the spite, the venom and the majority of the death threats.'

'Jesus, Malika! I've always wondered who all the bloody death-threateners were. It's you!'

'A lot of the time. I mean, there's plenty of nutters, obviously. We just make it look like the whole country's made up of them. We deliberately sow confusion and discord. We made cis people think that trans people were coming to get them and that Team UK was going to help them.'

'Jesus, Malika. That's *horrible*. Don't you feel bad?'

Malika thought about this for a moment. 'I *didn't* actually. Not at first. I'm not like you, Sally. I don't want to fix the world. I think the world's fucked so I might as well enjoy it while it lasts. You do understand I was being paid a *lot* of money? I mean a *lot*. And people have become such self-righteous arseholes, special pleading whingers, they deserve a bit of a stir-up. People take themselves so *seriously*. Anyway, that's the game on the net, isn't it? Every man for himself. They lie. You lie. Everybody lies. So what? The bigger the better. There aren't any rules any more. So why should I feel bad about not following them?'

Clegg was starting to remember very clearly why she and Malika had fallen out of friendship in the first place. 'So when something bad happened to one identity group or another you'd see that as an opportunity, right?'

'Absolutely. Julian would come to me – he's my boss by the way and, full disclosure, currently also my lover, which, of course, is how I ended up in such deep shit.'

'You *sleep* with this bastard?'

'Yeah. I regret that now. A lot. But you have *no idea* how rich he is. We used *private planes*. Wouldn't you find that a turn-on? No? Oh, well, different strokes, I suppose. Anyway, he'd come to me and say, "Oh, this black woman Latifa Joseph's been murdered. Let's stir that up a bit, make it look like the cops care more about a white trans woman than—"'

'Oh, my God, Malika, it was you who created #IamLatifa?'

'Julian did, or a member of his black-arts team. He calls them the Fishing Fleet. They fish for evidence of outrage, then use it as bait to catch shoals of voters. It's my job to locate the appropriate target audience, which is a mathematical problem. I write the algorithms that locate the Facebook addresses of the people we're trying to wind up. You remember that feminist historian who got killed?'

Malika was letting it all out now. It felt good to tell the truth for once.

'Cressida Baynes?' Clegg said. 'Please don't tell me you created #RememberThem.'

Malika actually laughed. Maybe the cocktail and the Krug 2011 were having an effect. 'No. Even Julian couldn't have made that up. I mean, trying to prosecute Samuel Pepys? Really? Because *that*'s going to help today's victims of sexual assault, isn't it? Except not.'

'Actually, I think Cressida Baynes was making a really good point. We need to understand how deep the roots of patriarchal entitlement are.'

'Oh, for Christ's sake, Sally, grow the fuck up!'

For a moment they were both seventeen again. Then Malika remembered that she was describing treason to a policewoman. And she needed to get this over with. The club was filling. Loud voices. Flashing faces. Every newcomer could be another messenger from Julian, and next time the gift might not be quite as pleasant as vintage champagne.

'Anyway, the point is we picked up on her campaign and we spun it. It was us who said she was trying to sue the Glorious Dead and take the British Empire to a tribunal under the terms of the 1965 Race Relations Act.'

'Jesus!'

'Yes! *But the point is . . .*' and now Malika leaned in once more '. . . it was *actually* the Russians. It's been the Russians all along. Our discord is their discord. When Baynes got murdered and the feminists started claiming that all men were murderers, ninety per cent of the internet traffic on that was generated by us – but really it was ninety per cent Vladimir Putin! He was stirring the UK pot via a criminal gang who are paymasters to *my boss*. My boyfriend! When that weird homophobic Christian couple killed themselves because of an online gay campaign? Remember that? Most of the online abuse wasn't from *actual* gay people at all. It was us. It was from the Russians, stirring up Middle England to righteous fury.'

'And *Rainbow Island*?' Clegg asked. 'Was it you who generated all that anger? LGBT against straight? Straight against LGBT?'

'A lot of it. Although sometimes you only have to start the ball rolling. A lot of people really are that nasty. But after the actual murders we *really* got stuck in. Made it look almost as if Team UK had killed Jay-Jay themselves by caving in to gay and trans fascists and ruining *Love Island*, which was *such* a good show, actually, before it went all PC. Did you see how Bunter Jolly worked all that identity stuff in his speech? Never thought he had the brains. He didn't know it was the Russians who gave him the ammunition.'

Clegg didn't say anything for a moment. She was thinking. Thinking hard.

'Anyway,' Malika went on, 'never mind what we do. The point is that I want to blow the whistle. But obviously I want to do it in a way that squares me with the authorities and without the Russian thugs or my boyfriend, Julian, knowing it was me. That's why I need your advice. I want you to make enquiries on my behalf. Do some sort of deal for me. Find out who I need to tell and let them know that I need protection and, if possible, anonymity. Tell them I won't incriminate myself in any—'

'Malika?' Clegg interrupted urgently. 'I'm going to ask you a question and I want you to think hard before you answer. These campaigns of disinformation you're telling me about. A lot of it seems to have been about reacting to some pretty awful events. Murders and suicides, of which there have been rather a lot recently.'

'Yes. That's true,' Malika agreed.

'How quickly would you say your friend Julian and his Fishing Fleet were able to react to these situations? I mean after Wotan Orc Slayer died, for instance? Or Cressida? Or Jay-Jay? How long was it before Julian supplied you with the first slew of skewed outrage to feed into your algorithms?'

'Oh, very quickly,' she said. 'They were incredibly good at their job.'

'How quickly?'

'Within hours. An hour, actually. The Fishing Fleet were always very impressive. Their reaction time was off the scale.'

'Clearly. So within an hour of Cressida Baynes being killed, you were able to alert millions of Facebook accounts with the fake news that feminists were blaming all men for her murder? And within an hour of Wotan Orc Slayer's death being announced, you were able to tell the world that crazed feminists had killed an innocent man?'

'Yes. That's right. Same for Jay-Jay. I may even have been given the first England Out posts laying Jay-Jay's deaths at Team UK's door *as* the news broke, now I come to think of it.'

Clegg stared at her old school friend. Now it was Clegg who found herself glancing over her shoulder to check she could not be overheard. 'Malika,' she said, 'doesn't that suggest to you those inflammatory posts must have been prepared *before* the news broke?'

For a moment Malika seemed confused. 'Yes,' she replied. 'I suppose it does. Except that would mean . . .'

Clegg completed Malika's sentence for her: '. . . that your boy-friend Julian knew the murders were going to happen.'

The penny dropped. Malika's jaw dropped with it. Her eyes were wide with alarm. 'Oh, fuck,' she said. 'I never thought of that.'

'I think you should.'

68. Stake Out

MATLOCK, CLEGG and Taylor had taken up position in an empty apartment block opposite Julian's residential warehouse. With binoculars, they had sight of the front door. It had been exactly twenty-two hours since Clegg had returned to Scotland Yard at the end of her evening at Soho House.

Matlock and Taylor had been waiting for her.

She'd texted from her cab: *Don't go home. Coming back to Scotland Yard. Have sensational news.*

And she had. She had found out who was responsible for the ten deaths that, until recently, only Matlock had even considered to be connected.

'The Russian Secret Service,' she had announced proudly, having first ushered Matlock and Taylor to a quiet corner of the Situation Room, which, despite the lateness of the hour, was still buzzing with video research. 'Our murderer is only Vladimir fucking Putin! Or, at least, that's who's employing him.'

At first they both thought it was a wind-up, naturally, but once Clegg had told them about her conversation with Malika Rajput, chief programmer at Communication Sandwich, neither Matlock nor Taylor could deny that it all made chilling sense. The revelation that Clegg's old school friend's job involved feeding Russian-controlled disinformation into the referendum debate – disinformation that exploited the divisive nature of the various killings but which had been prepared *before* the killings occurred – was stunning. But also grimly logical.

After all, it had worked. The nation was far more fractured and angry than it had been when either the murders or the referendum campaign had begun. Bunter Jolly's speech had been all about that.

And when they heard the details that Malika had given Clegg about her boss Julian Carter and their trip to Russia they all knew that they had taken a massive step closer to catching their culprits.

But how to do it? How to capture trained Russian assassins of whom there was literally no physical evidence?

All they had so far was the verbal testimony of one very nervous whistle-blower. What was more, the crucial parts of that testimony were circumstantial: Malika Rajput had known nothing about any murders. The only story she had to offer was her conviction that the England Out campaign was being funded by Russians. It was Clegg who had made the presumption that the same shadowy operatives were actually killing people to provide their divisive 'identity' strategy with a bit of extra edge.

'Russian cyber-interference in Western elections isn't news,' Matlock said. 'It's been going on at least since Trump and Brexit. Nobody really bothers about it much any more, as far as I can see. They used to at least have parliamentary inquiries after the event but they achieved so little I don't think anybody would have the energy to go through it all again. They just presume it's going on and live with it.'

'Yeah, but they wouldn't if they knew that things had got a bit more proactive, would they?' Clegg asked.

Matlock thought they probably would. The Russians had shot down a commercial jumbo jet and nobody had done anything about it. Nobody cared about anything because nobody really believed anything. But that wasn't his problem. He was a copper, not a politician, and all he was concerned about was catching the criminals.

But they had no proof. Everything they had was 100 per cent supposition.

'And the killers have left no traces whatsoever,' Matlock observed ruefully, 'which has been the problem from the beginning. At least we now know how they got to be so good at their job. These are trained professional assassins with the resources of the most proactive spy network in the world behind them. It's not like the old days when the Russians were crap, wandering around poisoning people with umbrellas and door knobs, then getting photographed at airports. They've certainly raised their game since then, haven't they? I mean, they even managed to get into the *Rainbow Island* villa and kill Jay-Jay without giving themselves away.'

'They just pulled out the fuse, snuck in, did the business and snuck out. Pretty brilliant, no argument,' said Taylor. 'So I doubt they're going to start giving themselves away now.'

'So what do we do, boss?' Clegg asked.

'Whatever we do, we have to do it now,' Matlock said. 'The referendum is only three days away. After which I think we can presume they'll close down their little operation for a while. That means the killers have either already left the country, or are preparing to leave . . . or . . .'

'Planning one more hit? Just to get it over the line,' Taylor said. 'They haven't stirred up the disabled lobby yet. Or the plus-sized or the vegans. If I was a fat veggie in a wheelchair I'd be nervous.'

'Not funny, Barry,' Matlock said. 'We need to act at once. The key is clearly this Julian Carter bastard. He's the connection, the only Brit who knows the whole story.'

'Do we pull him?' Clegg asked.

'For what? We don't have anything except our suspicions and Malika's story about a piss-up in Russia. You can be sure Carter's buried his money trail deep. It'd take months to dig it up, if we ever did. He'd say Malika was a fantasist, making it all up. That he'd just had a few vodkas with some old Russian mates. A story that, of course, they'd corroborate. If we pull him, he'll laugh in our faces. Meantime we'll have blown the one tiny advantage we have on him, which is that we know his game and he doesn't know we know.'

'And we'd also have blown Malika's cover,' Clegg added. 'We don't want her to be the next unconnected identical blow on the back of the head.'

'Exactly,' Matlock agreed. 'We can't get Carter to cooperate with us until we've got something to make him want to play ball. That means proof he's working with Russians, and since we know we're not going to find any, our only hope is a confession. Sally, you need to meet your old friend again. Preferably tonight. Latest tomorrow.'

'All right, boss,' Clegg said. 'I'll text her. She's not going to like it. She looked pretty scared.'

That conversation had taken place on the previous evening.

The night of Malika's revelations.

Now, twenty hours later, the three of them were sitting in the empty apartment building opposite Julian's warehouse, all wearing earphones.

69. Setting the Trap

WHEN MALIKA got back to the apartment after her old friends' reunion she was very pleased to find that Julian was already asleep.

She needed time to think.

The interpretation that Sally Clegg had put on Julian's Russian activities had increased the fear in which she held her boyfriend *a thousandfold*. She'd known he was in bed with serious gangster types, but the discovery that his whole propaganda operation was based on a series of cold-blooded strategic murders revealed a horrifying new level to his criminal depravity.

At first she'd struggled not to believe it even of him. Perhaps somehow he hadn't known. And yet, deep down, she knew he had. How could he not? He was preparing reactions to murders that he must have understood had not yet occurred.

When she and Clegg had parted, Clegg had told her that she would take advice from her superior and promised to respond as soon as she could with a plan of action.

'I'll send some sort of message by one o'clock this morning,' Clegg had promised.

And so Malika sat in the lounge area of the vast open-plan apartment, completely alone apart from the accomplice to serial murder sleeping in the bed beyond the roll-top bath. She had her phone in her hand and checked it over and over again to be sure that it was on mute.

The message came at twelve forty-five. They wanted another meeting. Fuck. Really?

Got to be tomorrow, Clegg texted. *You say when. Where. We'll come.*

So easy to demand.

Not so easy to arrange. It was a working day. She and Julian would travel to the office together. She'd work there all day. He'd take her to lunch. He always took her to lunch: it was their unbreakable ritual.

'Never skip lunch,' he'd say. 'Prince of meals. So much jollier, more hopeful, *sprightlier* than Old King Dinner. A civilized man treats a decent breakfast as an occasional luxury but a decent lunch as a daily necessity.'

She'd always liked that. Lunch was fun and classy. Old-school. A glass of wine, a really nice one-dish meal. Plus perhaps a bite of cheese. A universe away from the hurried Pret wrap at the desk that the world had got so used to. Julian knew she liked it too. Even now that he made her skin crawl, she still enjoyed their lunches. Every day a new little restaurant to discover – Julian's knowledge of London dining was just ridiculous. She still found that attractive about him. They both looked forward to lunch. If she cried off at short notice he'd definitely wonder why.

Then he'd remember that she'd been drinking with a police-woman the night before.

But Malika did yoga.

She loved her yoga. It meant a lot to her, and she'd been strong in her resolve not to allow Julian to insist she give it up, as he'd insisted she give up numerous other parts of her separate life as he had continued his creepy ownership project.

'What do you want to go to a public class for? You're rich,' he said. 'I'll pay for a private teacher, the best. She can come here.'

But Malika had stayed strong. She liked classes. They were social.

Her work involved long hours of private concentration. Her home life revolved exclusively round Julian. Without her classes she'd scarcely speak to anybody her age from one day to the next.

Yoga was hers and she had insisted on keeping it. 'I don't want a home teacher,' she'd said. 'And have you seen me suspended in a downward dog? No way! I'm not having you sitting there with a glass of Scotch, perving at me while I grunt and groan on the mat. Yoga is *not* a spectator sport. Quite apart from anything else, you sometimes can't help farting and I have *never* farted in front of a boy in my entire life and I never will. I like to keep my mystery.'

She'd won her argument, and her yoga classes had provided her with her only periods of peace and tranquillity in what had become a tense, nervous existence. She'd book a class tomorrow. But she knew it would be neither peaceful nor tranquil.

She texted back to Clegg, *4 p.m.*, and named a café near the dance studio where her yoga was held. Best to keep the meeting in the vicinity of the lie in case he offered to drop her off.

Having sent her text she joined Julian in bed. But she hardly slept. It was a horrible feeling to be naked under sheets with a killer.

She did her best to be bright and cheerful in the morning and equally so on the way to work. Fortunately Julian had never been a big morning guy.

She casually mentioned yoga over lunch.

'Yeah, sorry, got to leave early. Didn't I mention it? Julian, I *need* this class. It keeps me sane.'

He'd seemed happy enough and, fortunately, didn't offer to drive her.

Sally Clegg and Matlock were waiting for her when she arrived.

She didn't know what she'd expected Sally Clegg's boss to be like, maybe something like Matt Damon in the *Bourne* movies. Certainly not shambling Mick Matlock, a craggy old geezer in a

T-shirt, skinny jeans and a woolly hat. She thought he looked a bit like The Edge from U2 – she'd never heard of Bono until a month before but they were Julian's favourite band. Malika was sort of relieved. Matlock looked so normal. So ordinary. Maybe things weren't so scary after all.

Then he told her what he wanted her to do.

Which was entrap Julian.

He'd got straight to the point. 'We have to find a way of establishing some leverage over Julian Carter – who is currently invulnerable,' Matlock had explained, as they sipped their cappuccinos. 'Our best hope is to send you in with a wire and for you to try to extract some sort of admission out of him, which we record.'

Malika could scarcely believe what she was being asked to do. 'Are you fucking joking me?'

'I'm afraid not. It's the only way we can do this.'

'Of course! Why didn't I think of it myself? Just extract an admission of being an accessory to murder!' Malika protested. 'He'd never do that – ever. He's not an idiot. He's never talked about that to me. What's he going to think if I try to bring it up? Out of the blue? Particularly the day after I spent the evening with a policewoman.'

Matlock assured her that he didn't require her to probe him on the idea that the various deaths had been murders. All he needed was for him to talk about the Russian connection, which was knowledge he and Malika already shared. 'If we have audio of him admitting to being in the pay of a foreign power while working for England Out, that's proof of treason. Theoretically he could do life. Once we have that, we can bring him in and offer him a plea bargain. Trade his Russian connections for a lighter sentence, maybe no sentence at all if he's prepared to point us to the killers.'

Malika was entirely terrified at the prospect of what she was being asked to do. She tried to refuse. 'No! This is too much. I brought you the information. I only wanted to find the right person to tell it to, then hide at the bottom of a deep hole till Julian's arrested. I don't have to get involved with this. Trying to entrap him? With a wire? He's a very dangerous man and a proud one. Also, he thinks I'm in love with him. If he discovers I've betrayed him there's no telling what he'll do.'

'He won't discover it. We still call it a wire but there's no wires involved. These days, we use a tiny audio bug. It'll be stitched into your clothing.'

'No, it fucking won't!' Malika exclaimed. 'Is this even legal? Isn't it entrapment? Actually, who cares if it is or it isn't? I'm not doing it.'

Matlock assured her that what he was asking her to do was a legal manoeuvre and that they would be listening in at all times. If she would just attempt this one thing for them, her part in the whole business would be over. Tonight. 'Otherwise,' he added significantly, 'the only person we have anything on, Malika, is you.'

'What?'

'Your confession. To DC Clegg. That you have been knowingly working for Russian intelligence. It's only your word against hers admittedly, but she's a policewoman so any judge would favour her evidence. It'd certainly be enough for us to hold you while we started to dig. And when we found evidence, Malika, which in the end we would, you could get five years.'

It was a very nasty trick to pull and Clegg was furious with Matlock for pulling it. But, as he explained to her afterwards, he'd felt he had no choice. They were hunting a killer who had already killed ten times and might very soon strike again.

'I really doubt you're in any danger from Carter himself,' Matlock said. 'He's just the Russians' tame English posh boy. The respectable face of a very dirty little game. He's no ruthless killer.'

'You really don't know him, Chief Inspector.'

But Malika knew she had no choice. It was either help them get Julian or be arrested herself.

They kitted her out there and then.

Clegg took her to the toilet of the café and secured a tiny transmitter in the strap of Malika's bra. 'That way even if you have to take it off, hopefully you can drop it close enough for it to still pick up audio,' Clegg explained.

'Thanks. Very comforting, you serious, *serious* bitch, Sally. You're pimping me. I'm being pimped by the fucking police.'

'We just need you to get him talking.' Clegg avoided meeting her old friend's eye. 'We'll be listening nearby and the moment we've recorded enough to incriminate him we'll come straight over and arrest him. Once we can threaten him with aiding a foreign power we'll have the leverage we need to sweat him into turning in the killers. And you'll be a hero. They'll probably make a film.'

70. The End of a Relationship

MALIKA RETURNED to Julian's apartment in the early evening. The transmitter in her bra felt like a great throbbing sign announcing her intention to betray him.

'Good yoga class?' he asked.

'Mm. I really needed it. You're working me seriously hard at the office.'

'And making you serious dosh.'

'Oh, yeah. Love that.'

He took her bag from her and kissed her.

'I work you hard in lots of ways, don't I, baby bunny?' he said. 'Some more pleasurable than others.'

'Oh, *yeah*. Love that too.'

He'd already opened a bottle of wine and poured her a glass.

They made small-talk, chatted through the various projects of the day. He asked about her mother. She asked about his bad back, which sometimes troubled him.

He suggested a spot of dinner. 'We could ring for something.'

'Maybe later.'

She had to find a way to turn the conversation towards Russia. And yet she had the overwhelming sensation that even mentioning it would sound like a clanging alarm.

In the end she could think of no better method than simply to dive in. 'When are you going to take me back to St Petersburg?' she said. 'And Moscow, by the way, which I still haven't visited, even though you promised.'

It was a bold start and she felt it sounded horribly false. But he didn't seem to notice anything amiss.

'Oh, any time soon,' he said. 'The referendum's about over and things will *so* calm down then. I wouldn't mind a holiday too. Vodka and the Bolshoi. Lovely.'

'But would we have to see your horrible chums? I could really do without that. I felt like your prostitute.'

'They're all right, Malika darling. Don't be such a snob. They're colleagues.'

'They're criminals, *darling.*'

He didn't reply. Damn, if he'd said, 'Yes,' in some way it would have been a start. She tried again. 'How on earth did you even get involved with a couple of thugs like that? You never told me.'

Come *on*, she thought. Give me something.

He didn't.

'I've told you. They're colleagues.'

Christ, this was hard. That arsehole policeman had talked about it like she only had to ask and he'd make a full confession. He was across the street right now. Listening. She hoped he was realizing how tough this was going to be. She tried again.

'Yeah. Colleagues, right. Except when they're not being gangsters they work for Vladimir bloody Putin. Which is scary even to *say*. Have you ever met him?'

He looked at her. Was there suspicion in his eyes? Or was she just being paranoid? It could, of course, be both.

'No, I've never met him. I've been in the same room as him. But it was a very big room. We didn't meet.'

'Well, I guess he can't know all the people who corrupt elections for him *personally.*'

Fuck. That was a straight pitch at entrapment right there. Would he spot it? She'd tried to say it casually but in her head it sounded guilty as hell.

'Oh, let's not talk, shall we, bunny?' Julian said. 'I'm pretty tired.'

Let's not talk. Great. She had a tape-recorder in her bra and he didn't want to talk.

'I know what I want to do,' he said. And he kissed her again. She returned the kiss. There was nothing else to do. Her first effort at soliciting incriminating evidence had failed. Perhaps he'd be more amenable post-coitus.

He started to undress her, taking off her clothes in the lounge area. The bed was fully ten metres away across a vast expanse of polished floor, plus a huge iron bath. Way out of range of her transmitting device. If he undressed her here, then fucked her in the bed, anything she got him to say would go unrecorded. He'd unzipped her dress. It fell to her ankles. Her bra would be next. She could not afford to be separated from her bra.

'Let's go to bed,' she breathed into his ear, and tried to move, but he held her.

'I want to undress you here, under the skylight. The red evening sun is so pretty on your skin. Turns it to copper.'

She had to let him, of course. Theirs was not a relationship that allowed for the denial of such a request. He reached behind her back while he kissed her and undid it single-handed, like the expert he was. It fell to the floor, her precious, precious bra, her escape route from this appalling situation and it was no longer attached to her person. She was naked now – she hadn't been wearing knickers. That was deliberate: she knew he liked it. Better than anything from Agent Provocateur.

Then he took her hand and turned to lead her towards the bed. She tried to stand her ground. To stay close to her bra.

'No, let's make love here,' she said, 'in the evening sun.'

'I thought you wanted to go to bed?'

'That was before you said that beautiful thing about my copper skin.'

A good effort. He smiled. Had she succeeded? No, she hadn't.

'The sun'll be gone in five minutes, old scout, and anyway I can't fuck on floors any more. My knees, you know.'

'I'll go on top,' she said, trying to push him down. It sounded a bit weird and she knew it.

He did too.

'You're in a funny mood tonight,' he said. 'Come to bed.'

Further resistance would definitely look suspicious. She had no choice but to give in. She allowed herself to be led naked to the bed. Ten metres away from her transmitter.

Still, at least now a bunch of police officers wouldn't get to hear her having sex to which she must now succumb and must also appear to enjoy. He liked her to shout a bit when she came (or faked coming, which had been the case since Russia). To call him Daddy. He liked her to ask for it good and hard right there in her tight little pussy, Daddy.

She was happy not to be overheard in that particular performance.

Her plan was to get through it. Give him fifteen minutes of after-sex baby-girl talk, then go and get him some wine. On her way to the fridge she'd idly tidy up a little bit. She'd pick up her dress and drape it on the couch. Equally casually she'd pick up her bra, probably couldn't risk putting it on. That would look strange. No obvious need. They were in bed mode now. Drinking wine. Chatting. Why put back on the day's undies? If she was going to put anything on it'd be a loose sweatshirt, not her bra. But she could probably get away with absent-mindedly scooping it up in her hand as she returned with the wine. And idly dropping it on the floor beside the bed. Which would hopefully place the bra close enough for the moment when she gritted her teeth and returned to the horrible business of trying to get him to talk about his Russian employers.

That was the plan. But she never got the chance to carry it out. She did the first bit. The fucking. And the second bit, the post-coital baby talk, which she whispered in a little-girl voice while struggling not to gag.

'That was the best yet, baby. You're like a man of twenty when you do me. Your little baby girl loves getting nailed by her great big strong daddy.'

But when she made to get out of bed he stopped her. 'Don't go. Stay here.'

'I'm coming back,' she said, as casually as she could manage. 'Just getting your wine, darling. You've earned it.'

'No. Don't go. I don't need wine.'

'I do.'

'No. No wine. Let's have a little music.'

He reached for his phone. Julian loved his music. He had surround-sound speakers everywhere. He pressed his Spotify and side one of *The Joshua Tree* filled the vast attic space from one end to the other.

Malika could only stay where she was. Put her arms around him. Cuddle him. Try to relax him. 'Why won't Daddy let his little girl have wine?'

'Good yoga class?' he asked.

She stopped cuddling, trying not to show that she was now on her guard.

'You asked me that.'

'Mm. Thought I'd ask you again. Give you another chance to answer.'

'Answer what?'

'How was yoga?'

Could he sense her tension? How could he not? She tried to cover her nerves by adopting a firmer tone.

'Well. Like I said before, Julian, it was a great class. What's this about? Why can't I get a glass of wine?'

'Vigorous? Did she put you through it?'

Malika didn't answer. Fear had gripped her.

'She always does, doesn't she?' he went on. 'Quite the firm task-mistress.'

Malika tried to speak casually, not betray that she was now very scared. What did he know? 'Well, you have to feel it a bit,' she said. 'No pain, no gain and all that.'

But she could see he wasn't interested in her answer. He had his own.

'It's only that when I peeked inside your kit bag, just after you got home, while I was pouring the wine, your stuff was all fresh and folded. Not sweaty. Not crumpled. Not disturbed at all.'

He touched his phone. The music got a little louder.

'I . . . I'm neat,' Malika replied. 'You know that. What's this about? We had a relaxing class today. Meditation. Anusara technique.'

'So not vigorous, then? No pain and no gain?'

'No. And I didn't sweat and I folded my stuff in my bag because I thought I wouldn't bother washing it before the next class since it was hardly used. Is that good enough for you, Julian?'

It wasn't a bad effort off the cuff. But it turned out to be pointless. He already knew.

'No, not good enough, darling, and may I just add that you've broken my heart?'

'What? No! What are you saying, Daddy? I love you!'

'Please don't demean yourself, Malika. It's embarrassing. I had you followed today. I did that because of last night. When you came home I wasn't asleep. I watched you. I watched you sit and sit. And think and think. And then you got a text. Which you replied to, then deleted both the text and your reply. I know you deleted them because when I looked this morning they weren't there.'

'Julian, please, I can—'

'No, you can't, darling. You can't explain. But I can. You didn't go to yoga today. You met your friend again. And she brought a friend. Another policeman. Quite a famous one, actually. I've seen him on the television. Extraordinary that he'd come himself. Knowing he could be recognized. But that, of course, is policemen all over. Seriously fucking stupid.'

'You followed me?'

'I had you followed. And photographed. Would you like to see the pictures? I could send them to your phone.'

Malika didn't bother to reply. She was thinking hard. Could she run for it? She was almost naked but so what? Better naked on a pavement than dead in an apartment. But they always kept the front door locked. There were two dead locks to turn and the chain to disengage. He'd be on her before she ever got it open, and even if she did, they were eight floors up. He'd catch her before she could get down to the ground. So, run to the kitchen, perhaps, and grab a knife? That would have to be a very last resort. He was in good shape and much stronger than her. She really didn't fancy her chances with him in a fight. Even if she managed to secure a weapon. Besides, the kitchen was full of weapons: he could secure one too.

All she could do was sit naked in the bed beside him, wait and see.

'So you came back from your little meeting and you kissed me and you fucked me,' Julian went on. 'What was your plan, I wonder? Well. You asked me about my Russian friends. Are you wired perhaps? Did you hope to record me?'

Jesus, he was a clever bastard. He'd worked the whole thing out.

'Won't work now. You're naked, aren't you? No wire on your lovely copper-coloured body, old scout, unless it's up your arse. I didn't go there, did I? You never let me. Perhaps I will in a minute. Or is it in your clothes? The ones you didn't want me to take off before we got to bed? The ones you wanted to stay close to when you suggested we make love on a hard wooden floor?'

Jesus, the guy was a fucking mind-reader. He'd absolutely been playing with her.

Julian turned the music up a little more.

'I'll check later. Is there a bug sewn into your dress? Perhaps you've got a wired bra. That's funny, isn't it? A wired bra, sort of a pun. It'll be a sad thing that, going through your clothes. Your lovely lingerie. The stuff I bought you. After you're gone.'

'Gone?'

'I loved you, old scout. And you ruined everything, you stupid fucking bitch.'

'Julian, please.'

There was a knock at the door. A loud, firm knock. Loud enough to punch through the throbbing music emanating from a phalanx of state-of-the-art speakers.

'Friends of mine,' Julian said. 'Russian friends.'

She knew she had to make a run for the living area. To grab her bra and scream into it for help. The bra that was ten metres away. Maybe a scream would have reached it from the bed but not with that music playing.

He was clever, turning it up like that.

She made her move.

But he was ready and stopped her easily, grabbed her arm. Spun her round and punched her in the face. God, he was strong. And he knew how to punch. Private-school training, of course. They still boxed. Although it seemed they no longer taught them never to hit girls. Another depressing aspect of the new gender egalitarianism. He knocked her off the bed and before she could get up he was on her. Spinning her underneath him into an armlock and pinning her face to the floor.

'Ssh, my little spy. No one's going to hear you. Listen to the music.'

Bono still hadn't found what he was looking for but Julian certainly had, and so had the Russians knocking at the door.

She started a scream. With his free hand Julian grabbed her hair and smashed her face into the floor. She thought perhaps her nose was broken. Perhaps some teeth. There was blood in her mouth. She could no longer scream even if she wanted to.

The music seemed to be getting louder.

Julian hauled her to her feet and half marched, half dragged her towards the front door. Before they were even midway across the room she felt herself losing consciousness.

She was aware of him dropping her and of hitting the floor a second time. Then nothing.

71. How It Ended

A T FIRST Matlock, Clegg and Taylor had been congratulating each other that everything was working out well. The transmitter was delivering super audio. They'd listened to Malika returning home. The small-talk. Her noble efforts to move the conversation on to Russia.

'Good try, but she's started too soon,' Matlock muttered. 'She should have left it a bit.'

They heard Julian say he didn't want to talk. They'd registered the beginning of their lovemaking.

They could picture the scene as he began to undress her and they heard her efforts to stay connected with her bra.

'Impressive girl, this,' Matlock said. 'I think she's going to work out fine.'

They'd understood that Malika had failed to stay with the transmitter and had lost audio as Julian insisted they retreat to the bed.

Then silence. They could see that the transmitter was still working but there was no sound close enough for it to transmit.

They could only sit and wait. After about forty minutes they heard music.

'Fuck,' said Matlock. 'Music. That's the last thing we need. Mind you, U2's *The Joshua Tree* is a great album.'

'"Dad" music,' said Clegg. 'Definitely his choice, not hers.'

Matlock began to feel uneasy.

Then the music got louder.

'Is that deliberate?' Clegg said. 'Do you think he suspects something?'

They didn't have long to think about it because at that point Taylor, who was watching through the binoculars, spoke up.

'There's two blokes entering the building.'

Matlock grabbed his own pair of binoculars. 'Oh, God,' he said. 'Is that a Spurs shirt? Tell me it isn't.'

Taylor looked hard. 'Actually, I think it is,' he said. 'It's one of their away strips.'

For maybe half of one second Matlock stood frozen. Then he grabbed his radio.

'Armed response required urgently,' he barked into it, then, handing Clegg the radio, he said, 'Give them the address.'

With that he ran for the stairwell and began to clatter down the stairs towards the exit.

Clegg snapped the address into the radio, then she and Taylor followed.

Outside the street was empty. Matlock charged across and through the still open front door of Julian's warehouse building.

The apartment was on the top floor. He knew that.

Lift or stairs? He could see from the display that the lift was at the top. Clearly it had just delivered the two intruders, one of whom was wearing the same relatively unusual shirt as a man who had been noted at three of the murder sites.

Matlock took the stairs three at a time. Seconds later Clegg and Taylor followed him up.

As they emerged on the top floor they saw an open front door. The door to Julian's apartment.

Charging in, they found him in front of them.

Stretched out on the floor, blood seeping from a single blow to the back of his head. Beyond him Malika was just regaining consciousness. Her face was bloody but she was definitely alive.

They heard a door slam. Running to the window, Clegg saw two figures emerge from the building just as a car arrived to pick them up. Clearly the killers had been descending in the lift while the three police officers had been ascending the stairs. Shortly after that, the first of the armed units arrived. Way too late for Julian or to catch his killers.

72. Afterwards

MATLOCK WAS never able to say for sure why the two Russian agents hadn't killed Malika as well. His best guess was that that was not what they had been tasked to do. He had an idea that Russian secret agents might be pretty obedient to orders. You would be, working for a totalitarian state. His theory was that Julian Carter had exhausted his usefulness. The referendum was occurring the following day and Communication Sandwich's mischief-making was done. Carter had known every aspect of the Russian operation. He was also compromised: his call for help in disposing of his girlfriend would have been enough alone to convince his controllers that he had become a liability and a huge risk to their ongoing UK operations. So when he had requested that they kill Malika for him they'd decided to kill him instead. Malika was not a threat. She'd never had contact with any of them beyond an innocent dinner in Moscow. Why kill her? Particularly since she was unconscious and therefore hadn't seen them.

Of course, it was also possible that Matlock's arrival had saved her. The killers might have been about to finish her off when they heard him running up the stairs. Matlock took some pride in that possibility. And that he could still run up eight flights, three steps at a time.

The two killers escaped, and although MI5 were later able to identify them, they had long since been spirited back to Russia. Putin, of course, denied all knowledge of any dirty-tricks operation, immediately claiming that MI5 had committed the murders in order to blame it on the Russians.

Malika made a full recovery from her injuries and subsequently cooperated with the police investigation into electoral fraud. This led to Tommy Spoon and Xavier Arron being summoned to appear before a parliamentary inquiry, during which they were extremely strutty, shouty and rude. Nothing came of it. Nobody really cared. Malika never told anybody about her Geneva bank account, which only she, Julian and the bank knew about. A month or two after she had recovered from her broken nose she quietly began withdrawing the money, considering it the least she deserved. A quarter of a million Swiss francs was quite a decent severance bonus, particularly considering the pound had fallen so far through the floor by that time that the money converted to more than three million quid.

In other exciting news for Malika, Let's Do Lunch Films acquired the rights to her story and cast a famous and beautiful Indian actress in the role of Malika. It was all looking very positive, until objections were voiced from members of the mathematician community, who complained bitterly that the role should have gone to a *genuine* mathematician. Let's Do Lunch were accused of indulging in cultural appropriation and failing to celebrate the vibrant and separate mathematician identity. There was a Twitterstorm of protest and the project went instantly toxic. Tom and Bill dropped it like a hot cake.

Hayley and Narsti's affair ran its course and ended by mutual agreement. Contrary to Hayley's worst fears, Narsti didn't complain to Human Resources. Instead he told her he hoped they could still be friends and even offered to leave the team if his presence would make her feel uncomfortable. An offer that Hayley, of course, didn't accept. In an effort to once again reinvent a winning formula for her franchise, Hayley decided the next series of *Love Island* should be a celebrity one. However, such was the toxic nature of the brand after the Jay-Jay murders, that she couldn't get any celebrities to agree to take part. In an inspired move, she decided to use entirely ordinary people and claim that they were celebrities in the hope that nobody would notice. Since nobody has ever heard of any of the celebrities that go on that type of celebrity show anyway, the ruse worked brilliantly.

Mick Matlock retired from police work. He'd been intending to do a few more years but changed his mind. The death of Cressida Baynes had done nothing to diminish the public's desire for retrospective justice, and when he found himself tasked with pursuing the prosecution of Richard II, who in 1396 had married Isabella of Valois, who had been only six at the time, he just thought, Fuck it, and left. He's enjoying more time with Nancy and trying to get his school punk band (Sticky Zit) back together for a reunion gig.

Clegg and Taylor still work together, and with Matlock gone, they can both sit in the front of the car. Clegg has still not brought up the gender disparity in their tea-making and bringing of biscuits but she is really intending to do so soon.

England Out narrowly won the referendum but the process of trying to disentangle the United Kingdom proved so long and so complicated, the sunlit uplands so elusive, that eventually everybody just quietly forgot about it and Britain kept on bumbling on.

None of the three big beasts of England Out fulfilled their leadership ambitions. A still wounded and divided party saw them as wreckers and opted to pursue 'stability and strength' instead, sticking with the PM who had caused all the trouble in the first place. Bunter Jolly is now a regular guest host on satirical news programmes; Plantagenet Greased-Hogg presents documentaries for the Heritage and History Channel and Guppy Toad went on *Strictly*. He was the first contestant in that series to be voted off.

Samuel Pepys got six years and his name was entered in the sex offenders' register.

TWO BROTHERS

Berlin, 1920.

Two babies are born. Brothers in all but blood, united and indivisible, sharing everything.

But as Germany marches towards the Third Reich and the horrors of world war can both of them survive the cataclysm that is to come?

TIME AND TIME AGAIN

June 1914.

Hugh Stanton knows that a great and terrible war is coming. A collective madness that will kill millions and bring misery to countless more in the century to come. He knows this because, for him, that century is already history. Somehow he must change it.

The war will begin with a single bullet.

But can another single bullet prevent it?